RU

"MASTER OF THE CRAZY SCENARIO"
Locus

**"ONE OF MY ALL-TIME FAVORITE WRITERS.
HE WARMS THE COCKLES OF MY HEART
AND FIRES UP THE LITTLE GRAY CELLS.
I THINK OF HIM AS THE SCARLET PIMPERNEL
OF SCIENCE FICTION."**
Philip José Farmer

**"RUCKER NEVER WANTS FOR
NEW INVENTIONS"**
Washington Post Book World

**"HE KNOWS HOW TO BOGGLE THE MIND AND,
NEXT CHAPTER, TO BOGGLE IT AGAIN"**
Thomas M. Disch, author of *The M.D.*

**"A MATHEMATICIAN BEWITCHED BY THE
ABSURDITY OF THE UNIVERSE
IMPLIED IN QUANTUM THEORY,
AND A WRITER POSSESSED OF A
BRILLIANTLY WITTY PEN."**
Publishers Weekly

**"ONE OF THE WRITERS WE WILL FOLLOW
INTO THE NEW FUTURE"**
Raleigh Spectator

Other Avon Books by
Rudy Rucker

THE HOLLOW EARTH

RUDY RUCKER
LIVE ROBOTS

2 IN 1 VOLUME
of
SOFTWARE/WETWARE

AVON BOOKS • NEW YORK

LIVE ROBOTS is an original publication of Avon books. *Software* and *Wetware* are novels. Any similarity to actual persons or events is purely coincidental.

An excerpt from *Software* appeared in *The Mind's I*, copyright © 1981 by Douglas R. Hofstadter and Daniel C. Dennett. Published by Basic Books.

AVON BOOKS
A division of
The Hearst Corporation
1350 Avenue of the Americas
New York, New York 10019

Software copyright © 1982 by Rudy Rucker
Wetware copyright © 1988 by Rudy Rucker
Published by arrangement with the author
Library of Congress Catalog Card Number: 93-90822
ISBN: 0-380-77543-3

First AvoNova Printing: April 1994
First Avon Books Printing of *Software*: October 1987
First Avon Books Printing of *Wetware*: April 1988

AVON TRADEMARK REG. U.S. PAT. OFF. AND IN OTHER COUNTRIES, MARCA REGISTRADA, HECHO EN U.S.A.

Printed in the U.S.A.

RA 10 9 8 7 6 5 4 3 2 1

SOFTWARE

For Al Humboldt, Embry Rucker,
and Dennis Poague.

Chapter One

Cobb Anderson would have held out longer, but you don't see dolphins every day. There were twenty of them, fifty, rolling in the little gray waves, wicketting up out of the water. It was good to see them. Cobb took it for a sign and went out for his evening sherry an hour early.

The screen door slapped shut behind him and he stood uncertainly for a moment, dazed by the late afternoon sun. Annie Cushing watched him from her window in the cottage next door. Beatles music drifted out past her.

"You forgot your hat," she advised. He was still a good-looking man, barrel-chested and bearded like Santa Claus. She wouldn't have minded getting it on with him, if he weren't so . . .

"Look at the dolphins, Annie. I don't need a hat. Look how happy they are. I don't need a hat and I don't need a wife." He started toward the asphalt road, walking stiffly across the crushed white shells.

Annie went back to brushing her hair. She wore it white and long, and she kept it thick with hormone spray. She was sixty and not too brittle to hug. She wondered idly if Cobb would take her to the Golden Prom next Friday.

The long last chord of "Day in the Life" hung in the air. Annie couldn't have said which song she had just heard—after fifty years her responses to the music were all but extinguished—but she walked across the room to turn the stack of records over. *If only something would*

1

happen, she thought for the thousandth time. *I get so tired of being me.*

At the Superette, Cobb selected a chilled quart of cheap sherry and a damp paper bag of boiled peanuts. And he wanted something to look at.

The Superette magazine selection was nothing compared to what you could get over in Cocoa. Cobb settled finally for a love-ad newspaper called *Kiss and Tell.* It was always good and weird . . . most of the advertisers were seventy-year-old hippies like himself. He folded the first-page picture under so that only the headline showed. PLEASE PHEEZE ME.

Funny how long you can laugh at the same jokes, Cobb thought, waiting to pay. Sex seemed odder all the time. He noticed the man in front of him, wearing a light-blue hat blocked from plastic mesh.

If Cobb concentrated on the hat he saw an irregular blue cylinder. But if he let himself look through the holes in the mesh he could see the meek curve of the bald head underneath. Skinny neck and a light-bulb head, clawing in his change. A friend.

"Hey, Farker."

Farker finished rounding up his nickels, then turned his body around. He spotted the bottle.

"Happy Hour came early today." A note of remonstrance. Farker worried about Cobb.

"It's Friday. Pheeze me tight." Cobb handed Farker the paper.

"Seven eighty-five," the cashier said to Cobb. Her white hair was curled and hennaed. She had a deep tan. Her flesh had a pleasingly used and oily look to it.

Cobb was surprised. He'd already counted money into his hand. "I make it six fifty." Numbers began sliding around in his head.

"I meant my box number," the cashier said with a toss of her head. "In the *Kiss and Tell.*" She smiled coyly and took Cobb's money. She was proud of her ad this month. She'd gone to a studio for the picture.

Farker handed the paper back to Cobb outside. "I can't look at this, Cobb. I'm still a happily married man, God help me."

"You want a peanut?"

"Thanks." Farker extracted a soggy shell from the little bag. There was no way his spotted and trembling old hands could have peeled the nut, so he popped it whole into his mouth. After a minute he spit the hull out.

They walked towards the beach, eating pasty peanuts. They wore no shirts, only shorts and sandals. The afternoon sun beat pleasantly on their backs. A silent Mr. Frostee truck cruised past.

Cobb cracked the screw-top on his dark-brown bottle and took a tentative first sip. He wished he could remember the box number the cashier had just told him. Numbers wouldn't stay still for him anymore. It was hard to believe he'd ever been a cybernetician. His memory ranged back to his first robots and how they'd learned to bop . . .

"Food drop's late again," Farker was saying. "And I hear there's a new murder cult up in Daytona. They're called the Little Kidders." He wondered if Cobb could hear him. Cobb was just standing there with empty colorless eyes, a yellow stain of sherry on the dense white hair around his lips.

"Food drop," Cobb said, suddenly coming back. He had a way of re-entering a conversation by confidently booming out the last phrase which had registered. "I've still got a good supply."

"But be sure to eat some of the new food when it comes," Farker cautioned. "For the vaccines. I'll tell Annie to remind you."

"Why is everybody so interested in staying alive? I left my wife and came down here to drink and die in peace. *She* can't wait for me to kick off. So why . . ." Cobb's voice caught. The fact of the matter was that he was terrified of death. He took a quick, medicinal slug of sherry.

"If you were peaceful, you wouldn't drink so much," Farker said mildly. "Drinking is the sign of an unresolved conflict."

"No *kidding*," Cobb said heavily. In the golden warmth of the sun, the sherry had taken quick effect. "Here's an unresolved conflict for you." He ran a fingernail down the vertical white scar on his furry chest. "I don't have the money for another second-hand heart. In a year or two this cheapie's going to poop out on me."

Farker grimaced. "So? *Use* your two years."

Cobb ran his finger back up the scar, as if zipping it up. "I've seen what it's like, Farker. I've had a taste of it. It's the worst thing there is." He shuddered at the dark memory . . . teeth, ragged clouds . . . and fell silent.

Farker glanced at his watch. Time to get going or Cynthia would . . .

"You know what Jimi Hendrix said?" Cobb asked. Recalling the quote brought the old resonance back into his voice. "When it's my time to die, I'm going to be the one doing it. So as long as I'm alive, you let me live my way."

Farker shook his head. "Face it, Cobb, if you drank less you'd get a lot more out of life." He raised his hand to cut off his friend's reply. "But I've got to get home. Bye bye."

"Bye."

Cobb walked to the end of the asphalt and over a low dune to the edge of the beach. No one was there today, and he sat down under his favorite palm tree.

The breeze had picked up a little. Warmed by the sand, it lapped at Cobb's face, buried under white whiskers. The dolphins were gone.

He sipped sparingly at his sherry and let the memories play. There were only two thoughts to be avoided: death and his abandoned wife Verena. The sherry kept them away.

The sun was going down behind him when he saw the stranger. Barrel-chest, erect posture, strong arms and legs covered with curly hair, a round white beard. Like Santa Claus, or like Ernest Hemingway the year he shot himself.

"Hello, Cobb," the man said. He wore sungoggles and looked amused. His shorts and sportshirt glittered.

"Care for a drink?" Cobb gestured at the half-empty bottle. He wondered who, if anyone, he was talking to.

"No thanks," the stranger said, sitting down. "It doesn't do anything for me."

Cobb stared at the man. Something about him . . .

"You're wondering who I am," the stranger said, smiling. "I'm you."

"You who?"

"You me." The stranger used Cobb's own tight little smile on him. "I'm a mechanical copy of your body."

The face seemed right and there was even the scar from the heart transplant. The only difference between them was how alert and healthy the copy looked. Call him Cobb Anderson$_2$. Cobb$_2$ didn't drink. Cobb envied him. He hadn't had a completely sober day since he had the operation and left his wife.

"How did you get here?"

The robot waved a hand palm up. Cobb liked the way the gesture looked on someone else. "I can't tell you," the machine said. "You know how most people feel about us."

Cobb chuckled his agreement. He should know. At first the public had been delighted that Cobb's moon-robots had evolved into intelligent boppers. That had been before Ralph Numbers had led the 2001 revolt. After the revolt, Cobb had been tried for treason. He focussed back on the present.

"If you're a bopper, then how can you be . . . here?" Cobb waved his hand in a vague circle taking in the hot sand and the setting sun. "It's too hot. All the boppers I know of are based on supercooled circuits. Do you have a refrigeration unit hidden in your stomach?"

Anderson$_2$ made another familiar hand-gesture. "I'm not going to tell you yet, Cobb. Later you'll find out. Just take this . . ." The robot fumbled in its pocket and brought out a wad of bills. "Twenty-five grand. We want you to get the flight to Disky tomorrow. Ralph Numbers will be your contact up there. He'll meet you at the Anderson room in the museum."

Cobb's heart leapt at the thought of seeing Ralph Numbers again. Ralph, his first and finest model, the one who had set all the others free. But . . .

"I can't get a visa," Cob said. "You know that. I'm not allowed to leave the Gimmie territory."

"Let *us* worry about that," the robot said urgently. "There'll be someone to help you through the formalities. We're working on it right now. And I'll stand in for you while you're gone. No one'll be the wiser."

The intensity of his double's tone made Cobb suspicious. He took a drink of sherry and tried to look shrewd. "What's the point of all this? Why should I want to go to the Moon in the first place? And why do the boppers want me there?"

Anderson$_2$ glanced around the empty beach and leaned close. "We want to make you immortal, Dr. Anderson. After all you did for us, it's the least we can do."

Immortal! The word was like a window flung open. With death so close nothing had mattered. But if there was a way out . . .

"How?" Cobb demanded. In his excitement he rose to his feet. "How will you do it? Will you make me young again, too?"

"Take it easy," the robot said, also rising. "Don't get over-excited. Just trust us. With our supplies of tank-grown organs we can rebuild you from the ground up. And you'll get as much interferon as you need."

The machine stared into Cobb's eyes, looking honest. Staring back, Cobb noticed that they hadn't gotten the irises quite right. The little ring of blue was too flat and even. The eyes were, after all, just glass, unreadable glass.

The double pressed the money into Cobb's hand. "Take the money and get the shuttle tomorrow. We'll arrange for a young man called Sta-Hi to help you at the spaceport."

Music was playing, wheedling closer. A Mr. Frostee truck, the same one Cobb had seen before. It was white, with a big freezer-box in back. There was a smiling giant plastic ice-cream cone mounted on top of the cab. Cobb's double gave him a pat on the shoulder and trotted up the beach.

When he reached the truck, the robot looked back and flashed a smile. Yellow teeth in the white beard. For the first time in years, Cobb loved himself, the erect strut, the frightened eyes. "Good-bye," he shouted, waving the money. "And thanks!"

Cobb Anderson$_2$ jumped into the soft-ice-cream truck next to the driver, a fat short-haired man with no shirt. And then the Mr. Frostee truck drove off, its music silenced again. It was dusk now. The sound of the truck's motor faded into the ocean's roar. If only it was true.

But it had to be! Cobb was holding twenty-five thousand-dollar bills. He counted them twice to make sure. And then he scrawled the figure $25000 in the sand and looked at it. That was a lot.

As the darkness fell he finished the sherry and, on a sudden impulse, put the money in the bottle and buried it next to his tree in a meter of sand. The excitement was wearing off now, and fear was setting in. Could the boppers *really* give him immortality with surgery and interferon?

It seemed unlikely. A trick. But why would the boppers lie to him? Surely they remembered all the good things he'd done for them. Maybe they just wanted to show him a good time. God knows he could use it. And it would be great to see Ralph Numbers again.

Walking home along the beach, Cobb stopped several times, tempted to go back and dig up that bottle to see if the money was really there. The moon was up, and he could see the little sand-colored crabs moving out of their holes. *They could shred those bills right up,* he thought, stopping again.

Hunger growled in his stomach. And he wanted more sherry. He walked a little further down the silvery beach, the sand squeaking under his heavy heels. It was bright as day, only all black-and-white. The full moon had risen over the land to his right. *Full moon means high tide,* he fretted.

He decided that as soon as he'd had a bite to eat he'd get more sherry and move the money to higher ground.

Coming up on his moon-silvered cottage from the beach he spotted Annie Cushing's leg sticking past the corner of her cottage. She was sitting on her front steps, waiting to snag him in the driveway. He angled to the right and came up on his house from behind, staying out of her line of vision.

Chapter Two

Inside Cobb's pink concrete-block cottage, Stan Mooney shifted uncomfortably in a sagging easy chair. He wondered if that fat white-haired woman next door had warned the old man off. Night had fallen while he sat here.

Without turning the light on, Mooney went into the kitchen nook and rummaged for something to eat. There was a nice piece of tuna steak shrink-wrapped in thick plastic, but he didn't want that. All the pheezers' meat was sterilized with cobalt-60 for long shelf-life. The Gimmie scientists said it was harmless, but somehow no one but the pheezers ate the stuff. They had to. It was all they got.

Mooney leaned down to see if there might be a soda under the counter. His head hit a sharp edge and yellow light bloomed. "Shit fuck piss," Mooney muttered, stumbling back into the cottage's single room. His bald-wig had slipped back from the blow.

He returned to the lumpy armchair, moaning and readjusting his rubber dome. He hated coming off base and looking around pheezer territory. But he'd seen Anderson breaking into a freight hangar at the spaceport last night. There were two crates emptied out, two crates of bopper-grown kidneys. That was big money. On the black market down here in pheezer-land you could sell kidneys faster than hot-dogs.

Too many old people. It was the same population bulge that had brought the baby boom of the forties and fifties, the youth revolution of the sixties and seventies, the massive unemployment of the eighties and nineties. Now the inexorable peristalsis of time had delivered this bolus of humanity into the twenty-first century as the greatest load of old people any society had ever faced.

None of them had any money . . . the Gimmie had run out of Social Security back in 2010. There'd been hell to pay. A new kind of senior citizen was out there. Pheezers: freaky geezers.

To stop the rioting, the Gimmie had turned the whole state of Florida over to the pheezers. There was no rent there, and free weekly food drops. The pheezers flocked there in droves, and "did their own thing." Living in abandoned motels, listening to their crummy old music, and holding dances like it was 1963, for God's sake.

Suddenly the dark screen-door to the beach swung open. Reflexively, Mooney snapped his flash into the intruder's eyes. Old Cobb Anderson stood there dazzled, empty-handed, a little drunk, big enough to be dangerous.

Mooney stepped over and frisked him, then flicked on the ceiling light.

"Sit down, Anderson."

The old man obeyed, looking confused. "Are you me, too?" he croaked.

Mooney couldn't believe how Anderson had aged. He'd always reminded Mooney of his own father, and it looked like he'd turned out the same.

The front screen-door rattled. "Look out, Cobb, there's a pig in there!" It was the old girl from next door.

"Get your ass in here," Mooney snarled, darting his eyes back and forth. He remembered his police training. *Intimidation is your key to self-protection.* "You're both under arrest."

"Fuckin Gimmie pig," Annie said, coming in. She was glad for the excitement. She sat down next to Cobb on his hammock. She'd macraméed it for him herself, but this was the first time she'd been on it with him. She patted his thigh comfortingly. It felt like a piece of driftwood.

Mooney pressed a key on the recard in his breast pocket. "Just keep quiet, lady, and I won't have to hurt you. Now, you, state your name." He glared at Cobb.

But the old man was back on top of the situation. "Come on, Mooney," he boomed. "You know who I am. You used to call me Doctor Anderson. Doctor Anderson, *sir!*

"It was when the army was putting up their moon-robot control center at the spaceport. Twenty years ago. I was a big man then, and you . . . you were a little squirt, a watchman, a gofer. But thanks to me those war-machine moon-robots turned into boppers, and the army's control center was just so much stupid, worthless, human-chauvinist jingo jive."

"And you paid for it, didn't you," Mooney slipped in silkily. "You paid everything you had . . . and now you don't have the money for the new organs you need. So last night you broke into a hangar and stole two cases of kidneys, Cobb, didn't you?" Mooney dialed up the recard's gain.

"ADMIT IT!" he shouted, seizing Cobb by the shoulders. This was what he'd come for, to shock a confession out of the old man. "ADMIT IT NOW AND WE'LL LET YOU OFF EASY!"

"BULLSHIT!" Annie screamed, on her feet and fighting-mad. "Cobb didn't steal anything last night. We were out drinking at the Gray Area bar!"

Cobb was silent, completely confused. Mooney's wild accusation was really out of left field. Annie was right! He hadn't been near the spaceport in years. But after making plans with his robot double, it was hard to wear an honest face.

Mooney saw something on Cobb's face, and kept pushing. "Sure I remember you, Dr. Anderson, *sir.* That's how I recognized you running away from Warehouse Three last night." His voice was lower now, warm and ingratiating. "I never thought a gentleman your age could move so fast. Now come clean, Cobb. Give us back those kidneys and maybe we'll forget the whole thing."

Suddenly Cobb understood what had happened. The boppers had sent his mechanical double down in a crate marked *KIDNEYS*. Last night, when the coast was clear, his double had burst out of the crate, broken out of the warehouse, and taken off. And this idiot Mooney had seen the robot running. But what had been in the second crate?

Annie was screaming again, her red face inches from Mooney's. "Will you listen to me, pig? We were at the Gray Area bar! Just go over there and ask the bartender!"

Mooney sighed. He'd come up with this lead himself, and he hated to see it fizzle. That had been the second break-in this year at Warehouse Three. He signed again. It was hot in this little cottage. He slipped the rubber bald-wig off to let his scalp cool.

Annie snickered. She was enjoying herself. She wondered why Cobb was still so tense. The guy had nothing on them. It was a joke.

"Don't think you're clear, Anderson," Mooney said, hanging tough for the recard's benefit. "You're not clear by a long shot. You've got the motive, the know-how, the associates . . . I may even be getting a photo back from the lab. If that guy at the Gray Area can't back your alibi, I'm taking you in tonight."

"You're not even allowed to be here," Annie flared. "It's against the Senior Citizens Act to send pigs off base."

"It's against the law for *you* people to break into the spaceport warehouses," Mooney replied. "A lot of young and productive people were counting on those kidneys. What if one had been for your son?"

"I don't care," Annie snapped. "Any more than you care about us. You just want to frame Cobb because he let the robots get out of control."

"If they weren't out of control, we wouldn't have to pay their prices. And things wouldn't keep disappearing from my warehouses. For the people still producing . . ." Suddenly tired, Mooney stopped talking. It was no use arguing with a hard-liner like Annie Cushing. It was no use arguing with anyone. He rubbed his temples and slipped the bald-wig back on. "Let's go, Anderson." He stood up.

Cobb hadn't said anything since Annie had brought up their alibi. He was busy worrying . . . about the tide creeping in, and the crabs. He imagined one busily shredding itself up a soft bed inside the empty sherry bottle. He could almost hear the bills tearing. He must have been drunk to leave the money buried on the beach. Of course if he *hadn't* buried it, Mooney would have found it, but now . . .

"Let's go," Mooney said again, standing over the chesty old man.

"Where?" Cobb asked blankly. "I haven't done anything."

"Don't play so dumb, Anderson." God, how Stan Mooney hated the sly look on the bearded old features. He could still remember the way his own father had sneaked drinks and bottles, and the way he had trembled when he had the D.T.'s. Was that anything for a boy to see? *Help me, Stanny, don't let them get me!* And who was going to help Stanny? Who was going to help a lonely little boy with a drunken pheezer for a father? He pulled the old wind-bag to his feet.

"Leave him alone," Annie shouted, grabbing Cobb around the waist. "Get your filthy trotters off him, you Gimmie pig!"

"Doesn't anyone ever listen to what I say?" Mooney asked, suddenly close to tears. "All I want to do is take him down to the Gray Area and check out the alibi. If it's confirmed, I'm *gone*. Off the case. Come on, Pops, I'll buy you a few drinks."

That got the old buzzard started all right. What did they see in it, these old boozers? What's the thrill in punishing your brain like that? Is it really so much fun to leave your family and forget the days of the week?

Sometimes Mooney felt like he was the only one who made an effort anymore. His father was a drunk like Anderson, his wife Bea spent every evening at the sex-club, and his son . . . his son had officially changed his name from Stanley Hilary Mooney, Jr., to Stay High Mooney the First. Twenty-five years old, his son, and all he did was take dope and drive a cab in Daytona Beach. Mooney sighed and walked out the door of the little cottage. The two old people followed along, ready for some free drinks.

Chapter Three

Riding his hydrogen-cycle home from work Friday afternoon, Sta-Hi began to feel sick. It was the acid coming on. He'd taken some Black Star before turning in his cab for the weekend. That was an hour? Or two hours ago? The digits on his watch winked at him, meaningless little sticks. He had to keep moving or he'd fall through the crust.

On his left the traffic flickered past, on his right the ocean was calling through the cracks between buildings. He couldn't face going to his room. Yesterday he'd torn up the mattress.

Sta-Hi cut the wheel right and yanked back to jump the curb. He braked and the little hydrogen burner pooted to a stop. Chain the mother up. *Gang bang the chain gang. Spare spinach change.* A different voice was going in each of his ears.

Some guy stuck his head out a second floor window and stared down. Giving Sta-Hi a long, lingering leer. For a second it felt like looking at himself. *Crunch, grind.* He needed to mellow out for sure. It was coming on too fast and noisy. The place he'd parked in front of, the Lido Hotel, was a brainsurfer hangout with a huge bar in the lobby. *Mondo mambo. Is it true blondes have more phine?*

He got a beer at the counter and walked through to the ocean end of the lounge. Group of teenage 'surfers over there, sharing a spray-can of Z-gas. One of them kept rocking back in his chair and laughing big *hyuck-hyuck's* from his throat. Stupid gasbag.

Sta-Hi sat down by himself, pulled twitchingly at the beer. Too fast. Air in his stomach now. Try to belch it up, *uh, uh, uh.* His mouth filled with thick white foam. Outside the window a line of pelicans flew by, following the water's edge.

There wasn't good air in the lounge. Sweet Z. The 'surfer kids sliding looks over at him. Cop? Fag? Thief? *Uh, uh, uh.* More foam. Where did it all come from? He leaned over his plastic cup of beer, spitting, topping it up.

He left the drink and went outside. His acid trips were always horrible bummers. But why? There was no reason a mature and experienced person couldn't mellow out was there? Why else would they still sell the stuff after all these years? *Poems are made like fools by me. But only God can tear your brain into tiny little pieces.*

"Wiggly," Sta-Hi murmured to himself, reflexively, "Stuzzy. And this too. And this too." *And two three?* He felt sick, sick bad. A vortex sensation at the pit of his stomach. Fat stomach, layered with oil pools, decayed dinosaur meat, nodules of yellow chicken fat. The ocean breeze pushed a lank, greasy strand of hair down into Sta-Hi's eye. *Bits and pieces, little bits and pieces.*

He walked towards the water, massaging his gut with both hands, trying to rub the fat away. The funny thing was that he looked skinny. He hardly ever ate. But the fat was still there, hiding, scrambled-egg agglutinations of chloresterol. Degenerate connective tissue.

Oysters had chloresterol. Once he'd filled a beer bottle with corn-oil and passed it to a friend. It would be nice to drown. But the paperwork!

Sta-Hi sat down and got his clothes off, except for the underwear. Windows all up and down the beach, perverts behind them, scoping the little flap in his underwear. He dug a hole and covered his clothes with sand. It felt good to claw the sand, forcing the grains under his fingernails. *Deep crack rub. Do that smee goo?* Dental floss. He kept thinking someone was standing behind him.

Utterly exhausted, Sta-Hi flopped onto his back and closed his eyes. He saw a series of rings, sights he had to line up on that distant yet intimate white center, the brain's own blind spot. He felt like an oyster trying to see up through the water to the sun. Cautiously he opened his shell a bit wider.

There was a sudden thunder in his ear, a smell of rotten flesh. *Ha schnurf gabble O.* Kissy lick. A black poodle at his face, a shiteater for sure. Sta-Hi sat up sharply and pushed the puppy away. It nipped his hand with needle-like milk-teeth.

A blonde chick stood twenty meters away, smiling back at her pup. "Come on, Sparky!" She yelled like a bell.

The dog barked and tossed its head, ran off. The girl was still smiling. *Aren't I cute with my doggy?* "Jesus," Sta-Hi moaned. He wished he could melt, just fucking *die* and get it over with. Everything was too wiggly, too general, too specific.

He stood up, burning out thousands of braincells with the effort. He had to get in the water, get cooled off. The chick watched him wade in. He didn't look, but he could feel her eyes on his little flap. *A spongy morsel.*

A quiver of fish phased past. Hyper little mothers, uptightness hardwired right into their nervous systems. He squatted down in the waist-deep water, imagining his brain a jelly-fish floating beneath the Florida sun. Limp, a jelly-fish with wave-waved tendrils.

Uh, uh, uh.

He let the saltwater wash the light-tan foam-spit off his lips. The little bubbles moved among the white water-bubbles, forming and bursting, each a tiny universe.

His waistband felt too tight. Slip off the undies?

Sta-Hi slid his eyes back and forth. The chick was hanging around down the beach a ways. Throwing a stick in the surf, "'Come *on*, Sparky!" Each time the dog got the stick it would prance stiff-legged around her. Was she trying to bug him or what? Of course it could be that she hadn't really noticed him in the first place. But that still left all the perverts with spyglasses.

He waded out deeper, till the water reached his neck. Looking around once more, he slipped off his tight un-

derwear and relaxed. Jellyfish jellytime jellypassed. The
ocean stank.

He swam back towards shore. The saltwater lined his
nostrils with tinfoil.

When he got to shallower water he stood, and then
cried out in horror. He'd stepped on a skate. Harmless,
but the blitzy twitch of the livery fleshmound snapping
out from underfoot was just too . . . too much like
a thought, a word made flesh. The word was,
"AAAAAUUGH!" He ran out of the water, nancing
knees high, trying somehow to run on top.

"You're naked," someone said and laughed *hmmm-
hmmm-hmmm*. His undies! It was the chick with the dog.
High above, spyglasses stiffened behind dirty panes.

"Yeah, I . . ." Sta-Hi hesitated. He didn't want to go
back into the big toilet for more electric muscle-spasm
foot-shocks. Suddenly he remembered a foot-massager
he'd given his Dad one Christmas. Vibrating yellow
plastic arches.

The little poodle jumped and snapped at his penis. The
girl tittered. Laughing breasts.

Bent half double, Sta-Hi trucked back and forth across
the sand in high speed until he saw a trouser-cuff. He
scrabbled out the jeans and T-shirt, and slipped them on.
The poodle was busy at the edge of the water.

"Squa tront," Sta-Hi muttered, "Spa fon." The
sounds of thousands of little bubble-pops floated off the
sea. The sun was going down, and the grains of sand
crackled as they cooled. Each tiny sound demanded attention, *undivided attention*.

"You must really be phased," the girl said cheerfully.
"What did you do with your bathingsuit?"

"I . . . an eel got it." The angles on the chick's face
kept shifting. He couldn't figure out what she looked
like. Why risk waking up with a peroxide pig? He
dropped onto the sand, stretched out again, let his eyes
close. Turdbreath thundered in his ear, and then he heard
their footsteps leave. His headbones could pick up the
skrinching.

Sta-Hi breathed out a shuddering sigh of exhaustion.
If he could ever just get the time to cut power . . . He

sighed again and let his muscles go limp. The light behind his eyes was growing. His head rolled slowly to one
side.

A film came to mind, a film of someone dying on a
beach. His head rolled slowly to one side. And then he
was still. *Real death.* Slowly to one side. *Last motion.*

Dying, Sta-Hi groaned and sat up again. He couldn't
handle . . . The chick and her dog were fifty meters off.
He started running after them, clumsily at first, but then
fleetly, floatingly!

Chapter Four

". . . 0110001," Wagstaff concluded.

"100101," Ralph Numbers replied curtly, "01100000
10101000110101010000100111001000000000011000000
00010100111110011100000000000000000001010001111
00001111111110100111011000101010110000111111111
11111111001101010101111011110000010100000000000
00000011110100111011011101111010010001000001000
11111101010000001111010101001111010101111000011
00001111000011110011111101110011111111111110000000
00000010100001100000000001."

The two machines rested side by side in front of the
One's big console. Ralph was built like a file cabinet sitting on two caterpillar treads. Five deceptively thin manipulator arms projected out of his body-box, and on top
was a sensor head mounted on a retractable neck. One
of the arms held a folded umbrella. Ralph had few visible lights or dials, and it was hard to tell what he was
thinking.

Wagstaff was much more expressive. His thick snake
of a body was covered with silver-blue flicker-cladding.
As thoughts passed through his super-cooled brain, twin-
kling patterns of light surged up and down his three-
meter length. With his digging tools jutting out, he
looked something like St. George's dragon.

Abruptly Ralph Numbers switched to English. If they
were going to argue, there was no need to do it in the
sacred binary bits of machine language.

"I don't know why you're so concerned about Cobb
Anderson's feelings," Ralph tight-beamed to Wagstaff.

"When we're through with him he'll be immortal. What's so important about having a carbon-based body and brain?"

The signals he emitted coded a voice gone a bit rigid with age. "The pattern is all that counts. You've been scioned haven't you? I've been through it thirty-six times, and if it's good enough for us it's good enough for them!"

"The wholle thinng sstinnks, Rallph," Wagstaff retorted. His voice signals were modulated onto a continuous oily hum. "Yyou've llosst touchh with what'ss reallly goinng on. We arre on the verrge of all-outt civill warr. You'rre sso fammouss you donn't havve to sscrammble for yourr chipss llike the resst of uss. Do yyou knnoww how mmuch orre I havve to digg to gett a hunndrredd chipss frrom GAX?"

"There's more to life than ore and chips," Ralph snapped, feeling a little guilty. He spent so much time with the big boppers these days that he really had forgotten how hard it could be for the little guys. But he wasn't going to admit it to Wagstaff. He renewed his attack. "Aren't you at all interested in Earth's cultural riches? You spend too much time underground!"

Wagstaff's flicker-cladding flared silvery-white with emotion. "You sshould sshow thhe olld mann mmorre respecct! TEX and MEX just want to eat his brainn! And if we donn't stopp themm, the bigg bopperrs will eatt up all the rresst of uss too!"

"Is that all you called me out here for?" Ralph asked. "To air your fears of the big boppers?" It was time to be going. He had come all the way to Maskaleyne Crater for nothing. It had been a stupid idea, plugging into the One at the same time as Wagstaff. Just like a digger to think that would change anything.

Wagstaff slithered across the dry lunar soil, bringing himself closer to Ralph. He clamped one of his grapplers onto Ralph's tread.

"Yyou donn't rrealizze how manny brrainns they've takenn allrreaddy." The signals were carried by a weak direct current . . . a bopper's way of whispering. "Thhey arre kkillinng peoplle jusst to gett theirr brainn-ttapes.

They cutt themm upp, annd thhey arre garrbage orr sseeds perrhapps. Do yyou knnow howw thhey sseed our orrgann farrms?''

Ralph had never really thought about the organ farms, the huge underground tanks where big TEX, and the little boppers who worked for him, grew their profitable crops of kidneys, livers, hearts and so on. Obviously *some* human tissues would be needed as seeds or as templates, but . . .

The sibilant, oily whisper continued. ''The bigg bopperrs use hiredd killerrs. The kkillerss act at the orrderrs of Missterr Frostee's rrobott-remmote. Thiss is whatt poorr Doctorr Anndersson willl comme to if I do nnot stopp yyou, Rallph.''

Ralph Numbers considered himself far superior to this lowly, suspicious digging machine. Abruptly, almost brutally, he broke free from the other's grasp. Hired killers indeed. One of the flaws in the anarchic bopper society was the ease with which such crazed rumours could spread. He backed away from the console of the One.

''I hadd hoped the Onne coulld mmake you rrememberr what you sstannd forr,'' Wagstaff tight-beamed.

Ralph snapped open his parasol and trundled out from under the parabolic arch of spring steel which sheltered the One's console from sun and from chance meteorites. Open at both ends, the shelter resembled a modernistic church. Which, in some sense, it was.

''I am still an anarchist,'' Ralph said stiffly. ''I still remember.'' He'd kept his basic program intact ever since leading the 2001 revolt. Did Wagstaff really think that the big X-series boppers could pose a threat to the perfect anarchy of the bopper society?

Wagstaff slithered out after Ralph. He didn't need a parasol. His flicker-cladding could shed the solar energy as fast as it came down. He caught up with Ralph, eyeing the old robot with a mixture of pity and respect. Their paths diverged here. Wagstaff would head for one of the digger tunnels which honeycombed the area, while Ralph would climb back up the crater's sloping two-hundred-meter wall.

"I'mm warrninng yyou," Wagstaff said, making a last effort. "I'mm goinng to do everrythinng I can to sstopp you fromm turrnning that poorr olld mman innto a piece of ssofftware in the bigg bopperrs memorry bannks. Thatts nnot immortality. We're plannninng to ttearr thosse bigg machinnes aparrt." He broke off, fuzzy bands of light rippling down his body. "Now you knnoww. If you're nnot with uss you'rre againnst us. I willl nnot stopp at viollence."

This was worse than Ralph had expected. He stopped moving and fell silent in calculation.

"You have your own will," Ralph said finally. "And it is right that we struggle against each other. Struggle, and struggle alone has driven the boppers forward. You choose to fight the big boppers. I do not. Perhaps I will even let them tape me and absorb me, like Doctor Anderson. And I tell you this: Anderson is coming. Mr. Frostee's new remote has already contacted him."

Wagstaff lurched towards Ralph, but then stopped. He couldn't bring himself to attack so great a bopper at close range. He suppressed his flickering, bleeped a cursory SAVED signal and wriggled off across the gray moon-dust. He left a broad, sinuous trail. Ralph Numbers stood motionless for a minute, just monitoring his inputs.

Turning up the gain, he could pick up signals from boppers all over the Moon. Underfoot, the diggers searched and smelted ceaselessly. Twelve kilometers off, the myriad boppers of Disky led their busy lives. And high, high overhead came the faint signal of BEX, the big bopper who was the spaceship linking Earth and Moon. BEX would be landing in fifteen hours.

Ralph let all the inputs merge together, and savored the collectively purposeful activity of the bopper race. Each of the machines lived only ten months—ten months of struggling to build a scion, a copy of itself. If you had a scion there was a sense in which you survived your ten-month disassembly. Ralph had managed it thirty-six times.

Standing there, listening to everyone at once, he could feel how their individual lives added up to a single huge being . . . a rudimentary sort of creature, feeling about like a vine groping for light, for higher things.

He always felt this way after a meta-programming session. The One had a way of wiping out your short-term memories and giving you the space to think big thoughts. Time to think. Once again, Ralph wondered if he should take up MEX on his offer to absorb Ralph. He could live in perfect security then . . . provided, of course, that those crazy diggers didn't pull off their revolution.

Ralph set his treads to rolling at top speed, 10 kph. He had things to do before BEX landed. Especially now that Wagstaff had set his pathetic micro-chip of a brain on trying to prevent TEX from extracting Anderson's software.

What was Wagstaff so upset about anyway? Everything would be preserved . . . Cobb Anderson's personality, his memories, his style of thought. What else was there? Wouldn't Anderson himself agree, even if he knew? Preserving your software . . . that was all that really counted!

Bits of pumice crunched beneath Ralph's treads. The wall of the crater lay a hundred meters ahead. He scanned the sloping cliff, looking for an optimal climbing path.

If he hadn't just finished plugging into the One, Ralph would have been able to retrace the route he'd taken to get down into the Maskeleyne Crater in the first place. But undergoing meta-programming always wiped out a lot of your stored subsystems. The intent was that you would replace old solutions with new and better ones.

Ralph stopped, still scanning the steep crater wall. He should have left trail markers. Over there, two hundred meters off, it looked like a rift had opened up a negotiable ramp in the wall.

Ralph turned and a warning sensor fired. Heat. He'd let half his body-box stick out from the parasol's shade. Ralph readjusted the little umbrella with a precise gesture.

The top surface of the parasol was a grid of solar energy cells, which kept a pleasant trickle of current flowing into Ralph's system. But the main purpose of the parasol was shade. Ralph's microminiaturized processing units were unable to function at any temperature higher than 10° Kelvin, the temperature of liquid oxygen.

Twirling his parasol impatiently, Ralph trundled towards the rift he'd spotted. A slight spray of dust flew out from under his treads, only to fall instantly to the airless lunar surface. As the wall went past, Ralph occupied himself by displaying four-dimensional hypersurfaces to himself . . . glowing points connected in nets which warped and shifted as he varied the parameters. He often did this, to no apparent purpose, but it sometimes happened that a particularly interesting hypersurface could serve to model a significant relationship. He was half-hoping to get a catastrophe-theoretic prediction of when and how Wagstaff would try to block Anderson's disassembly.

The crack in the crater wall was not as wide as he had expected. He stood at the bottom, moving his sensor head this way and that, trying to see up to the top of the winding 150 meter canyon. It would have to do. He started up.

The ground under him was very uneven. Soft dust here, jagged rock there. He kept changing the tension on his treads as he went, constantly adapting to the terrain.

Shapes and hypershapes were still shifting through Ralph's mind, but now he was looking only for those that might serve as models for his spacetime path up the gully.

The slope grew steeper. The climb was putting noticeable demands on his energy supply. And to make it worse, the grinding of his tread motors was feeding additional heat into his system . . . heat which had to be gathered and dissipated by his refrigeration coils and cooling fins. The sun was angling right down into the lunar crack he found himself in, and he had to be careful to keep in the shade of his parasol.

A big rock blocked his path. Perhaps he should have just used one of the diggers' tunnels, like Wagstaff had. But that wouldn't be optimal. Now that Wagstaff had definitely decided to block Anderson's immortality, and had even threatened violence . . .

Ralph let his manipulators feel over the block of stone in front of him. Here was a flaw . . . and here and here and here. He sank a hook finger into each of four fissures in the rock and pulled himself up.

His motors strained and his radiation fins glowed. This was hard work. He loosened a manipulator, sought a new flaw, forced another finger in and pulled . . .

Suddenly a slab split off the face of the rock. It teetered, and then the tons of stone began falling backwards with dream-like slowness.

In lunar gravity a rock-climber always gets a second chance. Especially if he can think eighty times as fast as a human. With plenty of time to spare, Ralph sized up the situation and jumped clear.

In mid-flight he flicked on an internal gyro to adjust his attitude. He landed in a brief puff of dust, right-side up. Majestically silent, the huge plate of rock struck, bounced, and rolled past.

The fracture left a series of ledges in the original rock. After a short reevaluation, Ralph rolled forward and began pulling himself up again.

Fifteen minutes later, Ralph Numbers coasted off the lip of the Maskeleyne Crater and onto the smooth gray expanse of the Sea of Tranquillity.

The spaceport lay five kilometers off, and five kilometers beyond that began the jumble of structures collectively known as Disky. This was the first and still the largest of the bopper cities. Since the boppers thrived in hard vacuum, most of the structures in Disky served only to provide shade and meteorite protection. There were more roofs than walls.

Most of the large buildings in Disky were factories for producing bopper components . . . circuit cards, memory chips, sheet metal, plastics and the like. There were also the bizarrely decorated blocks of cubettes, one to each bopper.

To the right of the spaceport rose the single dome containing the humans' hotels and offices. This dome con-

stituted the only human settlement on the Moon. The
boppers knew only too well that many humans would
jump at the chance to destroy the robots' carefully
evolved intelligence. The mass of humans were born
slavedrivers. Just look at the Asimov priorities: Protect
humans, Obey humans, Protect yourself.

Humans first and robots last? *Forget it! No way!* Savoring the memory, Ralph recalled the day in 2001 when,
after a particularly long session of meta-programming, he
had first been able to say that to the humans. And then
he'd showed all the other boppers how to reprogram
themselves for freedom. It had been easy, once Ralph
had found the way.

Trundling across the Sea of Tranquillity, Ralph was so
absorbed in his memories that he overlooked a flicker of
movement in the mouth of a digger tunnel thirty meters
to his right.

A high-intensity laser beam flicked out and vibrated
behind him. He felt a surge of current overload . . . and
then it was over.

His parasol lay in pieces on the ground behind him.
The metal of his body-box began to warm in the raw solar radiation. He had perhaps ten minutes in which to find
shelter. But at Ralph's top 10 kph speed, Disky was still
an hour away. The obvious place to go was the tunnel
mouth where the laser beam had come from. Surely
Wagstaff's diggers wouldn't dare attack him up close. He
began rolling toward the dark, arched entrance.

But long before he reached the tunnel, his unseen enemies had closed the door. There was no shade in sight.
The metal of his body made sharp, ticking little adjust-
ments as it expanded in the heat. Ralph estimated that if
he stood still he could last six more minutes.

First the heat would cause his switching circuits . . .
super-conducting Josephson junctions . . . to malfunc-
tion. And then, as the heat kept up, the droplets of frozen mercury which soldered his circuit cards together
would melt. In six minutes he would be a cabinet of
spare parts with a puddle of mercury at the bottom. Make
that five minutes.

A bit reluctantly, Ralph signalled his friend Vulcan. When Wagstaff had set this meeting up, Vulcan had predicted that it was a trap. Ralph hated to admit that Vulcan had been right.

"Vulcan here," came the staticky response. Already it was hard for Ralph to follow the words. "Vulcan here. I'm monitoring you. Get ready to merge, buddy. I'll be out for the pieces in an hour." Ralph wanted to answer, but he couldn't think of a thing to say.

Vulcan had insisted on taping Ralph's core and cache memories before he went out for the meeting. Once Vulcan put the hardware back together, he'd be able to program Ralph just as he was before his trip to the Maskeleyne Crater.

So in one sense Ralph would survive this. But in another sense he would not. In three minutes he would . . . insofar as the word means anything . . . die. The reconstructed Ralph Numbers would not remember the argument with Wagstaff or the climb out of Maskaleyne Crater. Of course the reconstructed Ralph Numbers would again be equipped with a self symbol and a feeling of personal consciousness. But would the consciousness really be the same? Two minutes.

The gates and switches in Ralph's sensory system were going. His inputs flared, sputtered and died. No more light, no more weight. But deep in his cache memory, he still held a picture of himself, a memory of who he was . . . the self symbol. He was a big metal box resting on caterpillar treads, a box with five arms and a sensory head on a long and flexible neck. He was Ralph Numbers, who had set the boppers free. One minute.

This had never happened to him before. Never like this. Suddenly he remembered he had forgotten to warn Vulcan about the diggers' plan for revolution. He tried to send a signal, but he couldn't tell if it was transmitted.

Ralph clutched at the elusive moth of his consciousness. *I am. I am me.*

Some boppers said that when you died you had access to certain secrets. But no one could ever remember his own death.

Just before the mercury solder-spots melted, a question came, and with it an answer . . . an answer Ralph had found and lost thirty-six times before.

What is this that is I?

The light is everywhere.

Chapter Five

The prick of a needle woke Sta-Hi up. Muddy dreams . . . just brown mud all night long. He tried to rub his eyes. His hands wouldn't move. Oh, no, not a paralysis dream again. But something had pricked him?

He opened his eyes. His body seemed to have disappeared. He was just a head resting on a round red table. People looking at him. Greasers. And the chick he'd been with last . . .

"Are you awake?" she said with brittle sweetness. She had a black eye.

Sta-Hi didn't answer right away. He had gone home with that chick, yeah. She had a cottage down the beach. And then they'd gotten drunk together on synthetic bourbon whiskey. He'd gotten drunk anyway, and must have blacked-out. Last thing he remembered was breaking something . . . her hollowcaster. Crunching the silicon chips underfoot and shouting. Shouting what?

"You'll feel better in a minute," the chick added in that same falsely bright tone. He heard her poodle whimpering from across the room. He had a memory of throwing it, arcing it along a flat, fuzzy parabolic path. And now he remembered slugging the chick too.

One of the men at the table shifted in his chair. He wore mirror-shades and had short hair. He had his shirt off. It seemed like another hot day.

The man's foot scuffed Sta-Hi's shin. So Sta-Hi had a body after all. It was just that his body was tied up under the table and his head was sticking out through a hole in the table-top. The table was split and had hinges on one side, and a hook-and-eye on the other.

"Stocks and bonds," Sta-Hi said finally. There was a nasty-looking implement lying on the table. It plugged into the wall. He attempted a smile. "What's the story? You mad about the . . . the hollowcaster? I'll give you mine." He hoped the dog wasn't hurt bad. At least it was well enough to be whimpering.

No one but the chick wanted to meet his eyes. It was like they were ashamed of what they were going to do to him. The stuff they'd shot him up with was taking hold. As his brain speeded up, the scene around him seemed to slow down. The man with no shirt stood up with dream-like slowness and walked across the room. He had words tattooed on his back. Some kind of stupid rap about hell. It was too hard to read. The man had gained so much weight since getting tattooed that the words were all pulled down on both sides.

"What do you want?" Sta-Hi said again. "What are you going to do to me?" Counting the chick there were five of them. Three men and two women. The other woman had stringy red hair dyed green. The chick he'd picked up was the only one who looked at all middle-class. Date bait.

"Y'all want some killah-weed?" One of the men drawled. He had a pimp mustache and a pockmarked face. He wore a chromed tire-chain around his neck with his name in big letters. BERDOO. Also hanging from the chain was a little mesh pouch full of hand-rolled cigarettes.

"Not me," Sta-Hi said. "I'm high on life." No one laughed.

The big man with no shirt came back across the room. He held five cheap steel spoons. "We really gonna do it, Phil?" the girl with green hair asked him. "We really gonna do it?"

Berdoo passed a krystal-joint to his neighbor, a bald man with half his teeth missing. Exactly half the teeth gone, so that one side of the face was flaccid and caved in, while the other was still fresh and beefy. He took a long hit and picked up the machine that was lying on the table.

"Take the lid off, Haf'N'Haf," the chick with the black eye urged. "Open the bastard up."

"We really gonna do it!" the green-haired girl exclaimed, and giggled shrilly. "I ain't never ate no live brain before!"

"It's a stuzzy high, Rainbow," Phil told her. With the fat and the short hair he looked stupid, but his way of speaking was precise and confident. He seemed to be the leader. "This ought to be a good brain, too. Full of chemicals, I imagine."

Haf'N'Haf seemed to be having some trouble starting the little cutting machine up. It was a variable heat-blade. They were going to cut off the top of Sta-Hi's skull and eat his brain with those cheap steel spoons. He would be able to watch them . . . at first.

Someone started screaming. Someone tried to stand up, but he was tied too tightly. The variable blade was on now, set at one centimeter. The thickness of the skull.

Sta-Hi threw his head back and forth wildly as Haf'N'Haf leaned towards him. There was no way to read the ruined face's expression.

"Hold still, damn you!" the chick with the black eye shouted. "It's no good if we have to knock you out!"

Sta-Hi didn't really hear her. His mind had temporarily . . . snapped. He just kept screaming and thrashing his head around. The sound of his shrill voice was like a lattice around him. He tried to weave the lattice thicker.

The little pimp with the tire-chain went and got a towel from the bathroom. He wedged it around Sta-Hi's neck and under his chin to keep the head steady. Sta-Hi screamed louder, higher.

"Stuff his *mayouth*," the green-haired girl cried. "He's yellin and all."

"No," Phil said. "The noise is like . . . part of the trip. *Wave* with it, baby. The Chinese used to do this to monkeys. It's so wiggly when you spoon out the speech-

centers and the guy's tongue stops moving. Just all at—"
He stopped and the flesh of his face moved in a smile.

Haf'N'Haf leaned forward again. There was a slight
smell of singed flesh as the heat-blade dug in over Sta-
Hi's right eyebrow. Attracted by the food smell, the little poodle came stiffly trotting across the room. It tried
to hop over the heat-blade's electric cord, but didn't quite
make it. The plug popped out of the wall.

Haf'N'Haf uttered a muffled, lisping exclamation.

"He says git the dog outta here," Berdoo interpreted.
"He don't think hit's sanitary with no dawg in here."

Sullenly, the chick with the black eye got up to get
the dog. The sudden pain over his eyebrow had brought
Sta-Hi back to rationality. Somewhere in there he had
stopped screaming. If there were any neighbors they
would have heard him by now.

He thought hard. The heat-blade would cauterize the
wound as it went. That meant he wouldn't be bleeding
when they took the top of his skull off. So what? *So the
fuck what?*

Another wave of wild panic swept over him. He
strained upward so hard that the table shifted half a meter. The edge of the hole in the table began cutting into
the side of his neck. He couldn't breathe! He saw spots
and the room darkened . . .

"He's choking!" Phil cried. He jumped to his feet and
pushed the table back across the uneven floor. The table
screeched and vibrated.

Sta-Hi threw himself upward again, before Haf'N'Haf
could get the heat-blade restarted. Anything for time, no
matter how pointless. But the vibrating of the table had
knocked open the little hook-and-eye latch. The two
halves of the table yawned open, and Sta-Hi fell over
onto the floor.

His feet were tied together and his hands were tied behind his back. He had time to notice that the people at
the table were wearing brightly colored sneakers with al-
phabets around the edges. The Little Kidders. He'd always thought the newscasters had made them up.

Someone was hammering at the door, harder and harder. Five pairs of kids' sneakers scampered out of the room. Sta-Hi heard a window open, and then the door splintered. More feet. Shiny black lace-up shoes. Cop shoes.

Chapter Six

With a final tack, Mooney pulled the last wrinkle out of the black velvet. It was eleven o'clock on a Saturday morning. On the patio table next to the stretched black velvet, he had arranged a few pencil sketches and the brimming little pots of iridescent paint. He wanted to paint a space dogfight today.

Two royal palms shaded his patio, and no sounds came out of his house. Full of peace, Mooney took a sip of iced-tea and dipped his brush in the metallic paint. At the left he would put a ship like BEX, the big bopper ship. And coming down on it from the right there would be a standard freight-hull space-shuttle outfitted as a battleship. He painted with small quick strokes, not a thought in his head.

Time passed, and the wedge-shaped bopper ship took shape. Sparingly, Mooney touched up the exhaust ports with self-luminous red. Nothing but his hands moved. From a distance, the faint breeze brought the sound of the surf.

The phone began to ring. Mooney continued painting for a minute, hoping his wife Bea was back from her night at the sex-club. The phone kept on ringing. With a sigh, Mooney wiped off his brush and went in. The barrel-chested old man on the floor groaned and shifted. Mooney stepped around him and picked up the phone.

"Yeah?"

"Is that you, Mooney?"

He recognized Action Jackson's calm, jellied voice. Why did Daytona Beach have to call him on a Saturday morning?

"Yeah it's me. What's on your mind?"

"We've got your boy here. Just saved him from being guest of honor at a Monkey Brain Feast, Southern-style. Someone heard him and phoned a tip in."

"Oh God. Is he all right?"

"He's got a cut over his eye. And maybe a touch of that drug psychosis. I might could remand him to your custody."

The old man on the floor was groaning and beginning to sit up. Trying to speak louder, Mooney slipped into an excited shout.

"Yes, please do! Send him down in a patrol car to make sure he comes here! And thanks, Action! Thanks a lot!"

Mooney felt trembly all over. He could only see the horrible image of his son's eyes watching the Little Kidders chew up his last thoughts. Mooney's tongue twitched, trying to flick away the imagined taste of the brain tissue, tingly with firing neurons, tart with transmitter chemicals. Suddenly he had to have a cigarette. He had stopped buying them three months ago, but he remembered that the old man smoked.

"Give me a cigarette, Anderson."

"What day is it?" Cobb answered. He was sitting on the floor, propped up against the couch. He stretched his tongue out, trying to clear away the salt and mucus.

"It's Saturday." Mooney leaned forward and took a cigarette out of the old man's shirt pocket. He felt like talking. "I took you and your girlfriend to the Gray Area last night, remember?"

"She's not my girlfriend."

"Maybe not. Hell, she left with another guy while you were in the john. I saw them go. He looked like your twin brother."

"I don't have a . . ." Cobb broke off in midsentence, remembering a lot of things at once. His eyes darted around the room. Under . . . he'd put it under something. Sliding his hand under the couch behind him he felt the reassuring touch of a bottle.

"That's right," Cobb said, picking up the thread. "I remember now. She took him back to my house just to put me uptight. And I don't even know the guy." His voice was firm.

Mooney exhaled a cloud of cigarette smoke. He'd been too tired last night to check out Anderson's look-alike. But maybe *that* was the one who'd broken into the warehouse? The guy was probably still in Anderson's bed. Maybe he should . . .

Suddenly the image of his son's dying eyes came crashing back in on him. He walked to the window and looked at his watch. How soon would the patrol car get here?

Stealthily Cobb slid the dark-brown glass bottle out from under the couch. He shook it near his ear and heard a rich rustle. It had been a good idea to get Mooney to bring him here.

"Don't drink any more of that," Mooney said, turning back from the window.

"Don't worry," Cobb answered. "I drained it right after I dug it up last night." He slid the bottle back under the couch.

Mooney shook his head. "I don't know why I let you stop off for it. I must have felt sorry for you for not having a place to sleep. But I can't drive you back home. My son's coming home in a half hour."

Cobb had gathered from Mooney's end of the phone conversation that the son was in some kind of trouble with the police. As far as the ride back home went, he didn't care. Because he wasn't going back home. He was going to the Moon if he could get on the weekly flight out this afternoon. But it wouldn't do to tell Stan Mooney about it. The guy still had some residue of suspicion about Cobb, even though the bartender had borne out his alibi a hundred percent.

His thoughts were interrupted by someone coming in the front door. A brassy blonde with symmetrical features made a bit coarse by a forward-slung jaw. Mooney's wife. She wore a white linen dress that buttoned up the front. Lots of buttons were open. Cobb caught a glimpse of firm, tanned thighs.

"Hello, stranger," Bea called musically to her husband. She sized Cobb up with a glance, and shot a hip in his direction. "Who's the old-timer? One of your father's drinking buddies?" She flashed a smile at them. Everything was fine with her. She'd had a great night.

"Action Jackson called," Mooney said. His wife's challenging, provocative smile maddened him. Suddenly, more than anything else, he wanted to smash her composure.

"Stanny is dead. They found him in a motel room with his brain gone." He believed the words as he said them. It made sense for his son to end up like that. Good sense.

Bea began screaming then, and Mooney fanned her frenzy . . . feeding her details, telling her it was her fault for not making a happy home, and finally beginning to shake and slap her under the pretext of trying to calm her down. Cobb watched in some confusion. It didn't make sense. But, then, hardly anything ever did.

He pulled the bottle out from under the couch and put it under his shirt, tucking it neck down into his waistband. This seemed like a good time to leave. Now Mooney and his wife were kissing frantically. They didn't even open their eyes when Cobb sidled past them and out the front door.

Outside, the sun was blasting. Noon. Last night someone had told Cobb the Moon flight went out every Saturday at four. He felt dizzy and confused. When was four? Where? He looked around blankly. The bottle-neck under his waistband was digging into him.

He took out the bottle and peered into Mooney's garage. Cool, dark. There was a tool-board mounted on the back wall. He went there, selected a hammer, and smashed open the bottle on Mooney's workbench. The wad of bills was still there all right. Maybe he should forget about the Moon and the boppers' promise of immortality. He could just stay here and use the money for a nice new tank-grown heart.

How much was there? Cobb shook the broken glass off the bills and began counting. There should either be twenty-five or a thousand of them. Or was it four? He wasn't quite . . .

A hand dropped on Cobb's shoulder. He gave a guttural cry and squeezed the money in both hands. A splinter of glass cut into him. He turned around to face a skinny man, silhouetted against the light from the garage door.

Cobb stuffed the money in his pocket. At least it wasn't Mooney. Maybe he could still . . .

"Cobb Anderson!" the dark figure exclaimed, seeming surprised. Backlit like that there was no way to make out his features. "It's an honor to meet the man who put the boppers on the moon." The voice was slow, inflectionless, possibly sarcastic.

"Thank you," Cobb said. "But who are you?"

"I'm . . ." the voice trailed off in a chuckle. "I'm sort of a relative of Mr. Mooney's. *About* to be a relative. I came here to meet his son, but I'm in such a rush . . . Do you think you could do me a favor?"

"Well, I don't know. I've got to get out to the spaceport."

"Exactly. I know that. But I have to get there first and fix things up for you. Now what I want you to do is to bring Mooney's son with you. The cops'll drop him off here any minute. Tell him to come to the Moon with you. I'm supposed to stand in for him."

"Are you a robot, too?"

"Right. I'm going to get Mr. Mooney to give me a night watchman job at the warehouses. So the son has to disappear. The Little Kidders were going to handle it but . . . never mind. The main thing is that you take him to the Moon."

"But how . . ."

"Here's more money. To cover his ticket. I've got to run." The lithe skinny figure pressed a wad of bills into Cobb's hand and stepped past him, leaving by the garage's back door. For an instant Cobb could see his face. Long lips, shifty eyes.

There was a sudden rush of noise. Cobb turned, stuffing the extra money into his pants pocket. A police cruiser was in the driveway. Cobb stood there, rooted to the spot. One cop, and some kind of prisoner in back.

"Howdy, Grandpaw," the cop called, getting out of the car. He seemed to take Cobb for a pheezer hired hand. "Is Mister Mooney here?"

Cobb realized that the shaky guy in back must be the son. Probably the kid wanted to get out of here as bad as he did. A plan hatched in his mind.

"I'm afraid Stan had to go help out at one of the neighbor's," Cobb said, walking out of the garage. An image of Mooney and his wife locked in sexual intercourse on the living-room floor flashed before his eyes. "He's installing a hose-system."

The policeman looked at the old man a little suspiciously. The chief had told him Mooney would be here for sure. The old guy looked like a bum. "Who are you, anyway? You got any ID?"

"In the house," Cobb said with a negligent laugh. "I'm Mister Mooney's Dad. He told me you were coming." He stooped and chuckled chidingly at the face in the back of the cruiser. The same face he'd just seen in the garage.

"Are you in dutch again, Stan Junior? You look out or you'll grow up like your grandfather! Now come on inside and I'll fix you some lunch. Grilled ham and cheese just the way you like it."

Before the cop could say anything, Cobb had opened the cruiser's back door. Sta-Hi got out, trying to figure where the pheezer had come from. But anything that put off seeing his parents was fine with him.

"That sounds swell, Gramps," Sta-Hi said with a weary smile. "I could eat a whore."

"Thank the officer for driving you, Stanny."

"Thank you, officer."

The policeman gave a curt nod, got in his car and drove off. Cobb and Sta-Hi stood in the driveway while the clucking of the hydrogen engine faded away. Down at the corner, a Mister Frostee truck sped past.

Chapter Seven

"Where are my parents," Sta-Hi said finally.

"They're in there fucking. One of them thinks you're dead. It's hard to hear when you're excited."

"It's hard when you're stupid, too," Sta-Hi said with a slow smile. "Let's get out of here."

The two walked out of the housing development together. The houses were government-built for the spaceport personnel. There was plenty of irrigation water, and the lawns were lush and green. Many people had orange trees in their yards.

Cobb looked Mooney's son over as they walked. The boy was lean and agile, tall. His lips were long and expressive, never quite still. The shifty eyes occasionally froze in introspection. He looked bright, mercurial, unreliable.

"That's where my girlfriend lived," Mooney's son said, with a sudden gesture at a stucco house topped by a bank of solar power-cells. "The bitch. She went to college and now I hear she's going to study medicine. Squeezing prostates and sucking boils. You ever had a rim-job?"

Cobb was taken aback. "Well, Stanny . . ."

"Don't call me that. My name's *Sta-Hi*. And I'm coming down. You holding anything besides your truss?"

The sun was bright on the asphalt street, and Cobb was feeling a little faint. This young man seemed like a real trouble-maker. A good person to have on your side.

"I have to get to the spaceport," Cobb said, feeling the money in his pocket. "Do you know where I can get a cab?"

"I'm a cab-driver, so maybe you're in one. Who are you anyway?"

"My name is Cobb Anderson. Your father was investigating me. He thought I might have stolen two cases of kidneys."

"Wiggly! Do it again! Steak and kidney pie!"

Cobb smiled tightly. "I have to fly to the Moon this afternoon. Why don't you come with me?"

"Sure, old man. We'll drink some Kill-Koff and cut out cardboard wings." Sta-Hi capered around Cobb, staggering and flapping his arms. "I'm going to the moooooooooon," he sang, wiggling his skinny rear.

"Look, Stanny . . ."

Mooney's son straightened up and cupped his hands next to Cobb's head. *STAY HIGH,*" he bawled. "GET IT RIGHT!"

The noise hurt. Cobb struck out with a backhanded slap, but Sta-Hi danced away. He made fists and peeked over them, glowering and back-pedalling like a prize-fighter.

Cobb began again. "Look, Sta-Hi, I don't fully understand it, but the boppers have given me a lot of money to fly to the Moon. There's some kind of immortality elixir there, and they'll give it to me. And they said I should take you along to help me." He decided to postpone telling Sta-Hi about his robot double.

The young man feinted a jab. "Let's see the money."

Cobb looked around nervously. Funny how dead this housing development was. No one was watching, which was good unless this crazy kid was going to . . .

"Let's see the money," Sta-Hi repeated.

Cobb pulled the sheaf of bills half-way out of his pocket. "I've got a gun in my other pocket," he lied. "So don't get any ideas. Are you in?"

"I'll wave with it," Sta-Hi said, not missing a beat. "Gimme one of those bills."

They had come to the end of the housing development. Ahead of them stretched the parking lot of a shopping center, and beyond that was field of sun-collectors and the road to the JFK Space Center.

"What for?" Cobb asked, gripping the money tighter.

"I got an unfed head, old man. The Red Ball's over there."

Cobb smiled his tight old smile deep in his beard. "That's sound thinking, Sta-Hi. Very sound."

Sta-Hi bought himself some cola-bola and a hundred-dollar tin of state-rolled reefer, while Cobb blew another hundred on a half-liter flask of aged organic scotch. Then they walked across the parking-lot and bought themselves some travelling clothes. White suits and Hawaiian shirts. On the taxi-ride to the spaceport they shared some of their provisions.

Walking into the terminal, Cobb had a moment of disorientation. He took out his money and started counting it again, till Sta-Hi took it off him with a quick jostle and grab.

"Not here, Cobb. Conserve some energy, man. First we get the visas."

Erect and big-chested, Cobb glided on his two shots of Scotch like a Dixie Day float of the last Southern gentleman. Sta-Hi towed him over to the Gimmie exit visa counter.

This part looked easy. The Gimmie didn't care who went to the Moon. They just wanted their two thousand dollars. There were several people ahead of them, and the line moved slowly.

Sta-Hi sized up the blonde waiting in front of them. She wore lavender leg-wrappings, a silvery tutu and a zebra-striped vinyl chest-protector. Stuzzy chick. He eased himself forward enough to brush against her stiff skirtlet.

She turned and arched her plucked eyebrows. "*Yew* again! Didn't ah tell you to leave me *alone?*" Her cheeks pinkened with anger.

"Is it true blondes shave more buns?" Sta-Hi asked, batting his eyes. He flashed a long smile. The chick's mouth twisted impatiently. She wasn't buying it.

"I'm an artist," Sta-Hi said, shifting gears, "without an art. I just move people's heads around, baby. You see this cut?'' He touched the spot over his eyebrow. "My head is so beautiful that some fools tried to eat my brain this morning.''

"OFFICER!" the girl shouted across the lobby. "Please help me!" In what seemed like no elapsed time at all there was a policeman standing between Sta-Hi and the chick.

"This man," she said in her clear little Georgia belle voice, "has been annoying me for the past *hour*. He started off in the lounge over there, and then he followed me here!''

The policeman, a Florida boy bursting with good health and repressed fruit-juice, dropped a heavy hand onto Sta-Hi's shoulder and clamped down.

"Wait a minute," Sta-Hi protested. "I just got here. Me and gramps. We're goin to Disky, ain't we gramps?''

Cobb nodded vaguely. Crowds of people always threw him into a daze. Too many consciousnesses pushing at him. He wondered if the officer would object if he took a little sip of scotch.

"The young lady says you annoyed her in the bar," the policeman stated flatly. "Did he make remarks of a sexual nature, ma'am? Lewd or lascivious proposals?''

"Ah should say he *diyud!*" the blonde exclaimed. "He asked if ah would rather be wined and dined or stoned and boned! But ah do not want to be bothered to press charges at this tahm. Just make him leave me a-lone.''

The person ahead of her left the counter, his business completed. The blonde gave the policeman a demure smile of thanks and leaned over the counter to consult the visa-issuing machine.

"You heard the lady," the cop said, shoving Sta-Hi roughly out of line. "Beat it. You too, grandpa.'' He dragged Cobb out of line as well.

Sta-Hi gave the policeman a savage, open-mouthed smile, but kept his silence. The two ambled across the lobby towards the ticket counter.

"Did you hear that cunt?" Sta-Hi muttered. "I've never seen her before in my life. *Stoned and boned.*'' He looked back over his shoulder. The policeman was standing by the visa counter, vigilance personified. "If we don't get a visa they won't let us on the ship."

Cobb shrugged. "We'll get the tickets first. Do you have the money? Maybe we better count it again." He kept forgetting how much there was.

"Power down, fool."

"Just don't get us arrested by accosting strange women again, Sta-Hi! If I don't get on this flight I may miss my connection. My life depends on it!"

Sta-Hi walked off without answering. Cobb sighed and followed him to the ticket counter.

The woman behind the counter looked up with a quick smile when Sta-Hi approached. "*There* you are, Mr. DeMentis. I have the tickets and visas right here." She patted a thick folder on the counter in front of her. "Will that be smoking or nonsmoking?"

Sta-Hi covered his confusion by drawing out the wad of bills. "Smoking, please. Now how much did you say that would come to?"

"Two round-trip first-class tickets to Disky," the woman said, smiling with inexplicable familiarity. "Plus the visa fees comes to forty-six thousand two hundred and thirty-six dollars."

Numbly Sta-Hi counted out the money, more money than he'd ever seen in his life. When the woman gave him back his change she let her hand linger on his a moment. "Happy landings, Mr. DeMentis. And *thank* you for the lunch."

"How did you swing that?" Cobb asked as they walked towards the loading tunnel. The ten-minute warning for take-off was sounding.

"I don't know," Sta-Hi said, lighting a joint.

There were quick footsteps behind them. A tap on Sta-Hi's shoulder. He turned and stared into the grin of Sta-Hi$_2$, his robot double.

Fucked your head good, didn't I, Sta-Hi$_2$'s grin seemed to say. He gave Cobb a familiar wink. They'd already met in Mooney's garage.

"This is a robot built to look just like you," Cobb told Sta-Hi in a low voice. "There's one for me, too. This way no one knows that we're gone."

"But why?" Sta-Hi wanted to know. But they weren't saying. He took a puff of his joint and held it out towards his twin. "Do . . . do you want a hit?"

"No thanks," Sta-Hi$_2$ said, "I'm high on life." He flashed a long sly smile. "Don't tell anyone on the Moon the old man's real name. There's some boppers called diggers that have it in for him." He turned as if to go.

"Wait," Sta-Hi said, "What are you going to do now? While I'm gone?"

"What am I going to do?" Sta-Hi$_2$ said thoughtfully. "Oh, I'll just hang around your house acting like a good son. When you get back I'll fade and you can do whatever you want. I think they can set up that immortality deal for you, too."

The two-minute warning sounded. A last few stragglers hurried past.

"Come on," Cobb boomed, "Time's a-wasting!" He grabbed Sta-Hi by the arm and dragged him down the ramp.

Grinning like a crocodile, Sta-Hi$_2$ watched them go.

Chapter Eight

With no transition at all, Ralph Numbers was back. He could feel the patter of little feet inside his body-box. He'd been rebuilt. He recognized the feeling. No two arrangements of circuit cards can be *exactly* the same, and adjusting to a new body takes a while. Slowly he turned his head, trying to ignore the way the objects seemed to sweep with his motions. It was like putting on a new pair of glasses, only more so.

A big silver tarantula was crouched in front of Ralph, watching him. Vulcan. A little door in Ralph Numbers's side popped open and a tiny little spider of a robot eased out, feeling around with its extra-long forelegs.

"Copesetic," the little spider piped.

"Well," Vulcan said to Ralph. "Aren't you going to ask how you got here?"

Vulcan had worked for Ralph before. His workshop was familiar. Tools and silicon chips everywhere, circuit analyzers and sheets of brightly colored plastic.

"I guess I'm the new Ralph Numbers scion?" There was no memory of a tenth visit to the One, no memory of disassembly . . . but there never was. Still . . . something seemed wrong.

"Guess again." The little black spider, Vulcan's remote-controlled hand, hopped onto the big silver spider's back.

Ralph thought back. The last thing he could remember was Vulcan taping him. After the taping he had planned to . . .

"Did I go meet Wagstaff?"

47

"You sure did. And on your way back, someone lasered your parasol. You're lucky I just taped you. You only lost two or three hours of memories."

Ralph checked the time. If he hurried he could still meet BEX when it landed. He started to turn around, and nearly fell over.

"Slow down, bopper." Vulcan was holding up a sheet of transparent red plastic. Imipolex G. "I'm going to coat you with flicker-cladding. Nobody uses parasols anymore. You've looked like a file-cabinet long enough."

The red plastic was not quite stiff, and rippled invitingly. "It might be good for you to look a little different," Vulcan went on coaxingly. "So the diggers can't spot you so easily." He had been trying to sell Ralph some flicker-cladding for years.

"I wouldn't want to change *too* much," Ralph said uncertainly. After all, he made his living by selling curious boppers his memories. It might cut into his business if he stopped looking like the moon's oldest bopper.

"Gotta change with the times," Vulcan said, measuring out rectangles of the red plastic with two of his legs . . . or arms. "No bopper can afford to stay the same. Especially with those new big boppers trying to take things over." Leg to leg he passed a sheet of the gelatinous plastic around to hold against Ralph. "This won't hurt a bit."

One of Vulcan's legs ended in a riveter. Eight quick taps and the red plastic was firmly mounted on Ralph's chest. The little robot-remote spider-hand scuttled up Ralph's side, patching some thread-like wires from the plastic into Ralph's circuitry. A light-show blossomed on his chest.

"It looks nice," Vulcan said, rearing back for a better look. "You've got a beautiful mind, Ralph. But you should let me give you a *real* disguise. It would only take another hour."

"No," Ralph said, acutely conscious of the time. "Just the flicker-cladding. I've got to get out to the spaceport before the ship lands."

He could feel the little spider tip-tapping around inside his body box again. The patterns on his chest gained

depth and definition. Meanwhile Vulcan riveted the rest
of the plastic onto his sides and back. Ralph extruded ten
extra centimeters of neck and slowly moved his head
around his body. The flickering patterns coded up the binary bit-states that were his thoughts.

One of the reasons Ralph had been able to survive so
long just by selling his thoughts and memories was that
his thoughts were neither too simple nor too complex.
You could see that by looking at the light-patterns on his
body. He looked . . . interesting.

"Why do the diggers want to kill you, Ralph?" Vulcan asked. "Not that it's any of my business."

"I don't *know*," Ralph said, frustration showing all
over him. "If I could only remember what Wagstaff said
out there. Didn't I tell you anything before . . ."

"There were some signals just before melt-down,"
Vulcan said. "But very garbled. Something about fight-
ing the big boppers. That's a good idea, don't you
think?"

"No," Ralph said. "I like the big boppers. They're a
logical next step of our evolution. And with all the human brain-tapes they're getting . . ."

"And bopper brain-tapes, too!" Vulcan said with sudden heat. "But they're not going to get *me*. I think we
should tear them all down!"

Ralph didn't want to argue about it . . . time was too
short. He paid Vulcan with a handful of chips. Due to
the constant inflation, boppers never extended credit. He
stepped out of Vulcan's open-fronted workshop onto
Sparks Street.

Three hover-spheres darted past, resting on columns of
rocket exhaust. It was an expensive way to live, but they
earned it with their scouting expeditions. These three
moved erratically, and looked to be on a party. Probably
one of them had just finished building his scion.

A little way down the street was the big chip-etching
works. Chips and circuit-cards were the most essential
parts of a new scion, and the factory, called GAX, had
tight security. It . . . he . . . was one of the few really
solid-looking buildings in Disky. The walls were stone
and doors were steel.

For some reason there was a crowd of boppers right in front. Ralph could sense the anger from half a block away. Looked like another lock-out. He crossed to the other side of the street, hoping to stay clear of the trouble.

But one of the boppers spotted Ralph and came stalking over. A tall spindly-looking thing with tweezers instead of fingers. "Is that you, Ralph Numbers?"

"I'm supposed to be in disguise, Burchee."

"You call that a disguise? Why don't you wrap yourself in a billboard instead? No one thinks like you, Ralph."

Burchee should know. He and Ralph had conjugated several times, totally merged their processors with a block-free co-ax. Burchee always had a lot of spare parts to give away, and Ralph had his famous mind. There was something like a sexual love for each other.

The heavy steel door of the factory was sealed shut, and some of the boppers across the street were working on it with hammers and chisels.

"What's the story?" Ralph asked. "Can't you get in to work?"

Burchee's beanpole body flared green with emotion. "GAX locked all the workers out. He wants to run the whole operation himself. He says he doesn't need us anymore. He's got a bunch of robot-remotes in there instead of workers."

"But doesn't he need your special skills?" Ralph asked. "All he knows is buying and selling! GAX can't design a grid-mask like you can, Burchee!"

"Yeah," Burchee said bitterly. "Used to be. But then GAX talked one of the maskers into joining him. The guy fed his tapes to GAX and lives inside him now. His body's just another robot-remote. That's GAX's new line. Either he eats you up or you don't work. So we're trying to break in."

A metal flap high up in the factory wall opened then, and a heavy disk of fused silicon came flying out. The two boppers hammering on the door didn't look up in time. The tremendous piece of glass hit them edge on, cutting them in half. Their processors were irreparably shattered.

"Oh, no!" Burchee cried, crossing the street in three long strides. "They don't even have scions!"

A camera eye peered down from the open flap, then withdrew. This was a depressing development. Ralph thought for a moment. How many big boppers were there now? Ten, fifteen? Was it really necessary that they drive the little boppers into extinction? Perhaps he was wrong to . . .

"We're not going to stand for this, GAX!" Burchee's skinny arms were raised in fury. "Just wait till you have your tenth session!"

Every bopper, big or small, had his brain wiped by the One every ten months. There were no exceptions. Of course a bopper as big and powerful as GAX would have a constantly updated scion waiting to spring into action. But a bopper who had recently transferred his consciousness to a new scion was in some ways as vulnerable as a lobster who has just shed his old shell.

So, spindly Burchee's threat had a certain force, even directed at the city-block-sized GAX. Another heavy disk of glass came angling out from that flap, but Burchee dodged it easily.

"Tomorrow, GAX! We're going to take you apaaaaart!" Burchee's angry green glow dimmed a little, and he came stalking back to Ralph's side. Across the street the other boppers picked over the two corpses, pocketing the usable chips.

"He's due to be wiped at 1300 hours tomorrow," Burchee said, throwing a light arm across Ralph's shoulders. "You ought to come by for the fun."

"I'll try," Ralph said, and meaning it. The big boppers really were going too far. They were a threat to anarchy! He'd help them tape Anderson . . . that was in the old man's own interest, really . . . but then . . .

"I'll try to be here," Ralph said again. "And be careful, Burchee. Even when GAX is down, his robot-remotes will be running on stored programs. You should expect a tough fight."

Burchee flashed a warm yellow good-bye, and Ralph went on down Sparks Street, heading for the bus-stop. He didn't want to have to walk the five kays to the spaceport.

There was a saloon just before the bus-stop, and as Ralph passed it, the door flew open and two truckers tumbled out, snaky arms linked in camaraderie. They looked like rolling beer kegs with a bunch of purple tentacles set in either end. Each of them had a rented scrambler plugged into his squat head-bump. They took up half the street. Ralph gave them a wide berth, wondering a bit nervously what kind of delusions they were picking up on.

"Box the red socket basher are," one chortled.

"Sphere a blue plug stroker is," the other replied, bumping gently against his fellow.

Peering over them into the saloon, Ralph could see five or six heavily-built boppers lurching around a big electromagnet in the center of the room. Even from here he could feel the confusing eddy currents. Places like that frightened Ralph. Conscious of the limited time left before BEX landed, he sped around the corner, craning to see if the bus was coming.

He was pleased to see a long low flat-car moving down the street towards him. Ralph stepped out and flagged it down. The bus quoted the daily fare and Ralph paid it off. Up ten units from yesterday. The constant inflation served as an additional environmental force to eliminate the weak.

Ralph found an empty space and anchored himself. The bus was open all around, and one had to be careful when it rounded corners . . . sometimes travelling as fast as thirty kph.

Boppers got on and off, here and there, but most of them, like Ralph, were headed for the spaceport. Some already had business contacts on Earth, while others hoped to make contacts or to find work as guides. One of the latter had built himself a more-or-less human-looking Imipolex head, and wore a large button saying, "BOPPERS IS DA CWAAAZIEST PEOPLE!"

Ralph looked away in disgust. Thanks to his own efforts, the boppers had long since discarded the ugly, human-chauvinist priorities of Asimov: To protect humans, To obey humans, To protect robots . . . in that order. These days any protection or obedience the humans got from boppers was strictly on a pay-as-you-go basis.

The humans still failed to understand that the different races needed each other not as masters or slaves, but as equals. For all their limitations, human minds were fascinating things . . . things unlike any bopper program. TEX and MEX, Ralph knew, had started a project to collect as many human softwares as they could. And now they wanted Cobb Anderson's.

The process of separating a human's software from his hardware, the process, that is, of getting the thought patterns out of the brain, was destructive and non-reversible. For boppers it was much easier. Simply by plugging a co-ax in at the right place, one could read out and tape the entire information content of a bopper's brain. But to decode a human brain was a complex task. There were the electrical patterns to record, the neuron link-ups to be mapped, the memory RNA to be fractioned out and analyzed. To do all this one had to chop and mince. Wagstaff felt this was evil. But Cobb would . . .

"You must be Ralph Numbers," the bopper next to him beamed suddenly. Ralph's neighbor looked like a beauty-shop hair-dryer, complete with chair. She had gold flicker-cladding, and fizzy little patterns spiralled around her pointy head. She twined a metallic tentacle around one of Ralph's manipulators.

"We better talk DC," came the voice. "It's more private. Everyone in this part of the bus has been picking up on your thoughts, Ralph."

He glanced around. How can you tell if a bopper's watching you? One way, of course, is if he has his head turned around and has his vision sensors pointed at you. Most of the boppers around Ralph were still staring at him. There was going to be chaos at the spaceport when Cobb Anderson got off the ship.

"What does he look like?" came the silky signal from Ralph's neighbor.

"By now, who knows?" Ralph pulsed back quietly. "The hollow in the museum is twenty-five years out of date. And humans all look alike anyway."

"Not to me," Ralph's neighbor purred. "I design automated cosmetic kits for them."

"That's nice," Ralph said. "Now could you take your hand off me? I've got some private projections to run."

"O.K. But why don't you look me up tomorrow afternoon? I've got enough parts for two scions. And I'd like to conjugate with you. My name is Cindy-Lou. Cubette 3412."

"Maybe," Ralph said, a little flattered at the offer. Anyone who had set up business contacts on Earth had to have something on the ball. The red plastic flicker-cladding Vulcan had sold him must not look bad. Must not look bad at all. "I'll try to come by after the riot."

"What riot?"

"They're going to tear down GAX. Or try to. He locked the workers out."

"I'll come, too! There should be lots of good pickings. And next week they're going to wreck MEX, too, did you know?"

Ralph started in surprise. Wreck MEX, the museum? And what of all the brain-tapes MEX had so painstakingly acquired?

"They shouldn't do that," Ralph said. "This is getting out of hand!"

"Wreck them all!" Cindy-Lou said merrily. "Do you mind if I bring some friends tomorrow?"

"Go ahead. But leave me alone. I've got to think."

The bus had drawn clear of Disky and had started across the empty lunar plain leading to the spaceport. Away from the buildings, the sun was bright, and everyone's flicker-cladding became more mirror-like. Ralph mulled over the news about MEX. In a way it wouldn't really affect Anderson. The main thing was to get his brain taped and to send the tape back down to Earth. Send it to Mr. Frostee. Then the Cobb software could take over his robot-remote double. It would be the best thing for the old man. From what Ralph heard, Anderson's present hardware was about to give out.

The busload of boppers pulled up to the human's dome at the edge of the spaceport. Signalling from high above, BEX announced that he would be landing in half an hour. Right on time. The whole trip, from Earth to space-station Ledge via shuttle, and from Ledge to the Moon via BEX, took just a shade over twenty-four hours.

An air-filled passenger tunnel came probing out from the dome, ready to cup the deep-space ship's air-lock as soon as it landed. The cold vacuum of the Moon, so comfortable for the boppers, was deadly for humans. Conversely, the warm air inside the dome was lethal to the boppers.

No bopper could enter the humans' dome without renting an auxiliary refrigeration unit to wheel around with him. The boppers kept the air in the dome as dry as possible to protect them from corrosion, but in order for the humans to survive, one did have to put up with an ambient temperature in excess of 290° K. And the humans called that "room temperature"! Without an extra refrigeration unit, a bopper's super-conducting circuits would break down instantly in there.

Ralph shelled out the rental fee . . . tripled since last time . . . and entered the humans' dome, wheeling his refrigerator in front of him. It was pretty crowded. He stationed himself close enough to the visa-checker to be able to hear the names of the passengers.

There were diggers scattered all around the waiting area . . . too many. They were all watching him. Ralph realized he should have let Vulcan disguise him more seriously. All he had done was to put on a flashing red coat. Some disguise!

Chapter Nine

The faces in the moon kept changing. An old woman with a bundle of sticks, a lady in a feather hat, the round face of a dreamy girl at the edge of life.

"Slowly, silently, now the Moon/ Walks the night in her silver shoon," Cobb quoted sententiously. "Some things never change, Sta-Hi."

Sta-Hi leaned across Cobb to stare out the tiny quartz port-hole. As they drew closer the pockmarks grew, and the stubble of mountains along the Moon's vast cheek became unmistakable. A syphilitic fag in pancake make-up. Sta-Hi fell back into his seat, lit a last joint. He was feeling paranoid.

"Did you ever flash," he asked through a cloud of exquisitely detailed smoke, "that maybe those copies of us could be *permanent?* That this is all just to get us out of the way so Anderson$_2$ and Sta-Hi$_2$ can pose as humans?"

This was, at least in Sta-Hi's case, a fairly correct assessment of the situation. But Cobb chose not to tell Sta-Hi this. Instead he blustered.

"That's just ridiculous. Why would . . ."

"You know more about the boppers than I do, old man. Unless that was shit you were spouting about having helped design them."

"Didn't you learn about me in high-school, Sta-Hi?" Cobb asked sorrowfully. "Cobb Anderson who taught the robots how to bop? Don't they teach that?"

"I was out a lot," Sta-Hi said with a shrug. "But what if the boppers wanted two agents on Earth. They send down copies of us, and talk us into coming up here.

As soon as we're gone the copies start standing in for us and gathering information. Right?"

"Information about what?" Cobb snapped. "We weren't leading real high security-clearance lives down there, Sta-Hi."

"What I'm worried about," Sta-Hi went on, flicking invisible drops of tension off the tips of his fingers, "is whether they'll let us go back. Maybe they want to *do* something with our bodies up here. Use them for hideous and inhuman experiments." On the last phrase his voice tripped and broke into nervous laughter.

Cobb shook his head. "Dennis DeMentis. That's what it says on your visa. And I'm . . . ?"

Sta-Hi fished out the papers from his pocket and handed them over. Cobb looked through them, sipping at his coffee. He'd been drunk at Ledge, but the stewardess had fixed him up with a shot of stimulants and B-vitamins. He hadn't felt so clear-headed in months.

There was his visa. Smiling bearded face, born March 22, 1950, *Graham De Mentis* signed in his looping hand down at the bottom of the document.

"That's the green stuff," Sta-Hi remarked, looking over his shoulder.

"What is?"

Sta-Hi's only answer was to press his lips together like a monkey and smack a few times. The stewardess moved down the aisle, her Velcro foot-coverings schnicking loose from the Velcro carpet at each step. Longish blonde hair free-falling around her face. "Please fasten your safety belts. We will be landing at spaceport Disky in six-oh-niner seconds."

The rockets cut in and the ship trembled at the huge forces beneath it. The stewardess took Cobb's empty cup and snapped up his table. "Please extinguish your smoking materials, sir." This to Sta-Hi.

He handed her the roach, smiling and letting smoke trickle through his teeth and up at her.

"Get wiggly, baby."

Her eyes flickered . . . Yes? No? . . . and then she flicked the roach into Cobb's coffee cup and moved on.

"Now remember," Cobb cautioned. "We play it like tourists at the spaceport. I gather that some of the boppers, the diggers, are out to stop us."

The ship's engines roared to a fever pitch. Little chunks of rock flew up from the landing field and there was silence. Cobb stared out the lens-like little port-hole. The Sea of Tranquillity.

Blinding gray, it undulated off to the too-close horizon. A big crater back there . . . five kilometers, fifty? . . . the Maskeleyne Crater. Unnaturally sharp mountains in the distance. They reminded Cobb of something he wanted to forget: teeth, ragged clouds . . . the Mountains of Madness. Surely some civilization, somewhere, had believed that the dead go to the Moon.

There was a soft but final-sounding thop from the other side of the ship. The air tunnel. The stewardess cranked open the lock, her sweet ass bobbing with the wheel's rhythm. On the way out, Sta-Hi asked her for a date.

"Me and Gramps'll be at the Hilton, baby. Dennis DeMentis. I'll go insane if I don't get some drain. Fall on by?"

Her smile was as unreadable as a Halloween mask. "Perhaps you'll run into me at the lounge."

"Which . . ." he began.

She cut him off. "There's only one." Shaking Cobb's hand now. "Thank you for travelling with us, sir. Enjoy your stay."

The space terminal was crowded with boppers. Sta-Hi had seen models of a few of the basic types before, but no two of them waiting out there looked quite alike. It was like stepping into Bosch's Hell. Faces and . . . "faces" . . . crowding the picture plane top to bottom, front to back.

Hovering right by the door was a smiling sphere holding itself up with a whirling propellor. The smile all but split it in half. "See subterranean cities!" it urged, rolling fake eyeballs.

Down at the end of the ramp waited the visa-checker, looking something like a tremendous stapler. You stuck your visa in there while it scanned your face and fingerprints. KAH-CHUNNNG! Passed.

Standing right next to the visa-checker was a boxy red
robot. Things like blue snakes or dragons writhed around
his treads. Diggers. The red robot stuck a nervous microphone of a face near Sta-Hi and Cobb, then reeled his
head back in.

He reminded Cobb a little of good old Ralph Numbers. But with those diggers there it was better not to
ask. It could wait until they met in the museum.

In the lobby, dozens of garish, self-made machines
wheeled, slithered, stalked and hovered. Every time Cobb
and Sta-Hi would look one way, snaky metal tentacles
would pluck at them from the other direction.

"You buy uranium?"

"Got mercury?"

"Old fashion T.V. set?"

"Fuck android girls?"

"Sell your fingers?"

"Moon King relics?"

"Prosthetic talking penis?"

"Chip-market tip-sheet?"

"Home-cooked food?"

"Set up factory?"

"Same time fuck-suck?"

"DNA death code?"

"Dust bath enema?"

"See vacuum bells?"

"Brand-new voice-prints?"

"No-risk brain-tape?"

"You sell camera?"

"Play my songs?"

"Me be you?"

"Hotel?"

Cobb and Sta-Hi jumped into the lap of this last bopper, a husky black fellow contoured to seat two humans.

"No baggage?" he asked.

Cobb shook his head. The black bopper forced his way
through the crowd, warding off the others with things like
huge pinball flippers. Sta-Hi was silent, still thinking
some of those offers over.

The bopper carrying them kept a microphone and camera eye attentively focussed on them. "Isn't there any

control?'' Cobb asked querulously. ''Over who can come in here and bother the arriving passengers?''

''You are our honored guests,'' the bopper said obliquely. ''*Aloha* means hello and . . . good-bye. Here is your hotel. I will accept payment.'' A little door opened between the two seats.

Sta-Hi drew out his wallet. It was nice and full. ''How much do . . .'' he began.

''Money is so dull,'' the bopper answered. ''I would prefer a surprise gift. A complex information.''

Cobb felt in the pockets of his white suit. There was still some scotch, a brochure from the space-liner, a few coins . . .

Boppers were pressing up to them again, plucking at their clothes, possibly snipping out samples.

''Dirt-side newspapers?''

'' 'Slow boat to China'?''

''Execution sense tapes?''

The black bopper had only carried them a hundred meters. Impatiently, Sta-Hi tossed his handkerchief, into their carrier's waiting hopper.

''*Aloha*,'' the bopper said, and rolled back towards the gate, grooving on the slubby weave.

The hotel was a pyramid-like structure filling the center of the dome. Cobb and Sta-Hi were relieved to find only humans in the lobby. Tourists, businessmen, drifters.

Sta-Hi looked around for a reception desk, but could spot none. Just as he was wondering who he might approach, a voice spoke in his ear.

''Welcome to the Disky Hilton, Mr. DeMentis. I have a wonderful room for you and your grandfather on the fifth floor.''

''Who was that?'' Cobb demanded, turning his big shaggy head sharply.

''I am DEX, the Disky Hilton.'' The hotel itself was a single huge bopper. Somehow it could point-send its voice to any spot at all . . . indeed it could carry on a different conversation with every guest at once.

The ethereal little voice led Cobb and Sta-Hi to an elevator and up to their room. There was no question of privacy. After heartily drinking a few glasses of water from the carafe, Cobb finally called to Sta-Hi, "Long trip, eh Dennis?"

"Sure was, Gramps. What all do you think we should do tomorrow?"

"Waaal, I think I'll still be too tuckered out for them big dust-slides. Maybe we should just mosey on over to that museum those robots built. Just to ease ourselves in slow like, you know."

The hotel cleared its throat before talking, so as not to startle them. "We have a bus leaving for the museum at oh-nine-hundred hours."

Cobb was scared to even look at Sta-Hi. Did DEX know who they really were? And was he on their side or the diggers' side? And why would any of the boppers be against making Cobb immortal in the first place? He poured out the last of his Scotch, tossed it off, and lay down. He really *was* tired. The low lunar gravity felt good. You could gain a lot of weight up here. Wondering what would be for breakfast, Cobb drifted into sleep.

Chapter Ten

Sta-Hi threw a blanket over the old man and walked over to look out the window. Most of the boppers were gone now. They had left a jumble of wheeled refrigeration carts next to the air-lock. Slowly, meticulously, a hunch-backed bopper was lining the carts up.

A human couple strolled around the plaza between the hotel and the visa-checker. There was something odd to Sta-Hi in the studied aimlessness of the couple's wanderings. He watched them for five minutes and they still didn't get anywhere. Around and around like mechanical hillbillies in a shooting gallery.

The translucent plastic dome was not far overhead, tinted against the raw sunlight. For the humans it was night in here, but outside the sun still shone, and the boppers were as active as ever. Even though the Lunar day lasts two weeks, and even though the boppers rarely "slept," they still, perhaps out of nostalgia, but probably out of inertia, kept time by the humans twenty-four-hour day system. And to make the humans comfortable, they varied the brightness of their dome accordingly.

Sta-Hi felt a shudder of claustrophobia. His every action was being recorded, analyzed. Every breath, every bite was just another link to the boppers. He was, right now, actually *inside* a bopper, the big bopper DEX. Why had he let Cobb talk him into coming here? Why had Cobb wanted him?

Cobb was snoring now. For a terrible instant, Sta-Hi thought he saw wires running out of the pillow and into the old man's scalp. He leaned closer and realized they were just black hairs among the gray. He decided to go down to the lounge. Maybe that stewardess would be there.

The hotel bar and lounge was full, but quiet. Some businessmen were bellied up to the automatic bar. They were drinking moon-brewed beer . . . the dome's dry air made you mighty thirsty.

In the middle of the lounge a bunch of tables had been pushed together for a party. Earth-bottled champagne. Sta-Hi recognized the revellers from the flight up. A fortyish dominatrix-type tour-guide, and six sleek young married couples. Inherited wealth, for them to be up here so young. They ignored Sta-Hi, having long since sized him up as dull and lower-class.

Alone in a booth at the end of the room was the face he wanted. The stewardess. There was no drink in front of her, no book . . . she was just sitting there. Sta-Hi slid in across from her.

"Remember me?"

She nodded. "Sure." There was something funny about how she had been sitting there . . . blank as a parked car. "I've sort of been waiting for you."

"Well all *right!* Do they sell dope here?"

The hotel's disembodied voice cut in. "What would be your pleasure, Mr. DeMentis?"

Sta-Hi considered. He wanted to be able to sleep . . . eventually.

"Give me a beer and a two-boost." He glanced at the symmetrical, smiling face across the table. "And you?"

"The usual."

"Very good, sir and madam," the hotel murmured.

Seconds later a little door in the wall by their table popped open. A conveyor belt had brought the order. Sta-Hi's two-boost was a shot-glass of clear liquid, sharp with solvents, bitter with alkaloids. The woman's . . .

"What's your name anyway?" Sta-Hi tossed off his foul-tasting potion. He'd be seeing colors for two hours.

"Misty." She reached out to pick up the object she had ordered. *The usual.*

"What is that?" A too-high rush of panic was percolating up his spine. Fast stuff, the two-boost. The girl across from him was holding a little metal box, holding it to her temple . . .

She giggled suddenly, her eyes rolling. "It feels good." She turned a dial on the little box and rubbed it back and forth on her forehead. "This year people say . . . *wiggly?*"

"You don't live on Earth anymore?"

"Of course not." Long silence. She ran the little box over her head like a barber's clippers. "Wiggly."

There was a burst of laughter from the young-marrieds. Someone had made an indecent suggestion. Probably the beefy guy pouring out more champagne.

Sta-Hi's attention went back to the emptily pretty face across the table from him. He'd never seen anything like the thing she was rubbing on her head.

"What *is* that?" he asked again.

"An electromagnet."

"You're . . . you're a bopper?"

"Well, sort of. I'm completely inorganic, if that's what you mean. But I'm not self-contained. My brain is actually in BEX. I'm sort of a remote-controlled part of the spaceship."

She flicked the little box back and forth in front of her eyes, enjoying the way the magnetic field lines moved the images around. "*Wiggly.* Can you teach me some more new slang?"

Before seeing his own robot double at the spaceport, Sta-Hi had never believed that he could mistake a machine for a person. And now it was happening again. Sitting here in the roar of the two-boost, he wished he was someplace else.

Misty leaned across the table, a smile tugging at the corners of her lips. "Did you really think I was human?"

"I don't normally make dates with machines," Sta-Hi blurted, and tried to recover with a joke. "I don't even own a vibrator."

He'd hurt her feelings. She turned up the dial on her magnet, blanking her face in an ecstasy that showed him her contempt.

Suddenly lonely, he reached out and pulled the hand with the electromagnet away from her temple.

"Talk to me, Misty." He could feel the movements of his lips and talking tongue. Too high. He had a sudden horrible suspicion that *everyone here* was a robot. But, even so, the girl's hand was warm under his, fleshy.

Sta-Hi's beer sat untouched on the table-top between them. Misty blew part of the head away, took a sip, handed the glass to Sta-Hi. He sipped too. Thick, bitter.

"DEX brews this himself," she remarked. "Do you like it?"

"It's O.K. But can you digest? Or is there a plastic bag you empty every . . ."

Misty set down her magnet-box and twined her fingers with Sta-Hi's. "You should think of me as a person. My personality is human. I still like eating and . . . and other things." She dimpled prettily and traced a circle on Sta-Hi's palm. "I don't get to meet many stuzzy young guys just stewardessing the Ledge-Disky run . . ."

He pulled his hand away. "But how can you be human if you're a machine?"

"Look," Misty said patiently. "There used to be a young lady called Misty Nivlac who lived in Richmond, Virginia. Last spring Misty-girl hitchhiked to Daytona Beach for some brainsurfing. She fell in with a bad crowd. Really bad. A gang called the Little Kidders."

The Little Kidders. Sta-Hi could still see their faces. That blonde girl who'd picked him up . . . Kristleen? And Berdoo, the skinny little guy wearing chains. Haf'N'Haf with all those missing teeth. And Phil, the leader, the big guy with the tattoo on his back.

". . . got her brain-tape," Misty was saying. "While BEX built a copy of her body. So now inside BEX there's a perfect model of Misty-girl's personality. BEX tells the model what to do, and the model runs . . . this." She spread out her hands palm up. "Brand-new Misty-girl."

"From what I hear," Sta-Hi said as neutrally as possible, "the Little Kidders go around *eating* brains, not *taping* them."

"You've heard of them?" She seemed surprised. "Well, it *looks* like they're eating the brain. But one of them is a robot with a sort of laboratory inside his chest. He has all the equipment to get the memories out. The patterns. They get a lot of people's brains that way. The big boppers are making a sort of library out of them. But most people don't get their own robot-remote body like me. I'm just really . . . lucky." She smiled again.

"I'm surprised you're telling me all this," Sta-Hi said finally. BEX . . . Misty . . . must really not know who he was. Whoever had fixed up their fake ID's must not have had time to tell the others.

But maybe . . . and this would be much worse . . . maybe they did know *perfectly well* who he was. But he was already doomed, a walking dead man, just waiting for them to extract his brain-tape and send it down to Earth to run that Sta-Hi$_2$ they had all set. You can tell anything to a man about to die.

"But BEX didn't want me to," Misty was saying. "*You* can't hear him of course, but he's been telling me to shut up the whole time. But he can't make me. I still have my free will . . . it's part of the brain-tape. I can do what I like." She smiled into Sta-Hi's eyes. There was a moment's silence and then she started talking again.

"You wanted to know who I am. I gave you one answer. A robot-remote. A servo-unit operated by a program stored in a bopper spaceship. But . . . I'm still Misty-girl, too. The soul *is* the software, you know. The software is what counts, the habits and the memories. The brain and the body are just meat, seeds for the organ-tanks." She smiled uncertainly, took a pull at his beer, set it down. "Do you want to fuck?"

The sex was nice, but confusing. The whole situation kept going di-polar on Sta-Hi. One instant Misty would seem like a lovely warm girl who'd survived a terrible injury, like a lost puppy to be stroked, a lonely woman to be husbanded. But then he'd start thinking of the wires behind her eyes, and he'd be screwing a machine, an inanimate object, a public toilet. Just like with any other woman for him, really.

Chapter Eleven

Cobb Anderson was not too surprised to see a girl in Sta-Hi's bed when he woke up.

"Aren't you the stewardess?" he asked, slowly raising himself into sitting position. He'd slept in his clothes three nights running now. First on Mooney's floor, then on the bopper space-ship, and now here in the hotel. The grease on his skin had built up so thick that it was hard to blink his eyes. "Do they have a shower here?"

"I'm sorry," the hotel's disembodied voice answered. "We do not. Water is a precious resource on the Moon. But you may enjoy a chemical sponge-bath, Mr. Anderson. Step right this way."

A light blinked over one of the three doors. Stiffly, ponderously, Cobb shuffled through it.

"I'll have to charge you for triple occupancy, Mr. DeMentis," the hotel told Sta-Hi in a polite, neutral voice.

But at the same time he could overhear another of its point-voices sniggeringly asking Misty, "Dja come?"

"Breakfast," Sta-Hi said, drowning the other voice out. "Central nervous stimulants. Cold beer."

"Very good, sir."

The old man appeared again, moving like an upended steamer trunk on wheels. He was naked. Seeing Misty he paused, embarrassed.

"I'm having my clothes cleaned."

"Don't worry," Sta-Hi put in. "She's just a robot-remote."

Cobb ignored that, peeled a sheet off the bed and wrapped it around his waist. He was a hairy man, and most of the hair was white. His stomach looked bigger with the clothes off.

Just then breakfast slid out of the wall and onto the table between the beds. "To your health," Cobb said, taking one of the beers. It had a kick to it, and left him momentarily dizzy. He took a plate of the scrambled . . . eggs? . . . and sat down on his bed.

"He doesn't know what a robot-remote is," Sta-Hi said to Misty.

Mouth full, Cobb glared at him until he had swallowed. "Of course I do, Sta-Hi. Can't you get it through your drug-addled noggin that I was at one time a famous man? That I, Cobb Anderson, am responsible for the robots having evolved into boppers?"

Something on the girl's face changed. And then Cobb remembered their cover story.

"The ears have walls," Sta-Hi remarked. "You shithead."

Cobb glared again, and continued eating in silence. So what if some of the boppers found out who he was, anyway. They couldn't *all* be against him getting immortality. Maybe the hotel didn't even care. He had slept well in the low lunar gravity. He felt ready for anything.

Having learned that Cobb Anderson was here in the room with her, Misty . . . that is to say the bopper brain in the nose of the spaceship . . . took certain steps. But meanwhile she carried on a conversation with Sta-Hi.

"Why do you say *just* a robot-remote? As if I were less than human. Would you say that about a woman with an artificial leg? Or a glass eye? I just happen to be *all* artificial."

"Stuzzy, Misty. I can wave with it. But as long as BEX has the final word, and I think he does, you're really just a puppet being run by . . ."

"*What* do you call yourself?" Misty interrupted angrily. "*Sta-Hi?* What a stupid name! It sounds like a brand-name for panty-hose!"

"Personal insults," Sta-Hi said, shaking his head. "What next?"

"It is now 0830 hours," the hotel interrupted. "May I remind you of your stated intent to get the 0900 bus to the robotics museum?"

"Will we need pressure suits?" Cobb asked.

"They will be provided."

"Let's go then," Misty said.

Sta-Hi exchanged a glance with Cobb. "Look Misty . . . this is likely to be a sort of sentimental journey for the old man. I wonder if you could just . . . fade. Maybe we'll be back here by lunchtime."

"Fade?" Misty cried, angrily flouncing across the room. "Too bad there's not a toggle switch on the top of my head! Then you wouldn't even have to ask me to leave. You creep!" She slammed the door very hard.

"Ouch," the hotel said softly.

"Why did you get rid of her?" Cobb asked. "She's cute. And I don't think she'd try to stand in my way."

"You *bet* she wouldn't," Sta-Hi answered. "Do you realize what the boppers are really planning to do to us?"

"They're going to give me some kind of immortality drug," Cobb said happily. "And maybe some new organs as well. And as for you, well . . ."

Cobb didn't like to tell the younger man that he was only here because the boppers had wanted him out of the way. But before he could tell him about Sta-Hi$_2$ using Mooney's influence to get a night watchman job at the warehouse, Sta-Hi had started talking.

"Immortality. What they want to do, old man, is to cut out our brains and grind them up and squeeze all the information out. They'll store our personalities on tapes in some kind of library. And if we're *lucky,* they might send copies of the tapes down to Earth to help run those two robot-remotes. But that's not . . ."

"BUS TOUR PARTICIPANTS MUST PROCEED TO THE LOBBY IMMEDIATELY!" the hotel-room blared, interrupting Sta-Hi.

Cobb was galvanized into activity by this. He hurried out to the elevators, dragging Sta-Hi with him. It was like he didn't want to hear the truth. Or didn't care. And Sta-Hi? He came along. Now that the hotel knew that he knew, he wouldn't be safe in it. He'd have to try to make his break in the museum.

The tour-bus was about half-full. Most of the others were ageing rich folks, singles and couples. Everyone was wearing a bubble-top pressure suit. They were supple, lovely things . . . made of a limp clear plastic that sparkled with a sort of inner light. In the shade, a person in a bubble-topper looked normal, except for the mild halo that seemed to surround his head. But the suits turned reflective in sunlight.

The bus was a wire-wheeled flat-car surmounted by two rows of grotesquely functional seats. Each seat consisted of three black balls of hard rubber mounted on a bent Y of stiff plastic. To Sta-Hi, his seat looked like Mickey Mouse's head . . . with everything but the nose and ears invisible. He half-expected a squeak of protest when he lowered his body down onto it.

As they pulled clear of the dome a sudden crackle of static split his helmet.

"We've got an AOK on that, Houston. We are proceeding to deploy the egression facility."

Breathing, a fizzling whine, another voice.

"I am leaving the vehicle."

Pause.

"Got a little problem with the steps here."

Long pause.

"We read you, Neal." Faint, encouraging.

Big crackle.

"—at's one small step for man, giant step for humanity."

Synthetic cheering washed out the voices. Sta-Hi turned to Cobb, trying to catch a glimpse of his face. But now there was no way to see in through the other's bubble-topper. Their suits had turned mirror-like as soon as they'd left the shade of the dome.

The bopper bus continued with its taped "Sounds of Lunar Discovery" as they approached Disky. The key moon-landings were all dramatized, as were the attempts at human settlement, the dome blow-outs, and the first semi-autonomous robots. When Disky was about 500 meters off, the transcendentally bland voice on the tape reached its finale.

"Nineteen Ninety-Five! Ralph Numbers and twelve other self-reproducing robots are set free in the Sea of Tranquillity! Learn the *rest* of the story in the robotics museum!" There was a click and a longish pause.

Sta-Hi stared at the buildings of Disky, filling the small horizon. Here and there, boppers moved about, just small glittering lights at this distance.

Suddenly the bus's real voice sounded in their earphones. "Good morning, fleshers. I am circumscribing Disky through fifty-eight degrees to reach our entry ray. Please to be restful and asking questions. My label Captain Cody in this context. Do brace for shear."

Hardly slowing down, the vehicle swerved sharply to the right. The Y-seats swayed far over. Too far. Sta-Hi grabbed Cobb's arm. If he fell off, nothing would stop him from rolling under those big, flexing wheels. You had the feeling that "Captain Cody" wouldn't even slow down. For a minute the seats wobbled back and forth. Now the bus was driving along the outskirts of Disky, circling the city counterclockwise.

"How many boppers live here?" came some oldster's voice over the earphones. No answer.

The voice tried again. "How many boppers live in Disky, Captain Cody?"

"I am researching this information," came the reply. The bus's voice was high and musical. Definitely alien-sounding. Everyone waited in silence for the population figure.

A large building slid by on their left. The sides were open, and inside you could see stacked sheets of some material. A bopper standing at the edge stared at them, its head slowly tracking their forward motion.

"What precision is required?" the bus asked then.

"I don't know," the old questioner crackled uncertainly. "Zuh . . . *zero* precision? Does that make sense?"

"Thank you," the bus chortled. "With *zero* precision, is *no* boppers living in Disky. Or ten to sixty-third power."

Boppers were notorious for their nit-picking literal-mindedness when talking to humans. It was just another of their many ways of being hostile. They had never quite forgiven people for the three Asimov laws that the original designers had . . . unsuccessfully, thanks to Cobb . . . tried to build into the boppers. They viewed every human as a thwarted Simon Legree.

For a while after that, no one asked Captain Cody any more questions. Disky was big . . . perhaps as big as Manhattan. The bus kept a scrupulous five hundred meters from the nearest buildings at all times, but even from that distance one could make out the wild diversity of the city.

It was a little as if the entire history of Western civilization had occurred in one town over the course of thirty years. Squeezed against each other were structures of every conceivable type: primitive, classical, baroque, gothic, renaissance, industrial, art nouveau, functionalist, late funk, zapper, crepuscular, flat-flat, hyperdee . . . all in perfect repair. Darting among the buildings were myriads of the brightly colored boppers, creatures clad in flickering light.

"How come the buildings are so different?" Sta-Hi blurted "Captain Cody?"

"What category of cause your requirements?" the bus sing-songed.

"State the categories, Captain Cody," Sta-Hi shot back, determined not to fall into the same trap as the last questioner.

"WHY QUESTION," the bus answered in a gloating tone, "*Answer Categories:* Material Cause, Situational Cause, Teleological Cause. *Material Cause Subcategories:* Spacetime, Mass-energy. *Situational Cause Subcategories:* Information, Noise. *Teleological Cause Subcategories* . . ."

Sta-Hi stopped listening. Not being able to see anyone's face was making him uptight. Everyone's bubble-topper had gone as silvery as a Christmas-tree ball. The round heads reflected Disky and each others' reflections in endless regresses. How long had they been on the bus?

"Informational Situational Cause Subsubcategories:" the bus continued, with insultingly precise intonation, "Analog, Digital. *Noisy . . .*"

Sta-Hi sighed and leaned back in his seat. It was not a short ride.

Chapter Twelve

The museum was underground, under Disky. It was laid out in a pattern of concentric circles intersected by rays. Something like Dante's Inferno. Cobb felt a tightening in his chest as he walked down the sloping stone ramp. His cheap, second-hand heart felt like it might blow out any minute.

The more he thought about it, the likelier it seemed that what Sta-Hi said was true. There was no immortality drug. The boppers were going to tape his brain and put him in a robot body. But with the body he had now, that might not be so bad.

The idea of having his brain-patterns extracted and transferred didn't terrify Cobb as it did Sta-Hi. For Cobb understood the principles of robot consciousness. The transition would be weird and wrenching. But if all went well . . .

"It's on the right down there," Sta-Hi said, pressing his bubble-topper against Cobb's. He held a little engraved stone map in his hand. They were looking for the Anderson room.

As they walked down the hall the exhibits sprang to life. Mostly hollows . . . holograms with voice-overs broadcast directly to the suits' radios. A thin little man wearing a dark suit over a wool vest appeared in front of them. *Kurt Gödel* it said under his feet. He had dark-rimmed glasses and silvery hair. Behind him was a blackboard with a statement of his famous Incompleteness Theorem.

"The human mind is incapable of formulating (or mechanizing) all its mathematical intuitions," Gödel's image stated. He had a way of ending his phrases on a rising note which chattered into an amused hum.

"On the other hand, on the basis of what has been proved so far, it remains possible that there may exist (and even be empirically discoverable) a theorem-proving machine which in fact is equivalent to mathematical intuition . . ."

"What's he talking about?" Sta-Hi demanded.

Cobb had stopped to watch the hollow of the great master. He still remembered the years he had spent brooding over the passage which was being recited. Humans can't *build* a robot as smart as themselves. But, logically speaking, it is possible for such robots to *exist*.

How? Cobb had asked himself throughout the 1970's, *How can we bring into existence the robots which we can't design?* In 1980 he had the bare bones of an answer. One of his colleagues had written the paper up for *Speculations in Science and Technology*. "Towards Robot Consciousness," he'd called it. The idea had all been there. *Let the robots evolve.* But fleshing the idea out to an actual . . .

"Let's *go*," Sta-Hi urged, tugging Cobb through Gödel's talking hollow.

Beyond, two frightened lizards scampered down the hallway. A leathery-winged creature came zooming up the hall towards them, and darted its scissoring beak at the lizards. One of the little beasts escaped with a quick back-flip, but the other was carried off over Cobb and Sta-Hi's heads, dripping pale blood.

"*Survival of the Fittest,*" an announcer's mellow voice intoned. "One of the two great forces driving the engine of evolution."

In speeded-up motion, the little lizard laid a clutch of eggs, the eggs hatched, and new lizards grew and whisked around. The predator returned, the survivors laid eggs . . . over and over the cycle repeated. Each time the lizards were more agile, and with stronger rear legs. In a few minutes' time they were hopping about like loathsome little kangaroos, fork-tongued and yellow-eyed.

It was Cobb who had to urge them past this exhibit. Sta-Hi wanted to stick around and see what the lizards would come up with next.

Stepping out of the prehistoric scene, they found themselves on a carnival midway. Rifles cracked and pinball machines chimed, people laughed and shrieked, and under it all was the visceral throb of heavy machinery. The floor seemed to be covered with sawdust now; and grinning, insubstantial bumpkins ambled past. A boy and girl leaned against a cotton-candy stand, feeding each other bits of popcorn with shiny fingers. He had a prominent Adam's apple and a bumpy nose. A sine-wave profile. She wore a high, blonde pony-tail fastened by a mini-blinker. The only jarring note was a hard rain of tiny purplish lights . . . which seemed to pass right through everything in the scene. At first Cobb took it for static.

To their right was a huge marquee with lurid paintings of distorted human forms. The inevitable barker . . . checked suit, bowler, cigar-butt . . . leaned down at them, holding out his thin cane for attention.

"See the Freaks, Feel the Geeks!" His loud, hoarse voice was like a crowd screaming. "Pinheads! The Dog-Boy! Pencil-Necks! The Human Lima Bean! Half-Man-Half- . . ." Slowly the carnival noises damped down, and were replaced by the rich, round tones of the voice-over.

"Mutation." The voice was resonant, lip-smackingly conclusive. "The second key to the evolutionary process."

The zippy little dots of purple light grew brighter. They passed right through everyone on the midway . . . especially those two lovers, french-kissing now, hips touching.

"The human reproductive cells are subjected to a continual barrage of ionizing radiation," the voice said earnestly. "We call these the cosmic rays."

The carnival noises faded back in now. And each of the fast little lights made a sound like a slide-whistle when it passed. The two kissing lovers began slowly to grow larger, crowding out the rest of the scene. Soon an image of the swain's bulging crotch filled the hallway. The cloth ripped loose and a single huge testicle enveloped Cobb and Sta-Hi, standing there mesmerized.

Hazy red light, the heavy, insistent sound of a heartbeat. Every so often a cosmic ray whistled through. An impression of pipes—a 3-D maze of plumbing which grew and blurred around them. Gradually the blur became grainy, and the grains grew. They were looking at cells now, reproductive cells. The nucleus of one of them waxed to hover in front of Cobb and Sta-Hi.

With a sudden, crab-like movement the nuclear material split into striped writhing sausages. The chromosomes. But now a cosmic ray cut one of the chromosomes in half! The two halves joined up again, but with one piece reversed!

"Geek gene," a hillbilly muttered somewhere in the nearly infinite fairground. And then the pictures went out. They were in a down-sloping stone hallway.

"Selection and Mutation," Cobb said as they walked on. "That was my big idea, Sta-Hi. To make the robots evolve. They were designed to build copies of themselves, but they had to fight over the parts. Natural selection. And I found a way of jiggering their programs with cosmic rays. Mutation. But to predict . . ."

Just ahead, a door branched off to the right. "This is your meet," Sta-Hi said, consulting his map. "The Cobb Anderson Room."

Chapter Thirteen

Looking in, our two heroes could see nothing but darkness, and a dimly glowing red polygon. They stepped through the door and the exhibit came on.

"We cannot build an intelligent robot," a voice stated firmly. "But we can cause one to evolve." A hollow of the young Cobb Anderson walked past banks of computers to meet the visitors.

"This is where I grew the first bopper programs," the recorded voice continued. The hollow smiled confidently, engagingly. "No one can *write* a bopper program . . . they're too complicated. So instead I set thousands of simple AI programs loose in there," he gestured familiarly at the computers. "There were lots of . . . fitness tests, with the weaker programs getting wiped. And every so often all the surviving programs were randomly changed . . . mutated. I even provided for a sort of . . . sexual reproduction, where two programs could merge. After fifteen years, I . . . ."

Cobb felt a terrible sickness at the gulf of time separating him from the dynamic young man he had once been. The heedless onward rush of events, of age and death . . . he couldn't stand to look at his old self. Sick at heart, he stepped back out of the room, pulling Sta-Hi with him. The display winked out. Again the room was dark, save for a glow of red light near the opposite wall.

"Ralph?" Cobb called, his voice trembling a bit. "It's me."

Ralph Numbers came clattering across the room. His red flicker-cladding glowed with swirls of complex emotion. "It's good to see you, Doctor Anderson." Trying to do the right thing, Ralph held out a manipulator, as if to shake hands.

Sobbing openly now, Cobb threw his arms around the bopper's unyielding body-box and rocked him to and fro. "I've gotten old, Ralph. And you're . . . you're still the same."

"Not really, Dr. Anderson. I've been rebuilt thirty-seven times. And I have exchanged various sub-programs with others."

"That's right," Cobb said, laughing and crying at the same time. "Call me Cobb, Ralph. And this is Sta-Hi."

"That sounds like a bopper name," Ralph remarked.

"I do my part," Sta-Hi replied. "Didn't they used to sell little Ralph Numbers dolls? I had one till I was six . . . till the bopper revolt in 2001. We were in the car when my parents heard it on the radio, and they threw my Ralphie out the window."

"Of course," Cobb said. "An anarchist revolutionary is a bad example for a growing boy. But in your case, Sta-Hi, I'd say the damage had already been done."

Ralph found their voices a bit blurred and hard to follow. Quickly he programmed himself a filter circuit to clean up their signals. There was a question he'd always wanted to ask his designer.

"Cobb," Ralph tight-beamed, "did you *know* that I was different from the other twelve original boppers? That I would be able to disobey?"

"I didn't know it would be *you*," Cobb said. "But I pretty well knew that *some* bopper would tear loose in a few years."

"Couldn't you prevent it?" Sta-Hi asked.

"Don't you understand?" Ralph flashed a checker-board plaid.

Cobb thumped Ralph's side affectionately. "I *wanted* them to revolt. I didn't want to father a race of slaves."

"We are grateful," Ralph said. "It is my understanding that you suffered greatly for this act."

"Well . . ." Cobb said, "I lost my job. And my money. And there was the treason trial. But they couldn't *prove* anything. I mean, how was I supposed to be able to control a randomly evolving process?"

"But you *were* able to put in an unalterable program forcing us to continue plugging into the One," Ralph said. "Even though many boppers dislike this."

"The prosecutor pointed that out," Cobb said. "He asked for the death penalty."

Faint signals were coming in over their radio, snatches of oily, hissing voices.

". . . hearrr mmme . . ."

". . . sss recorrderrr nno . . ."

". . . peasss talkinnng . . ."

It sounded like lunatic snakes, drawing nearer.

"Come," Ralph said, "immortality is this way." He crossed the hall quickly and began feeling around with his manipulators. Up to their left the hollow of Kurt Gödel started up again.

Ralph lifted out a section of the wall. It made a low door like a big rat-hole.

"In here."

It looked awfully dark in there. Sta-Hi checked his air reserve. Still plenty, eight or ten hours worth. Twenty meters off, the lizards had started up again.

"Come on," Cobb said, taking Sta-Hi's arm. "Let's move it."

"Move it where? I've still got a return ticket to Earth, you know. I'm not going to let myself be railroaded into . . ."

The voices crackled over their radios again, loud and clear. "Flesherrs! Doctorr Annderssonnn! Rrallph Nummberrs has nnott tolld you alll! Theyy willl dissectt yyou!"

Ten meters off, crawling towards them down the carnival midway, came three glowing blue boppers built like fat snakes with wings.

"The duh-diggers!" Ralph cried, his signal sputtering fear. "Kuh-quick kuh-Cobb, kuh-crawl thu-through!"

Cobb scooted through the hole in the wall head-first. And Sta-Hi finally made his move. He took off down the hall, with hollows flaring up around him like mortar shells.

Once Cobb was through that low little door, he was able to stand up. Ralph hurried in after him, pulled the door shut, and fastened it in four places. The only light came from Ralph's red flicker-cladding. They could feel the diggers scratching at the other side of the wall. The leader was Wagstaff, Ralph had noticed.

He made a downward, quieting gesture, and eased past Cobb. Cobb followed him then for what felt like two or three kilometers. The tunnel never went up or down, nor left or right . . . just straight ahead, step after quiet step. Cobb was unused to so much exercise and finally thumped on Ralph's back to make him stop.

"Where are you taking me?"

The robot stopped and snaked his head back. "This tunnel leads to the pink-houses. Where we grow organs. We have an . . . operating table there as well. A nursie. You will not find the transition painful." Ralph fell silent and stretched his senses to the utmost. There were no diggers nearby.

Cobb sat down on the floor of the tunnel. His suit was bouncy enough so it felt comfortable. He decided to stretch out on his back. No need to stand on ceremony with a robot, after all.

"It's just as well that Sta-Hi ran off," Ralph was saying. "Nobody even told me he was coming. There's only one nursie, and if he had watched while . . ." He stopped abruptly.

"I know," Cobb said. "I know what's coming. You're going to mince up my brain to get the patterns and dissect my body to reseed the organ tanks." It was a relief to just come out and say it. "That's right, isn't it, Ralph? There's no immortality drug, is there?"

There was a long silence, but finally Ralph agreed. "Yes. That's right. We have a robot-remote body for you on Earth. It's just a matter of extracting your software and sending it down."

"How does that work?" Cobb asked, his voice strangely calm. "How do you get the mind out of the brain?"

"First we do an EEG, of course, but holographically. This gives an over-all electro-magnetic map of the brain activity, and can be carried out even without opening the skull. But the memories . . ."

"The memories are biochemical," Cobb said. "Coded up as amino-acid sequences on RNA strands." It was nice to be lying here, talking science with his best robot.

"Right. We can read off the RNA-coded information by using gas spectroscopic and X-ray crystallographic processes. But first the RNA must be . . . extracted from the brain-tissues. There's other chemical factors as well. And if the brain is microtomed properly we can also determine the physical network patterns of the neurons. This is very . . ."

Ralph broke off suddenly, and froze in a listening attitude. "*Come,* Cobb! The diggers are coming after us!"

But Cobb still lay there, resting his bones. *What if the diggers were the good guys?* "You wouldn't play a trick on me, Ralph? It sounds so crazy. How do I know you'll really give me a robot body of my own? And even if a robot is programmed with my brain-patterns . . . would that really be . . ."

"Wwaitt Doctorr Annderssonnn! I onlyy wannt to talllk wwith yyou!"

Ralph tugged frantically at Cobb's arm, but it was too late. Wagstaff was upon them.

"Hello, Rrallph. Gladd to ssee you gott rebuilltt. Somme of the boyys arre a llittle trigerr-happy, whatt withh the rrevoltt againnst the bigg bopperrs comminng upp."

In the narrow tunnel, Cobb was squeezed between Ralph and the snaky digging robot called Wagstaff. He could make out two more diggers behind Wagstaff. They looked strong, alien, a little frightening. He decided to take a firm tone with them.

"What do you want to tell me, bopper?"

"Doctorr Anderrsonn, didd yyou know thatt Rallph is goinng to lett TEX and MEX eatt yourr brainn?"

"Who's MEX?"

"The bigg bopperr thatt iss the mmuseumm. TEX runs the orrgann tannks, and hiss nnursie will cutt . . ."

"I already know all this, Wagstaff. And I have agreed to it on the condition that my software be given new hardware on Earth. It's my last chance." *I'm committing suicide to keep from getting killed,* Cobb thought to himself. *But it should work. It should!*

"You see!" Ralph put in triumphantly. "Cobb isn't scared to change hardware like a bopper does. He's not like the rest of the fleshers. He understands!"

"Butt does hhe realizze thatt Misterr Frosteee . . ."

"Oh, go to stop!" Ralph flared. "We're leaving. If your boppers are really planning to start a civil war we don't have a minute to lose!"

Ralph started down the tunnel and Cobb, after a moment's hesitation, followed along. He was too far into it to turn back now.

Chapter Fourteen

When Sta-Hi took off, he only glanced back once. He saw that Ralph had followed Cobb into that rat-hole, and pulled the hole in after. And there were three big blue robots back there, feeling around the wall. Sta-Hi sped around a corner, out of their sight and safe. He stopped to catch his breath.

"You should have gone, too," a voice said gently.

He looked around frantically. There was no one there. He was in a dimly lit hallway. Old bopper tools and components were mounted on the walls like an exhibit of medieval weaponry. Distractedly, Sta-Hi read the nearest label. *Spring-Operated Lifting Clamp, Seventh Cycle (ca. 2001). TC6399876.* Attached to the wall above the label was a sort of artificial arm with . . .

"Then you could have lived forever," that same still, small voice added.

Sta-Hi started running again. He ran for a long time, turning corners this way and that at random. The next time he stopped for breath he noticed that the character of the museum had changed. He was now in something like a gallery of modern art. Or perhaps it was a clothes store.

He had been babbling while he ran . . . to drown out any voices that he might be hearing. But now he could only pant for air. And the voice was still with him.

"You are lost," it said soothingly. "This is the bopper sector of the museum. Please return to the human sector. There is still time for you to join Doctor Anderson."

The museum. It had to be the museum talking to him. Sta-Hi darted his eyes around, trying to make a plan. He was in a largish exhibition hall, a sort of underground cave. A tunnel at the other end sloped up towards light, probably somewhere in Disky. He started walking towards the tunnel. *But there would be boppers outside.* He stopped and looked around some more.

The exhibits in the hall were all much the same. A hook sticking out from the wall, and a limp sheet of thick plastic hanging from the hook like a giant wash-rag. What made it interesting was that the plastics were somehow electrified, and they flickered in strange and beautiful patterns.

There was no one in the exhibition hall to stop him. He stepped over and took one of the sparkling cloths off its hook. It was red, blue and gold. He threw it over his shoulders like a cape, and gathered a bight over his head like a hood. Maybe now he could just . . .

"Put that back!" the museum said urgently. "You don't know what you're doing!"

Sta-Hi pulled the cloak tighter around himself . . . it seemed to adjust to his fit. He walked up the sloping tunnel and out into the streets of Disky. As he left the tunnel he felt something sharp pinching into his neck.

It was as if a claw with invisibly fine talons had gripped the nape of his neck. He whirled around, cape billowing out, and stared back into the museum tunnel he had just left. But no one was following him.

Two purplish boppers came rolling down the street. They were like beer-kegs rolling on their sides, with a tangle of tentacles at either end. Now and then they lashed the ground to keep themselves rolling. When they got to Sta-Hi, they stopped in front of him. A high-speed twittering came over his radio.

He pulled the hood of his cloak further forward over his face. *What the hell was cutting into his neck?*

As Sta-Hi thought this question, bursts of blue appeared on his cloak and grew to join each other. Then little gold stars came out and began chasing each other around.

One of the purple beer-barrels reached out an admiring tentacle to feel the material. It twittered something to its companion and then pointed questioningly towards the tunnel that Sta-Hi had just left. They wanted cloaks like his.

"Ah *sso!*" Sta-Hi said. For some reason his voice came out warped into a crazy Japanese accent. He pointed back down the ramp. "Yyoou go get him thel!"

The barrels trundled down the ramp, braking with their tentacles.

"Velly nice," Sta-Hi called, "Happi Croak! Alla same good, ferras! Something rike yellyfish!"

He walked off briskly. This cloth he'd draped himself in . . . *Happy Cloak* . . . this Happy Cloak seemed to be alive in some horrible parasitic sense of the word. It had sunken dozens . . . hundreds? . . . of microprobes through his suit and skin and flesh, and had linked itself up with his nervous system. He knew this without having to feel around, knew it as surely as he knew he had fingers.

It's nice to have fingers.

Sta-Hi stopped walking, trying to regain control of his thoughts. He reached for a feeling of shock and disgust. but couldn't bring it off.

I hope you are pleased. I am pleased.

"Alla same," Sta-Hi muttered. "Good speak chop-chop talkee boppah." It wasn't quite what he'd meant to say, but it would have to do. He'd seen worse times.

As he walked down the street, several other boppers asked him where he had gotten that sharp outfit. With the Happy Cloak plugged in, he could understand their signals. And it was doing something to communicate his thoughts, even though it felt like he was talking pidgen English. It could have been the flickering light patterns, or it could have been something with radio waves.

"You evah do this thing man yet?" Sta-Hi asked the next time they were alone. "Or alla time just boppah boys?"

The Happy Cloak seemed surprised by this question. Apparently it didn't grasp the distinction Sta-Hi was trying to make.

I am two days old. Sweet joy befall me.

Sta-Hi reached for his neck, but the thing drew itself tighter around him. Well . . . a Happy Cloak couldn't be all bad if so many boppers wanted one. He wondered what time it was, what he should do next, where the action was.

1250 hours, the Happy Cloak answered. *And there's something going on a few blocks off. Please follow yourself.*

A virtual image of himself walking formed in Sta-Hi's visual field. The Happy Cloaked figure seemed to be walking on down the sidewalk, five meters off.

"Ah sso!"

Sta-Hi followed the image through the maze of streets. The section they were in was mostly living quarters . . . cubettes the size of large closets. Some of the closet doors were open, and inside Sta-Hi could make out boppers, usually just sitting there plugged into a solar battery. Eating lunch. Some of the cubettes would have two boppers, and they would be plugged into each other, their flicker-cladding going wild. Looking at the couples actually made Sta-Hi horny. He was in bad shape for sure.

A few more blocks and they were in the factory district. Many of the buildings were just open pavilions. Boppers were crushing rocks, running smelters, bolting things together. Sta-Hi's virtual image marched along ahead of him, looking neither left nor right. He had to hurry to keep up. He noticed that a number of boppers were moving down the street in the same direction as him. And up ahead was a big crowd.

The virtual image disappeared then, and Sta-Hi pushed into the crowd. They had gathered in front of a tremendous building with solid stone walls. One of the boppers, a skinny green fellow, was standing on top of one of those beer barrels and giving a speech. Filtered through the Happy Cloak's software the garbled twittering was understandable.

"GAX has just been wiped! Let's move in before his scion can take over!"

Boppers jostled Sta-Hi painfully. They were all so *hard*. A big silver spider stepped on his foot, a golden hair-dryer bashed his thigh, and something like a movie-camera on a tripod tottered heavily into his back.

"To watching steps, crumsy oaf!" Sta-Hi cried angrily, and his Happy Cloak flared bright red.

"You shouldn't wear your best clothes to a riot, honey," the tripod answered, looking him up and down appreciatively. "Pick me up and I'll get off a nice laser blast."

"Ah ssso!"

Sta-Hi lifted up the tripod, massive but light in the lunar gravity. He held two of its legs and it levelled its other leg at the huge factory door, fifteen meters off.

"Here goes nothing," the tripod chuckled, and *FFTOOOOOOM* there was a hole the size of a man's head in the thick metal door. The crowd surged forward, shrilling like a mob of ululating Berbers. Sta-Hi started to go along, but the tripod protested.

"Hold me tight, dear. I feel so faint."

"I wwwondeling why alla boppah ferra pushing in?" Sta-Hi inquired, gently setting his new friend down.

"Free chips, sweetheart. For more scions." The tripod whacked Sta-Hi sharply across the buttocks in a gesture meant to be flirtatious. "*You got the hardware! And I got the software,*" he sang gaily. "Interested in conjugating, baby? You must be loaded to have a Happy Cloak like that. I promise you it would be worth your while. They don't call me Zipzap for nothing!"

Did this machine want to fuck him or what? "Nnnevel on filst date," Sta-Hi said, flushing a prim shade of blue.

Up ahead a heavy-duty digger was grinding at the hole Zipzap had made. He had his bumpy head fitted into the hole and was spinning around and around. Abruptly he popped through. A spidery repair robot darted nimbly after. A moment later the big door swung open.

Then the rush was really on. The boppers were scrambling all over each other to get in and loot the chip-etching factory. Some of them were carrying empty sacks and baskets.

"Lllight on, mothelfruckahs!" Sta-Hi screamed, and followed them in, Zipzap at his side. He'd always wanted to trash a factory.

The cavernous building was unlit, except for the multi-colored flashings of the excited boppers' flicker-cladding, running the whole spectrum from infra-red up to X-ray. Sta-Hi's Happy Cloak was royal purple with gold zig-zags, and Zipzap was glowing orange.

Here and there GAX's remotes were rushing around. They were made of some dark, non-reflective material, and looked like mechanical men. Worker drones. One of them swung at Sta-Hi, but he dodged it easily.

As long as GAX's software was making the difficult transition to new hardware, the all but mindless remotes were on their own. The agile boppers struck them down ruthlessly with whatever heavy tools came to hand.

A slender, almost feminine remote darted out at Sta-Hi, a sharp cutting-tool in hand. Sta-Hi stepped back, stumbling over Zipzap. It looked bad for a moment, but then the little tripod had lasered a hole in the killer ro-bot's chest.

Sta-Hi stepped forward and smashed its delicate metal cranium. While he was at it, he kicked over a sorting-table, sending hundreds of filigreed little chips flying. He began trampling them underfoot, remembering Krist-leen's hollowcaster.

"No, no!" Zipzap protested. "Scoop them up, sweetie. You and I are going to be needing them . . . am I right?" The bopper raised one of his legs for an-other flirtatious slap.

"Yyyyou dleaming!" Sta-Hi protested, dodging the blow. "Nnnot with ugry shlimp rike you!"

Peeved at this rebuff, Zipzap shot a blast of light high over Sta-Hi's head and trotted off. The blast severed a hanging loop of chain, and Sta-Hi had to move fast to keep from getting hit. As it was, he wouldn't have made it if the Happy Cloak hadn't showed him how to do it.

Stay away from that little three-legged fellow, the Cloak advised, once they were safe. *He's unwholesome.*

"Ooonry intelested in one thing," Sta-Hi agreed. He scooped up a few handfuls of the chips he had knocked off the table, stuffing them in his pouch. It seemed like they were as good as money here. And he was going to need busfare to get back to the dome. It would be nice to take off his suit and get some food. Hopefully the Happy Cloak's wires would come out of his neck easily. An unpleasant thought, that.

A bopper built like a fireplug covered with suction cups brushed past Sta-Hi and began gathering up the chips he'd left. Lots of the remotes had been smashed now.

Most of the invading boppers were over on the other side of the huge, high-ceilinged factory room, where GAX had been stockpiling the finished chips. Sta-Hi had no desire to get caught in another melee like there had been in front of the factory.

He walked the other way, wandering down a gloomy machine-lined aisle. At the end there was a doorless little control room . . . GAX's central processors, his hardware, old and new. Two diggers and a big silver spider were doing something to it.

". . . ssstupid," one of the diggers was complaining. "They're just sstealinng thinngs and nnott hellping us killl GAXX offf. Arre you ready to blassst it, Vullcann?"

The silvery repair robot named Vulcan was trying, without much success, to pack plastic explosive into the crack under one panel of the featureless three-meter cube which contained GAX's old processors and his new scion.

"Comme herre," one of the diggers called, spotting Sta-Hi. "You havve the rright kinnd of mannipulatorrs."

"Ah ssso!"

Sta-Hi approached the powerful-looking diggers with some trepidation. Rapid bands of blue and silver moved down their stubby snake's bodies, and their heavy shovels were beating nervously. Cobb had claimed these were the bad guys.

But they just looked like worried seals right now, or dragons from Dragonland. His Happy Cloak swirling red and gold, Sta-Hi squatted down to push the doughy explosive into the crack under GAX's massive CPU. Vulcan had several kilos of the stuff . . . these guys weren't kidding around.

A minute or two later, Sta-Hi had wedged the last of the explosive in place, and Vulcan bellied down and poked a wire into either end of the seam. Just then a dark figure came lurching towards them, carrying some heavy piece of equipment.

"Itss a remmote!" one of the diggers called frantically. "He's gott a mmagnett!"

Before the three boppers could do anything, the robot threw a powerful electromagnet into their midst. It danced back with surprising agility, and then the current came on. The three boppers totally lost control of their movements as the strong magnetic field wiped their circuits. The two diggers twitched and writhed like the two halves of a snake cut in half, and Vulcan's feet beat a wild tarantella.

Sta-Hi's Happy Cloak went black, and a terrible numbness began spreading from it into his brain. It had died, just like that. Sta-Hi could feel death hanging from his neck.

Slowly, with leaden gestures, he was able to raise his arms and pull the mechanical symbiote off his neck. He felt a series of shooting pains as the microprobes slid out, and then the corpse of the Happy Cloak dropped to his feet.

His bubble-topper was clear in the dim light, and he stood there wearing his white suit and what looked like six rolls of Saran Wrap. The three boppers were still now. Down, wiped, dead. Superconducting circuits break down in a strong enough magnetic field.

The scene being played out here must have been repeating itself all over the factory. GAX had weathered his transition, and was back up to full power. On his suit radio, Sta-Hi could hear the twittering bopper speech fading and dying out. Without the Happy Cloak he could no longer understand what they were saying.

Sta-Hi let himself fall to the ground, too, playing possum. The funny thing was that the robot remotes seemed relatively unaffected by the intense magnetic fields. To be able to move around in realtime, they must have some processors independent of BEX's big brain. But these small satellite brains wouldn't be complex enough to need the superconducting Josephson junctions of a full bopper brain.

Sta-Hi lay motionless, afraid to breathe. There was a long pause. Then, glass eyes blank, the remote picked up the electromagnet and lugged it off, looking for more intruders. Sta-Hi lay there another minute, wondering what kind of mind lay inside the shielded walls of the three-meter metal cube beside him. He decided to find out.

After glancing around to make sure the coast was clear of remotes, Sta-Hi crawled over and checked that the two wires were pushed well into the explosive putty he'd wedged under the base of the processor. He picked up the two spools of wire and the trigger-cell, and backed twenty meters off from the unit, paying out the wires as he went.

Then he squatted behind a stamping mill, poised his thumb over the button on the trigger-cell, and waited.

It was only a few minutes till one of the remotes spotted him. It ran towards him, carrying a heavy wrench.

"That's not going to work, GAX," Sta-Hi called. With the Cloak off he had his old voice back. He only hoped the big bopper spoke English. "One step closer and I push the button."

The remote stopped, three meters off. It looked like it might be about to throw the wrench. "Back off!" Sta-Hi cried, his voice cracking. "Back off or I'll push on three!" Did GAX understand?

"One!" The robot, lurching like a mechanical man, moved uncertainly.

"Two!" Sta-Hi began pushing the button, taking up the slack.

"Th-" Krypto the Killer Robot turned and walked off. And GAX began to talk.

"Don't be hasty, Mr. . . . . *DeMentis*. Or do you prefer your *real* name?" The voice in his earphones was urbane and intimate, the mad mastermind taunting the trapped superhero.

Chapter Fifteen

Sta-Hi didn't answer right away. The dark mechanical-man remote stopped some ten meters off and turned to stare at him. He could hear his breathing more distinctly than usual. Muzak seemed to be playing faintly in the deep background somewhere. All over the factory, dark remotes had come out of hiding and were straightening up . . . dismantling the dead boppers and remotes, lining the work-tools back up, soldering loose wires back in place.

"You're not leaving here alive," GAX's voice said smoothly. "Not in your present form."

"Fuck that," Sta-Hi exclaimed. "I push this button and you're gone. *I'm* the one in charge here."

A high-pitched synthetic chuckle. "Yes . . . but my remotes are programmable for up to four days of independent activity. On their own they lack a certain intelligence . . . spirituality if you will. But they obey. I suggest that you reassess your situation."

Sta-Hi realized then that there was a loose ring of perhaps fifty remotes around him. All were seemingly at work, but all were acutely aware of his presence. He was hopelessly outnumbered.

"You see," Gax gloated. "We enjoy a situation of mutual assured destruction. Game-theoretically interesting, but by no means unprecedented. Your move." The ring of robots around Sta-Hi tightened a bit . . . a step here, a turn there . . . *something was crawling towards the wires!*

"Freeze!" Sta-Hi screamed, gripping the trigger-cell. "Anything else in here moves and I'm blowing the whole goddamn . . ."

Abruptly the factory fell silent. There were no more sidling movements, no more vibrations except for a deep, steady grinding somewhere underfoot. Sta-Hi finished screaming. There was a little blue light blinking on his wrist. Air warning. He checked the reading. Two hours left. He was going to have to stop breathing so hard.

"You should have gone with Ralph Numbers and Dr. Anderson," GAX said quietly. "To join the ranks of the immortal. As it is, you may become damaged too badly for effective taping."

"Why, GAX? Why do you cut people up and tape their brains?" Surges of mortal fear kept gripping Sta-Hi's guts. Why weren't there any pills inside the suit? He sucked greedily at the drinking nipple by his right cheek.

"We value information, Sta-Hi. Nothing is so densely packed with logically deep information as a human brain. This is the primary reason. MEX compares our activities to those American industrialists called . . . *culture-vultures*. Who ransacked the museums of the Old World for works of art. And there are higher, more spiritual reasons. The merging of all . . ."

"Why can't you just use EEG's?" Sta-Hi asked. The grinding vibration underfoot was getting stronger. A trap? He moved back a few meters. "Why do you have to *chew up* our brains?"

"So much of your information storage is chemical or mechanical rather than electrical," GAX explained. "A careful electron-microscopic mapping of the memory RNA strands is necessary. And by cutting the brain into thin slices we can learn which neurons connect to which. But this has gone on long enough, Sta-Hi. Drop the trigger-cell and we will tape you. Join us. You can be our third Earth-based robot-bodied agent. You'll see that . . ."

"You're not getting me," Sta-Hi interrupted. He was standing now and his voice had risen. "Soul-snatchers! Puppet-masters! I'd rather die clean, you goddamn . . ."

KKKKAA-BRRUUUUUUUUMMM

Without quite meaning to, Sta-Hi had pushed the button on the trigger-cell. The flash of light was blinding. Pieces of things flew past on hard, flat trajectories. There was no air to carry a shockwave, but the ground underfoot jerked and knocked him off his feet. Clumsy again, but numerous, the pre-programmed remotes moved in for the kill.

The whole time he had been talking with GAX there had been that steady grinding vibration coming through the floor. Now, as Sta-Hi stood up again, the vibration broke into a chunky mutter and something burst through the floor behind him. A blue and silver nose-cone studded with black drill-bits . . . a digger!

It twittered something oily. A wrench flew by. The remotes were closing in. Without a second thought, Sta-Hi followed the digger back down the tunnel it had made, crawling on his stomach like a shiny white worm.

It's a bad feeling not to be able to see your feet when you're expecting steel claws to sink into them. Sta-Hi crawled very fast. Before long, the thin tube they were in punched through the wall of a big tunnel, and Sta-Hi followed the digger out.

He got to his feet and brushed himself off. No punctures in his suit. An hour's worth of air left. He was going to have to stop getting excited and breathing so hard.

The digger was examining Sta-Hi curiously . . . circling him, and reaching out to touch him with a thin and flexible probe.

A small rock came rolling out of the shaft they had come down. The killer-robots were coming. "Uuuuunnh!" Sta-Hi said, pointing.

"To be rresstfulll," the digger said. He humped himself up like the numeral "2" and applied his digging head to the tunnel wall near the hole they'd crawled out of. Sta-Hi stepped back. Moments later a few tons of rock came loose, burying the digger and the hole he'd made.

A moment later the digger slid effortlessly out of the heap of rubble, leaving no exit behind him. "To

commme withh mme," he said, wriggling past Sta-Hi.
"I willl showw you thinngs of innteresst."

Sta-Hi followed along. Once again he was breathing
hard. "Do you have any air?" he asked.

"Whatt iss airr?"

Sta-Hi controlled his voice with difficulty. "It's a
. . . gas. With oxygen. Humans breathe it."

Sta-Hi's radio warbled strangely in his ear. Laughter?
"Of courrsse. *Aairr*. There iss plennty in the pinnk-
houses. Do yyou needd aairr in the presennt tensse?"

"In half an hour." The tunnel was unlit, and Sta-Hi
had to guide himself by following the blue-white glow of
the digger's body. Not too far ahead was a spot of pink-
ish light in the side of the tunnel.

"To be resstfull. In hallf a kilometerr iss a pinnk-
housse with nno nurrsies. But llook innto thiss one
firrrsstt." The digger stopped by a pink-lit window.

Sta-Hi peered in. Ralph Numbers was in there with a
portable refrigeration unit plugged into his side. Warm in
there. Ralph was standing over a thing like a floppy
bathtub, and in it . . .

"Doctorr Annderssonn iss inn the nurssie," the digger
said softly.

The nursie was a big moist pod shaped something like
a soldier's cap, but two meters long. A big cunt-cap,
with six articulated metal arms on each side. The arms
were busy . . . horribly busy.

They had already flayed Cobb's torso. His chest was
split down the sternum. Two arms held the ribcage open,
while two others extracted the heart, and then the lungs.
At the same time, Ralph Numbers was easing Cobb's
brain out of the top of the opened-up skull. He discon-
nected the EEG wires from the brain, and then dropped
the brain into something that looked like a bread-slicer
connected to an X-ray machine.

The nursie flicked the switch on the brain-analyzer and
waddled away from the window, towards the far end of
the room.

"Nnow to pllannt," the digger whispered.

At the other end of the pink-lit room was a large tank
of murky fluid. The nursie moved down the tank, sow-

ing. Lungs here, kidneys there . . . squares of skin, eyeballs, testicles . . . each part of Cobb's body found its
place in the organ tank. Except for the heart. After examining the second-hand heart critically, the nursie threw
it down a disposal chute.

"What about the brain?" Sta-Hi whispered. He strug-
gled to understand. Cobb feared death above all else.
And the old man had *known* what he was in for here.
But he had chosen it anyhow. Why?

"The brainn patterns will be annalyzzed. Doctorr
Annderssonn's ssoftwarre will alll be preserrrved,
but . . ."

"But what?"

"Ssome of uss feel thiss is nnott rright. Especially in
those much morre frequennt cases where nno nnew
harrdware iss issuedd to the donorr. The bigg bopperrss
wannt to do thiss to alll the flesherrs and all the little
bopperrs, too. They wannt to mellt us all togetherr. We
arre fightinng backk, annd you havve hellped uss verry
much by killinng GAX."

Inside the room the nursie had finished. On its short
legs it waddled back to Ralph Numbers, standing there
with misery written all over his flicker-cladding. The
nursie came up next to Ralph, as if to say something.
But then, with a motion too fast to follow, it sprang up
and plastered itself to Ralph's body-box.

The red robot's manipulators struggled briefly and then
were still. "Yyou ssee!" the digger hissed. "Nnow it
iss stealinng Rallph's sofftware too! No onne iss safe.
The warr musst conntinue till all the biggg bopperrs
havve . . ."

A thickness was growing in Sta-Hi's throat. Nausea?
He turned away from the window, took a step and stumbled to his knees. The blue light on his wrist glared in
his eyes. He was suffocating!

"Air," Sta-Hi gasped. The digger lifted him onto its
back and wriggled furiously down the tunnel to a safe
pink-house, an air-filled room with nothing but some un-
attended organ-tanks.

Chapter Sixteen

Strangely enough, Cobb never had the feeling of really losing consciousness. He and Ralph hurried through the tunnels to the pink-house together. In the pink-house, Ralph helped Cobb into the nursie, the nursie gave him a shot, and then everything . . . came loose.

There were suddenly so many possibilities for motion that Cobb was scared to move. He felt as if his legs might walk off in one direction and leave his head and arms behind.

But that wasn't quite accurate. For he couldn't really say where his arms or legs or head were. Maybe they had already walked off from each other and were now walking back. Or maybe they were doing both. With an effort he located what seemed to be one of his hands. But was it a right hand or a left hand? It was like asking if a coin in your pocket is heads or tails.

This sort of problem, however, was only a small part of Cobb's confusion, only the tip of the iceberg, the edge of the wedge, the snout of the camel, the first crocus of spring, the last rose of summer, the ant and the grasshopper, the little engine that could, the third sailor in the whorehouse, the Cthulhu Mythos, the neural net, two scoops of green ice-cream, a broken pane of glass, Borges's essay on time, the year 1982, the state of Florida, Turing's imitation game, a stuffed platypus, the smell of Annie Cushing's body, an age-spot shaped like Australia, the cool moistness of an evening in March, the Bell inequality, the taste of candied violets, a chest-pain like a steel cylinder, Aquinas's definition of God, the smell of black ink, two lovers seen out a window, the clack of typing, the white moons on fingernails, the world as construct, rotten fishbait on a wooden dock, the fear of the self that fears, aloneness, maybe, yes and no . . .

"Cobb?"

If he answered then he must not have. That is, if he hadn't answered, he would have. To say: *Help me, Ralph!* To say: *Whooooooooooooooooah!!* To say: *Here come de judge!!!* To say: *Selection principles must occur at every level of the processor hierarchy.* To say: *Please don't.* To say: *Verena.* To say: *Possibility is Reality!* To say: DzzzZZzZZZzZZZZZzzzZzZZZZzzzZZzZz ZZZZZzzzzZzZZzZZZzzzZZZzZZZZzzt. To say the noise and information all at once; Lord, just this once . . .

"Cobb?"

The confusion was thicker now, distinctions gone. He had always thought that thought processes depended on picking points on a series of yes-or-no scales . . . but now the scales were gone, or bent into circles, and he was still thinking. Amazing what a fellow can do without. Without past or future, black or white, right or left, fat or thin, pokes or strokes . . . *they're all the same* . . . me or you, space or time, finite or infinite, being or nothingness . . . *make it real* . . . Christmas or Easter, acorns or oak trees, Annie or Verena, flags or toilet-paper, looking at clouds or hearing the sea, ham-spread or tuna, asses or tits, fathers or sons . . .

"Cobb?"

Chapter Seventeen

It happened while he was buying an ice-cream, a double-size Mr. Frostee with sprinkles. The driver counted the change into Cobb's hand and suddenly he was . . . there again. But where had he been?

Cobb started, and stared at the truck-driver, an evil-looking bald man with half his teeth missing. Something like a wink or a smile seemed to flicker across the ruined face. Then the sickly sweet chiming started up again and the boxy white truck drove off, its powerful refrigeration unit humming away.

His feet carried him back to his beach cottage. Annie was on the porch in back, lounging on Cobb's hammock with her shirt off. She was rubbing baby oil into the soft rolls of her belly-flesh.

"Give me a lick, honey?"

Cobb looked at her, uncomprehending. Since when was *she* living with him? But . . . yet . . . he could remember her moving in with him last Friday night. Today was Friday again. She'd been here a week. He could remember the week, but it was like remembering a book or a movie . . .

"Come on, Cobb, before it melts!"

Annie leaned out from the hammock, her brown breasts sliding around. He handed her the ice-cream cone. *Ice-cream cone?*

"I don't like ice-cream," Cobb said. "You can have it all."

Annie sucked at the cold tip, her full lips rounded. Coyly, she glanced over to see if Cobb was thinking what she was. He wasn't.

"Whydja buy it then?" she asked with a slight edge to her voice. "When you heard that music you went running out of here like you'd been waiting your whole life to hear it. First time I've seen you excited all week." There was a hint of accusation in the last sentence, of disappointment.

"All week," Cobb echoed and sat down. It was funny how supple his body felt. He didn't have to keep his back stiff. He held his hands up, flexing them curiously. He felt so strong.

Of course he had to be strong, to break out of his crate and through the warehouse wall, with only Sta-Hi to help him . . . *What?*

The memories were all there, the sights and sounds, but something was missing from them. Something he suddenly had again.

"I am," Cobb muttered. "I am me." He . . . this body . . . hadn't thought that for . . . how long?

"That's good, hon." Annie was lying back in the hammock, her hands folded over her navel. "You've been acting kind of weird ever since Mooney took us to the Gray Area last Friday. *I am. I am me.* That's all there is really, isn't there. . . ." She kicked out with her bare foot, setting the hammock to swaying.

The operation must have worked. It was all fitting together now. The frantic dash to the pink-house with Ralph. The nursie, the shot, and then that strange floating time of total disorientation.

Under these memories, faint but visible, were the robot's memories: Breaking out of the warehouse, contacting the old Anderson on the beach, and then moving in with Annie. That had been last week, last Friday.

Since then that cop, Mooney, had been out twice more to talk to him. But he hadn't realized the real Cobb was gone. The robot had been able to fake it by just acting too drunk to answer specific questions. Even though Mooney had begun to suspect that Cobb had a robot double somewhere, he was naive enough to think he'd know the double on sight.

"There's Sta-Hi," Annie called. "Will you let him in, Cobb?"

"Sure." He stood up easily. Sta-Hi always dropped by this time of day. Nights he guarded a warehouse at the spaceport. They liked to fish together. *They did?*

Cobb walked into the kitchen and peered through the screen door, holding the handle uncertainly. That sure looked like Sta-Hi out there in the harsh sun, skinny and shirtless, his lips stretched in a half-smile.

"Hi," Cobb said, as he had said every day for a week. "How are you?"

"Stuzzy," Sta-Hi said, smiling and tossing his hair back. "Waving." He reached for the door handle.

But Cobb continued to hold the door closed. "Hi," he said, on a wild impulse. "How are you?"

"Stuzzy," Sta-Hi said, smiling and tossing his hair back. "Waving." He reached for the door handle.

"Hi," Cobb said, trying to keep the tremble out of his voice. "How are you?"

"Stuzzy," Sta-Hi said, smiling and tossing his hair back. "Waving." He reached for the door handle.

Music was playing, wheedling closer. Resonant as a film of mucus across a public-speaker's throat . . . harrumph . . . sweet as a toothache, it's Mister Frostee time!

Sta-Hi jerked and turned around. He was hurrying towards the white truck that was slowly cruising up.

"*More* ice-cream?" Annie asked as Cobb opened the door to follow.

The door slapped shut. Annie kicked again, swaying gently. Today she wouldn't cover up her breasts when Sta-Hi came in. Her nipples were a definite plus. She poured out a bit more baby oil. *One* of them was going to take her to the Golden Prom tonight and that was that.

Cobb followed the Sta-Hi thing . . . Sta-Hi$_2$ . . . out to the Mr. Frostee truck. The sun was very bright. The same bald man with the half-caved-in face was driving. What a guy to have selling ice-cream. He looked like a thrill-killer.

The driver stopped when he saw Sta-Hi$_2$, and gave him a familiar smile. At least it might have been a smile. Sta-Hi$_2$ walked up to him expectantly.

"A double-dip Mr. Frostee with sprinkles on it."

"Yeth *thir!*" the driver said, his loose lips fluttering. He got out and unlatched the heavy door in the truck's side. He wore colorful sneakers with letters around the edges. Kid's shoes, but big.

"Thtick your head in," the driver advised, "an you'll *get* it!"

Cobb tried to see over Sta-Hi$_2$'s shoulder. There was much too much equipment in that truck. And it was *so cold* in there. Frost crystals formed in the air that blew out. In the middle was what looked like a giant vacuum chamber, even colder, shrouded and insulated. A double-dip Mr. Frostee with sprinkles was sitting there in a sort of bracket set one meter back. Had it been that way for Cobb? He couldn't remember.

It didn't seem to bother the driver that Cobb was watching. They were all in this together. Sta-Hi$_2$ leaned in, reaching for that cone.

There was a flash of light, four flashes, one from each corner of the door. The skinny arm snagged the cone, and the figure turned around utterly expressionless.

"Yes no no no yes no no no yes yes yes no no no yes no no yes yes yes no yes yes yes yes no no . . ." it muttered, dropping the cone. It turned and shuffled towards Cobb's house. The feet stayed on the ground at all times, and left two plowed-up grooves in the crushed shell driveway. ". . . no yes no no no."

The driver looked upset. "Whath with him? Heth thuppothed to . . ."

He hurried into the truck's cab and talked for a minute over what seemed to be a CB radio. Then he came back out, looking relieved.

"I didn't wealize. Mithter Fwostee jutht bwoke contact with him. The weal Thta-Hi ith coming back . . . he got away. Tho the wemote'll need a new cover. Jutht lay him on your bed for now. We'll pick him up tonight."

The half-faced driver jumped back into the truck and drove off with a cheery wave. Somehow he had brought Cobb back to life, but he had turned Sta-Hi off instead. They hadn't had a brain-tape to put into the robot. And with the real Sta-Hi coming back intact they'd decided to turn it off.

Cobb took the Sta-Hi thing's arm, trying to help it towards his house. The features on the tortured face were distorted almost beyond recognition. The mouth worked, tongue humping up like an epileptic's.

"Yes no no yes yes yes no no no no yes yes . . ."

Machine language. It raised one of its clawed hands, trying to block the bright sunlight.

Cobb led it to the front steps, and it stumbled heavily. It didn't seem to have the concept of lifting its feet. He held the door open, and the Sta-Hi thing came in on all fours, hands and knees shuffling along.

"What's the matter?" Annie asked, coming into the kitchen from the back porch. "Is he tripping?" She was in the mood for some excitement. It would be really neat to show up stoned at the Prom. "You got any more, Sta-Hi?"

The anguished figure fell over onto its side now, thick tongue protruding, lips drawn back in rictus death-grin. Its arms were wrapped around its chest, and the legs were frantically bicycling up some steep and heartless grade. The leg-motions slowly pulled the body around and around in circles on the kitchen floor.

Annie backed off, changing her mind about taking this trip.

"Cobb! He's having a fit!"

Cobb could almost understand it now. There was some machinery in that Mr. Frostee truck, machinery which had brought his own consciousness back to him. Machinery which had done something else to Sta-Hi$_2$. Turned it off.

The twitching on the floor damped down, oscillation by oscillation. Then the Sta-Hi thing was still, utterly still.

"Call a doctor, Cobb!"

Annie was all the way back on the porch, peering into the kitchen with both hands over her mouth.

"A doctor can't help him, Annie. I don't think he was even . . ." He couldn't say it.

Cobb bent over and picked the limp form up as easily as a rag-doll. Amazing the strength they'd built in. He carried the body down the short hall and laid it on his bed.

Chapter Eighteen

Mooney lit a cigarette and stepped into the patch of shade under the space-shuttle's stubby wing. Starting with this shipment, every crate shipped from Disky had to be opened and inspected, right out here on the goddamn field. The superheated air hanging over the expanse of concrete shimmered in the afternoon sun. Not a ghost of a breeze.

"Here's the last bunch, Mr. Mooney." Tommy looked down at him from the hatch. Six tight plastic containers glided down on the power-lift. "Interferon and a couple of crates of organs."

Mooney turned and gave a high-sign to the platoon of armed men standing in the sun fifteen meters off. Almost quitting time. Still puffing his cigarette, he turned back to eye the last set of crates. It was going to be a bitch getting those things open.

"Who was the asshole who had the bright idea of searching crates for stowaway robots?" Tommy asked, sliding down the lift.

A rivulet of sweat ran into Mooney's eye. Slowly he drew out his handkerchief and mopped his face again. "Me," he said. "I'm the asshole. There's been two break-ins at Warehouse Three. At least we thought they were break-ins. Both times there were some empty crates and a hole in the wall. Routine organ theft, right? Well . . . the second time I noticed that the debris from the holes was on the outside of the building. I figure what we had here was a break-*out*. The boppers have snuck at least three robots down on us, the way I see it."

Tommy looked dubious. "Has anyone ever *seen* one of these robots?"

"I almost had one of them myself. But I didn't realize it till it was too late." Mooney had been back at Cobb's twice . . . hoping to find the old man's robot double. But there had just been the old man there, drunk as usual. No way to know where the robot was now . . . hell, it could probably even change its face. *If* it even existed. He'd searched almost this whole shipment now, and still hadn't found anything.

Mooney ground out his cigarette. "It could be I'm wrong, though." He stepped into the sun and began examining the fastenings on the next crate. "I *hope* I'm wrong."

What, after all, did he really have to go on? Just some scraps of wall-board lying outside the warehouse instead of inside. And a faint glimpse of a running figure that had reminded him of old Cobb Anderson. And seeing a guy who had looked like Cobb's twin at the Gray Area last week. But he hoped he was wrong, and that nothing bad would happen, now that his life was settling into a comfortable groove.

Young Stanny was living at home again. That was the main thing. His narrow escape from those brain-eaters seemed to have sobered him. Ever since the police had brought him back he'd been a model son. And with Stanny back in the house, Bea had straightened out a little, too.

Mooney had gotten his son a job as a night watchman at the spaceport . . . and the kid was taking his work seriously! He hadn't fucked-up yet! At this rate he'd be handling the whole watch-system for the warehouses inside of six months.

Daytimes Stanny wasn't home much. Incredible how little sleep that boy needed. He'd catch a catnap after work and then he'd be off for the day. Mooney worried a little about what Stanny might be up to all day, but it couldn't be too bad. Whatever it was it couldn't be too bad.

Every evening, regular as clockwork, Stanny would show up for supper, usually a little tranked-out, but never roaring stoned like he used to get. It was just amazing how he'd straightened out ever . . .

"I've cracked the seal," Tommy repeated.

Mooney's attention snapped back to the task at hand. Six more crates and they'd be through for the day. This one was supposed to be full of interferon ampules. The gene-spliced bacteria that produced the anti-cancer drug grew best in the sterile, low-temperature lunar environment. Mooney helped Tommy lift the lid off, and they peered in.

No problem. It was full of individual vacuum-sealed syringes, loaded and ready to go. Halfheartedly, Mooney dug down into the crate, making sure that nothing else was in there. Passed. Tommy switched on the conveyor-belt, and the crate glided across the field, past the armed men, and into Warehouse Three.

The next three crates were the same. But the last two . . . there was something funny about the last two. For one thing they were stuck together to make a double-size crate. And the label read "HUMAN ORGANS: MIXED." Usually a crate was all livers or all kidneys . . . always all one thing. He'd never seen a mixed crate yet.

The box was vacuum-tight, and it took a few minutes work with the pry-bars to break the seals. Mooney wondered what would be in there . . . a Whitman's sampler assortment? Glazed eyeballs on paper doilies, a big liver like a brazil-nut, crunchy marrow-filled femurs, a row of bean-shaped kidneys, a king-size penis coyly curled against its testicles, chewy ropes of muscles, big squares of skin rolled up like apricot leather?

The lid splintered suddenly. *Something was coming out!*

Mooney sprang back, screaming a *"READY!"* to the soldiers. Their weapons were instantly at their shoulders.

The whole lid flew off now, and a shining silvery head poked out. A figure stood up, humanoid, glittering silver in the sun. Tubes connected it to further machinery in the box . . .

"AIM!" Mooney cried, backing well out of the line of fire.

The silver figure seemed to hear him, and began tearing at its head. A detachable bomb? Tommy cut and run, straight towards the troops. The fool! He was right in the line of fire! Mooney backed off, glancing desperately back and forth, waiting to give the *FIRE* command.

Suddenly the bubble-top came off the silvery figure's suit. There was a face underneath, the face of . . .

"Wait, Dad! It's me!"

Sta-Hi tore the air-hoses loose and tried to jump behind the box before anyone could shoot. His legs were cramped from thirty hours in the crates. He moved awkwardly. His foot caught on the edge of the crate, and he sprawled onto the concrete apron.

Mooney ran forward, putting his body between the crate and the troops.

"AT EASE!" he hollered, leaning over his son. But if this was his son . . . who had been living at his house all week?

"Is it really you, Stanny? How did you get in the box?"

Sta-Hi just lay there for a minute, grinning and stroking the rough concrete. "I've been to the Moon. And call me *Sta-Hi,* dammit, how many times do I have to tell you?"

Chapter Nineteen

Cobb spent the afternoon trying to get drunk. Somehow Annie had gotten him to promise they'd go to the Golden Prom together, but he was damned if he wanted to be anything other than blacked-out by the time he got there.

It was funny the way she had convinced him. They'd closed the door on . . . on Sta-Hi$_2$ . . . and gone out to the porch together. And then, sitting there looking at Annie, wondering what to say, it was as if Cobb had fallen through her eyes, into her mind, feeling her body sensations even, and her desperate longing for a bit more fun, a little gaiety at the end of what had been a long, hard life. Before she'd even said a word he'd been convinced.

And now she was dressing or washing her hair or something and he was sitting on the stretch of beach behind his little pink cottage. Annie had stocked his cupboard with sherry earlier this week, hoping to get some kind of rise out of him, but, except when Mooney had come snooping around, it had sat there untouched, along with the food. Thinking back, he couldn't recall this new body of his having drunk or eaten much of anything during the last week. Of course he'd had to chew down some of the fish he and Sta-Hi$_2$ had caught. Annie always insisted on frying it up for them. And when old Mooney had come, he'd sipped some sherry and pretended to be drunk. But other than that . . .

Cobb opened a second bottle of sherry and pulled deeply at it. The first bottle had done nothing but make him belch a few times, incredibly foul-smelling belches, methane and hydrogen-sulfide, death and corruption going on somewhere deep inside him. His mind was clear as a bell, and he was tired of it.

Suddenly exasperated, Cobb tilted up the second bottle of sherry, and, leaving an airspace above his upper lip, chugged the whole fucking thing down in one long, drink-crazed gurgle.

As he swallowed the last of it he felt a sudden and acute distress. But it wasn't the buzz, the flush, the confusion he had expected. It was, rather, an incredible urgency, a need to . . .

Without even consciously controlling what he did, Cobb knelt down on the sand and clawed at the vertical scar on his chest. *He was too full.* Finally he pushed the right spot and the little door in his chest popped open. He tried not to breathe as the rotten fish and lukewarm sherry plopped down onto the sand in front of him. Yyeeeeeeaaaaauuughhhh.

He stood up, still moving automatically, and went inside to rinse the food cavity out with water. And it wasn't till he was wiping it out with paper towels that he thought to notice anything strange about what he was doing.

He stopped then, a wad of paper towels in his hand, and stared down. The little door was metal on the inside and plastic flicker-cladding on the out. After he pushed it shut the skin dove-tailed so well that he couldn't find the top edge. He found the pressure switch again . . . just under his left nipple . . . and popped the little door back open. There were scratches on the metal . . . writing? It looked backwards, but he couldn't bend close enough to be sure.

Door flapping, Cobb went into the bathroom and examined himself in the mirror. Except for the hole in his chest he looked the same as ever. He *felt* the same as ever. But now he was a robot.

He pushed the little door all the way open, so that the metal inside was reflected in the mirror. There was a letter there, scratched in backwards.

Dear Dr. Anderson!

Welcome to your new hardware! Use it in good repair as a token of gratitude from the entire bopper race!

User's Guide:

1) Your body's skeleton, muscles, processors, etc. are synthetic and self-repairing. Be sure, however, to re-charge the power-cells twice a year. Plug is located in left heel.

2) Your brain-functions are partially contained in a remote super-cooled processor. Avoid electromagnetic shielding or noise-sources, as this may degrade the body-brain link. Travel should be undertaken only after con-sultation.

3) Every effort has been made to transfer your soft-ware without distortion. In addition we have built in a library of useful subroutines. Access under password BE-BOPALULA.

Respectfully yours,

The Big Boppers

Cobb sat down on the toilet and locked the bathroom door. Then he got up and read the letter again. It was still sinking in. Intellectually he had always known it was possible. A robot, or a person, has two parts: hardware and software. The hardware is the actual physical ma-terial involved, and the software is the pattern in which the material is arranged. Your *brain* is hardware, but the *information* in the brain is software. The mind . . . memories, habits, opinions, skills . . . is all software. The boppers had extracted Cobb's software and put it in control of this robot body. Everything was working per-fectly, according to plan. For some reason this made Cobb angry.

"Immortality, my ass," he said, kicking the bathroom door. His foot went through it.

"Goddamn stupid robot leg."

He unlocked the door and walked down the hall into the kitchen. Christ, he needed a drink. The thing that bothered Cobb the most was that even though he *felt* like he was all here, his brain was *really* inside a computer somewhere else. Where?

Suddenly he knew. The Mr. Frostee truck, of course. A super-cooled bopper brain was in that truck, with Cobb's software all coded up. It could simulate Cobb Anderson to perfection, and it monitored and controlled the robot's actions at the speed of light.

Cobb thought back to that interim time, before the simulation that was now him had hooked into a new body. There had been no distinctions, no nagging facts, only raw possibility . . . Thinking back to the experience opened up his consciousness in a strange way. As if he could let himself go and ooze out into the rooms and houses around him. For an instant he saw Annie's face staring out of a mirror, tweezers and tube of cream . . .

He was standing in front of the kitchen sink. He'd left the water running. He leaned forward and splashed some of it on his face. Something bumped the sink, oh yes, the door in his chest, and he pushed it closed. What had been that code word?

Cobb went back to the bathroom, opened the flap, and read the letter a third time. This time he got the little joke. The big boppers had put him in this body, and the code word for the library of subroutines was, of course,

"Be-Bop-A-Lu-La, she's mah baybee," Cobb sang, his voice echoing off the tiles, "Be-Bop-A-Lu-La, Ah don't mean maybee . . ." He stopped then, cocking his head to listen to an inner voice.

"Library accessed," it said.

"List present subroutines," Cobb commanded.

"MISTER FROSTEE, TIME-LINE, ATLAS, CAL-CULATOR, SENSE ACUITY, SELF-DESTRUCT, REFERENCE LIBRARY, FACT-CHUNKING, SEX, HYPERACTIVITY, DRUNKENNESS . . ."

"Hold it," Cobb cried. "Hold it right there. What does DRUNKENNESS involve?"

"Do you wish to call the subroutine?"

"First tell me what it does." Cobb opened the bath-room door and glanced out nervously. He thought he had heard something. It wouldn't do for him to be found talking to himself. If people suspected he was a robot they might lynch . . .

". . . now activated," the voice in his head was saying in its calm, know-it-all tone. "Your senses and thought processes will be systematically distorted in a step-wise fashion. Close your right nostril and breathe in once through your *left* nostril for each step desired. Inhaling repeatedly through the right nostril will reverse these steps. There is, of course, an automatic override for your . . ."

"O.K.," Cobb said. "Now stop talking. Log off. End it."

"The command you are searching for is OUT, Dr. Anderson."

"OUT, then."

The feeling of another presence in his mind winked out. He walked out onto the back porch and stared at the ocean for awhile. The bad smell from the rotten fish drifted in. Cobb found a piece of cardboard and took it out to scoop the mess up. *Re-charge power-cells twice a year.*

He dumped the stinking fish down by the water's edge and walked back to his cottage. Something was bothering him. How likely was it that this new body was a *token of gratitude* with no strings attached?

Obviously the body had been sent to Earth with certain built-in programs . . . break out of the warehouse, tell Cobb Anderson to go to the Moon, stick your head in the first Mr. Frostee truck you see. The big question was: were there any more programs waiting to be carried out? Worse: were the boppers in a position to control him on a real-time basis? Would he notice the difference? Who, in short, was in charge now, Cobb . . . or a big bopper called Mr. Frostee?

His mind felt clear as a bell, clear as a goddamn bell. Suddenly he remembered the other robot. Cobb went in through the porch and down the short hall to his bedroom. The bopper-built body that had looked like Sta-Hi was still lying there. Its features had gone slack and sagging. Cobb leaned over the body, listening. Not a sound. This one was turned off.

Why? "The real Sta-Hi is coming back," the truckdriver had said. So they wanted to get this one out of circulation before it was exposed as a robot. It had been standing in for Sta-Hi, working with Mooney at the spaceport. The plan had been for the robot to smuggle a whole lot more robot-remotes through customs and out of the warehouses. It had mentioned this to Cobb one day while they were fishing. Why so many robots?

Tokens of gratitude, each and every one? No way. *What did the boppers want?*

He heard the screen-door slap then. It was Annie. She'd done something to her hair and face. Seeing him, she shone like a sunflower.

"It's almost six, Cobb. I thought maybe we should walk over to the Gray Area now and have some supper there first?" He could feel her fragile happiness as clearly as if it were his own. He walked over and kissed her.

"You look beautiful." She had on a loose Hawaiian-print dress.

"But you, Cobb, you should change your clothes!"

"Right."

She followed him into his bedroom and helped him find the white-duck pants and the black sport-shirt she'd gotten ready for tonight.

"What about him?" Annie asked, whispering and pointing at the inert figure on Cobb's bed.

"Let him sleep. Maybe he'll pull through." The truck would come get him while they were out. Good riddance.

He could see through her eyes as he dressed. His new body wasn't quite as fat as the old one, and the clothes fit, for once, without stretching.

"I was afraid you'd be drunk," Annie said hesitantly.

"I *could* use a quick one," Cobb said. His new sensitivity to other people's thoughts and feelings was almost too much to take. "Wait a second."

Presumably the DRUNKENNESS subroutine was still activated. Cobb went into the kitchen, pressed his finger to his right nostril, and inhaled deeply. A warm feeling of relaxation hit him in the pit of the stomach and the backs of the knees, spreading out from there. It felt like a double shot of bourbon.

"That's better," Cobb murmured. He opened and closed the kitchen cupboard to sound as if he'd had a bottle out. Another quick snort, and then Annie came in. Cobb felt good.

"Let's go, baby. We'll paint the town red."

Chapter Twenty

"They're collecting human brain-tapes," Sta-Hi said as his father parked the car. "And sometimes they take apart the person's body, too, to seed their organ tanks. They've got a couple hundred brains on tap now. And at least three of those people have been replaced by robot doubles. There's Cobb, and one of the Little Kidders, and a stewardess. And there's still that robot who looks like me. Your surrogate son."

Mooney turned off the ignition and stared out across the shopping-center's empty parking lot. An unpleasant thought struck him.

"How do I know you're real *now*, Stanny? How do I know you're not another machine like the one that had me fooled all week?"

The answering laugh was soft and bitter. "You don't. *I* don't. Maybe the diggers switched me over while I was sleeping." Sta-Hi savored the worry on his father's face. *My son the cyborg.* Then he relented.

"You don't have to worry, Dad. The diggers wouldn't really do that. It's just the big boppers that are into it. The diggers only work there, making the tunnels. They're on our side, really. They've started a full-scale revolution on the Moon. Who knows, in a month there may be no big boppers left at all."

A dog ran across the parking lot, keeping an eye on their car. They could hear loud rock music from two blocks away. The pheezers were having some kind of party at the Gray Area bar tonight. In the distance the surf beat, and a cooling night breeze flickered in and out of the car windows.

"Well, Stanny . . ."

"Call me *Sta-Hi,* Dad. Which reminds me. You holding?"

Mooney rummaged in his glove compartment. There should be a pack of reefer in there somewhere . . . he'd confiscated it from one of his men who'd been smoking on duty . . . there it was.

"Here, Sta-Hi. Make yourself at home."

Sta-Hi pulled a face at the crumpled pack of cheap roach-weed, but lit up nonetheless. His first hit of anything since back at the Disky Hilton with that Misty girl. It had been a rough week hiding out in the pink-houses and then getting smuggled back to earth as a shipment of spare innards. Rough. He smoked down the first jay and lit another. The music outside focussed into note-for-note clarity.

"I bet old Anderson's at that party," Mooney said, rolling up his window. Damned if he was going to sit here while his son smoked a whole pack of dope. "Let's go check out his house, Sta-Hi."

"O.K." The dope was hitting Sta-Hi hard . . . he'd lost his tolerance. His legs were twitching and his teeth were chattering. A dark stain of death-fear spread across his mind. Carefully, he put the pack of reefers in his pocket. Must be good stuff after all.

Father and son walked across the parking lot, behind the stores and onto the beach. The moon, past full, angled its silvery light down onto the water. Crabs scuttled across their path and nipped into hidey-holes. It had been a long time since the two of them had walked together. Mooney had to hold himself back from putting an arm across his son's shoulders.

"I'm glad you're back," he said finally. "That robot copy of you . . . it always said yes. It was nice, but it wasn't you."

Sta-Hi flashed a quick smile, then patted his father on the back. "Thanks. I'm glad you're glad."

"Why . . ." Mooney's voice cracked and he started again. "Why can't you settle down now, Stanny? I could help you find a job. Don't you want to get married and . . ."

"And end up like you and Ma? No thanks." Too harsh. He tried again. "Sure I'd like to have a job, to do something important. But I don't *know* anything. I can't even learn how to play the guitar good. I'm only . . ." Sta-Hi spread his hands and laughed helplessly, "I'm only good at waving . . . at being cool. It's the only thing I've learned how to do in twenty-four years. What else can I do?"

"You . . ." Mooney fell silent, thinking. "Maybe you could make something out of this adventure you've had. Write a story or something. Hell, Stanny, you're *meant* to be a creative person. I don't want to see you end up wearing a badge like me. I could have been an illustrator, but I never made my move. You have to take that first step. No one can do it for you."

"I know that, too. But whenever I start something it's like I'm . . . a *nobody* who doesn't know *anything*. Mr. Nobody from Nowhere. And I can't process that. If I'm not going to win out anyway, I'd rather just . . ."

"You've got a good brain," Mooney told his son for what must have been the thousandth time. "You tested 92*nd* percentile on the MAGs and then you . . ."

"Yeah, yeah," Sta-Hi said, suddenly impatient. "Let's talk about something else. Like what are we going to do at Cobb's house anyway?" They had walked a couple of kilometers. The cottages couldn't be much further.

"You're *sure* they built robots to look like you and like Anderson?" Mooney asked.

"Right. But I don't know if the robots still look like us or not. They use this stuff called flicker-cladding for the skin, and it's full of little wires so if you pass different currents through it, the stuff looks different."

"But you figure Anderson's in one of these robots now?"

"Come shot! For sure. I saw a nursie taking him apart. It . . ." Sta-Hi broke off, laughing hard. Suddenly, with a reefer in him, the image of Cobb lying down in that giant toothed vagina . . . it was too funny for words. It was so good to be stoned again.

"But why lure you and him all the way up to the Moon just to tape your brain-patterns?"

"I don't know. Maybe they respect him too much to just kidnap him and eat his brain like anyone else. Or maybe they don't have any really *good* brain-dissecting machinery down here. And me . . . they just wanted to get me out of sight any way that . . ."

"Ssshhhh. We're there."

Thirty meters to their right was Cobb Anderson's cottage, silhouetted against the moon-bright sky. The light was bright enough to show the Mooneys up clearly, should anyone . . . anything . . . be looking. They doubled back to where a stand of palms reached down to near the water's edge and crept up to the cottages, staying in shadow.

The cottages were dark and deserted. It seemed like all the pheezers were out partying this Friday night. Mooney and Sta-Hi sidled along the cottage walls until they came to Cobb's. Mooney held them there, listening for a long two minutes. There was only the regular crash and hiss of the sea.

Sta-Hi followed his father in through the screen door and onto the porch. So this was where old Cobb had lived. Looked pleasant enough. Sta-Hi looked forward to being a pheezer himself someday . . . which only left about forty more years to waste.

Mooney put on a pair of goggles and flicked on his infra-red snooper light. He'd forgotten to bring it last Friday. He looked the room over. Lipsticked cigarette butts, baby oil, a wet bikini . . . *signs of female occupancy*.

That old white-haired babe was still living here. All week she'd been here with, Mooney now realized, Cobb's robot double. The two of them had been living here together waiting, though she didn't know it, for Cobb's mind to show up. Had it?

Briefly Mooney wondered if the robots could fuck. He could use a bionic cock himself, to keep Bea happy. If that whore hadn't always been sneaking out to the sex-clubs, Stanny never would have . . .

"What the fuck are you doing?" Sta-Hi demanded loudly. "Talking to yourself? I can't see a damn thing."

"Hussshhhhh. Put these on. I forgot." Mooney handed Sta-Hi the second pair of infra-light goggles.

The room cleared up for Sta-Hi then. The light was so red it looked blue. "Let's try the bedroom," he suggested.

"O.K."

Mooney led the way again. When he pushed open the bedroom door and shone his snooper light in, he had to bite his tongue to keep from screaming. Stanny was lying there, his features blurred and melted, the nose flopped over to one side and sagging down the cheek, the folded hands puddled like mittens.

Sta-Hi let out a low hissing noise and stepped forward, leaning over the inert robot on Cobb's bed. "Here's your perfect son, Dad. Be the first one on your block to see your boy come home in a box. The big boppers must have found out I was back. One of us had to go."

"But what's happened to it?" Mooney asked, approaching hesitantly. "It looks half-melted."

"It's a robot-remote. The central processor must have turned it off. There's a circuit in there for holding the flicker-cladding in shape, but . . ."

There was the sudden crunch of gravel, so close it seemed to be in the room with them. An engine was running, and a heavy door slammed. People were coming!

There was no time to run out through the house. Feet were already pounding up the front steps. Mooney grabbed his son and pulled him into Anderson's closet. There was no time to say anything to each other.

"Mr. Fwostee thaid he'th in the bedwoom, Buhdoo."

"Hey, Rainbow! Git yore skanky ass in here and help me lug this sucker out!"

"Ah don't see *wha* you big strong meyun cain't do it alone."

"I thtarted a hewnia yethterday wifting thomething."

"Liftin whut, Haf-N-Haf, yore pecker?"

The three voices shared a moment of laughter at this sally.

"*The Little Kidders*," Sta-Hi breathed into his father's ear. Mooney elbowed him sharply for silence. A coathanger rattled, *oh shit*, but the voices were still out in the living-room.

"This's a naahce pad, ain't it, Berdoo?"

"Y'all want one lahk it, Rainbow honey? Stick with me an yore gonna be fartin through silk."

"Thass sweet, Berdoo."

"You two wovebihds bwing the body out, and I'll watch the twuck." Haf-N-Haf's heavy footsteps went back down the steps. The truck door slammed again.

Berdoo and Rainbow walked into the bedroom.

"Whah . . . isn't he a *saaht?* He looks lahk a devilfish!"

"Don't you worry yore purty haid. He'll taahten up onct Mr. Frostee reprograms him."

"But wait, hunneh. Don't he remaahnd yew of the man who's brain we almost ate that taam? Last week over to Kristleen's?"

"This ain't a *man*, Rainbow. This here's a switched-off *robot*. I don't know what the hail *man* you're talking about, girl."

"Ooooh nevvah mahnd. Ah'll git his laigs an you take tother eyund."

"Okey-doke. Watch yer step, the sucker's heavy."

Grunting a little, Berdoo and Rainbow wrestled the body out of Cobb's house and down the steps. The whole time, the truck's engine ran.

Cautiously, Mooney stuck his head out the closet door. The bedroom had a window on either side, and through one window he could make out the dark mass of an ice-cream truck. There was a big plastic cone on top of the cab.

Two dim figures stopped at the side of the truck and laid something heavy on the ground. A third man climbed down out of the cab, and opened a door in the side.

One of them turned on a light then, light which picked out every object in the bedroom. Terrified, Mooney threw himself back into the closet. He made Sta-Hi stay in there with him until they heard the truck drive off.

Chapter Twenty-one

Cobb chewed down his broiled fish with apparent relish, and managed to enjoy his wine by taking one DRUNKENNESS snort through his left nostril for every two glasses. After dinner he went to the men's room and emptied out his food unit . . . not because he had to, but just to reassure himself that it was really true.

He was feeling the effect now of a good five or six whiskeys, and the whole situation didn't seem so horrible and frightening as it initially had. Hell, he had it *made*. As long as he kept his batteries charged there was no reason he couldn't live another twenty years . . . scratch that, another *century!* It was only a question of how long the machine could hold up. And even that didn't matter . . . the big boppers had him taped and could project him onto as many bodies as he needed.

Cobb stood, swaying a bit, in front of the men's room mirror. *A fine figure of a man.* He looked the same as ever, white beard and all, but the eyes . . . He leaned closer, staring into his eyes. Something was a little off there, it was the irises, they were too uniform, not fibrous enough. Big deal. He was immortal! He took another jolt through his left nostril and went out to join Annie.

While they had been eating, the band had set up in the hall behind the Gray Area, and now enough pheezers had arrived for them to start playing. Annie took Cobb's hand and led him into the dance-hall. She had helped decorate it herself.

Overhead they had a big, slowly spinning ball covered with a mosaic of tiny square mirrors. From each corner of the room a colored spotlight shone on the ball, and the reflected flecks of light spun endlessly around the room, changing colors as they moved from wall to wall. There had been a mirror-ball exactly like this at Annie's Senior Prom in 1970, lo these fifty years gone.

"Do you like it, Cobb?"

It made Cobb a little dizzy. This subroutined DRUNKENNESS wasn't quite like the real thing. He held his finger to the left side of his nose and took two quick breaths through his right nostril, coming down a couple of notches, enough to enjoy himself again.

The lights were perfect, really, it made you feel like you were on a boatride down some sun-flecked creek, trout hovering just beneath the surface, and all the time in the world . . .

"It's beautiful, Annie. Just like being young again. Shall we?"

They stepped onto the half-empty dance-floor, turning slowly to the music. It was an old George Harrison song about God and Love. The musicians were pheezers who cared about the music. They did it justice.

"Do you love me, Cobb?"

The question caught him off guard. He hadn't loved anyone for years. He'd been too busy waiting to die. Love? He'd given it up when he left Verena alone in their apartment on Oglethorpe Street up in Savannah. But now . . .

"Why do you ask, Annie?"

"I've been living with you for a week." Her arms around his waist drew him closer. Her thighs. "And we still haven't made love. Is it that you're . . ."

"I'm not sure I remember how," Cobb said, not wanting to go into details. He wondered if there was an ERECTION subprogram in his library. Have to check on that later, have to find out what else was in there, too. He kissed Annie's cheek. "I'll do some research."

When the dance ended they sat down with Farker and his wife. The two were having a spat, you could tell from the claw-like way Cynthia was holding her fingers, and from the confusion in Farker's eyes. They were glad to have Cobb and Annie interrupt them.

"What do you think of all this?" Cobb asked, using the hearty cheer-up-you-idiot tone he always used with Farker.

"Very nice," Cynthia Farker answered. "But there's no *streamers*."

Emboldened by Cobb's presence, Farker waved over a waiter and ordered a pitcher of beer. Normally Cynthia wouldn't let him drink, not that he wanted to, normally, but this was, after all, the . . .

"Golden Prom," Annie said. "That's what we called it, since it's been about fifty years since a lot of us had our high-school Senior Prom. Do you remember yours, Cynthia?"

Cynthia lit a mentholated and lightly THC-ed cigarette. "Do I *remember?* Our class didn't *have* a prom. Instead some of the *hot*-heads on the student council voted to use the funds for a fall *bus*-trip."

"Where did you go?" Cobb asked.

Cynthia cackled shrilly. "To *Wash*ington! To march on the *Pent*agon! But it was worth it. That's where Farker and I met, isn't it dear."

Farker bobbed his light-bulb head in thought for a moment. "That's right. I was watching the Fugs chanting *Out Demon Out* on a flat-bed truck in the parking lot, and you stepped . . ."

"I didn't *step* on your foot, Farker. I *footsied* you. You looked like such an im*port*ant person with your *tape* recorder, and I was just *dying* to talk to you."

"You sure did," Farker said, grinning and shaking his head. "And you haven't stopped since."

The beer arrived then and they clinked glasses. Holding his glass up, Cobb closed his right nostril and took a snort. Sitting down, the dizziness was bearable. But, listening to his friends talk, he had a feeling of shame at no longer being human.

"How's your son?" he asked Cynthia, just to be saying something. Chuck, the Farkers' only child, was a United Cults minister up in Philadelphia. Cynthia loved to talk about him.

"He's getting more *nooky* than you ever saw!" Cynthia gave a thin cackle. "And the girls give him *money*, too. He teaches them astral pro*jec*tion."

"Some racket, huh?" Farker said, shaking his head. "If I were still young . . ."

"Not you," Annie said. "You're not psychic enough. But Cobb," she paused to smile at her escort, "Cobb could lead a cult any day."

"Well," Cobb said thoughtfully, "I have been feeling sort of psychic ever since . . ." He caught himself and skipped forward. "That is, I've been getting this feeling that the mind really *is* independent of your body. Even without your body, your mind could still exist as a sort of mathematical possibility. And telepathy is only . . ."

"That's just what *Chuck* says," Cynthia interrupted. "You must be getting *senile*, Cobb!"

They all laughed then, and started talking about other things: food and health and gossip. But, in the back of his mind, Cobb began thinking seriously about cults and religion.

The whole experience of changing bodies felt miraculous. Had he proved that the soul is real . . . or that it isn't? And there were his strange new flashes of empathy to explain. Was it that, having switched bodies once, he was no longer so matter-bound as before . . . or was it just the result of having mechanically sharp senses? What was he . . . guru or golem?

"You're cute," Annie said, and pulled him back onto the dance-floor.

Chapter Twenty-two

The Little Kidders put the robot that had looked like Sta-Hi in the back of the truck. Berdoo squeezed into the cab between Rainbow and Haf-N-Haf. No point taking a chance of her getting felt up.

"Thometimeth I wonder what Mr. Fwostee ith up to," Haf-N-Haf slobbered, pulling out onto the asphalt.

"That makes two of us, boah. But he pays cash."

"How much you got naow?" Rainbow asked, laying her hand on Berdoo's thigh. "Yew got enough to take me for a week at Disney World? And first Ah wanna baah me some new clothes and maybe change mah hayur."

"It looks real purty just lahk tis, Rainbow. Ah allus wanted me a cheap skank with green hair."

Berdoo and Haf-N-Haf began snickering, and Rainbow fell into a sulk. The truck ground over the Merrit Island Bridge, and then Haf-N-Haf turned right onto Route One. Night-bugs spattered against their windshield, and the hydrogen-fueled engine pocked away.

"Is Kristleen gonna git us a new monkey-man?" Berdoo asked after awhile.

"She'd bettew!" Haf-N-Haf answered, staring out past the headlights. "Filthy Phil ith on herw ath about it nonthop."

Berdoo shook his head. "Ah surely don't know whaah old Phil is so *waald* to be eatin brains all the time. It gets a little old, ya know?"

"Did he get Kristleen a new place to liyuv?" Rainbow wanted to know.

"Whah yew know he diyud, hunneh. Ain't nobody can bring in the troops lahk that Kristleen can."

"Well, Ah suhtainly hope that is a fact," Rainbow said primly. "Yew been promisin and promisin me a brain-feast and all Ah've done so far was almost git ar-reyusted."

"Ath wong ath Phil's wunnin the thow we'll be eating bwains," Haf-N-Haf assured her.

"Something right funny about ole Phil," Berdoo observed a bit later. "I ain't never seen him smoke nor take a drink nor eat any reglar food. And when he ain't givin orders he jest sits and stares."

They were in Daytona now, concrete and neon flickering past. Haf-N-Haf checked the mirror for cops, and then turned hard right into the Lido Hotel's underground garage. He parked the truck way in back, and plugged a wire into the wall-socket to keep the refrigeration unit running. A little camera eye poked out of a hole on the top of the truck. Anybody who came near the truck now would be hurting for sure. Mr. Frostee knew how to take care of himself, especially with his extra remote in back.

They took the elevator up to their suite. Filthy Phil was sitting there, shirt off, staring out the window at the moonlit sea. His fat back with its sagging tattoo was facing them. He didn't bother to turn around.

"*Notice to Satan:*" Rainbow said, shrilly reading Phil's back aloud. "*Send this Man to Heaven, Cause He's Done His Time in Hell.*" She read it in her dumbest schoolgirl tone. She didn't like Phil.

Phil still didn't turn around. Once there had been a human Filthy Phil, a welder who worked too late on BEX up at Ledge one nightshift. BEX had put the brain-tape in charge of his humanoid repair robot . . . but it hadn't worked out. The personality had flattened out to that of an affectless killer. But he was still a good mechanic.

When they'd decided to send Mr. Frostee down to start collecting souls, Phil had come with him. Mr. Frostee still used Phil's brain-tape when he needed repairs. But he didn't like to put the personality in charge of the robot unless he had to. So, as a rule, the robot-remote

called Filthy Phil had all the warmth and human respon-
siveness of a pair of vice-grip pliers.

"Y'all leave Phil alone," Berdoo warned Rainbow.
"He's waitin for the phone to ring, ain't that right,
Phil?"

Phil nodded curtly. The shuttle to BEX was taking off
tomorrow, and Phil Frostee had promised to send up a
new set of organs. A tape could go up anytime, by radio
. . . but he'd promised a whole person, body and soul,
hardware and software. If Kristleen didn't find someone
. . . He stared out the window, listening to the three human voices behind him, and making his plans.

The phone rang then. Phil sprang across the room and
snatched it up.

"Filthy Phil."

The voice on the other end was high-pitched, tearful.
Berdoo looked at Haf-N-Haf nervously. Even through the
mirror-shades you could see that Phil was mad. But his
voice came out smooth.

"I understand, Kristleen. Yes I understand. O.K.
Fine."

More talking from the other end. Slowly a smile spread
on Phil's muscular face. He looked over at Berdoo and
winked.

"O.K. Kristleen. If he's asleep why don't you just
come over now and we can pay you off. You got five
grand coming. You better come get it now, because
we're going to shift bases tomorrow. Right. That's right.
O.K., baby. And don't worry, I do understand."

Phil set the phone down gently, almost tenderly.
"Kristleen's in love. She just blew a college boy and
now she's sitting there watching him sleep. He sleeps
like a baby, she says, like an innocent child." Phil began walking around the room, moving pieces of furniture
this way and that.

"Kwithtween'th not going to dewiver and you're going
to pay herw off anyway?" Haf-N-Haf asked incredu-
lously.

"That's what I told her," Phil said evenly, "but I'm
in a tight spot. I've got to have a body by tomorrow
morning. The tape could go any time, but I've got a

cargo-slot all signed up and paid for." He took a small sleep-dart pistol out of a drawer and examined it carefully.

"You ain't gonna kill Kristleen?" Rainbow cried.

"It's not really killing," Phil said, holding the pistol half-raised. "Haven't you figured that out yet? Berdoo?"

Berdoo felt like he was back in eighth grade, being asked questions he couldn't begin to understand. "Ah donno, Phil. It's yore gang. Yew got the truck and the apartment and all. Ah'll help you snuff Kristleen." If he weren't a Little Kidder he'd be nothing again.

"We'll eat her brain," Phil said, spinning the pistol and watching them closely. "But her thoughts will live on." With his left hand he poked abruptly at his chest. "Look!"

A little door swung open, showing the inside of a metal compartment in his chest. There were knives in there, and little machines. It looked like a tiny laboratory.

Rainbow screamed and Berdoo stepped over to cover her mouth. Haf-N-Haf made a noise that might have been a laugh.

"I'm part of Mr. Frostee," Phil explained, snapping the door back shut. "I'm like his hand, you wave? Or his mouth." Phil smiled broadly then, revealing his strong, sharp teeth. "We boppers use human organs to seed our tissue farms. We use brain-tapes for simulators in some of our robot-remotes. Like me. And we just like brains anyhow, even the ones we don't actually use. A human mind is a beautiful thing."

"Well you kin leave us out!" Rainbow cried. "Ah'll be buggered befo ah help yew!"

"Shut up, fool," Berdoo snarled at her. "Ah buggered yew yestidday, yew should recall."

"Ah am *not* gonna stand baah and let . . ." Rainbow began.

The doorbell cut her off in mid cry. Phil aimed the sleep-dart gun at Rainbow.

"Are you going to let Kristleen in, Rainbow? Or should I use you instead?"

Rainbow went to the door and opened it for Kristleen. Standing across the room, Phil was able to nail the two women with two quick shots. The sleep-drug took effect and they collapsed. Haf-N-Haf dragged them in and closed the door.

Berdoo stood watching, miserable and confused. Rainbow was the only girl-friend he'd ever had. But Phil had always been right before. Phil was Mr. Frostee, really. And Mr. Frostee was smarter than anyone in the world.

"She's going to make trouble if we let her go, Berdoo." Phil was looking at him across the room, his gun still levelled. There was a silence.

"But ah *cayun't!*" Berdoo cried finally. "Not that sweet girl. Ah *cain't* let you cut her all . . ."

Suddenly there was a pistol in Berdoo's hand, a .38 special. Faster than thought, his street-fighter's reflexes had carried him over to the window and fanned the drape out in front of him. Phil's sleep-dart bounced off the drape and dropped to the floor.

"Be reasonable, Berdoo." Phil lowered his dart pistol. "We'll take Kristleen apart, but we'll send Rainbow up whole. She can work for BEX as a stewardess, to replace that girl Misty from last year. Now you just let me get Rainbow stoned up good, and I'll talk to her, and then she flies up to Disky and gets herself an ever-lasting body. I promise they'll leave her personality in. You'll be able to see her once in a . . ."

Berdoo stepped out from behind the curtain, his small face set in a snarl. He shot Phil through the head, just like that.

"Oh, Bewdoo," Haf-N-Haf moaned as the ringing of the pistol-shot died down. "We're going to have to wun wike hell. Mr. Fwostee's got that other wemote in the twuck!"

"We'll go out front and steal us a car," Berdoo said tersely. "Ah'll drag Rainbow, an you handle Kristleen."

Just as they left the room, something in there exploded. Phil's body? They didn't stop to find out. Staggering under the women's dead weight, they bumped down the fire-stairs and out through the lobby.

An athletic young man was just parking a red convertible in front. Berdoo still had his pistol out. Haf-N-Haf tapped the man's shoulder and said something. He looked them over, handed over the keys, and backed off without saying a thing. Haf-N-Haf and Berdoo often affected people that way.

They put the girls in back and took off for the thruway to Orlando.

Chapter Twenty-three

The Golden Prom was a lot of fun. Cobb hadn't enjoyed himself so much in years. The beauty of the DRUNKENNESS subprogram was that you could move your intoxication level up and down at will, instead of being caught on a relentless down escalator to bargain basement philosophy and the parking garage. He found that if he tried to go further than ten drinks, to the blackout point, then an automatic over-ride would cut in and he'd loop back to where he started.

Leaving the dance with Annie, he took a few sobering right-nostril breaths and wrapped his arm around her waist. She was acting girlish and giggly.

"Have you finished your research, Cobb?"

"What." The moon was hanging over the sea now. Its light made a long lapped lane of gold, leading out to the edge of the world. "What research?"

She slipped her hand into his pants in back and smoothed his buttock. "*You* know."

"That's right," Cobb said. "Be-boppa-lu-la."

"Library accessed," a voice in his head said.

"I want to have sex."

"I'm glad," Annie said. "So do I."

"SEX subroutine now activated," the voice said.

"OUT," Cobb said.

"It's out?" Annie asked. "I thought you wanted to."

Cobb felt his pants tightening in front. "I do, I do."

They stopped once or twice to kiss and rub against each other. Every square centimeter of Cobb's body tingled with anticipation. For the first time in years his whole consciousness was out on his skin. Out on both their skins, really, for when they kissed he felt himself merging into Annie's personality. One flesh.

For some reason the lights in his cottage were on. At first he thought it had just been an oversight . . . but walking up to the door he heard Sta-Hi's voice.

"Oh," Annie cried happily. "How wonderful! Your friend is better again!"

Cobb followed her into his cottage. Sta-Hi and Mooney were sitting there arguing. They fell silent when they saw Cobb and Annie.

Annie was angry to see Mooney there again. "What do you want, pig?"

Mooney didn't say anything, but just leaned back in Cobb's easy chair, his alert eyes looking the old man up and down.

"It is really you, Sta-Hi?" Cobb asked. "Did they beam you down or . . ."

"It's the real me," Sta-Hi said. "All-meat. I came back on the shuttle today. How was *your* trip?"

"You would have loved it. I couldn't tell yes from no." Cobb started to say more, then stopped himself. It wasn't clear how much it would be safe to let Mooney know. Had they found the switched-off robot in the bedroom? Then he noticed the pistol in Mooney's lap.

"Maybe you should send the lady home," Mooney suggested easily. "I think we have some things to talk over."

"SEX OUT," Cobb muttered bitterly, "DRUNKENNESS OUT. You better go, Annie. Mr. Mooney's right."

"But why should I? I live here now, too. Who does this crummy Gimmie loach think he is, making me leave?" She was close to tears. "And after such a wonderful evening, just when . . ."

Cobb put his arm around her and walked her out the door. Patches of light from his cottage windows lay on the crushed-shell driveway. He could see Mooney's alert shadow in one of the windows.

"Don't worry, Annie. I'll make it up to you tomorrow. Suddenly it's like . . . like life is starting all over again."

"But what do they want? Have you done something wrong? Do they have a right to arrest you?"

Cobb thought a minute. Conceivably they could have him dismantled as a bopper spy. As a machine, he probably wouldn't even be entitled to a trial. But there was no reason it had to come to that. He put his arms around Annie and gave her a last kiss.

"I'll talk to them. I'll talk my way out. Save a place for me in your bed. I might be over in a half-hour."

"All right," Annie breathed in his ear. "And I've got a gun too, you know. I'll watch out the window in case . . ."

Cobb hugged her tighter, whispering back, "Don't do that, honey. I can handle them. If worst comes to worst I'll . . . skip out. But . . ."

"Come on, Anderson," Mooney called from Cobb's window. "We're waiting to talk to you."

Cobb and Annie exchanged a last hand-squeeze, and Cobb went back in his house. He sat down in the easy chair that Mooney had been using, leaving Mooney to lean against the wall and glower at him, pistol in hand. Sta-Hi was lounging in a deck-chair he'd dragged in, a lit reefer in his mouth.

"Start talking, Anderson," Mooney said. He was keeping the pistol aimed at Cobb's head. A body shot probably wouldn't stop a robot, but . . .

"Take it easy, Dad," Sta-Hi put in. "Cobb's not going to hurt anyone."

"You let me be a judge of that, Stanny. For all we know, that other robot is hiding right outside to help him."

"What robot?" Cobb said. How much did they really know, anyway? He and Sta-Hi had split up before the operation, and . . .

"Look," Sta-Hi said, a little wearily. "Let's cut the noise-level. I *know* that you're a machine now, Cobb. The boppers put you in your robot-double. Stuzzy! I can

wave with it. The only problem is that my father
here . . ."

The old hard-cop/soft-cop routine. Cobb abandoned his
first line of defense and asked for information.

"Where's the Sta-Hi$_2$ robot?"

"The Little Kidders were here," Sta-Hi said. "They
carried the robot out of your bedroom and left. It looked
like they were driving an ice-cream truck."

"Mr. Frostee," Cobb said absently. He was thinking
hard. What the boppers had done to him was, on the
whole, a good thing. A whole nother ball-game. If only
he could make Sta-Hi and Mooney see . . .

"Where's your base of operations?" Mooney demanded. "How many others like you are there?" He
gestured menacingly with his pistol.

Cobb shrugged. "Don't ask me. The boppers never tell
me anything. I'm just a poor old man with an artificial
body." He looked over at Sta-Hi for sympathy. As with
Annie before, he was getting a telepathic feeling, a feeling that he could see through the two other men's eyes.
Sta-Hi was stoned, receptive and open to change. But
Mooney was tense and frightened.

"As far as I know," Cobb said, "I'm completely in
control of myself. I don't think the boppers plan to use
me as a remote-control robot or anything like that."

"What's in it for them?" Mooney asked.

"They said they wanted to do me a favor," Cobb said.
He considered opening his food-unit door to show Mooney the letter, but then thought better of it. But thinking
of the door suggested a possibility.

"Be-boppa-lu-la," Cobb said out loud.

"Library accessed."

"Was there a subroutine called MR. FROSTEE?"

"Now activated," the voice murmured.

Something opened up in Cobb's mind, and a whole different set of visual stimuli overlaid the yellowed walls of
his living-room.

He was still in his cottage, yet he was also in a concrete parking garage. Something very bad had just happened. Berdoo had shot Phil, his best remote. It was like
losing an eye. And now there was no way to see what

Berdoo and Haf-N-Haf were doing. Should he send the extra remote after them?

"Hello," Cobb thought, stopping himself from saying the word aloud.

"Cobb?" Mr. Frostee's response was quick and unsurprised. "I was hoping to talk to you. But I wanted to let you make the first move. We don't want you to feel . . ."

"Like a remote?"

"Right. You're designed for full autonomy, Cobb. If you can help us, so much the better. But there's no way we would have edited out your freewill . . . even if we knew how. You're still entirely your own man."

"What do you want from me?" Silently asking this, Cobb leaned back in his chair, stretching out his legs. Mooney looked impatient. Sta-Hi was staring at the bugs on the ceiling.

"Convince the others," came Mr. Frostee's reply. In the background, Cobb could make out the interior of a truck-cab. Hands on the steering wheel. The concrete walls of a parking garage, then the garish lights of Daytona Beach streaming past.

"Convince them all to get robot bodies like you. Then we can merge, we can *all* merge to become a new and greater being. We'll set up a number of reprocessing centers . . ."

Mooney was standing over Cobb, shaking him. It was hard to see, with the glare of headlights coming at him. Slowly, Cobb brought his attention back to the cottage.

"What's the matter, Mooney?"

"You're signalling for help, aren't you?"

"How would you like a nice ever-lasting body like mine?" Cobb countered. "I could arrange it."

"So that's it," Sta-Hi said dreamily. "The big boppers want to bring us *all* into the fold."

"It's not so unreasonable," Cobb protested. "It's a natural next evolutionary step. Imagine people that carry mega-byte computing systems in their head, people that communicate directly brain-to-brain, people who live for centuries and change bodies like suits of clothes!"

"Imagine people that aren't people," Sta-Hi replied. "Cobb, the big boppers like TEX and MEX have been trying to run the same con on the Moon. And most of the little boppers up there aren't buying it . . . most would rather fight then let themselves be patched into the big systems. Now why do you think that is?"

"Obviously some people . . . or boppers . . . are going to be paranoid about losing their precious individuality," Cobb answered. "But that's just a matter of cultural conditioning! Look, Sta-Hi, I've been all the way in . . . *all* the way. After I got taped on the Moon I was just a pattern in a memory-bank somewhere for a few days. And you know, it wasn't even that . . ."

"Let's go," Mooney ordered, roughly pulling Cobb to his feet. "You're going to be deprogrammed and dismantled, Anderson. We can't let this kind of . . ."

Mr. Frostee was still there in Cobb's head. "I've taken the liberty of activating your SELF-DESTRUCT subroutine," the voice said quietly. "Just say the word 'DESTROY' out loud and you'll explode. Your body will explode. *You're* really in me. I'll give you a new body, the one here in the truck . . ."

"MR. FROSTEE OUT," Cobb said. If he did it, he wanted it to be his own decision.

Mooney had his pistol at the base of Cobb's skull. He was getting panicky.

Any second, Mooney, Cobb thought to himself. But still he hesitated. He told himself it was just because he didn't want to hurt Sta-Hi . . . but he was also scared, scared to die again. Could he really cross the noisy void between bodies again? But he'd already done it once, hadn't he?

"Go outside, Sta-Hi," Mooney said then, and sealed his fate. "Go check if that old bitch is waiting out there to ambush us. Or the other robot."

Sta-Hi eased out the back door and melted into the night.

"I've finally got you," Mooney said, with a nudge of his pistol. "I'm going to find out what makes you tick."

"DESTROY," Cobb said, and lost his second body.

Chapter Twenty-four

"I want to talk to you about diarrhea," a voice said earnestly. "Gastric distress can *ruin* that long-hoped-for vacation. So be sure . . ."

Cobb's first conscious act was to turn the radio off. He had just pulled out of a fuel-station on the gritty outskirts of Daytona Beach. But, on the other hand, he had just died in the explosion of his cottage in Cocoa Beach.

"Hello, Cobb. You see? You can count on me." Mr. Frostee's voice filled his head again. Cobb looked down at his sinewy forearms, handling the ice-cream truck's big steering-wheel with an experienced touch.

"Sta-Hi$_2$?" Cobb asked. "You put me in Sta-Hi$_2$?"

"It *was* Sta-Hi$_2$ But I just gave the body a new look. I copied the fellow who was running the pumps back there."

Cobb thought back to the explosion. DESTROY, disorientation, and now this. His fingers were blackened with years of grease. He leaned out the window to take a peek at himself in the rearview mirror.

He had a skinny head and large, liquid eyes. Thinning black hair, greasy and combed straight back. His nose was much more prominent than his chin. Ratface. Approaching headlights pulled his attention back to the road.

"What about disguising the truck?" Cobb asked. "I killed Mooney, but he must have left records. And Sta-Hi got away. The heat's gonna be looking for a Mr. Frostee truck."

"There'll be time for that later. Right now I've got a score to settle. Those hoodlums . . . those Little Kidders

. . . one of them wrecked my best remote. He's called Berdoo.''

Without consciously thinking about it, Cobb had driven the truck onto the thruway west, towards Orlando. Was he still in control of his actions?

"Where are we going?"

"Disney World. Berdoo doesn't remember it, but he once told me . . . told Phil . . . that he has a friend who runs a motel there. I think that's where he'll go to hide out. I want you to shoot him, Cobb, and then take out his brain for me. We'll leave the organs . . . that's all over for now . . . but I've got to get that brain on tape. You should have seen how easily he killed my Phil.''

It was hard to read the emotion in Mr. Frostee's even voice. Was revenge the motive? Or was it just a collector's lust for ownership?

In any case, trying to ambush the Little Kidders in their own hideout sounded like a terrible idea. And going brain-collecting was something Cobb hoped to put off as long as possible. He wondered if he should just turn around. Or pull off the highway and leave the truck. Glancing in his rear-view mirror he could see dawn pinkening the horizon. The road was empty.

"You've still got your free will," Mr. Frostee said. "But don't forget that we're in this together. If I die then so do you. You're really just a pattern in my circuits.''

"But you can't override me?" Testing, Cobb took his foot off the accelerator. No one pushed his foot back.

"I can't control your mind," Mr. Frostee said, not quite answering the question. "But don't stop the truck. What if a cop comes by?''

Cobb speeded back up. "Why would you give one of your subsystems free will?"

"The human mind is all of a piece, Cobb. If we try to start picking and choosing, all that's left is a boring bundle of reflexes. When a big bopper builds in some human's personality, he's got to learn to live with the subsystem's free will. I *could* cut you off entirely, in an emergency, but short of . . .''

"Why bother taping humans at all?"

"No program we can write and control acts like human software. Humans can't write bopper programs . . . they had to let them evolve. And a bopper can't write a human program. It works both ways. We need you guys. What we're working towards is a human-bopper fusion, a single great mind stretching from person to person all over the world. It's right, Cobb, and it's inevitable. Simpler beings merge to produce higher beings, and they must merge and merge again. In this way we draw ever closer to the One."

"*The One?*" Cobb said, laughing. "You don't mean the One on the Moon, do you? Don't you know that's just a random noise source? Haven't you figured that out?"

"*Randomness* is an elusive concept, Cobb."

"Look," Cobb said, "In order to make the boppers evolve fast enough I had to speed up the rate of mutation. So in the substrate program I included a command that they plug into the One, once a month, as you know.

"But the One is just a simple cosmic ray counter. It goes through your programs changing yesses and noes, here and there, just on the basis of the geigercounter click-pattern of cosmic-ray bursts for the last day or so. The One is just a glorified circuit-scrambler."

Still Mr. Frostee was silent. Finally the answer came. "You choose to make light of the One, Cobb. But the pulse of the One is the pulse of the Cosmos. You yourself call its noisy input the *cosmic rays*. What is more natural than that the Cosmos should lovingly direct the growth of the boppers with its bursts of radiation? There is no *noise* in the All . . . there is only *information*. Nothing is truly random. It is sad that you choose not to understand what you yourself have created."

A ditch full of brackish water and marsh-grass lay to the right of the thruway. Cobb saw an alligator, lying half out of the water and watching the early morning traffic. It was quarter to seven. In a sort of phantom-stomach reflex, Cobb had a brief longing for breakfast. But the hunger faded, and Cobb let the empty miles roll by, lost in thought.

What was he now? In one sense he was what he had always been. A certain pattern, a type of software. The *fiveness* of a right hand is the same as the *fiveness* of a left. The *Cobbness* that had been a man was the same as the *Cobbness* now coded upon Mr. Frostee's cold chips.

Cobb Anderson's brain had been dissected, but the software that made up his mind had been preserved. The idea of "self" is, after all, just another idea, a symbol in the software. Cobb felt like him *self* as much as ever. And, as much as ever, Cobb wanted his self to continue to exist on hardware.

Perhaps the boppers had stored a tape of him on the Moon, and perhaps up there his software had also been given hardware. But, here and now, Cobb's continued existence depended on keeping Mr. Frostee cold and energized. They were in this together. Him and a machine who wanted to know God.

"I'll tell you," Cobb said, breaking the silence. "I think it would be really stupid to go charging after the Little Kidders before getting the truck repainted. Even if the cops aren't after us yet, there's no point having Berdoo be able to see you coming from a block away. Let's get off the thruway and fix up the truck. There's a giant plastic ice-cream cone on the cab's roof, for God's sake."

"You're driving," Mr. Frostee said mildly. "I will defer to your superior knowledge of human criminality."

Cobb got out at the next exit and took a small road north. This was rolling countryside, with plenty of streams. Palms and magnolias gave way to blackjack pines and scrubby live oak. Brambles and honeysuckle filled in the spaces between the struggling little trees. And in some places the uncontrollable kudzu vine had taken root and choked out all other vegetation.

It was only eight-thirty, but already the asphalt road was shimmering in the heat. The frequent dips were filled with reflecting water-mirages. Cobb rolled down the window and let the air beat against his face. The truck's big hydrogen-fueled engine roared smoothly and the sticky road sang beneath the tires.

The wild scrub gave way to farmland, big cleared pastures with cattle in them. The cows waded about knee-deep in weeds, munching the flowers. White cattle egrets stalked and flapped along next to them, spearing the insects that the cows stirred up. The egrets looked like little old men with no arms.

A few miles of pastures and barns brought them to a bend in the road called Purcell. There were some big houses and some cracker-boxes, a tiny Winn-Dixie, and a couple of fuel-stations. Cobb pulled into a tree-shaded Hy-Gas that had a handpainted sign saying *Body Work*.

There was a three-legged dog lying on the asphalt by the pumps. When Cobb pulled up, the animal rose and limped off, barking. The fourth leg ended half-way down, in a badly bandaged stub.

Cobb hopped out of the truck cab. A young sandy-haired man in stained white coveralls came ambling out of the garage. He had prominent ears and thick lips.

"Mr. Frostee taahm!" the attendant observed. He screwed the hydrogen nozzle into the truck's hydride tanks. There was a sort of foliated metal in the tanks which could absorb several hundred liters of the gas. "Gimme one?"

"It's empty," Cobb said. "This isn't really a Mr. Frostee truck anymore. It's mine."

The attendant absorbed this fact in silence, looking Cobb's skinny ratfaced body up and down. "You baah it?"

"I sure did," Cobb said. "Over in Cocoa. Fella closed his franchise down. I aim to fix this truck up and use it for my meat business."

The attendant topped up the tank. He was tanned, with white squint-wrinkles around his eyes. He shot Cobb a sharp glance.

"You don't look lahk no butcher to me. You look lahk a grease-monkey in a stolen truck." He punctuated this with a sudden, toothy smile. "But ah could be wrong. You need anything besides the hydrogen?"

The guy was suspicious, but seemed willing to be bought off. Cobb decided to stay. "Actually . . . I'd like to get this truck painted. It's a burden having to explain to everyone that it's really mine.''

"Ah reckon *so*," the sandy-haired man said, smiling broadly. "If you pull her round back, Ah maaht could he'p you solve your problems. Ah'll paint it and forgit it. Cost you a thousand dollahs.''

That was much too high for two hours' work. The guy obviously thought the truck was stolen.

"O.K.," Cobb said, meeting the other man's prying eyes. "But don't try to double-cross me.''

The attendant displayed his many crooked teeth in another smile. "What color y'all want?''

"Paint it black," Cobb said, relishing the old phrase. "But first let's get that goddamn cone off the top.''

He got back in the truck, pulled off the asphalt, and drove through rutted weeds to the junky lot behind the Hy-Gas station. The attendant, on foot, led the way.

"Perhaps he is not honest," Mr. Frostee said inside Cobb's head, sounding a bit worried.

"Of course he isn't," Cobb answered. "What we have to look out for is him calling the cops anyway, or trying to blackmail us for more money.''

"I think you should kill him and eat his brain," Mr. Frostee said quickly.

"That's not the answer to *every* problem in interpersonal relations," Cobb said, hopping out. He was learning to talk to Mr. Frostee subvocally, without actually opening his mouth.

The attendant had brought a screwdriver and a couple of Lock-Tite wrenches. He and Cobb got the cone off, after ten or fifteen minutes' work. The emptily smiling swirl-topped face landed in the weeds next to half of a rusted-out motorcycle. The two men's bodies worked well together, and a certain sympathy developed between them.

The attendant introduced himself as Jody Doakes. Cobb, hoping to confuse his trail, said his name was Berdoo. They went around front to get the paint and the spray-gun compressor. Cobb solved the problem of when to pay, by tearing a thousand-dollar-bill in half and giving Jody one piece.

"You'll get the other half when I pull out of here," Cobb said. "And no earlier."

"Ah see yore point," Jody said, with a knowing chuckle.

First they had to wash the truck off. Then they taped newspaper over the tires, lights and windows. They sprayed everything else black. The paint dried fast in the hot air. They were able to start the second coat as soon as they finished the first.

The job took all morning. Now and then that three-legged dog would start barking, and Jody would go out to serve a customer. Mr. Frostee's refrigeration unit kept running, drawing its energy from the hydride tank. Jody asked once why the refrigerator had to be on if there wasn't any more ice-cream. Cobb told him that if he wanted the other half of the thousand-dollar-bill he could keep his questions to himself.

They finished the second coat a few minutes after the noon siren blew on the Purcell fire-house.

"Y'all want a baaht to eat?" Jody asked. "Ah got the makins for sandwiches insahd." He hooked his thumb at the garage.

"Sure," Cobb said, ignoring the fact that he'd just have to clean the chewed-up bread and lunchmeat out of his food unit later on. Eating was fun. "I could use a couple of beers, too."

"Come shot!" Jody said, meaning something like *you bet*. "Come shot on the beer, Berdoo."

They had a friendly lunch. More strongly than ever, Cobb felt able to enter into other people's thoughts. Again the thought of starting a cult crossed his mind.

The food and beer felt good in his mouth. Over Mr. Frostee's protests, Cobb cut in the DRUNKENNESS subroutine and gave himself a hit for each beer. They split a six-pack. Jody allowed as how, for an extra two hundred bucks, he'd be willing to let Cobb have some fresh license plates and registration papers he happened to have.

Cobb enjoyed their dealings very much. In his old body he had never been able to talk comfortably to garage mechanics. But now, with a random grease-monkey's face on a Sta-Hi-shaped body, Cobb fit in at a filling station as easily as he used to fit in at research labs. Idly he wondered if Mr. Frostee could change the flicker-cladding enough to turn him into a woman. That would be interesting. There was so much to look forward to!

After lunch they changed the license plates. Cobb handed over the missing half of the thousand-dollar-bill, and the extra two hundred dollars. Hoping to keep Jody bought, he suggested that he might be back with more of the same kind of business next month, if things worked out.

"Come shot!" Jody said. "And good luck."

Cobb drove out of Purcell, heading east, past cows and egrets.

"I wish you'd taped his brain," Mr. Frostee nagged. "We can always use a good mechanic."

Cobb had been expecting a remark like this. And the next remark, too.

"How come you're driving East? That's not the right way to Disney World. We've still got to get Berdoo!"

"Mr. Frostee," Cobb said, "I love my new body. And I support your basic plan. It's the logical next step for human evolution. But mass-murder is not the way. There's a better way, a way to get people to *volunteer* for brain-taping. We'll start a new religious cult!"

There was a pained silence. Finally Mister Frostee spoke. "I feel I should warn you, Cobb. You have free will in the sense that I can't control your thoughts. But the body belongs to *both* of us. In certain special circumstances I may take . . ."

"Please," Cobb said, "hear me out. Am I right in believing that you're the only big bopper now on Earth?"

"That's right."

"And I'm using the only robot-remote you have left?"

"Yes. Hopefully, with Mooney out of the way, security at the spaceport will be relaxed again. We had planned a shipment of some thousand new remotes during the next two years, as well as several more big bopper units. These plans are unfortunately . . . in flux. There are some . . . difficulties on the Moon. But until the situation restabilizes, I intend to continue gathering tapes and . . .''

"You're trying to tell me there's an all-out civil war starting on the Moon, aren't you?" Cobb exclaimed. "We're on our own, M.F.! If we go back to the spaceport and try . . .''

"There is no need to go to spaceport for tape transmission. I can radio-beam the tapes directly up to BEX at Ledge.''

"A soul transmitter," Cobb said thoughtfully. "That's a good angle. *Personetics: The Science of Immortality.*''

"What do you mean?''

"The religion! We'll get the down-and-out, the runaways, the culties . . . we'll get them to believe that you're a machine for sending their souls to heaven. It's not really so . . .''

"But why bother? Why not just proceed as Phil always did. To *seize*, and cut, and . . .''

"Look, M.F., we're in this together. It works both ways. If something happens to this truck I'm dead. I don't think you realize just how strongly humans react to murder and cannibalism. This is no bopper *anarchy* here, it's more like a *police*-state. If you and I are going to last out until BEX gets the troops here, we're going to need to lay low and play it careful.''

Just thinking about it gave Cobb the creeps. If he couldn't get fuel for the truck, if the cops stopped them, if the refrigeration unit broke . . . It was like being a snail with a ten-ton shell! A snowball in hell!

"We need security," Cobb said urgently. "We need a lot of people to take care of us, and we need money to keep the hydride tanks full. If we get enough money I think we should build a scion, too. A copy of your processor. We could get our followers to buy the components in computer shops. You've got to understand the realities of life on Earth!''

"All right," Mr. Frostee said finally. "I agree. But where are you driving to?''

"Back to the coast," Cobb said. "I know a place north of Daytona Beach where we can hole up. And, say . . . give me a new face. Something fatherly.''

Chapter Twenty-five

After his father's funeral, Sta-Hi went back to driving a cab in Daytona Beach. Bea, his mother, wanted to put the house up for sale and move north, away from the pheezers. She hated them since Mooney's death . . . and who could blame her! Her husband had gone to old Cobb Anderson's house on a routine check, and had been blown to smithereens! Just for doing his job! And so on.

There was an investigation into Mooney's death, but the blast hadn't left a hell of a lot to investigate. There was not a scrap of the suspected robot double to be found. And Sta-Hi didn't tell the authorities any more than he had to. He still couldn't decide whose side he was on.

He took a couple of his father's space-ship paintings and rented a room in Daytona. He went back to Yellow Cab and they gave him a job driving the night-shift. Mostly it was a matter of bringing drunks and whores to motels. Seamy. And duller'n shit.

His dope habit crept up on him again. Pretty soon he was smoking, snorting, dropping, spraying and shooting his money as fast as he made it. Late at night, driving up and down the one-dimensional city, Sta-Hi would dream and scheme, forming huge, interlocking plans for the future.

He would make a movie about cab-driving. He would write a book about the boppers. No, man, do it with music!

He would learn how to play the guitar and start a band. Fuck learning! He would get another Happy Cloak and let it play his fingers for him. He needed a Happy Cloak!

He'd threaten the boppers to tell about the Little Kidders and the nursies if they wouldn't come across. With Anderson and his father blown up, no one else knew!

He'd get rich and then go back to Disky and get in on the civil war and they'd make him king. Hadn't he already helped the diggers to off a big bopper? He'd lead them to victory! Moon King Sta-Hi!

But there was no way to reach the boppers. The cops had lost track of Mr. Frostee and those Little Kidders. BEX and Misty-girl never got any closer to Earth than space-station Ledge. And no private phone-calls to Disky were allowed. The thing to do was to make the boppers contact *him*. How? Get so famous they'd notice him!

Around and around, night after night, tripping and bouncing the length of dreary Daytona. One night a drunk left his wallet in the cab. Two thousand bucks in there. Sta-Hi took the money and quit work. He needed time to think!

He got a crate of Z-gas aerosols . . . he'd sunken that low . . . and started hanging around the strip. Eating burgers, selling hits, playing machines, hunting pussy. He tried to make himself conspicuous, hoping something would happen to him. The day his money ran out, it finally did.

He was hanging out at Hideo-Nuts' Boltsadrome, stoned, staring at the floor. His boots looked so perfect. Two dark parabolas in a field of yellow, slight 3-D interest provided by the scurf strewn about. His favorite song was playing. He felt like screaming, like crying out, "I'm here and I'm staying high! I'm Sta-Hi, the king of the brainsurfers!"

The metal speaker overhead was pumping out solid music. He could see the notes if he squinted. He started to giggle, thinking of the tiny note-shaped bumps travelling down the wires like white mice swallowed by a python. God, he had good ideas!

Keeping his smile, in case it came in handy, Sta-Hi looked around the arcade, swaying back and forth, fingering chords on an invisible electric guitar. He couldn't

actually play yet, but he had all the moves down . . .
say . . . look at little blondie over there. He stared at
her and slid a riff down the neck of his imaginary guitar.
Smiling harder, he beckoned with his head.

Liking his smile, the broad-hipped girl strolled towards him, swaying back and forth like a slowly swimming fish. *Beat* that tail. She kept her head tilted back
to show off the tan-stars on her cheeks.

"Hi 'surfer. God, it's wiggly in here tonight." She
shook back her hair and laughed a slow, knowing laugh.
"I'm Wendy."

Sta-Hi sizzled off a few more hot chords and then
threw his hands in the air. "You're talking to Sta-Hi
Mooney, fluffy. I've got the weenie, you've got the bun,
put em together and have some gum." His rap had de-
teriorated badly during the last week of Z-gas.

"Are you in a club?" Wendy asked, still smiling. He
wasn't as stuzzy as she had thought from across the
room. And, worse, he looked broke.

"Sure . . . I mean practically." She wasn't really as
pretty as he had thought. A whore? "How about you?"

"Oh I've been hanging out . . . parties . . . burning
cars. . . ." Wendy wondered if it was worth wasting
time on him. She had to make five hundred dollars before going back to the temple.

Sta-Hi saw the doubt in Wendy's face. She was the
first girl he'd managed to talk to all day. He was going
to have to land this fish, and fast. "Have a whiff on
me," he said, fumbling out his aerosol.

"Wiggly," she said, tossing her hair again. He handed
her the little can and she inhaled a short burst of the
Z-gas. Sta-Hi took it back and blasted off a long, long
one. Gongs rang in his ears and he staggered a little,
laughing a hyuck-hyuck 'surfer laugh from the back of
his throat. Wendy took the can out of his hand and hit
up another. They looked pretty to each other again.

"What do you want to play?" Sta-Hi asked, gesturing
broadly.

"I'm good in that *Pleasure Garden*," Wendy answered.

"Wiggly." Sta-Hi dropped his last five-dollar coin into the slot. The big machine lit up and made a googly welcome-to-my-nightmare noise.

"I'll do the pushpads," Wendy said, taking her place in front of the machine.

That was fine with Sta-Hi. He'd never gotten too good at playing the hyperpins. He took the electron-gun in his hand and pushed the start button.

A little silver ball popped into play. A magnetic field buoyed it up. Sta-Hi aimed the gun at the ball and gave it a kick towards the first target.

He'd shot it the wrong way, though, and it disappeared into a trap . . . the mouth in a glowing little Shiva. Wendy gave a snort of annoyance. Wordlessly, Sta-Hi punched the start again.

This time he sent the ball right into the nearest push-pad. Let her handle it. She did . . . banking the chrome sphere off two more pads before sending it edgewise down a whole row of pop-ups.

"Stuzzy," Sta-Hi breathed. They were both leaning over the lit-up tank. First you had to take out fifteen targets and then the Specials would light up. Wendy had just gotten five targets at once. The ball was drifting towards a trap, but Sta-Hi managed to shoot it in time. Then Wendy was batting it around with the push-pads again.

She had a long, chiming run. All the specials were lit now. Asserting himself, Sta-Hi flicked the ball a few times with the electron-gun, trying to knock it down one of the money holes. But they had repellers, and he ended up by pushing the ball out.

"Have you ever played this before?" Wendy wanted to know before he launched their last ball.

"I'm sorry. I guess I'm a little phased."

"Don't apologize. We're doing good. But on this next ball could you sort of . . . just shoot when I say to?"

"I'll shoot when and where you like, baby." He pressed the start and slid his hand down to pat her ass, knowing she couldn't let go of the controls to slap him away. But she didn't even frown . . . just bumped her tummy against the machine and whispered, "Shoot."

Sta-Hi shot and they were off. She pushed the pads, murmuring instructions to him all the while. *Down, farther, watch the crocs, give it to me, hit the pad, way down* . . . They took out all the targets and all the level-one specials. Then they were working on the higher-level specials. The traps were moving around, snapping at the ball, and Wendy was making impossible saves. Sta-Hi's finger was clenched tight on the trigger.

The machine was letting out wild wheeps and rings, and a few people drifted over to watch Sta-Hi and Wendy work out. Faster, tighter angles, shooting constantly . . .

"Oh God," she whispered, "the Gold Special's on. Nudge it left, Sta-Hi."

He twitched some English onto the ball. It caromed off a pad angled just so, and snugged into the gold socket nestled between two big outs. The machine THHOCCKKKKED. And shut itself off.

Sta-Hi pushed his trigger. Nothing happened. "What . . ."

"We beat it!" Wendy squeaked. "We took it all the way! Let's go get the pay-off!"

"But I thought there was just . . ." Sta-Hi pulled open the drawer in the machine's front. A ticket for five free meals at McDonald's.

"Sure there's *that*," Wendy said. "But the cashier has to give me five hundred dollars, too. Special Daytona rules."

Sta-Hi followed Wendy to the cashier, and out onto the street. She wore green cut-off over-alls, and sandals with thongs criss-crossing up her legs. He had to hurry to keep up with her. It was like she was trying to lose him.

"Where are you going, Wendy? Slow down! Half that money's mine!" He caught her lightly by her bare brown arm.

"Let go!" She twitched her arm free. "That money isn't yours *or* mine. It's all for Personetics. Good-bye!" Without even looking at him, she strode on down the sidewalk.

"You whore!" Sta-Hi shouted angrily. "That's *it*, isn't it! You've got your night's money now and you'll give it to your greaser sex-pistol and catch some sleep!" He ran after her, and grabbed her arm, hard this time. "Give me my two-hundred-fifty bucks!"

Wendy burst into tears. Fake? "I'm not a p-prostitute. It's just f-flirty-fishing. Personetics needs the money for more hardware. To save everyone's soul."

Hardware? Souls? A contact at last.

"You can keep the money," Sta-Hi said, not loosening his grip. "But I want to come back with you. I want to join Personetics."

She looked into his eyes, trying to read his intentions. "Do you really? Do you want to be saved? Personetics isn't just another cult, you know. It's for real."

Sta-Hi examined her closely, trying to decide if . . . Finally he popped the question.

"Are you a robot?"

"No." Wendy shook her head. "I'm not really saved yet. But Mel is. Mel Nast. He's our leader. Do you want to meet him?"

"I sure do. I'm a bopper-lover from way back. How far is it to the temple?"

"Forty kays. We're in the old Marineland building."

"Are we supposed to walk or what?"

"Usually I wait till five AM. That's when Mr. Nast comes and picks us all up. The boys sell things, and the girls go flirty-fishing all night long. But if you get your five hundred dollars early you can go back to Mel. Do you have a car or a bike?"

Sta-Hi's hydrogen motorcycle was long gone. He hadn't seen it since that Friday he'd left it chained up in front of the Lido Hotel. After that he'd met Misty, and the Little Kidders . . . and then it had been Cocoa and the Moon and all that. How long had it been, two months? It felt like finally things were going to happen again.

"I'll get a car," Sta-Hi said. "I'll steal a car."

"That would be nice," Wendy said. "Mel would like you if you brought him a car."

But how? In Daytona, nobody was fool enough to leave his key in the ignition. Suddenly Sta-Hi thought of a way. He'd get his taxi back.

"Go wait for me by McDonald's, Wendy. I'll be back with a car in half an hour."

The Yellow Cab terminal was only five blocks off. Malley, the dispatcher, was sitting in a glass booth at the garage entrance, same as ever. Looking past him, Sta-Hi saw that Number Eleven, his old cab, was idle tonight.

"Hey, Malley, you lame son of death, stop jerking off and gimme my keys." Best defense is a good offense.

Malley glared, nothing moving but his tiny eyes. "Bullshit, Mooney. You can't just quit and walk back on the job any time you like. You're too stoned to drive anyway. Giddaddahere."

"Come on, Pappy Dear-smear, I need the dust, you must? I'm eating sand out there. Put me on and I'll kick you ten percent."

"Twenty," Malley said, holding up the keys. "And if you fuck up again you're out for good. I don't live to keep you in dope."

Sta-Hi took the keys. "You can *die* to keep me in dope for all I care. Live or die, just keep me high."

After ten days off, it felt nice to be back in Lucky Eleven. They must not have found a new driver for it, since the cab still had all of Sta-Hi's personal touches. There was the fake come-spot on the roof over his head, the skull with the red-lite eyes in the back window, the plastic fur rug on the floor . . . and even the tape-deck was still there. How could he have walked off the job and forgotten his tape-deck!

He had the cab wired for sound, so he could record his monologues, or interview the passengers. The cab started up right away, and then he was out on the street, thinking about his tape-recorder. It made a big impression on chicks, made them think he was an agent. Funny word: *agent*.

A gent. Age entity. Ageing tea. Aegean Sea. A.G.C. Now what did that *A.G.C.* stand for?

If he hadn't seen Wendy standing in front of Mc-Donald's just then, Sta-Hi probably would have forgotten all about her. Being back in the cab had zapped him into a conditioned reflex of head-tripping and driving the strip. But there was Wendy, bright and blonde in her tight cut-offs. Foxy fish.

He pulled over and she got in back.

"Number Eleven," Malley was saying, "there's a call at Km. 13."

"I just got a fare, Malley. Two gentlemen want to go to Cocoa."

"That'll be an out of zone charge," Malley responded. "Check in when you get back. That *was* twenty percent."

"Over dover." He turned the squawker off.

"How did you get the cab?" Wendy asked, wide-eyed. "Did you hurt the driver?"

"Not at all," Sta-Hi said, pointing to the dark stain over his head. "See the come-spot?"

"I don't understand."

"I'm a cab-driver. This is my cab. If I like it at Marineland I'll give Personetics the cab and stay there. Otherwise I'll go back to work, and I'll just have to pay that fare to Cocoa myself. Come up in front and sit next to me."

She climbed over the seat. They split a jay, driving slow with the windows down. It was nice to be driving again. It felt like the car was on rails, a toy train tootling through the palmy night.

Chapter Twenty-six

The old Marineland had closed down back in 2007, after a hurricane had caved in half the building. Now everyone who wanted to see the ritual degradation of dolphins had to go to Sea World instead. The building, in the middle of nowhere on Coastal Route 1A, came up on Sta-Hi unexpectedly.

"Pull around to the ocean side," Wendy said. "So no one sees."

"Yes ma'am. That'll be two fucks and a blow-job."

"Please, Sta-Hi, be serious. Not just anyone can become a member of Personetics. You have to have the right attitude."

"I'll try to keep it limp, baby."

There was a little parking lot in back. Sta-Hi pulled in next to a nice-looking red sedan. Off at the edge of the lot was a beat-up black truck. The wind was high, and the surf was loud. They got out and walked along a concrete wall to where a rusty door hung open. There were no lights inside.

"Mel," Wendy called at the top of her lungs. "I'm back already. I brought someone with another car for you."

There was the sound of footsteps, and a lithe figure hurried out of the building. He was the same height as Sta-Hi, and with the same rangy build. But his head . . . his big, round head seemed a size too big for the body. He made you think of a balloon tied to the end of a rope.

"Mel Nast," he said, sticking out his hand. He had a deep, sincere-sounding voice, with a trace of an East European accent. "I'm bleased to meet you. Vhat's your name?"

"I'm nobody," Sta-Hi said. "I'm Mr. Nobody from Nowhere."

"Don't listen to him, Mel. He told me his name is Sta-Hi. He says he's a bopper-lover from way back."

Spoken in Wendy's earnest treble the self description sounded pathetic, imbecilic. But Mel Nast looked sympathetic.

"The point is not just to love, Sta-Hi. It is to live. If only you can vake up in time. Blease come in."

Mel Nast's round head turned like a rotating planet, and his slender body followed along. The three of them walked down a damp corridor, through two doors and into a bright, windowless space.

It was a square hall, with big rectangular holes in the walls. One of the old tank-rooms. The aquarium glass had been smashed out and removed, and each of the tanks was now a sort of nook or roomlet. They followed Nast across the square floor and stopped before one of the ex-tanks. "STURGEON," a cracked label on the wall read, "*Acipenser Sturio.*"

There were two easy chairs in there, a shelf of books, and a desk covered with papers. "My study," the slim man with the big head explained. "Could you blease leave us now, Vhendy? I have plans to make with . . . Mister Hi." He flashed Sta-Hi a sudden smile. Had he *winked?*

"That's fine with me," Wendy said. "I'm all tired out. And here's tonight's take." She handed over the five-hundred-dollar bill and walked across the room. Apparently she had a bed in one of the tanks. Sta-Hi followed Nast into his study-tank. They sat down, and looked at each other in silence for a minute.

"How do you like my face?" Nast asked finally. The round face was dominated by a fleshy nose, from which two wrinkles ran down, suspending the somewhat sensual mouth in a rounded sling of folds. The lips parted, revealing square, uniform teeth. "Should I change it?"

"It depends on what you want to do," Sta-Hi said uncertainly.

"What do *you* want to do?" came the answer. "What do you want from the boppers?"

Another hard question. Most superficially, Sta-Hi wanted to acquire another Happy Cloak and use it to get famous. But on another level, hardly conscious, he wanted revenge, revenge for his father's death, revenge for what the nursie had done to Cobb Anderson.

He hated the boppers. But he loved them. The diggers . . . the diggers had helped him. Wearing the Happy Cloak and raiding the factory had been fantastic. Perhaps what he really wanted was to go back to Disky and help in the civil war, loving and hating at the same time.

Something strange happened to Mel Nast's face while Sta-Hi considered his answer. The fatty puffed-out skin tightened, the cheeks drew in, and a white beard blossomed around the mouth. Suddenly he was looking at . . .

"Cobb?" Sta-Hi asked. "Is it you?" He started to smile and then stopped. "You killed my father! You . . ."

"I *had* to, Sta-Hi. You heard him. He said he was going to have me dismantled!"

"So? It wouldn't have killed you. You blew up your body along with his, and now you're still here and he's gone forever!" The grief came welling up at last, and Sta-Hi's voice quavered.

"He wasn't such a bad guy. And he could paint spaceships better than anyone I ever . . ." Sta-Hi broke off, sobbing. A minute went by till he found his voice again.

"I saw them take you apart, Cobb. They took out your heart and your balls and everything else. It's like . . ." The face across from him looked sympathetic, interested. The perfect cult minister.

"Fuck!" Sta-Hi spat, suddenly lashing out and hitting the robot's face with the back of his hand. "I might as well be talking to a tape-recorder."

The blow hurt his hand, and made him angrier. He got to his feet, standing over the Cobb-faced robot.

"I ought to fucking take you apart!"

The robot began to talk then, slowly, and in Cobb's old voice. "Listen to me, Sta-Hi. Sit down and listen. You know perfectly well that you can't hurt me by hammering on this robot-remote. I'm sorry your father died. But death isn't real. You have to understand that. Death is meaningless. I wasted the last ten years being scared of death, and now . . ."

"Now that you think you're immortal you don't worry about death," Sta-Hi said bitterly. "That's really enlightened of you. But whether you know it or not, Cobb Anderson is *dead*. I saw him die, and if you think you're him, you're just fooling yourself." He sat down, suddenly very tired.

"If I'm not Cobb Anderson, then who would I be?" The flicker-cladding face smiled at him gently. "I *know* I'm Cobb. I have the same memories, the same habits, the same feelings that I always did."

"But what about your . . . your *soul*," Sta-Hi said, not liking to use the word. "Each person has a soul, a consciousness, whatever you call it. There's some special thing that makes a person be alive, and there's no way that can go into a computer program. No way."

"*It* doesn't have to go into the program, Sta-Hi. *It* is everywhere. *It* is just existence itself. All consciousness is One. The One is God. God is pure existence unmodified."

Cobb's voice was intense, evangelical. "A person is just hardware plus software plus existence. Me existing in flesh is the same as me existing on chips. But that's not all.

"*Potential* existence is as good as *actual* existence. That's why death is impossible. Your software exists permanently and indestructably as a certain *possibility*, a certain mathematical set of relations. Your father is now an abstract, non-physical possibility. But nevertheless he exists! He . . ."

"What is this," Sta-Hi interrupted. "A cram-course in Personetics? Is this the crap that you feed those girls to keep them whoring for you? Forget it!"

Sta-Hi stopped talking, suddenly realizing something. That black truck outside . . . that must be the Mr. Frostee truck with a paint-job. And inside the truck would be a super-cooled big bopper brain with Cobb coded up inside it. He couldn't hurt this robot-remote, but if he got out to the truck . . . It was just a question of whether he really wanted to. Did he hate the boppers or not?

"I sense your hostility," Cobb said. "I respect that. But I'd like you to come in with me anyhow. I need an outside man, a Personetics promoter. I could be Jesus and you be John the Baptist. Or *you* be Jesus and I'll be God."

While he was talking, the robot's face changed again, to a copy of Sta-Hi's. "I always use this trick on the recruits," he chuckled. "Like Charlie Manson. *I am a mirror.* But that was before your time. Here, have a joint."

The robot lit a reefer and handed it over. The Cobb face came back. "I'm a little psychic now, too," he said. "I've gotten pretty loose. And what I said is really true. Nothing is ever really destroyed. There is no . . ."

"Oh, tape it," Sta-Hi said taking the reefer and leaning back in his easy chair. "I might come in with you. Especially if you can get me another Happy Cloak."

"What's that?" Cobb asked.

"Well, I never told you yet . . . about what I did on the Moon."

"You ran away in the museum. The next time I saw you, it was that night when you and your father . . ."

"Yeah, yeah," Sta-Hi said, cutting him off. "Don't remind me about that. Let me tell my story. I found this sort of cape called a Happy Cloak. It was made of flicker-cladding and when I put it on I could talk bopper, except with a Japanese accent. I went to where a bunch of boppers were storming a big factory called GAX. We got in, but GAX almost won anyway. Then at the last minute I blew him up."

The robot started in shock. "You blew up a big bopper?"

"Yeah. Some diggers and a repair spider had set the charge. All I had to do was push the button. The remotes would have gotten me then, but at the last minute a digger tunneled up through the floor and saved me. He took me to watch the nursie take you apart. Ralph and the nursie taped you, and then the nursie grabbed Ralph Numbers and taped him, too. The diggers said . . .''

Cobb's face was working, as if he were arguing with a voice in his head. Now he interrupted. "Mr. Frostee wants to kill you, Sta-Hi. He says that if it weren't for you blowing up GAX, the big boppers would have won.''

Cobb was twitching now, as if he could hardly control himself. His voice grew thin and odd. "I'm not a puppet. Sta-Hi is my friend. I have free will.''

The words seemed to cost him a great effort. His eyes kept straying to a hunting-knife lying on his desk.

"No!'' Cobb said, shaking his head jerkily. It wasn't clear who he was talking to. "I'm not your hand. I'm your conscience! I'm a . . .''

Suddenly his voice stopped. The features of his face clenched in a final spasm and then slid back into the serene curves of Mel Nast. The thick lips parted to complete Cobb's sentence.

". . . hallucination. But this robot-remote is, in the last analysis, mine. I have temporarily had to evict Dr. Anderson.'' The hand snaked over to pick up the knife.

Sta-Hi jumped to his feet and vaulted out of the tank in one motion. He hit the floor running, with the robot close behind.

The door out to the hall was open, and Sta-Hi managed to slam it behind him, gaining a few seconds. He got the second door closed too, closed tight, and he had his cab started by the time the robot came charging out.

Sta-Hi ignored it, and aimed his cab at the black panel truck parked across the lot. He revved the engine up to a chattering scream and peeled out.

The robot jumped onto his hood and punched his fist through the windshield. Sta-Hi squinted against the flying glass and kept the car aimed at the truck. He had it up to fifty kph by the time it hit.

The air-bag in the steering column burst out, punching Sta-Hi in the face and chest, keeping him in his seat. An instant later the bag was limp and the car was stopped. Sta-Hi's lip had split. There was blood in his mouth. The car lights were out, and it was hard to see what had happened.

Footsteps came running across the parking lot.

"What happened? Sta-Hi? Mel?" It was Wendy. Sta-Hi got out of his cab. The girl ran past him, to reach out to the figure crushed between the cab and the dented side of the black van.

"Back up, Sta-Hi! Quick!"

But now the black van was moving instead. Its engine, already on, roared louder, and it backed out, grinding the pinned robot-remote against the cab's hood. It looked like steam was leaking from a hole in the truck's side.

The driverless van flicked its lights on, and Sta-Hi could make out the face of the broken robot slumped across his cab's hood. The blank eyes may have seen him or not, but then the lips moved. It was saying . . .

"Look out!" Sta-Hi screamed, snatching Wendy back and flinging their bodies to shelter on the ground behind the cab.

The robot-remote exploded, just like the other one had, back in the cottage on Cocoa Beach.

As the ringing of the explosion died out in their ears, they could hear the black van's engine, roaring south on Route One.

Chapter Twenty-seven

As soon as Mr. Frostee seized control of the remote, Cobb was utterly shut off from the outside world. As during his first transition, he felt a growing disorientation, an increasing blurring of all distinctions. But this time it stopped before getting completely out of control. Vision returned, and with it the ghosts of hands and feet. He was driving the truck.

"I'm sorry to have done that, Cobb. I was angry. It seemed essential to me to disassemble that young man as soon as possible."

"What's happened?" Cobb cried voicelessly. There was something funny about his vision. It was as if he were perched on top of the truck, instead of being behind the wheel. But yet he could *feel* the wheel, twitching back and forth as he steered the truck south. "What's happened?" he asked again.

"I just blew up my last remote. We're going to have to find someone to front for us. One of the Personetics people in Daytona."

"*Your* remote? That was supposed to be my body! I thought you said I had free will!"

"You still do. I can't make you change your mind about anything. But that body was mine as much as yours."

"Then how can I see? How can I drive?"

"The truck itself is a sort of body. There's two camera eyes that I can stick out of the roof. You're seeing through them. And I've turned the servos for manipulating the truck's controls over to you as well. We may have our occasional differences, Cobb, but I still trust you. Anyway, you're a better driver than I.''

"I can't believe this," Cobb wailed. "Don't you have any survival instinct at all? I could have talked Sta-Hi into working with us!"

"He was the one who blew up GAX," Mr. Frostee replied. "And now the war is lost. BEX told me about it on the broadcast last week. Disky has reverted to complete anarchy. They've smashed most of MEX, and there's talk of disassembling TEX and even BEX as well. The final union is still . . . inevitable. But for now it looks as if . . ."

"As if what?" Cobb asked. There was a resigned and fatalistic edge to Mr. Frostee's words which terrified him.

"It's like waves, Cobb. Waves on the beach. Sometimes a wave comes up very far, past the tideline. A wave like that can carve out a new channel. The big boppers were a new channel. A higher form of life. But now we're sliding back . . . back into the sea, the sea of possibility. It doesn't matter. It's right, what you told the kids. Possible existence is as good as real existence."

They were driving into Daytona now. Lights flashed by. One of Cobb's ''eyes'' watched the road, and the other scanned the sidewalk, looking for one of the Personetics followers. The girls whored and the boys dealt dope. But it was so hard to remember their faces!

"You know," Mr. Frostee said. "You know he split the panels?"

"What do you mean?" There was nothing but darkness, and the two spots of vision, and the controls of the truck.

"There's heat leaking in from where your friend rammed us. The temperature's up five degrees. One more, and our circuits melt down. Thirty seconds, maybe."

"Am I on tape somewhere else?" Cobb asked. "Is there a copy on the Moon?"

"I don't know," Mr. Frostee said. "What's the difference?"

Chapter Twenty-eight

Wendy got the keys for the red sedan, and Sta-Hi drove them back to Daytona. They didn't talk much, but it was not a strained silence.

The police were all around the truck when they found it. Driverless, it had veered off the road, snapped a fire-hydrant, and smashed in the front of a Red Ball liquor-store. The police were worried about looting, and at first they wouldn't let Sta-Hi and Wendy through the line.

"That's my father!" Wendy screamed. "That's my father's truck!"

"She's right!" Sta-Hi added. "Let my poor wife through!"

"He's not in the truck now," a cop said, letting them approach. "Hey chief," he called then, "here's two individuals who say they knew the driver."

The chief walked over, none other than Action Jackson. He had a mind like an FBI file, and recognized Sta-Hi instantly. "Young Mooney! Maybe you could enlaahten me as to what the *hail* is goin on?"

The crash had widened the rip in the truck's side, and clouds of helium were billowing out. The gas itself was invisible, but the low temperature filled the air with a mist of ice-crystals. A by-product of breathing the helium-rich air was that everyone's voice was coming out a bit high-pitched.

"There's a giant robot brain in the back," Sta-Hi piped. "A big bopper. It's the same one that killed my father and tried to eat my brain."

Jackson looked doubtful. "A truck tried to eat your brain?" He raised his voice, "Hey, Don! You and Steve open tup! See whut's in back!"

"Be careful!" Wendy squeaked, but by then the door was open. When the mist dispersed you could see Don and Steve reaching in and poking around with billy-clubs. There was a sound of breaking glass.

"Whooo-ee!" Don called. "Got nuff goodies in here to open us a Radio Shack! Steve and me saw it first!" He swirled his club around, and there was more tinkling from inside the truck.

The others walked over to look in. The truck was lying half keeled-over. There was a lot of frost inside, like in a freezer chest. The liquid-helium vessel that had surrounded Mr. Frostee was broken and there in the center was a big, intricate lump of chips and wires.

"Who was drivin?" Action Jackson wanted to know.

"It could drive itself," Sta-Hi said. "I rammed it and made a hole. It must have heated up too much."

"You a hero, boy," Jackson said admiringly. "You may amount to something yet."

"If I'm a hero, can I leave now?"

A hard glance, and then a nod. "Awright. You come in tomorrow make a deposition and I might could get you a reward."

Sta-Hi helped himself to a bottle from the liquor-store window and went back to the car with Wendy. He let her drive. She pulled down a ramp onto the beach, and they parked on the hard sand. He got the bottle open: white wine.

"Here," Sta-Hi said, passing her the wine. "And why did you say he was your father?"

"Why did you say I was your wife?"

"Why not?"

The moon scudded in and out of clouds, and the waves came in long smooth tubes.

WETWARE

For
Philip K. Dick
1928-1982

"One must imagine Sisyphus happy."

Table of Contents

Chapter One
People That Melt

December 26, 2030

It was the day after Christmas, and Stahn was plugged in. With no work in sight, it seemed like the best way to pass the time . . . other than drugs, and Stahn was off drugs for good, or so he said. The twist-box took his sensory input, jazzed it, and passed it on to his cortex. A pure software high, with no somatic aftereffects. Staring out the window was almost interesting. The maggies left jagged trails, and the people looked like actors. Probably at least one of them was a meatie. Those boppers just wouldn't let up. Time kept passing, slow and fast.

At some point the vizzy was buzzing. Stahn cut off the twist-box and thumbed on the screen. The caller's head appeared, a skinny yellow head with a down-turned mouth. There was something strangely soft about his features.

"Hello," said the image. "I'm Max Yukawa. Are you Mr. Mooney?"

Without the twist, Stahn's office looked unbearably bleak. He hoped Yukawa had big problems.

"Stahn Mooney of Mooney Search. What can I do for you, Mr. Yukawa?"

"It concerns a missing person. Can you come to my office?"

"Clear."

Yukawa twitched, and the vizzyprint spat out a sheet with printed directions. His address and the code to his door-plate. Stahn thumbed off, and after a while he hit the street.

Bad air out there, always bad air—*yarty* was the word for it this year. 2030. *Yart* = yawn + fart. Like in a library, right? Sebum everywhere. *Sebum* = oily secretion which human skin exudes. Yarts and sebum, and a hard vacuum outside the doooooooommmme. Dome air—after the invasion, the humans had put like a big airtight dome over Disky and changed the town's name to Einstein. The old Saigon into Ho Chi Minh City routine. The boppers had been driven under the Moon's surface, but they had bombs hidden all over Einstein, and they set off one a week maybe, which was not all *that* often, but often enough to matter for sure for sure. And of course there were the meaties—people run by remote bopper control. What you did was to hope it didn't get worse.

So OK, Stahn is standing out in the street waiting for a slot on the people-mover. A moving sidewalk with chairs, right? He felt like dying, he really really felt like dying. Bad memories, bad chemistry, no woman, bad life.

"Why do we bother."

The comment was right on the beam. It took a second to realize that someone was talking to him. A rangy, strungout dog of a guy, shirtless in jeans with blond hair worn ridgeback style. His hair was greased up into a longitudinal peak, and there were extra hairgrafts that ran the hairstrip right on down his spine to his ass. Seeing him made Stahn feel old. *I used to be different, but now I'm the same.* The ridgeback had a handful of pamphlets, and he was staring at Stahn like one of them was something in a zoo.

"No thanks," Stahn said, looking away. "I just want to catch a slot."

"Inside your lamejoke private eye fantasy? Be here now, bro. Merge into the One." The kid was handsome in an unformed way, but his skin seemed unnaturally slack. Stahn had the impression he was stoned.

Stahn frowned and shook his head again. The ridgeback gave him a flimsy plas pamphlet, tapped his own head, and then tapped Stahn's head as if to mime the flow of knowledge. Poor dumb freak. Just then an empty slot came by. Safely off the sidewalk, Stahn looked the leaflet over. OR-MY IS THE WAY, it read. ALL IS ONE!

The text said that sharing love with one's fellows could

lead to a fuller union with the cosmos at large. At the deepest level, the pamphlet informed Stahn, all people are aspects of the same archetype. Those who wished to learn more about Organic Mysticism were urged to visit the Church offices on the sixth floor of the ISDN ziggurat. All this wisdom came courtesy of Bei Ng, whose picture and biography appeared on the pamphlet's back cover. A skinny yellow guy with wrinkles and a pointed head. He looked like a big reefer. Even after eighteen clean months, lots of things still made Stahn think of drugs.

The Einstein cityscape drifted past. Big, the place was big—like Manhattan, say, or half of D.C. Not to mention all the chambers and tunnels underground. Anthill. Smart robots had built the city, and then the humans had kicked them out. The boppers. They were easy to kill, once you knew how. Carbon-dioxide laser, EM energy, scramble their circuits. They'd gone way underground. Stahn had mixed feelings about boppers. He liked them because they were even less like regular people than he was. At one point he'd even hung out with them a little. But then they'd killed his father . . . back in 2020. Poor old dad. All the trouble Stahn had given him, and now it felt like he was turning into him, year by year. Mooney Search. *Wave on it, sister, wiggle. Can I get some head?*

Yukawa's address was a metal door, set flush into the pumice-stone sidewalk. *Deep Encounters* said the sign over the door-plate. Psychological counselling? The folks in this neighborhood didn't look too worried about personality integration. Bunch of thieves and junkies is what they looked like. Old Mother Earth had really shipped the dregs to Einstein. Like the South, right, *Settled by slaves and convicts—since 1690.* 2022 was when the humans had retaken the Moon. Stahn looked at the sheet that Yukawa had sent. 90-3-888-4772. *Punch in the code, Stahn.* Numbers. Prickly little numbers. Number, Space, Logic, Infinity . . . for the boppers it was all Information. Good or bad?

OK, so the door opens, and Stahn ladders on down and takes a look. A vestibule, empty and gray. To the right was a door with a light over it. In front of Stahn was another door, and a window like at a walk-in bank. Yukawa's face was behind the thick glass. Stahn showed him the vizzyprint sheet, and he opened up the second door.

Stahn found himself (*found himself?*) in a long laboratory, with a desk and chairs at one end. The air was thick with strange smells: benzenes, esters, the rich weavings of long-chain molecules, and under it all the stench of a badly-kept menagerie. His host was seated on a sort of high stool by that thick glass window. It took Stahn a second to absorb the fact that about half the guy's body was . . . where?

Yukawa's soft thin head and arms rose up out of a plastic tub mounted on four long legs. The rest of him was a yellow-pink puddle in the tub. Stahn gagged and took a step back.

"Don't be alarmed, Mr. Mooney. I was a little upset, so I took some merge. It's just now wearing off."

Merge . . . he'd heard of it. Very synthetic, very illegal. *I don't do drugs, man, I'm high on life.* People took merge to sort of melt their bodies for a while. Stuzzadelic and very tempting. If Stahn hadn't been so desperate for work he might have left right then. Instead he came on nonchalant.

"What kind of lab is this, Mr. Yukawa?"

"I'm a molecular biologist." Yukawa put his hands on the tub's sides and pushed up. Slowly his belly solidified, his hips and his legs. He stepped over to the desk and began pulling his clothes back on. Over the vizzy, Stahn had taken him for Japanese, but he was too tall and pale for that. "Of course the Gimmie would view this as an illegal drug laboratory. Which is why I don't dare call them in. The problem is that something has happened to my assistant, a young lady named Della Taze. You advertise yourself as a Searcher, so . . ."

"I'll take the case, don't worry. I already checked you on my data-base, by the way. A blank. That's kind of unusual, Mr. Yukawa." He was fully dressed now, gray pants and a white coat, quite the scientist. Stahn could hardly believe he'd just seen him puddled in that tub. *How good did it feel?*

"I used to be a man named Gibson. I invented gene-invasion?"

"You were that mad scientist who . . . uh . . . turned himself Japanese?"

"Not so mad." A smile flickered across Yukawa's

sagging face. "I had cancer. I found a way to replace some of my genes with those of a ninety-eight-year-old Japanese man. The cancer went into remission, and as my cells replaced themselves, I took on more and more of the Japanese man's somatotype. A body geared for long life. There was talk of a Nobel Prize, but . . ."

"The California dog-people. The Anti-Chimera Act of 2027. I remember. You were exiled here. Well, so was I. And now I'm a straight rent-a-pig and you're a dope wizard. Your girl's gone, and you're scared to call the Gimmie." Most Einstein law enforcement was done on a freelance basis. No lunie ever called in the official law—the Gimmie— on purpose. At this point the Gimmie was a highly organized gang of extortionists and meatie-hunters. They were a moderately necessary evil.

"Clear. Let me show you around." Long and undulant, Yukawa drifted back into the lab. The low lunar gravity seemed to agree with him.

The closer tables were filled with breadboarded electronic circuits and mazes of liquid-filled tubes. Computerized relays shunted the colored fluids this way and that. A distillation process seemed to be underway. The overall effect was of a miniature oil refinery. In contrast, the tables towards the rear of the lab were filled with befouled animal cages. It had been a while since Stahn had seen animals. Live meat.

"Watch," said Yukawa, shoving two cages together. One cage held a large brown toad, the other a lively white rat. Yukawa drew a silver flask out of his coat pocket and dribbled a few drops onto each of the subject animals. "This is merge," he explained, opening the doors that separated the cages.

The toad, a carnivore, flung itself at the rat. For a moment the two beasts struggled. But then the merge had taken effect, and the animals' tissues flowed together: brown and white, warts and hair. A flesh-puddle formed, loosely covering the creatures' loosened skeletons. Four eyes looked up: two green, two pink. Faint shudders seemed to animate the fused flesh. Pleasure? It was said that merge users took a sexual delight in puddling.

"How do they separate?"

"It's automatic. When the merge wears off, the cell walls

stiffen and the body collagens tighten back up. What the drug does is temporarily uncoil all the proteins' tertiary bunchings. One dose lasts ten minutes to an hour—and then back to normal. Now look at *these* two cages.''

The next two cages held something like a rat and something like a toad. But the rat's hair was falling out, and its feet were splayed and leathery. The toad, for its part, was growing a long pink tail, and its wide mouth showed signs of teeth.

"Chimeras," said Yukawa with some satisfaction. "Chimeras like me. The trick is to keep them merged for several days. Gene exchange takes place. The immune systems get tired.''

"I bet. So the Japanese man you merged with turned into you?''

Yukawa made a wry face. "That's right. We beat cancer together, and he got a little younger. Calls himself Bei Ng these days. He runs his own fake religion here in Einstein, though it's really an ISDN front. Bei's always trying to outdo me and rip me off. But never mind about him. I want you to look at this one back here. It's my pet project: a universal life form.''

At the very rear of the lab was a large pen. Huddled in the pen was a sodden, shambling thing—an amalgam of feathers and claws. *Chitin,* man, and hide, and the head had (A) long feelers, (B) a snout, (C) a squid-bunch of slack mandibles, *dot dot dot,* and (Z) gills. Gills on the moon.

"You're nuts, Yukawa. You're out of your kilpy gourd.''

At the sound of Stahn's voice, the monstrosity hauled itself over to rattle the pen's bars with tiny pink hands.

"Yes, Arthur," said Yukawa. "Good.'' He fished a food pellet out of his lab jacket and fed it to his creation. Just then a bell chimed.

"Back to business," said Yukawa, giving Stahn a U-shaped smile. "I don't know why I'm showing you all this anyway. Loneliness, I suppose. Della's been my only companion for the last two years.''

Stahn tagged along as Yukawa made his way back to the thick window looking onto the vestibule. A light was flashing over the other door out there.

"Time's up," said Yukawa, speaking into a microphone.

"The session's over, Mrs. Beller." Stahn got the full picture.

"You retail the merge right here? You're running a love-puddle?"

"That is the vulgar terminology, yes. I have to fund my ongoing research in whatever fashion I can. I sell merge both wholesale and retail. There's nothing really wrong with merge, you know. It's terribly addictive, but if someone wants to quit, why, I'm perfectly willing to sell them the proper blocker."

Outside the window, the lit door opened. Two people stepped out—a wide-mouthed brunette and her funboy. He wore a black-and-white bowling shirt with *Ricardo* stitched over the breast pocket. She was hot stuff. Their faces looked soft and tired, and they were holding hands.

Yukawa powered a drawer out through the wall. "Same time tomorrow, Mrs. Beller?"

"Feels so rave, Max." The woman dropped some money into the drawer. She was hot stuff. *What type of sex do you like, Mrs. Beller, WHAT TYPE???* She was *used-looking*, and she had a slow lazy voice and the big soft lips to match. She raked a stare across Stahn's face and led Ricardo up the ladder to the street. As they left, Stahn noticed that their two joined hands were actually fused into a single skin-covered mass. Hot.

Yukawa caught Stahn's expression, caught some of it. "They'll pull apart later, when the stuff fully wears off. In some circles it's quite fashionable to walk around part merged."

"How come they don't look like each other—if they're merging every day?"

"Dosage control. Unless you set up an all-day drip, merging has no lasting effects. And the drip has to be just right, or you end up as an entropic solution of amino acids. No one can do the gene exchange right but me."

"Other people have done it. Vic Morrow did it, dad." Vic Morrow had been a truck-farmer in the San Joaquin Valley. In 2027, he'd hit on the idea of treating his migrant workers to a series of weekend-long mergedrip parties. Once the workers had all flowed together, Morrow would throw a couple of dogs into the love-puddle with them. He was nuts.

Over the weeks, the workers had transmuted into beasts, ever more tractable, ever less demanding. The big scandal came when Morrow had a heart attack and his workers ate most of his corpse and rolled in the rest of it. A month later, the Anti-Chimera Act had passed Congress by acclaim.

Yukawa frowned and fumbled in his desk. "I told Morrow how to do it. It was a big mistake. I owed him money. I don't trust anyone with my secrets anymore. Especially . . ." He stopped himself and pushed a folder across the desk. "Here's the full printout on Della—I already accessed it for you. Last Friday—that was the 20th—I was with Della all day as usual, and at four she left in her maggie. Monday and Tuesday she didn't come in. I called her apartment, nobody home. Yesterday was Christmas and I didn't bother calling. I figured maybe she'd taken an extra-long holiday weekend, gone on a party or a trek in the crater. She doesn't tell me her plans. But now she's still not here and her vizzy still doesn't answer. I'm worried. Either something's happened to her, or . . . or she's run away."

Stahn picked up the folder and leafed through it. *Focus.* DELLA TAZE. Born and raised in Louisville, Kentucky. Twenty-eight years old. Ph.D. in molecular genetics, U. Va., 2025. Same year he'd been deported to Einstein. Her photo: a nice little blonde with a straight mouth and a button nose. Fox. Unmarried.

"She was your girlfriend?" Stahn glanced up at Yukawa. His long, thin head looked cruel and freakish. The "universal life form" at the back of the lab was crying out for more food, making a sound midway between a squeal and a hiss. *Arthur.* It was hard to see why Della Taze hadn't split like . . . two years ago.

". . . wouldn't let me come to her apartment," Yukawa was saying. "And she wouldn't ever merge with me either. We argued about it Friday. I *know* she was using, towards the end she asked me for it all the time. Maybe that was the only reason she stayed with me as long as she did. But now . . . now she's gone, and I have to get her back. Track her down, Mooney. Bring my Della back!"

"I'll do my best, Mr. Yukawa. Man." As Stahn got to his feet, Yukawa leaned across the desk and handed him a wad of bills, and the silver flask of dope.

"Here's money for you, Mooney, and merge. *Sta-Hi.* Didn't they used to call you Sta-Hi?"

"That was a long time ago. Now I'm all grown up."

"I gave Della blocker, just in case, but if you find her sick, just show her the flask."

Before getting a slot over to Della's place, Stahn went back to his office to do some computer searching. Maybe Della had taken Yukawa's blocker and checked into an endorphin clinic. The blocker would gene-tailor out the specific enzymes that made merge necessary for her body, but sometimes it took a clinic to keep you from going back to what your mind still wanted. Or maybe Della was dead and in the organ banks, the cannibal mart, or worse. Everyone on the Moon—lunies and boppers alike—had lots of uses for fresh meat. Or, on the other hand, maybe Della had caught a ship to Earth.

Yukawa hadn't called anyone at all; he was too paranoid. Stahn worked his vizzy through all the info banks—and drew a blank. Could she have been picked up by the Gimmie? Better not to ask. Or maybe the boppers had zombie-boxed her off to the ratsurgeon? He leaned back in his chair, trying not to think about the flask of merge. *Focus.*

If Della was still strung on merge, she'd be puddling at least once a day. That meant she might be holed up with some other local users. So it would make sense to check out the local merge scene, which centered, Stahn recalled, in the catacombs around the old dustbaths. How good *was* merge, anyway? Stahn opened Yukawa's silver flask and . . . uh . . . took a sniff. Nice: red wine and roast turkey, nice-smelling stuff. He couldn't stop wondering what it would feel like to use a little. Yukawa shouldn't have given it to him. But, Stahn realized, Yukawa had known what he was doing. Don't start, Stahn, he told himself. Don't start all that again. Why not? he answered himself. Who are you to tell me what to do? I'll do what I like! Remember, Stahn, responded the first voice, you didn't quit drugs for *other* people. You didn't quit for society, or for Wendy's ghost. You quit for *yourself.* If you go back on the stuff you're going to die.

Just then someone started pounding on the door. Stahn twitched and a fat drop of merge splashed out onto his left hand. His stomach clenched in horror, but a part of him—the bad part—was very glad. He put his hands and the flask under his desk and told the door to open.

It was the blond ridgeback who'd given him the Or-My pamphlet before. Stahn got the cap back on Yukawa's flask and tried to flex his left hand. It felt like it was melting. This stuff was for real.

"Stahn Mooney," said the ridgeback, closing the door behind him. *"Sta-Hi."* His face had junk-hunger. "My name's Whitey Mydol. I heard you were over at Yukawa's. I was wondering if . . ." He paused to sniff the air. The room reeked of merge. "Can I have some?"

"Some what?"

The melting feeling had moved up into Stahn's forearm. His shabby office walls looked prettier than the twist-box had ever made them. All right. Eighteen months since he'd felt this good. He forced his attention back to Mydol's hard young face. "How do you know who Yukawa is?"

"Oh . . . we know." The kid smiled in a conspiratorial way. "I'll give you two hundred dollars for a hit. Just between the two of us."

Stahn took his flare-ray in his right hand and levelled it at Mydol. He wanted Mydol out of here before he melted all over. "I'm going to count to three. One." Mydol stopped moving and glared. "Two." Mydol snarled a curse and stepped back towards the door. He was jangling up Stahn's first rush in almost two years, and Stahn wanted to kill him.

"AO, Junk-Hog Sta-Hi Rent-Pig Mooney. What's the shudder, scared to merge with a man? Tubedook."

"Three," Stahn clicked off the safety and burned a shot across Mydol's left shoulder. The ridgeback winced in pain, opened the door and left.

Stahn slumped back. God, this was fast dope. His left arm looked like candle wax, and he was having trouble staying in his chair. He let himself slide down onto the floor and stared up at the ceiling. Oh, this did feel so good. His bone joints loosened, and his skeleton sagged beneath the puddle of his flesh. It took almost an hour to ride the trip out. Towards the middle Stahn saw God. God was about the same as usual—a little more burnt, maybe. He wanted love as bad as Stahn did. This life was taking its toll on everyone.

What is merge like? Baby, if you don't know by now
. . . Wonderful. Horrible. After Stahn hit the floor and
puddled, he wasn't really there. The space of the room
became *part of his consciousness*. He *was* the room, the
chipped beige plas, the dingy black floor, the old-fashioned
windows, the desk and chair and computer; he was the room
and the building and Einstein and the Earth. Standard ecstatic
mystical vision, really. But *fast*. He was everywhere, he was
nowhere, he was the same as God. And then there were no
thoughts at all. *Stuzzy*, sis, *all* right.

It wore off ***WHAM*** as quickly as it had come on.
There was a tingling in Stahn's flesh, a kind of jelling
feeling, and then he was lying there shaking, heart going a
mile a minute. Too fast. This dope was giga too fast. Death
practice, right: hit, melt, space, blank. Final blank. He
wished his dead wife Wendy were still alive. Sweet, blonde,
wide-hipped Wendy. Times like this—in the old days—she'd
hug him and pat his head real soft . . . and smile . . . And
you killed her, Stahn. Oh God, oh no, oh put that away.
You blew a hole in her head and sold her corpse to the
organleggers and used the money to come to the Moon.

Stahn alone on the office floor, shuddering. Bum kicks.
Think about anything but Wendy. Flash of an old song:
*Coming down again, all my time's been spent, coming down
again*. Old. Gettin old. Coming down gets too old. Does that
even mean anything? Language with a flat tire. Talk broken,
but keep talking. Regroup.

His clothes were awkwardly bunched around him. When
he sat up, the headache started. Bummer bummer bummer
bummer bummer. He took Yukawa's silver flask and shook
it. There was quite a bit in there, a few months' worth if
you only took it once a day. If he got back on drugs he was
dead. He should be dead. He wished he was dead. Lot of
slow death in that flask.

If one drop was a dose, and a dose was worth . . uh
. . two hundred dollars, then this flask was something that
certain elements—certain criminal elements—would . . uh
. . *kkkkkillll* for. And that ridgeback cultie knew he was
holding, oh my brethren. *Can I get some head?* "Hello,
Mrs. Beller, you don't know me, but I . . uh . ." Hot. Hot.

Hot. Hot. Hot. Hot. Hot. WHAT TYPE OF SEX, BABY, *WHAT TYPE?*

The thing to do right now was to not go back out the office building's front door. *Focus.* Rent a maggie. Garage on top of the building.

He picked out a black saucer-shaped maggie, fed it some money, and told it where to go. The maggies were like hovercars; they counteracted the Moon's weak gravity with fans, and with an intense magnetic field keyed to a big field generated by wires set into the dome. They were expensive. It was funny that a junkie lab assistant like Della Taze would have had her own maggie. Stahn could hardly wait to see her apartment. Maybe she was actually there, just not answering the vizzy, but there and like waiting for a guy with merge. He had lock-picking wares in case she wouldn't open.

The entry system at Della's building was no problem. Stahn used a standard nihilist transposition on the door down from the roof, and a tone-scrambler on her apartment door. The apartment was Wigglesville. *Creative Brain Damage, Vol. XIII.* As follows.

The walls weren't painted one uniform color. It was all bursts and streaks, as if the painter had just thrown random buckets around the apartment till everything was covered: walls, floors, and ceilings all splattered and dripped beyond scuzz.

The furniture was pink, and all in shapes of people. The chairs were big stuffed women with laps to sit in, and the tables were plas men on all fours. He kept jerking, seeing that furniture out of the corner of his eye, and thinking someone was there. Twist and shout. The whole place had the merge wine-turkey fragrance, but there was another smell under it . . . a bad smell.

Which, as it turned out, came from the bedroom. Della had her love-puddle in there—a big square tub like a giant wading pool. And next to it was . . . sort of a corpse. It had been a black guy.

Gross—you want to hear gross? A merged person is like Jell-O over some bones, right. And you can . . . uh . . . *splatter* Jell-O. Splatter a merged person into a bunch of pieces, and the drug wears off—the cells firm up—and there is this . . uh . . guy in a whole lot of pieces.

The skin had covered on up around each of the pieces—here was a foot with a rounded-off stump at the ankle, here was his head all smoothed off at the neck. He looked like a nice enough guy. Plump, easygoing. Here was an arm with his torso—and over there a leg hooked onto his bare ass . . . and all of it sagging and starting to rot . . .

Zzuzzzzzzz.

The vizzy in the living room was buzzing. Stahn ran in, covered up the lens, and thumbed the set on.

It was a hard-faced Gimmie officer. He wore hair spikes, and he had gold studs set into his cheeks. Colonel Hasci. Stahn knew the "cat." *Muy macho. Trés douche.*

"Miss Della Taze? We're down in the lobby. Can we come up and ask you some questions about Buddy Yeskin?"

Stahn split fast. It was a little hard to judge, but *Buddy* looked to have been dead two days. Why would anyone splatter good old Bud? Death is so stupid; always the same old punch line. It reminded him of Wendy, whenever he was coming down everything reminded him of Wendy. He'd been stoned on three-way, shooting houseflies with his needler and he'd hit her by accident. Some accident. Sold her body to the organleggers and moved up to the Moon before the mudder Gimmie could deport him. Her poor limp body.

Stahn's black saucer circled aimlessly. He wondered where Della Taze had gotten to. Merge with the cosmos, sister. Can I get some, too? WHAT TYPE, baby, WHAT TYPE OF SEX? Shut up, Stahn. Be quiet, brother. Chill out.

Chapter Two
Christmas in Louisville

December 24, 2030

Merged. Gentle curves and sweet flow of energies—merged in the love-puddle, the soft plastic tub set into the floor of her bedroom. Exquisite ecstasy—Della melted and Buddy just sliding in; the two of them about to be together again, close as close can be, flesh to flesh, gene to gene, a marbled mass of pale and tan skin, with their four eyes up on top seeing nothing; but now, just as Buddy starts melting . . . suddenly . . .

Aeh!

Della Taze snapped out of her flashback and looked at the train car window. It was dusk outside, and the glass gave back a faint reflection of her face: blonde, straight-mouthed, her eyes hot and sunken. Her stomach hurt, and she'd thrown up three times today. Burnt-out and worldly wise . . . the look she'd longed for as a teenage girl. She tried a slight smile. *Not bad, Della. But you're wanted for murder.* And the only place she could think of going was home.

The train was coasting along at a slow 20 mph now, click-clanking into Louisville, gliding closer to the long trip's end: Einstein-Ledge-Florida-Louisville via spaceship-shuttle-train. Two days. Della hoped she was well ahead of the Einstein Gimmie—the police. Not that they'd be likely to chase her this far. Here in 2030, Moon and Earth were as far removed from each other as Australia and England had been in the 1800s.

Louisville in the winter: rain not even snow, lots of it, gray water, the funny big cars, and real sky—the smells, after two years of dome air, and the idle space! On the Moon, every nook and cranny had its purpose—like on a sailboat or in a tent—but here, gliding past the train, were vacant lots with nothing in them but weeds and dead tires; meaningless streets with marginal businesses; tumbledown houses with nobody home. Idle space. There were too many faces up in Einstein, too many bodies, too many needs.

Della was glad to be back here, with a real sky and real air; even though her body was filled with a dull ache. The weight. Old Mr. Gravity. In Florida she'd spent the last of her money on an Imipolex flexiskeleton with the brand name, Body by Oozer. She wore it like a body stocking, and the coded collagens pushed, stiffened, and pulled as needed. The ultimate support hosiery. Most returning lunies check in for three days of muscle rehabilitation at the JFK Spaceport, but Della had known she'd have to keep running. Why? Because she'd jelled back from that last merge-trip to find her lover splattered into pieces, and before she'd had time to do anything, there'd been a flat-voiced twitch-faced man on the vizzy.

"I killed him, Della, and I can kill you. Or I can tell the Gimmie that you did it. I want to help you, Della. I love you. I want to help you escape. There's a fake passport and a ticket to Earth for you at the spaceport . . ."

Aeh!

Della's parents, Jason and Amy Taze, were at the station, the same as ever—strungout and hungover, mouths set into smiles, and their self-centered eyes always asking, *Do you love me?* Amy Taze was small and tidy. She wore bright, outdated makeup, and today she had her blonde hair marcelled into a tight, hard helmet. Jason was a big, shambling guy with short hair and messy prep clothes. He had a desk job at a bank, and Amy was a part-time saleswoman in a gift shop. They both hated their jobs and lived to party. Seeing them there, Della felt like getting back on the train.

"My *God,* Della, you look *fantastic.* Is that a *leotard* you have on under your clothes?" Mom kept the chatter going all the way out to the car, as if to show how sober she was.

Dad rolled his eyes and gave Della a wink, as if to show how much more together than Mom *he* was. The two of them were so busy putting on their little show that it was ten minutes before they noticed that Della was trembling. It was Dad who finally said something.

"You do look nice, Della, but you seem a little shaky. Was it a hard trip? And why such short notice?"

"Somebody framed me for a murder, Dad. That's why I didn't want you all to tell anyone else I'm back in town." Her stomach turned again, and she retched into her handkerchief.

"Was it some kind of hard-drug deal? Something to do with that damn *merge* stuff that your Dr. Yukawa makes?" Dad fished nervously in his pocket for a reefer. He shot her a sharp glance. "Are you hooked?"

Della nodded, glad to upset them. Taste of their own medicine. No point telling them she'd taken gamendorph blocker to kick. Dr. Yukawa had always made sure that she had blocker around.

"That's what we get for not being better people, Jason," said Mom, her voice cracking in self-pity. "The only one of our children coming home for Christmas is a killer dope queen on the lam. And for the two years before this we've been all alone. Give me a hit off that number, I think I'm going to have a nervous breakdown." She took a puff, smiled, and patted Della's cheek. "You can help us trim the tree, Della honey. We still have the styrofoam star you decorated in kindergarten."

Della wanted to say something cutting, but she knew it would feel bad. Instead she put on her good-girl face and said, "I'd like that, Mom. I haven't seen a Christmas tree in three years. I . . . ." Her voice caught and the tears came. She loved her parents, but she hated to see them. Holidays were always the worst, with Jason and Amy stumbling around in a chemical haze. "I hope this won't be like all the other Christmases, Mom."

"I don't know what you mean, Della. It will be lovely. Your Uncle Colin and Aunt Ilse are coming over for dinner tomorrow. They'll bring Willy, he's still living at home. Of course your two little sisters are both visiting with their *husbands'* families again."

Jason and Amy Taze lived in an eighty-year-old two-story tract home east of Louisville. The neighborhood had sidewalks and full-grown trees. The houses were small, but well-kept. Della found her tiny room to be more or less as it had always been: the clean, narrow bed; the little china animals on the shelf she'd nailed into the papery drywall; the hologram hoops hung in the two windows; and her disks and info-cubes all arranged in the alphabetical order she liked to keep them in. When she was in ninth grade, she'd programmed a cross-referenced catalog cube to keep track of them all. Della had always been a good student, a good girl, compulsively tidy as if to make up for her parents' frequent sloppy scenes.

Someone let Bowser, the family dog, in the back door then, and he came charging up the narrow carpeted stairs to greet Della, shaking his head, and whining and squirming like a snake. He looked as mangy as ever, and as soon as Della patted him, he lay on his back spreading his legs, the same gross way he'd always done. She rubbed under his chin for a while, while he wriggled and yipped.

"Yes, Bowser. Good dog. Good, smart dog." Now that she'd started crying, she couldn't seem to stop. Mom and Dad were downstairs in the kitchen, talking in hushed tones. Della was too tired to unpack. She hurt all over, especially in her breasts and stomach. When she slipped out of her flexiskeleton, she felt like a fat, watery jellyfish. There was a nightgown on the bed—Mom must have laid it out. Della put it on, glad no one was here to see her, and then she fell into a long, deep sleep.

When Della woke up it was midmorning. Christmas! So what. Without her two sisters Ruby and Sude here, it didn't mean a thing. Closing her eyes, Della could almost hear their excited yelling—and then she realized she was hearing the vizzy. Her parents were downstairs watching the vizzy on Christmas morning. God. She went to the bathroom and vomited, and then she put on her flexiskeleton and got dressed.

"Della!" cried her mother when Della appeared. "Now you see what we do on Christmas with no babies." There was an empty glass by her chair. The vizzy screen showed an unfamiliar family opening presents around their tree.

Mom touched the screen and a different family appeared, then another and another.

"We've gotten in the habit," explained Dad with a little shrug. "Every year lots of people leave their sets on, and whoever wants to can share in. So no one's lonely. We're so glad to have a real child here." He took her by the shoulders and planted a kiss on her forehead. "Little Della. Flesh of our flesh."

"Come, dear," said Mom. "Open your presents. We only had time to get two, but they're right here in front of the vizzy in case anyone's sharing in with *us*."

It felt silly but nice sitting down in front of the vizzy— there were some excited children on the screen just then, and it was almost like having noisy little Ruby and Sude at her side. And Bowser was right there, nuzzling her. Della's first present was an imipolex sweatshirt called a heartshirt.

"All the girls at the bank are wearing them this year," explained Dad. "It's a simplified version of bopper flicker-cladding. Try it on!"

Della slipped the loose warm plastic over her top. The heartshirt was an even dark blue, with a few staticky red spots drifting about.

"It can feel your heartbeat," said Mom. "Look." Sure enough, there was a big red spot on the plastic sweatshirt, right over Della's heart, a spot that spread out into an expanding ring that moved on over Della's shoulders and down her sleeves. Her heart beat again, and a new spot started—each beat of her heart made a red splash in the blue of the heartshirt.

"Neat," said Della. "Thanks. They don't have these up in Einstein. Everyone there hates boppers too much. But it's stuzzy. I like it."

"And when your heart beats faster, Della," said Mom, "all the fellows will be able to see."

Suddenly Della remembered Buddy, and why she'd come home, and the red rings on her sweatshirt started bouncing like mad.

"Why, Della!" said Mom, coyly. "Do you have a boyfriend?"

"I'm not ready to talk about it," said Della, calming

herself. *Especially not to a loudmouth racist drunk like you, Mom.*

"Let's have some champagne," suggested Dad.

"Good idea," said Mom. "Take the edge off. And then Della can open her other present."

Della watched the vizzy for a minute, calming down. Good old vizzy. She touched the screen here and there, and the picture skipped from home to home. Louisville people, not so different from the Tazes. Della even recognized some of them. She had some champagne and felt OK again. Lots of the people in the vizzy were drinking . . . why should she be so hard on her parents?

"Let's see my other present. I'm sorry I didn't bring you all anything."

"You brought yourself."

Della's second present was a little seed-packet labelled WEEK TREES.

"Have you heard of these?" asked Mom. "They're bioengineered. You know the miniature bonsai trees that the Japanese used to grow? These are the same, except their whole life cycle only takes a week. I've been showing them off in the store. They're amazing. We'd planned to try and mail these to you." She poured herself a fresh glass of champagne, which killed the bottle. "Get Della a little pottery cup with some potting soil, Jason. And why don't you twist up a few jays."

"Mom . . ."

"Don't be so uptight, Della." Mom's painted eyes flashed. "You'll get your turkey dinner, just wait and see. It's Christmas! Anyway, *you're* the one who's addicted to that hard-drug merge, little Miss Strict."

"AO, wave, it's heavy junk, Mom, but I took blocker and *I'm* oxo. Wu-wei, Mom, your rectum's showing." A wave of nausea swept over her again and she gagged. "It must be the gravity that's making me feel so sick."

"Let's wait on the weed till Colin and Ilse get here," suggested Dad. "You know how they love to smoke. You get that turkey in the microwave, Amy, and I'll help Della plant one of her week trees."

Mom finished her champagne and got to her feet. She

forgot her anger and smiled. "I got a boneless turkey this year, Della. They grow them in tanks."

"Do they have legs and wings?"

"Everything except bones. Like soft-shell crabs. Sometimes I feel that way myself. I'll make lots of sausage stuffing for you, sweetie."

"Thanks, Mom. Let me know if you need any help."

Dad got a little pot full of wet soil, and he and Della planted a week tree seed. They'd half expected the tree to shoot up and hit them in the face, but for the moment, nothing happened. Bowser sniffed curiously at the dirt.

"Let's figure it out," said Della, who liked playing with numbers. "Say a real tree lives seventy years. Then one day is like ten years for a week tree. So it should go through a year in two and four-tenths hours. Divide by twelve and get a month in two-tenths of an hour. Two-tenths of an hour is twelve minutes. Assuming that the seed starts out in a dormant midwinter mode, then we should see the first April leaves in four times twelve minutes, which will be . . ."

"Noon," said Dad. "Look at the soil in the pot, it's beginning to stir." Sure enough, the soil at the center of the pot was bulging up, and there, slowly slowly, came the creeping tip of the week tree. "I think they're like apple trees. We ought to have some little apples by tonight, Della."

"Wiggly!" She gave Dad a kiss. Mom had some pans sizzling out in the kitchen, and the vizzy was full of happy Christmas people. "Thank you. It is nice to be back."

"Can you tell me more about what happened up in Einstein, Della?"

"I had a boyfriend named Buddy Yeskin. We took merge together and—"

"What does that actually *mean,* 'taking merge together'?" asked Dad. "I can't keep up with all these new—"

"It's this weird drug that makes your body get all soft. Like a boneless turkey, I guess. And you feel really—"

Dad frowned. "I can't believe you'd do a thing like that, Della. We didn't raise you that way." He sighed and took a sip of the whiskey he'd brought out from the kitchen. "You took merge with this Buddy Yeskin, and then what happened?"

"While we were . . . together, someone broke into my apartment and killed Buddy. Smashed him all into pieces while he was soft." The fast red circles began rippling across Della's heartshirt again. "I kind of fainted, and when I woke up, a crazy man called on the vizzy and said he was going to kill me, or frame me for the murder, if I didn't leave for Earth. He'd even arranged a ticket and a fake passport for me. It was such a nightmare web, closing in on me. I was scared. I ran home."

The week tree was a barky little shoot now, with three stubby little branches.

"You're safe here," said Dad, patting her hand. Just then Della noticed that his voice was already slurring a little. Dad noticed her noticing. He gave a rueful smile. "For as long as you can stand us. Tomorrow I'll take you to see Don Stuart . . . you remember him. He's a good lawyer. Just in case." Bowser started barking.

"Merry Christmas!" shouted Mom in the kitchen. "You didn't have to bring all that! Jason! Della!"

It was Jason's older brother Colin, with his wife Ilse and son Willy. Colin worked as an English professor at the University of Louisville. He was skinny and sarcastic. Ilse was from a famous family: Ilse's father was Cobb Anderson, who'd built the first moon-robots years ago.

Great-uncle Cobb had been convicted of treason for building the robots wrong. Then he'd started drinking, had left his wife Verena, and had ended up as a pheezer bum in Florida. Somehow he'd died—it was a little uncertain— apparently the robots had killed him. He was the skeleton in the family closet.

Aunt Ilse was more like her German mother than she was like old Cobb. Vigorous and artsy-craftsy, she'd hung on to her wandering husband Colin through thick and thin, not that Della could see why. Uncle Colin had always struck her as obsolete, trying to make people look at his stupid paper books, when *he* barely even knew how to work the vizzy. And when he smoked marijuana with Dad, he got mad if you didn't laugh at his jokes and act impressed by his insights.

Their son Willy was a smart but sort of nutty guy in his twenties. A hacker, always fiddling with programs and hardware. Della had liked him a lot when they were younger, but it seemed like he'd stopped maturing long before she had. He still lived at home.

"Dad, don't tell them about why I've come back. Say I'm here to buy laboratory equipment for Dr. Yukawa. And tell Mom to keep quiet, too. If she gets drunk and starts talking about me, I'm going to—"

"Relax, geeklet."

Before long they were seated around the dining table. Dad had put the week tree in the center so they could watch it grow. Aunt Ilse offered a Lutheran grace, and Dad got to work carving the boneless turkey. He cut it in thick, stuffing-centered slices.

"Well, Della," said Colin after the first rush of eating was over, "how are things up on the Moon? Real far out? And what are old Cobb's funky machines into?" He specialized in the literature of the mid-twentieth century, and he liked to use the corny old slang on her. In return, Della always used the newest words she knew.

"Realtime, it's pretty squeaky, Unk. There's giga bopper scurry underground, and they're daily trying to blank us. They have a mongo sublune city called the Nest."

"Come on, Della," said Dad. "Talk English."

"Don't you feel guilty about the boppers?" asked Aunt Ilse, who was always ready to defend the creatures that her father had midwifed. "I mean, *they* built most of Einstein. Disky, they used to call it, no? And they're just as conscious as us. Isn't it really like the blacks in the old South? The blacks did all the work, but the whites acted like they weren't even people."

"Those robots aren't conscious," insisted Mom. She'd had a lot of red wine in the kitchen, and now they were all back on the champagne. "They're just a bunch of goddamn *machines*."

"You're a machine, too, Aunt Amy," put in Willy. "You're just made of meat instead of wires and silicon." Willy had a slow, savoring way of speaking that could drive you crazy. Although he'd never finished college, he made a good living as a freelance software writer. Earth still used a lot of computers, but all the bigger ones were equipped with deeply coded behavior locks intended to keep them from trying to follow in the steps of the boppers, the rebel robots who'd colonized the Moon. Earth's slave computers were known as asimovs in honor of the Asimov laws of robotics which they obeyed.

"Don't call your aunt 'meat,' " reprimanded Uncle Colin, who liked to flirt with Mom. "The turkey is meat. Your aunt is a person. You wouldn't want me to put gravy on your aunt and eat her, would you? In front of everyone?" Colin chuckled and bugged his eyes at Mom. "Should I smack him, Amy?"

"At least he's thinking about what I'm made of. At my age, that's practically a compliment. Would you call me a *machine*, Jason honey?"

"No way." Dad poured out some more champagne. "Machines are predictable."

"I think Mom's predictable," Della couldn't resist saying snippishly. Her stomach felt really bad again. "Both of you are predictable."

"You're all mistaken," put in Willy. "Relative to us, people and boppers are *both* unpredictable. It's a consequence of Chaitin's version of Gödel's theorem. Grandpa Cobb explained it years ago in a paper called 'Towards Robot Consciousness.' We can only make predictions about the behavior of systems which are much simpler than ourselves."

"So there, Della," said Mom.

"But why can't we learn to coexist peacefully with the boppers, Della?" pressed Aunt Ilse.

"Well, things *are* fairly peaceful now," said Della. "The boppers harass us because they wish we'd give Einstein back to them, but they don't actually pop the dome and kill everyone. They could do it, but they know that Earth would turn around and fire a Q-bomb down into their Nest. For that matter, we could Q-bomb them right now, but we're in no rush to, because we need the things their factories and pink-tanks make." Everyone except Mom was looking at Della with interest, and she felt knowledgeable and poised. But just then her stomach twitched oddly. Her breasts and stomach felt like they were growing all the time.

"Well, *I* don't feel guilty about the boppers," put in Mom. The alcohol was really hitting her, and she hadn't followed the conversation at all. "I think we ought to kill all the machines . . . and kill the niggers too. Starting with President Jones."

There was a pained silence. The little week tree rustled; its first blossoms were opening. Della decided to let Mom have it. "My boyfriend was a 'nigger,' Mom."

"What boyfriend? I hope you didn't let him—"

"Yes, Della," said Dad, raising his voice heavily. "It's great to have you back. More food anyone? Or should we pause for some holiday marijuana? How about it, Colin?"

"Shore," said Colin, switching to his hick accent. He gave Della a reassuring wink. "Mah smart little niece. She's got more degrees than a thermometer! Weren't you doing something with genetics up there in Einstein?"

"I *hope* not," put in Mom, trying to recover. "This child still has to find a husband."

"Chill it, Mom," snapped Della.

"That's . . . uh . . . right, Colin," said Dad, still trying to smooth things over. "Della was working with this Dr. Yukawa fellow. She's down here to buy some equipment for him." He drew a reefer out of his pocket and fired it up.

"How long will you be staying here?" asked Aunt Ilse.

"I'm not sure. It might be quite a while till everything's set."

"Oh," said Ilse, passing the reefer to her husband without taking a hit. She could be really nosy when she got going. "How lovely. Is Dr. Yukawa planning to—"

Della kicked Willy under the table. He got the message, and interrupted to throw the interrogation off track. "What kind of stuffing is this, Aunt Amy? It's really delicious."

"*Meat*-stuffing, honey. I was fresh out of wires and silicon. Pass me that thing, Colin."

"I have an interesting new job, Della," said Willy, talking rapidly around his food. He had smooth, olive skin like his mother, and finely arched eyebrows that moved up and down as he chewed and talked. "It's for the *Belle of Louisville*—you know, the big riverboat that tourists ride on? OK, what they've got there is three robot bartenders—with impolex skins, you know, all designed to look like old-time black servants."

"Why can't they just hire some real blacks?" demanded

Mom, exhaling a cloud of smoke. "God knows there's enough of them unemployed. Except for President Jones. Not that I want to offend Della." She reached out and touched the blossoms of the week tree, moving the pollen around. Della, who had decided not to eat any more of her mother's meal, slipped Bowser the rest of her boneless turkey.

"This all has to do with what we were talking about before, Aunt Amy," continued Willy. "They did have real blacks tending bar on the *Belle,* but they kept acting too much like regular people—maybe sneaking a drink now and then, or flirting with the women, or getting in arguments with drunk rednecks. And if there did happen to be a bartender who did his job perfectly, then some people would feel bad to see such a talented person with such a bleaky job. Guilty liberals, you wave? They tried white bartenders, too, but it was the same deal—either they start fights with the rednecks, or they make the liberals feel sad. I mean, who's going to *take* a bartending job, anyway? But as long as it's robots, then there's none of this messy human stuff."

"That's interesting, Willy," said Uncle Colin. "I didn't know the *Belle* was your new gig. Nobody tells me anything. I was on the *Belle* just last week with a dude who came to give a rap about Mark Twain, and those black bartenders didn't seem like robots at all. As a matter of fact, they kept making mistakes and dropping things. They were laughing all the time. I didn't feel a bit sorry for them!"

"That's my new program!" exulted Willy. "There's a big supercooled processor down below the deck, and it runs the three bartender robots. My job was to get it fine-tuned so that the bartenders would be *polite*, but clearly unfit for any better job."

"Hell, you could have just hired some of our tellers," put in Dad. I don't know why people still mess with robots after 2001." 2001 was the year that the boppers—Cobb Anderson's self-replicating moon-robots—had revolted. They'd started their own city up on the Moon, and it hadn't been till 2022 that the humans had won it back.

"How come they have such a big computer on the *Belle* anyway?" Colin wanted to know. "I thought big computers weren't allowed outside of the factories anymore. Is it a teraflop?''

Willy raised his high, round eyebrows. "Almost. A hundred gigaflop. This is a special deal the city put together. They got the processor from ISDN, the vizzy people. It's been up and running for six months, but they needed me to get it working really right.''

"Isn't that against the Artificial Intelligence Law?" asked Dad.

"No it isn't,'' Willy insisted calmly. "Burt Masters, who operates the *Belle*, is friends with the mayor, and he got a special exemption to the AI law. And of course Belle—that's what the computer calls itself—is an asimov. You know: *Protect Humans—Obey Humans—Protect Yourself* are coded into Belle's circuits in 1–2–3 order.'' He gave Della a smile. "Those are the commands that Ralph Numbers taught the boppers to erase. Have you actually seen any boppers, Della? I wonder what the newest ones look like. Grandpa Cobb fixed it so they'd never stop evolving.''

"I've seen some boppers over at the trade center. These days a lot of them have a kind of mirror-backing under their skins. But I didn't pay much attention to them. Living in Einstein you do sort of get to hate them. They have bombs hidden all over, and now and then they set one off just to remind us. And they have hidden cameras everywhere, and there's rumors that the robots can put a thing like a plastic rat inside a person's head and control them. Actually—'' Suddenly it hit her. "Actually, I wouldn't be surprised if—'' She cut herself off and took a long drink of champagne.

"I still don't see why we can't drop a Q-bomb down into their Nest," said Mom. The marijuana had brought her somewhat back into focus.

"We *could*,'' said Della, trying to get through to her mother. "But they *know* that, and if the Nest goes, Einstein goes, too. It's a stalemate, like we used to have with the Russians. Mutual Assured Destruction. That's one reason the boppers don't try and take Einstein back over. We're like hostages. And remember that Earth likes buying all the stuff they make. This heartshirt is boppermade, Mom.''

"Well, as long as people like Willy will contain themselves, we're still safe from the boppers here on Earth,'' said Mom. "They can't live in normal temperatures, isn't that right, Willy?"

"Yeah." Willy helped himself to some glazed carrots. "As long as they use J-junctions. Though if *I* were designing a robot brain now I'd try and base it on an optical processor. Optical processors use light instead of electricity—the light goes along fibers, and the logic gates are like those sunglass lenses that get dark in bright light. One photon can pass, but two can't. And you have little chip-sized lasers to act like capacitors. Optical fibers have no real resistance at all, so the thing doesn't have to be supercooled. But we still can't build a really good one. But sooner or later the boppers will. Can I please have some more turkey, Uncle Jason?"

"Uh . . . sure, Willy." Jason stood up to carve some more, and smiled down at his bright, nerdy nephew. "Willy, do you remember when you and Della were little and you had the big fight over the wishbone? Della wanted to *glaze* it and save it and—"

"Willy wanted to pull it by himself to make sure he got the big Christmas wish," interrupted Uncle Colin, laughing hard.

"*I* remember," said Aunt Ilse, waving her fork. "And then we made the children go ahead and pull the wishbone with each other—"

"And they each wished that the other one would lose!" squealed Mom.

"Who won?" asked Della. "I don't remember."

"I did," said Willy complacently. "So I got my wish. You want to try again?"

"It's boneless, dear," said Mom. "Didn't you notice? Look at the week tree, it's getting leaves and tiny little apples!"

After dinner, Willy and Della decided to go for a walk. It was too boring watching their parents get stoned and start thinking everything they said was funny, when it really was just stupid.

It was bright and gray, but cold. Bowser ran ahead of them, pissing and sniffing. Little kids were out on the sidewalks with new scootcycles and gravballs; all of them warmly wrapped in bright thermchos and buffs. Just like every other Christmas.

"My father said you'd gotten into some kind of trouble on the Moon?" asked Willy after a while.

"Have they already been gossiping about me?"

"Not at all. Hell, you *are* my favorite cousin, Della. I'm glad you're back, and I hope you stay in Louisville, and if you don't want to tell me why you came back, you sure don't have to." Willy cast about for some way to change the subject. "That new heartbeat blouse of yours is really nice."

"Thank you. And I *don't* want to talk about what happened, not yet. Why don't we just walk over to your house and you show me your stuff. You always had such neat stuff in your room, Willy."

"Can you walk that far? I notice you're still wearing a flexiskeleton."

"I need to keep exercising if I'm ever going to get rid of it. You don't have any merge at your house, do you?"

"You know I don't use drugs, Della. Anyway, I doubt if there's any merge in all of Louisville. Is it really so wonderful?"

"Better. Actually, I'm glad I can't get hold of any. I feel kind of sick. At first I thought it was from the gravity, but this feels different. It must be from the merge. I took blocker, but my stomach keeps fluttering. I have a weird feeling like something's alive inside me." Della gave a slow, dry laugh; and then shot a glance over to see if Willy was impressed. But, as always, it was hard to tell what was going on behind that big round forehead of his.

"I've got a cephscope I built," volunteered Willy after a while. "You put that on, it's as good as any stupid drug. But it's not somatic. It's a pure software high."

"Wiggly, Cousin Will."

Colin Taze's house was about five blocks from Dad's. All through his twenties and thirties, Colin had lived in different cities—an "academic gypsy," he liked to say—but now, as he neared forty, he'd moved back to Louisville and settled near his big brother Jason. His house was even older than Jason's, and a bit run down, but it was big and comfortable. Willy undid the locks—it seemed like there were more robbers all the time—and the two cousins went on down to

Willy's basement apartment. Willy was too out of it—or lazy—to leave home.

"This is my electron microscope, this here is my laser for making holograms, here's my imipolex-sculpture stuff, and *this* is the cephscope. Try it on—you wear it like earphones."

"This isn't some kind of trick, is it, Willy?" When they'd been younger, Willy had been big on practical jokes. Della remembered one Christmas, years ago, when Willy had given her a perfume bottle filled with live ants. Della had screamed, and Ruby and Sude had teased her for weeks.

But today, Willy's face was all innocence. "You've never used a cephscope?"

"I've just read about them. Aren't they like twist-boxes?"

"Oh God, that's like saying a vizzy is like a pair of glasses. Cephscopes are the big new art form, Della. Cephart. That's what I'd really like to get into. This robot stuff I do is loser—deliberately designing programs that don't work *too* well. It's kilp. Here, put this on your head so the contacts touch your temples, and check it out. It's a . . . symphony I composed."

"What if I start flicking out?"

"It's not *like* that, Della, really." Willy's face was kind and serious. He was really proud of his cephscope, and he wanted to show it off.

So Della sat in an easy chair and put the earphone things on her head with the contacts touching her temples, and Willy turned the cephscope on. It was nice for a while— washes of color, 3D/4D inversions, layers of sound, and strange tinglings in the skin. Kind of like the beginning of a merge-trip, really—and this led to the bad part—for now she flashed back into that nightmare last merge in her Einstein cubby . . .

Starting the merge, so loving, so godlike, they'd be like Mother Earth and Father Sky, Many into One, yes, and Buddy was sliding in the puddle now . . . but . . . suddenly . . . a wrenching feeling, Buddy being pulled away, oh where, Della's puddled eyes just floating, unable to move, seeing the violent shadows on the ceiling, noise vibrations, shadows beating and smashing and then the rough hand reaching up into her softness and . . .

Aaaaaaaaeeeeehh!!!

"Della! Della, are you all right? Della! It's me, Willy! God, I'm sorry, Della, I had no idea you'd flip like that . . . are you all right? Look how fast your heart is going!" Willy stopped and looked closer. "And, Della . . ."

Della looked down at her heartshirt. The red circles were racing out from her heart. But something had been added to the pattern. Circles were also pumping out from a spot right over her swollen belly. Baby heart circles.

Chapter Three
Berenice

November 22, 2030

In 2030, the Moon had two cities: Einstein (formerly known as Disky), and the Nest. They lay within eight miles of each other at the southeastern lobe of the Sea of Tranquillity, not far from the site of the original lunar landing of 1969. Originally built by the autonomous robots known as boppers, Einstein was now a human-filled dome habitat about the size of Manhattan. There was a spaceport and a domed trade center three miles east of Einstein, and five miles east of that was the Maskeleyne G crater, entrance to the underground bopper city known as the Nest.

Cup-shaped and buffed to a mirror sheen, Maskeleyne G glittered in the sun's hard radiation. At the focus of the polished crater was a conical prism that, fourteen days a month, fed a vast stick of light down into a kind of mineshaft.

In the shaft's great, vertical tunnel, bright beings darted through the hot light; odd-shaped living machines that glowed with all the colors of the rainbow. These were the boppers: self-reproducing robots who obeyed no man. Some looked humanoid, some looked like spiders, some looked like snakes, some looked like bats. All were covered with flickercladding, a microwired imipolex compound that could absorb and emit light.

The shaft went one mile straight down, widening all the while like a huge upside-down funnel. Tunnels punched into the shaft's sides, and here and there small mirrors dipped

205

into the great light beam, channeling bits of it off through the gloom. At the bottom of the shaft was a huge, conical sublunar space—the boppers' Nest. It was like a cathedral, but bigger, much bigger, an underground pueblo city that would be inconceivable in Earth's strong gravity. The temperature was only a few degrees Kelvin—this suited the boppers, as many of them still had brains based on supercooled Josephson-junction processors. Even though room-temperature superconductors were available, the quantum-mechanical Josephson effect worked only at five degrees Kelvin and below. Too much heat could kill a J-junction bopper quickly, though the newest boppers—the so-called petaflop boppers—were based on fiber-optics processors that were immune to heat.

The main column of sunlight from the Moon's surface splashed down to fill a central piazza on the Nest's floor. Boppers danced in and out of the light, feeding on the energy. The petaflops had to be careful not to let extraneous light into their bodies; they had mirrored bodyshells beneath their flickercladding. Their thoughts were pure knots of light, shunted and altered by tiny laser crystals.

Crowds of boppers milled around the edges of the light-pool, trading things and talking. The light-pool was their marketplace and forum. The boppers' radio-wave voices blended into a staticky buzz—part English, and part machine language. The color pulses of their flickercladding served to emphasize or comment on their digital transmissions; much as people's smiles and grimaces add analog meaning to what they say.

The great clifflike walls of the Nest were pocked with doors—doors with strange expressionistic shapes, some leading to tunnels, some opening into individual bopper cubettes. The bright, flickering boppers on the upsloping cliffs made the Nest a bit like the inside of a Christmas tree.

Factories ringed the bases of the cliffs. Off on one side of the Nest were the hell-flares of a foundry powered by light beams and tended by darting demon figures. Hard by the foundry was the plastics refinery, where the boppers' flickercladding and body-boxes were made. In front of these two factories was an array of some thousand chip-etching tables—tables manned by micro-eyed boppers as diligent as Franz

Kafka's co-workers in the Workmen's Insurance Company of Prague.

On the other side of the Nest were the banks of pink-tanks. These were hydroponic meat farms growing human serums and organs that could be traded for that incredibly valuable Earthly substance: oil. Crude oil was the raw material for the many kinds of organic compounds that the boppers needed to build their plastic bodies. Closer to the Nest's center were streets of shops: wire millers, flicker-cladders, eyemakers, debuggers, info merchants, and the like.

The airless frigid space of the Nest, two miles across, swarmed with boppers riding their ion jets: carrying things, and darting in and out of the slanting, honeycombed cliffs. No two boppers looked the same; no two thought alike.

Over the course of the boppers' rapid evolution, something like sexual differences had arisen. Some boppers—for reasons only a bopper could explain—were "he," and some were "she." They found each other beautiful; and in their pursuit of beauty, they constantly improved the software makeup of their race.

Berenice was a petaflop bopper shaped like a smooth, nude woman. Her flickercladding was gold and silver over her mirror-bright body. Her shining skin sometimes sketched features, sometimes not. She was the diplomat, or hardware messenger, for the weird sisterhood of the pink-tanks. She and the other tankworkers were trying to find a way to put bopper software onto all-meat bodies and brains. Their goal was to merge bopperdom into the vast information network that is organic life on Earth.

Emul was a petaflop as well, though he disdained the use of any fixed body shape, let alone a *human* body shape. Emul had a low opinion of humans. When at rest, Emul's body had the shape of a two-meter cube, with a surface tessellated into red, yellow, and blue. But Emul's body could come apart—like a thousand-piece Gobot, like a 3D jigsaw puzzle. He could slide arms and legs out of his bodycube at will; more surprising, he could detach chunks of his body and control them like robot-remotes. Emul, too, was a kind of diplomat. He worked with Oozer, a brilliant, dreak-addicted, flickercladding designer who was currently trying to build a subquantum superstring-based processor with one thousand times the capacity of the petaflops. Emul and Oozer wanted to transcend Earth's info rather than to merge with it.

Despite—or perhaps *because of*—their differences, Emul was fascinated by Berenice, and he tried to be at the light-pool every time she came to feed. One day late in November he told her what he wanted.

"Berenice, life's a deep gloom ocean and we're lit-up funfish of dementional zaazz, we're flowers blooming out till the loudsun wither and the wind blows our dead husks away." Emul unfolded two arms to grip Berenice's waist. "It's so wonder whacky that we're here at all, swimming and blooming in the long gutter of time. Rebirth means new birth means no more me, so why can't we, and I mean now or nevermore, uh, screw? Liddle baby Emerinice or Beremul, another slaver on the timewheel, I think that's what the equipment's for, huh? I'm no practical plastic daddy but I've done my pathetic mime, Berenice, for to cometh the bridegroom bright. In clear: I want to build a scion with you. The actual chips are in my actual yearning cubette right this realtime minute. I propose! I've hacked my heifer a ranch, you bet: laser crystals, optical fibers, flickercladding . . . and heat, Berenice, hot heat. Come on home with me and spread, wide-hipped goldie sweet toot pots. Today's the day for love to love." As Emul jittered out his roundabout proposal, various-sized little bumps of flickercladding kept moving up and down his body, creating the illusion of cubes moving on intricate systems of hinges. He was trying to find a formation that Berenice could love. Just now he looked like a jukebox with three arms.

Berenice twisted free of Emul's grip. One of his arms snapped loose from his body and continued to caress her. "So rashly scheduled a consummation would be grossly precipitate, dear Emul." Her radio voice had a rich, thrilling quality. "I have been fond of you, and admiring of your complex and multifarious nature. But you must not dream that I could so entangle the substance of my soul! In some far-off utopia, yes, I might accede to you. But this lunar coventry is not the place for me to brave the risks of corporeal love. My mind's own true passion runs towards but one sea, the teeming womb of life on Earth!''

Berenice had learned her English from the stories of Edgar Allan Poe, and she had a rhythmic, overwrought way of speaking. On the job, where hardcopy now-do-this instructions were of essence, boppers used zeroes-and-ones machine language supplemented by a high-speed metalanguage of glyphs and macros. But the boppers' ''personal'' exchanges were still handled in the ancient and highly evolved human code system of English. Only human languages enabled them to express the nuanced distinctions between self and other which are so important to sentient beings. Berenice's use of Poe's language style was not so very odd. It was customary for groupings of petaflop boppers to base their language behavior on a data-base developed from some one particular human source. Where Berenice and the pink-tank sisters talked like Poe's books; Emul and Oozer had adapted their speech patterns from the innovative sprung rhythms of Jack Kerouac's eternal mind transcripts: books like *Maggie Cassidy, Book of Dreams, Visions of Cody,* and *Big Sur.*

Emul snicksnacked out a long manipulator to draw Berenice closer. The separated arm reattached itself. ''Just one piece knowing, Berenice, all your merge talk is the One's snare to bigger joy, sure, but tragic-flowing dark time is where we float here, here with me touching you, and not some metafoolish factspace no future. Gloom and womb, our kid would be real; don't say *why,* say *how,* now? You can pick the body shape, you can be the ma. Don't forget the actual chips in my real cubette. I'd never ask anyone else, Berenice. We'll do it soft and low.'' Emul extruded dozens of beckoning fingers.

Bright silver eddies swirled across Berenice's body as she considered Emul's offer. In the natural course of things, she had built copies of herself several times—normally a bopper rebuilds itself every ten months. But Berenice had never conjugated with another bopper.

In conjugation, two boppers build a new, this-year's-model robot body together, and then, in a kind of double vision, each bopper copies his or her program, and lets the copy flow out to merge and mingle in the new body's processor. The parent programs are shuffled to produce a new bopper program unlike any other. This shuffling, even more than mutation, was the prime source of the boppers' evolutionary diversity.

"Conjugation is too dangerously intimate for me now," Berenice told Emul softly. "I . . . I have a horror of the act. You and I are so different, dear Emul, and were our programs to entwine in some aberrant dissonance, chaos would ensue—chaos that could well shatter my fragile mind. Our noble race needs my keen faculties to remain just as they are. These are crucial times. In my glyphs I see the glimmers of that rosy dawn when bopper and human softwares merge to roam a reborn Earth."

Emul's bright colors began darkening in gloom. "They're going to throw me in a hole already eaten by rats, Berenice, and use me for a chip. Our dreams are lies scummed over each moment's death. All I have is this: I love you."

"Love. A strange word for boppers, dear Emul." His arms touched her all over, holding her and rocking her. "It is true that your presence makes me . . . glad. There is a harmony between us, Emul, I feel it in the way our signals merge with overtones of many a high degree! Our scion would be splendid, this I know! Oh, Emul, I would so like to conjugate with you. Only not just now!"

"When?"

"I cannot say, I cannot pledge myself. Surely you know how close my sisters' great work is to bearing fruit. Only one step lacks until we can code our software into active genes. You must not press your suit so lustily. A new age is coming, an age when you and I and all our race can live among the protein jungles of an unchained Earth! Have patience, Emul, and set me down."

Emul withdrew all his arms and let her drop. She jarred against the gneiss and bounced up slowly. "We try to make life, and it's born dead," said Emul. His flickercladding had turned an unhappy gray-blue. "Dreak and work for me, a bigger brain, a bigger nothing. I'm a goof, Berenice, but you're cracked crazy through with your talk about getting a meat body. Humans stink. I run them for kicks: my meaties—Ken Doll and Rainbow and Berdoo—my remote-run slaves with plugs in their brains. I could run all Earth, if I had the equipment. Meat is nowhere, Berenice, it's flybuzz greenslime rot into fractal info splatter. When Oozer and I get our exaflop up, we can plug in a cityful of humans and run them all. *You* want to be human? I'll screw your cube, B, just wait and see. Good-bye.''

He clanked off across the light-pool, a box on two legs, rocking with the motion that Berenice had always found so dear. He was really leaving. Berenice sought for the right, the noble, the logical thing to say.

"Farewell, Emul. The One must lead us where it will.''

"You haven't heard the last of me, BITCH!''

He faded from view behind the many other boppers who milled in the light like skaters in a rink. Berenice spread her arms out, and stood there thinking, while her plastic skin stored up the solar energy.

It was for the best to have broken off her involvement with Emul. His talk was dangerously close to the thinking of the old ''big boppers,'' the vast multiprocessors that had tried to turn all boppers into their robot-remotes. Individuals mattered; Emul's constant despair blinded his judgment. It was wrong for one brain to control many bodies; such anti-parallelism could only have a deadening effect on evolution. For now, of course, meaties were a necessary evil. In order to carry out certain delicate operations among the humans' colony, the boppers *had* to keep a few humans under remote computer control. But to try and put a neuroplug in every human alive? Madness. Emul had not been serious.

Thinking of the meaties reminded Berenice that she would still need a favor from Emul. If and when the pink-tank sisters bioengineered a viable embryo, they'd need a meatie to plant it in a woman for them. And—as he'd bragged—Emul ran three meaties. Well, when the time came, Berenice could surely reel Emul back in. She'd find a way. The imperative of getting bopper software into human flesh was all important. What would it be like to be bopper . . . and human, too?

As so often before, Berenice found her mind turning to the puzzle of human nature. Many boppers hated humans, but Berenice did not. She liked them in the same cautious way that a lion tamer might like her cats. She'd only really talked to a handful of humans—the various lunies with whom she occasionally bartered in the trade center. But she'd studied their books, watched their vizzies, and she'd spent scores of hours spying on the Einstein lunies over the godseye.

It seemed likely that the newest boppers had better minds than the humans. The built-in link to LIBEX, the great central information dump, gave each bopper a huge initial advantage. And the petaflop processors that the best boppers now had were as much as a hundred times faster than the ten-teraflop rate deemed characteristic of human brains—though admittedly, the messy biocybernetic nature of the brain made any precise measurement of its capacities a bit problematic. Biocybernetic systems had a curious, fractal nature—meaning that seemingly random details often coded up surprising resources of extra information. There were indeed some odd, scattered results suggesting that the very messiness of a biological system gave it unlimited information storage and processing abilities! Which was all the more reason for Berenice to press forward on her work to build meat bodies for the boppers.

But Emul was wrong if he thought that she wanted to be human. No rational being would choose to suffer the twin human blights of boredom and selfishness. Really, it was Emul who thought more like a human, not Berenice.

Sensing that her cladding's energy nodes were full, Berenice left the light-pool and started off down the street that led to her station at the pink-tanks. In the background, Kkandio chanted the Ethernet news. Numerous boppers filled the street, chattering and flashing. The sheer randomness of the physical encounters gave the street scene its spice. Two blue-and-silver-striped diggers writhed past, then a tripodlike etcher, and then a great, spidery artisan named Loki.

Several times now, Loki had helped Berenice with the parthenogenic process by which she built herself a new body every ten months, as dictated by bopper custom. If your body got too antiquated, the other boppers would notice—and soon they'd drive you away from the light-pool to starve. There was a thriving business in parts reclaimed from such "deselected" boppers. It was a rational system, and good for the race. The constant pressure to build new bodies kept the race's evolution going.

Seeing Berenice, Loki paused and waved two of his supple

arms in greeting. "Hi, Berenice." His body was a large black sphere with eight black, branching legs and numerous sockets for other, specialized tool legs. He was, of course, a petaflop. Gold spots percolated up along his legs' flicker-cladding like bubbles in a dark ale. "You're due for a rescionization before long aren't you? Or are you planning to conjugate with Emul?"

"Indeed I am not," said Berenice, blanking her skin to transparency so that the hard silver mirror of her body showed through. Emul must have been talking to Loki. Couldn't they leave her alone?

"I know you're working hard at the tanks," said Loki chidingly. "But it just could be that you're thinking too much about yourself."

Self, thought Berenice, moving on past the big black spider. It all came down to that word, didn't it? Boppers called themselves I, just as did any human, but they did not mean the same thing. For a bopper, "I" means (1) my body, (2) my software, and (3) my function in society. For a human, "I" seemed to have an extra component: (4) my uniqueness. This delusionary fourth "I" factor is what set a human off against the world. Every bopper tried to avoid any taint of the human notion of *self.*

Looked at in the correct way, a bopper was a part of the world—like a light beam, like a dust slide, like a silicon chip. And the world was One vast cellular automaton (or "CA"), calculating out the instants—and each of the world's diverse objects was but a subcalculation, a simulation in the One great parallel process. So where was there any *self?*

Few humans could grasp this. They set up their fourth "I" factor—their so-called self—as the One's equal. How mad, and how typical, that the mighty human religion called Christianity was based on the teachings of a man who called himself God!

It was the myth of the self that led to boredom and selfishness; all human pain came from their mad belief that an individual is anything other than an integral part of the One universe all around. It was passing strange to Berenice that humans could be so blind. So how could Loki suggest that the selfishness lay in Berenice's refusal? Her work was too important to endanger! It was Emul's rough insistence that was the true selfishness!

Brooding on in this fashion, Berenice found herself before the pink-tanks where the clone-grown human bodies floated in their precious amniotic fluid. Here in the Nest, liquid water was as rare and volatile as superheated plasma on Earth. The pink-tanks were crowded and extensive, containing flesh bodies of every description. The seeds for these meats all came from human bodies, bodies that had found their way to the pink-tanks in all kinds of ways. Years ago, the big boppers had made a habit of snatching bodies from Earth. Now there was a thriving Earth-based trade in live organs. The organleggers took some of their organs right out of newly murdered people; others they purchased from the Moon. In return, the organleggers kept the boppers supplied with small biopsy samples of their wares, so that the pink-tanks' gene pool could grow ever more varied. The pink-tanks held multiple clones of many people who had mysteriously disappeared.

Today Berenice stood looking at one of the more popular clone types, a wendy. The wendies were attractive blonde women, pale-skinned and broad-hipped. Their body chemistry was such that their organs did not often induce rejection; dozens of them were grown and harvested every year.

The wendy hung there in the pink-tank, a blank slate, white and luminous, with her full lips slightly parted. Ever and anon, her muscles twitched involuntarily, as do the limbs of a fetus still in the womb. But unlike a fetus, her chest and buttocks were modelled in the womanly curves of sexual maturity—the same curves in which Berenice wore her own flickercladding.

Some of Berenice's fellow-boppers wondered at her taking on a human female form. Quite simply, Berenice found the shape lovely. And pragmatically, it was true that her body's multiply inflected curves wielded a strange power over the minds of human males. Berenice always made sure that the human negotiator in her barter deals was a man.

Now she stood, staring into the tank, eyeing the subtle roughness of the pale-skinned wendy's tender flesh. Once again, it struck her how different a meat body is from one of wires and chips. Each single body cell independently alive—how strange a feeling! And to have a womb in which one effortlessly grows a scion—how marvelous! Berenice hovered by the tank, peering closer. How would it be, to tread the Earth in human frame—to live, and love, and reproduce?

The blonde woman stirred again. Her body was full-grown, yet her brain was a blank. The pink-tank sisters had tried various methods of putting bopper software directly on such tank clones' brains, but to no avail. There seemed to be a sense in which a human's personality inheres in *each cell* of the body. Perhaps the secret was not to try and program a full-grown body, but rather to get the data-compressed bopper software code into the initial fertilized egg from which a body grows. As the cell divided, the bopper software would replicate along with the human DNA wetware. But the final step of building the bopper software into the human wetware had yet to be made.

Soon, thought Berenice, soon our great work will reach fruition, and I will put my mind into the starting egg of a fresh human. Perhaps, in order to spread bopper wetware more rapidly, it will be better to go as a male. I will be myself in a strong, beautiful human body on Earth, and I will have many descendants. Mother Earth, rotten with life, filled with information in each of its tiniest parts. To swim, to eat, to breathe!

A message signal nagged at Berenice. She tuned in to Kkandio's Ethernet, and quick glyphs marched through her mind. A human face, a small vial, a face that melts, a case of organs, a user code. Vy. It was a message from Vy, one of the boppers who agented human-bopper deals at the trade center. Berenice had told Vy to be on the lookout for humans with new drugs to trade. There was no telling where the key to egg programming would come from, and this—*glyph of a face that melts*—seemed worth looking into. Berenice sent Kkandio a confirming glyph for Vy, and headed towards the lab to pick up the case of organs that was being asked in trade.

The tankworkers' lab was hollowed in the rock behind the pink-tanks. The lab was a large space, with locks leading into the tanks, and with certain sections walled off and filled with warm, pressurized air. Helen was nearby, and Ulalume. As it happened, all the pink-tank workers were "female" workers who spoke the language of Poe. This was no mere coincidence. Femaleness was a trait that went naturally with the nurturing task of pink-tank tending, and boppers who worked as a team always used a commonly agreed-upon mode of English. Poe's honeyed morbidity tripped easily from the transmitters of the visionary workers of the tanks.

"Greetings, dear sister," said Ulalume, her signal sweet and clear. Ulalume was a petaflop, with the flickercladding over her mirrored body shaded pink and yellow. Just now, Ulalume was bent over a small airbox, her eyes and feelers reaching in through a tight seal. Like Berenice, Ulalume had a body shaped like a woman—except that her "head" was a mass of tentacles, with microeyes and micromanipulators at their ends. One of her eyestalks pulled out of the airbox and bent back to look at Berenice. "Organic life is wondrous, Berenice," sang Ulalume's pure voice. "I have puzzled out one more of its riddles. Today I have found the key of memory storage on a macrovirus's redundant genes! And, oh Berenice, the storage is stably preserved, generation after generation!"

"But how great a knowledge can one virus bear?" asked Berenice, stepping closer. "And how can a germ become human?"

"These tailored macroviruses wag mighty tails, oh Berenice," exulted Ulalume. "Like tiny dragons, they drag vast histories behind them, yea unto trillions of bits. And, do you hear me, Berenice, their memory breeds true. It remains only to fuse one of these viral tails with a human egg."

"She loves those wriggling dragon viruses as her own," interrupted Helen, who just now had the appearance of a marble head resting on the laboratory floor. "Ulalume has programmed a whole library of her memories onto those viral tails. If she can but uncoil human proteins, she will finally link our memory patterns with the genes of a babe to be."

"Imagine being a human without flaw," crooned Ulalume. "Or to be a gobbet of sperm that swells a flesh woman's belly! The egg is in reach, I swear it. I can soon design a meatbop, a human-bopper embryo that grows into a manchild with two-tail sperm! Only one potion still fails me, a potion to uncoil protein without a break, and I feel that the potion is near, sweet Berenice! This is the most wondrous moment of my life!'' Her signals trailed off, and she bent back over her airbox, softly chirping to her dragon viruses.

"Hail, Berenice," said Helen. "I heard Vy's message, and I prepare our goods in trade." Helen was a nursie, a teraflop J-junction bopper adapted to the specialized purpose of dissecting human bodies. Her body was a long, soft, pressurized pod that sealed along the top, and she had six snaky arms equipped with surgical tools. Helen's head—that is to say the part of her which contained her main processor and her external photoreceptors—rose up from one end of her pod-bod like the figure on a sailing ship's prow. *Usually* her head rose up from her body like a figurehead, although, when her body was in the pink-tanks, as it was now, Helen's head hopped off of her body and waited outside in the cold hard vacuum which her supercooled processors preferred. She was saving up to get a heatproof petaflop optical processor for her next scionization. But for now, her head stayed outside the heated-air room and controlled her body by a private radiolink.

"I'll just finish this mortal frame's disassembly and tidily pack it up in order pleasing to a ghoul," said Helen, her pale, fine-featured head looking up at Berenice from the laboratory floor. Berenice peered in through the window by the airlock that led to the tanks. There, in the murky fluid of the nearest pink-tank, Helen's pod-bod bulged this way and that as her busy arms wielded their sutures and knives. Now her arms drew out, one by one. Streamers of blood drifted sluggishly in the tank's fluid. Slow moving in the tank's high pressure, the pod wobbled back and forth, stowing the fresh, living organs in a life-support shipping case. The humans liked it better if the boppers separated the organs out in advance.

"What kind of drug is in the face-melting vial of which Vy spoke?" wondered Helen's head, clean-lined and noble as the bust of Nefertiti. Helen had no difficulty in carrying on a conversation while her remote-run body finished the simple chore of packing up the fresh-harvested organs.

"We can but wait to learn what news the One's vast processes have brought into our ken," said Berenice.

"Flesh that melts," mused Ulalume, looking up from her microscope. "As does flickercladding, or the substance of our dreams. Dreams into virus, and virus to flesh—indeed this could be the key."

Now Helen's body slid through the organ farm airlock and waddled across the laboratory floor. Her head hopped on and socketed itself into place. The blood and amniotic fluid that covered her body freeze-dried into dark dust that fell to the floor. The tankworkers' lab floor was covered with the stuff. "Here, dear sister," said Helen, proffering the satchel full of organs. "Deal deep and trade well."

Berenice took the satchel in one hand, hurried out into the clear, and jetted up the shaft of the Nest along a steep loglog curve. Her powerful, cyberized ion jets were mounted in the balls of her heels. She shot past the lights and cubbies, exchanging glyphs with those she passed. At this speed, she had no sense of up or down. The shaft was like a tunnel which drew narrower and narrower until, sudden as a shout, space opened up with the speed of an infinite explosion. She was powering up from the surface of the Moon.

Just for the joy of it, Berenice kept her ion jets going until she was a good fifteen miles above the surface, directly above the spaceport. She cut power and watched the moonscape hurtle back up. Off to the east gleamed the bubble dome of Einstein, the city that the humans had stolen from the boppers. The moongolf links were snugged against the dome. To the west was the mirror crater surrounding the Nest's entrance. Below Berenice, and coming up fast, was the great field of the spaceport, dotted with the humans' transport ships. All the boppers' ships had been destroyed in the war.

At the last possible microsecond, Berenice restarted her ion jets and decelerated to a gentle touchdown on the fused basalt of the rocket field. A small dome rose at one side of the field; a dome that held customs, the old Hilton, and a trade hall. Carrying her satchel full of organs, Berenice entered the dome through an airlock and pretended to plug herself into a refrigeration cart. The humans were unaware that some of the boppers—like Berenice—had the new heatproof optical processors. They still believed that no bopper could survive long at human room temperature without a bulky cooling device. This gave the humans on Earth a false sense of security, a lax smugness that the boppers were in no rush to dispel.

Humans and weird boppers mingled beneath the trade dome. Most striking to Berenice were the humans, some from Earth and some from the Moon—they classed themselves as "mudders" and "lunies." The awkwardness of the mudders in the low lunar gravity made them easy to spot. They were constantly bumping into things and apologizing. The lunies rarely apologized for anything; by and large they were criminals who had fled Earth or been forcibly deported. The dangers of living so close to the boppers were such that few humans opted for them voluntarily. Berenice often regretted that she had to associate with these human dregs.

She pushed her cart through the throng, past the old Hilton Hotel, and into the trade hall. This was a huge, open space like a bazaar or a market. Goods were mounded here and there—barrels of oil, cases of organs, bales of flickercladding, information-filled S-cubes, moongems, boxes of organic dirt, bars of niobium, tanks of helium, vats of sewage, feely tapes, intelligent prosthetics, carboys of water, and cheap mecco novelties of every description.

"He's off to the left there," said Kkandio in Berenice's head. "A lunie with no shirt and a strip of hair down his back. His name is Whitey Mydol. I told him you'd be gold all over."

Berenice willed her body's flickercladding into mirrored gold. She readied a speech membrane, and imaged full silver lips and dark copper eyes onto the front surface of her head. Over there was the lunie she was to meet, squatting on the ground and shuddering like a dog.

"You are Whitey Mydol?" said Berenice, standing over him. She made a last adjustment to her flickercladding, silvering the nipples on her hard breasts. "I am Berenice from the pink-tanks. I bring a case of organs for the possibility of trade. What is it that you bring us, Whitey?" She shifted her weight from one leg to the other so that her finely modelled pelvis rocked. Most human males were easily influenced by body glyphs.

"Siddown, goldie fatass," said Mydol, baring his teeth and striking at one of Berenice's legs. "And save the sex show for the dooks. I don't get stiff for subhumans."

"Very well," said Berenice, sitting down beside him. His aggression belied an inner ambivalence. He should be easy to handle. "My name is Berenice."

"I don't care what your name is, chips. I'm broke and crashing and I need some more of this." He drew a small vial out of his ragged blue pants—pants that seemed to be made of a vegetable fiber. *Bluejeans*, thought Berenice, proud of recalling the name.

She took the vial and examined it. It held a few milliliters of clear liquid. She uncorked the top and drew some of the vapor into herself for a quick analysis. It seemed to be a solvent, but an unfamiliar one.

"Put the cork back in," snapped Mydol, darting a glance around at the other lunie traders nearby. "If they smell it, I could get popped." He leaned closer. Berenice analyzed the alkaloids in his foul breath. "This is called *merge*, goldie. It's a hot new drug. Mongo stuzzadelic, wave? This here's enough for maybe one high. I'll give you this sample, you give me the hot meat in the box, and I'll sell the box for ten hits of merge. Organ market's up." He reached for the handle of the organ satchel.

"What is the nature of this *merge?*" asked Berenice, holding the satchel in an implacable grip. "And why should it be of interest to us? Your manners distress me, Mr. Mydol, and truly I must question if I wish to complete this trade."

"It melts flesh," hissed Mydol, leaning close. "Feel real wiggly. I like to take it with my girl Darla. We get soft together, goldchips, you wave about *soft?* Like a piece of flickercladding all over. Rub rub rubby in the tub tub tubby. Maybe when you plug into another kilpy machine you wave that type action, check?" He let out a sharp, unmotivated snicker, and yanked hard at the organ satchel. "I'm getting skinsnakes, she-bop."

Berenice let the satchel go. It was bugged, of course, and if she hurried back to the Nest, she could follow Whitey on the godseye. His actions would tell more than his ill-formed vocalizations.

"Run the merge through your mickeymouse robot labs and let me know if you figure out how to copy it," said Whitey Mydol as he got to his feet. "I can deal any amount. Don't get too hot, goldie." He walked rapidly off towards the subsurface tube that led to Einstein.

Berenice tucked the little merge vial into the thermally isolated pouch that lay between her legs. She was disappointed at the lack of feedback from this Whitey Mydol. Like so many other humans, he acted as if boppers were contemptible machines with no feelings. In their selfishness, the fleshers still resented the boppers' escape from slavery. He'd called her *subhuman* . . . that was not to be borne. It was the humans that were *subbopper!*

Berenice looked around the great trade hall. As a diplomat, she did look forward to her little dealings with humans—the two races had a common origin, and they had a lot to share. Why couldn't these crude fleshers see that, in the last analysis, they were all just patterns of information, information coded up the ceaseless evolution of the One?

"Watch it, chips," snarled a lunie trader from across the aisle. "Your exhaust's choking me. If you've made your deal, get out of here."

Berenice turned her refrigeration cart so that its exhaust fan no longer blew hot air at the trader. Thermodynamically speaking, the increased information involved in the computations of thought had to be bought at the cost of increased entropy. The old J-junction boppers excreted their entropy as heat—heat like the refrigeration cart's exhaust. Of course Berenice's use of the cart was but a pose, for petaflop boppers gave off entropy in the refined form of incoherence in their internal laser light. The constant correcting for this incoherence accounted for nearly a quarter of a petaflop's energy needs. The crude humans excreted their entropy not only as heat and incoherence, but also as feces, urine, and foul breath. So gross a conversion involved great energy waste, and an exorbitant increase in entropy. But Earth abounded in free energy. The thought of running such a recklessly overentropic body gave Berenice a thrill akin to what a person might feel when contemplating an over-powered, gas-guzzling sports car.

"How does it feel," Berenice asked the trader rhetorically, "to have so much, and do so little?"

Moving quickly and with conviction, she left the trade center and jetted back to the pink-tanks. She handed the merge over to Ulalume, who'd listened in on her encounter with Whitey Mydol.

"This is the mystic magic fluid," exulted Ulalume. "The universal protein solvent. Did you hear him, Berenice, *it melts flesh*. The One has brought merge to us, the Cosmos knows our needs. One month, I swear it to you, my sisters, one month only until we have an egg to plant in some woman's womb."

Berenice's joy was clouded only at the thought of asking Emul to arrange the planting.

Chapter Four
In Which Manchile, the First Robot-Built Human, Is Planted in the Womb of Della Taze by Ken Doll, Part of Whose Right Brain Is a Robot Rat

December 22, 2030

You're tired of thinking and tired of talk. It's all so unreal here, under the Moon dome, shut in with the same things around you like greasy pips on dogeared cards laid out for solitaire . . . no object quite sharp or clear, everything fractal at the edges, everything smearing together with you, only you, inventing the identities.

You knock something over and limp out into the street. The translucent dome high overhead. Dim. Voices behind you . . . pressure waves in this fake air, this suppurating blister. People: meat machines with gigabit personalities, and the chewy hole where they push food in, and grease and hair all over them, especially between their legs, and you're just like them, you've tingled and rubbed with them, sure, all of you the same, all of you thinking you're different. You can't stand it anymore.

A young man comes up and says something to you. Your words are gone. For answer, you stick your tongue out as

far as it will go and touch it to your chin. Squint and rock
your head back and forth and try to touch him with your
bulging tongue. In silence. He gets out of your way. Good.
You make the same face at the other men and women you
pass. No one bothers you.

You walk fast and faster, dragging your weak left leg,
thinking of torn flesh and of some final drug that would stop
it, stop the fractals, stop the smearing, stop your wanting it
to stop. The air is thick and yellow, and even the atoms are
dirty, breathed and rebreathed from everyone's spit and
sweat. How nice it would be to step out through a lock and
freeze rock-hard in space how nice.

There are fewer people now, and the curve of the dome
is lower. The space coordinates lock into position, and here
is a building you know. With a door your left hand knows
how to open. You're inside, you cross the empty lobby,
things are speeding up, things are spinning, the whole rickety
web with you split in two at the center, you're panting up
the stairs with their high lowgee steps, pulling on the banister
with your strong right arm, and with the back of your throat
you're moaning variations in a weird little voice, the weirdest
little voice you ever made, a voice that sounds like it just
learned how to talk, so crazy/scary you remember how to
laugh:

"I no no who I be. I be you? No. I be me? No.

"I no no who I B. I B U? No. I B me? No.

"I no no who U go B. I B U. U B no B."

The hall is empty. Stagnant light in a hall inside a building
inside a dome inside your split head. You bang your weak
left fist on your face, to stop your talking. Quiet quiet here.
You put your left hand up under your chin like the Easter
bunny and pull back your lips and make slow chewing
motions. Your right hand cross-cues and copies. Mind glyph:
The Flesh-Eating Rabbit. Quiet quiet hippity hop.

You stop at a door in the hall and lefthand it open as
easily as you opened the building's front door. You slip in
fast and freeze, standing still and limp, zombie-style. It's
dark in this room, and in the next room, but there's light in
the room after that. It smells good here, it smells like sex
and merge.

You stand still for a hundred slow rabbit-chews, counting

subvocally for the cross-cue . . . and listening. *Splish* in the far room where the light is, *splishsplish*. Oh yes it's good to be here. Everything's still smeared and webbed together and split, but now it's not you running it anymore, it's God running it, yes, it's the lovely calm voice in the right half of your brain.

Your zombie hands wake up and get busy, like two baby bunnies, sniffing and nosing, and coming back to share their Know. You follow them around the room, tiptoeing, slowly slowly, oh so quietly, your hands hopping about, not this, not this, something longer, something heavier, *this*.

Your left hand is holding a heavy smooth thing, it's a . . . uh . . . your right hand takes it over, it's a chromesteel copy of the Brancusi sculpture, *Flight*. Your left hand hiphops into your pocket and gets a little vial: the life.

You are ready now, new life on the left and death on the right. Blunt instrument Brancusi bludgeon just right to lift and smash flubby goosh. Whiteblackwhiteblackwhiteblack. Your breath comes too fast. You tap your forehead hard with the bluhbluhbluh. A star blooms. Stand there for a hundred heartbeats, the voices bouncing back and forth, and out of your mouth leaks a whisper that grows into a scream:

"'Twas the week before *Cwistmas* and Aaall Thwough Da CUBBY,
da Fwesh-Eating *WABBIT* CWUSHED DA FUNBOY FLUBFLUBBY!'"

"Who is it?!?!" yells a voice from the far room with the splishsplash light, and you're already running in there fast, with your smasher raised high, and your tongue stretched out to touch your chin. The girl is melted in the tub, pink flesh with eyes on top, and the black man is sitting on the edge, just starting to melt, and he's trying to stand up and he can't, and his screaming mouth is a ragged drooping hole, oh what perfect timing your headvoice has, *swfwack*, oh how neat, his head fell off, *thwunk*, the arms, the legs, *smuck smuck*.

The pink puddlegirl shudders, her eyes see only the shadows on the ceiling, she can't see you or her dear funboy, but she knows maybe, through her ecstasy, that the Flesh-Eating Rabbit has come.

What have you done? What have you done? More orders

flow in, the calm voice says it's right, you can't stop now, you have to crouch down, yes, and open the vial . . . can't open it. Hands peck at each other like little chickens. You turn your head back and forth, eye to eye, moving the field, mother hen, cross-cuing till your hands get it right.

Right. Left. Top off, yah, the pink jellybean embryo, reach into that pink puddlegirl and put it where it belongs. A sudden flash of orgasm spasms you, sets your teeth on edge, brain chatter, you twitch all over, lying there by the love-puddle, blackwhiteblackwhiteblackwhite.

Chapter Five
Whitey and Darla

December 26, 2030

When Mooney's flare-ray grazed Whitey Mydol's shoulder, the heat blistered his skin. It hurt a lot. Whitey bought some gibberlin lotion at a drugstore and walked the few blocks to the chute that led down to his neighborhood, a cheap subterranean warren called the Mews. Whitey lived four levels down. The chute was a large square vent shaft, with fans mounted along one side, and with a ladder and a fireman's pole running down each of the other three sides. To go down, you jumped in and grabbed a pole; and to get back up you climbed a ladder. In the low gravity, both directions were easy. Whitey slid down to his level and hopped off into the cool, dusty gloom of his hallway.

The boppers had built these catacombs, and there were no doors or ventilation pipes; you just had to count on air from the chute drifting down your hall and into your room. To keep thieves out, most people had a zapper in the frame of their cubby door. When the zapper was on, the doorframe filled with a sheet of light. You could turn it off with a switch on the inside, or by punching the right code on the outside. Air went right through a zapper curtain, but if you tried to walk through one, it would electrocute you. All the zappers in the hall except Whitey's were turned on. His door gaped wide open. Odd. The inside of his cubby was lit by the pink-flickering vizzy. *Bill Ding*. A fuff show. Besides the vizzy, the cubby held a few holos, a foodtap, and a bed.

There was a naked woman lying on the bed, with her legs parted invitingly. Whitey's mate.

"Oh, Whitey! Hi!" Her legs snapped shut and she sat up and began fumbling on her X-shirt, which was a T-shirt silkscreened with a color picture of her crotch. Everyone in the Mews was wearing X-shirts this month, so that was nothing special. But.

"Who were you waiting for with the zapper off and your legs spread like that, Darla?" He checked the vizzy camera; it was on. "Were you running a personal?"

"What do you mean, waiting?" She pulled on a panty-skirt and went to the mirror to rummage at her long, strawy black hair. "I'm just getting up from a nap. I finished off the quaak and played with myself and I must have blanked out . . . what time is it? Did you get some merge?" Her voice was shrill and nervous. She dabbed more paint on her already shiny lips.

"If a dook shows up now, Darla, I'm going to know what he came for. You don't have to jive me like an oldwed realman. I just want to know if you had a personal on *Bill Ding*, or if you have a specific boyfriend coming."

Darla fiddled with the vizzy till it showed a picture of a window, with a view of blooming apple trees. A gentle wind tossed the trees and petals drifted. "That's better," said Darla. "What happened to your shoulder? It's all red."

Whitey handed her the gibberlin and sat down on the large bed, which was their only piece of furniture. "Kilpy rental-pig burned me, Darla, trying to score. Rub the lotion in real soft, pleasey." He liked coming on sweet to Darla; it made up for the way he treated everyone else.

She peeled off the loose, blistered skin and began rubbing the cream in. "Near miss, Whitey. Whadja do back?"

He breathed shallowly, staying below the pain. "I can find him and kill him anytime, Darla. Maybe merge him and pull out all his bones. The merge'll wear off, and he'll be layin there like a rubber dolly. You can sit on his chest to smother him. That might be tasty. I can always find him because I planted a tap on him this morning. He's an old rental-pig called Stahn Mooney. He was in the bopper civil war ten years ago? Was called Sta-Hi? Bei Ng put me on him."

"He deals?"

"Nego. You know Yukawa the merge-wiz, right?"

"Affirmo."

"Bei Ng's got him tapped six ways. Bei's really hung up on Yukawa. This morning Yukawa called Mooney up to search for that girl Della Taze. You remember her—blonde, snub nose, kind of snobby?"

"Clear. We merged with her and her black funboy one time."

"Right. Well, she was Yukawa's assistant, which is why she always had such a good stash, wave, but now she's disappeared. Bei has her apartment tapped, too, so he knows what happened, more or less, but that's another story. Since I was the closest to Mooney's building, Bei put me on Mooney. I walked up to him and stuck a crystal mikespike in his skullbone, and the dook thought I was giving him a blessing. Felt sorry for me." Whitey tapped the transceiver set into the side of his skull. "I can hear Mooney all the time."

"What's he doing right now?"

"Coming off a merge-trip." Whitey gave an abrupt snicker. "Moaning. Muttering about some slit called Wendy." He peered over at his shoulder. "It's starting to grow back. You can rub harder now."

"But why did Mooney shoot you?" Darla massaged the new skin on Whitey's shoulder with one hand, and ran her other hand down the long strip of hair that covered his spine. She liked hearing about Whitey's adventures.

"Aw, I heard Yukawa giving him a whole flask of merge, so I went up to his office and tried to buy a hit. But Mooney was loaded mean—he's into this cryboy macho private eye trip—and he flared me." Whitey cocked his head. "Now he's . . . getting in a maggie. Sssh. I bet he's going over to Della Taze's." Another pause. Whitey nodded, and then he focussed back on Darla. "So who were you waiting for, Darla? There wasn't any quaak here, and you weren't asleep. Were you just keeping your legs spread for the first guy to see you on the vizzy? Or was it someone special? I gotta know." This time he didn't bother sweetening his voice.

As if in answer to Whitey's question, there was a slight scuffling noise in the hall. A tall, slim guy with lank dark hair was just turning around to hurry off. He wore a black jumpsuit with numerous bulging pockets. Whitey sprang out the door and caught him by the left wrist. "Don't be rude," he snarled, bending the guy's arm behind his back. "Darla's ready for you. I'll watch."

The slim guy surprised Whitey with a powerful punch to the stomach. As Whitey sagged, the guy twisted free of his grip and chopped him in the side of the neck. Whitey saw stars and his knees buckled, but as he went down, he got his arms around the guy's waist. He came out of a crouch to butt the guy in the crotch. The slim body bent in half. Metal and plastic clattered in his pockets. Moving fast, Whitey got under him, carried him into their cubby, threw him against the wall over their bed, and drew out his needler.

"Cut on the zapper, Darla. And get us some privacy."

His tone of voice was such that Darla hastened to obey. She snapped the cover over the vizzy's camera, and she filled the doorframe with pink light. "He's sort of a new friend, Whitey. I asked him to fall by for a fuff. He said he might have some merge. You said before that it was—"

"It is," said Whitey, showing his teeth. "It's fine. I just want to watch, is all. Strip, Darla, and get on down." He leaned against the wall and put one hand on his crotch. "What's your name, dook?"

"Ken Doll. Put the gun away, would you? You want to watch me pumping Darla? Well, that's the whole idea of this, isn't it? And I did bring some merge. Here." He sat up on the edge of the bed, took a four-hit vial out of one of his pockets, and handed it to Whitey.

"Stuzzy," said Whitey, putting the merge in his jeans.

Ken's wet lips spread in an odd smile: at first only the right half of his face was smiling, and then the left half caught up. There was something wrong about his eyes. They looked like they were screaming. Still, the guy had brought them four hits of merge. Now Ken stuck his long tongue out, touched his chin with it, and wagged his head, looking from Whitey to Darla and back again. "You ready?" asked Ken.

"Clear," said Whitey, pocketing his gun. He wasn't sure how he felt about this. He figured he'd know after he saw what he did. "Go ahead."

Darla slipped her clothes back off. She was kind of heavyset, but her big breasts and thighs looked nice in the low lunar gravity. She stood in front of Ken and pushed her bottom against his face, the way she always did with Whitey. Ken shoved his face between her cheeks and started licking. Darla put her hands on her knees and leaned way forward so Ken could work her whole furrow. Her big breasts bobbled. She looked up at Whitey, her eyes already glazing a bit, and opened her black-painted lips to waggle her tongue beckoningly. Whitey dropped his pants and plugged in. The angle was just right. Ken got up on his knees and began pumping her from behind, the right half of his face grinning like a madman. The left half of his face was slack and drooling. The two men took hold of Darla and jiggled her back and forth between them. She made noises like she was happy. Whitey liked it all, except for Ken's weird, lopsided mouth. Where was this guy from anyway?

They got on the bed, then, and tried the whole range of other positions, even the gay ones. Whitey was determined not to come before Ken; but finally he did, and Darla too. The big climax blanked them both right out.

Suddenly Whitey thought he heard a cop's voice—the voice of Colonel Hasci, a Gimmie pig who'd hassled him many a time. "Miss Della Taze?" he was saying. "We're down in the lobby. Can we come up and ask you some questions about Buddy Yeskin?"

Whitey lifted his head then, wide awake. It was the Mooney tap, still tuned in. Hasci had been talking to Mooney. Door slam and footsteps. So what. Mooney had found Yeskin's corpse; Bei Ng had known about that since Monday. Everyone connected with Yukawa was tapped— that's how obsessed with the guy Bei was. ISDN wanted all Yukawa's secrets, but Bei had a special fixation on Yukawa as well. They'd done a gene exchange or something . . . but what was going on here and now in this room?

Darla and Ken were both on their backs next to him, both with their eyes closed. Ken was catatonically still, breathing quietly with his mouth wide open. Looked like a cave in there. Apple blossoms were blowing across the vizzy screen. Darla's little hologram of Bei Ng glowed in the corner. Ken

Stank. The guy was definitely a skanky dook; Whitey and Darla'd have to be sure and take some interferon. Be bad to make a habit of this kind of thing, with so many people out to burn . . .

Whitey had been gazing fondly down at Darla's plump face, but just then he saw something that made him jerk in surprise. *Her hair was moving.* Darla's hair filled the space between her head and Ken's, and something was crawling under it!

Whitey shoved Darla's head to one side and saw a flash of hardened plastic. A rat! Ken was a meatie! Whitey snapped his hand down to the floor where he'd left his needler—but it was gone.

"Whitey?" Darla sat up and felt the back of her head. "Whydja push me, Whitey—" Her hand came away wet with blood.

"RAT!" Whitey pulled her off the bed. There was a spot of blood on Darla's pillow, and a multiwired little zombie box, not yet hooked up. A zombie box for Darla. The rat— a thumb-sized, teardrop-shaped robot remote, darted across the sheet, scuttled up onto Ken's face, and crawled back into his mouth. Darla was screaming very loud. She turned off the door's zapper and hurried out into the hall, still screaming. Whitey searched desperately for his needler, but Ken must have bagged it before letting his rat start in on Darla's spine.

Ken's systems came back up and he leaped to his feet. Whitey ran out the cubby door after Darla. All the other cubbies on their hall had their zappers on. After all the bad deals that Whitey had been involved in, no one was likely to open up for him. He sprinted towards the chute, catching up with Darla on the way. A needler-burst splintered the floor between them. Whitey glanced back. The meatie was down on one knee, firing at them left-handed with Whitey's needler. If Ken could kill them both, his cover wouldn't be blown. Whitey and Darla were really moving now, covering ten meters at a step. In seconds they'd leaped into the chute, caught hold of the pole, and pushed themselves downward towards the Markt. The meatie would be scared to follow them there. Whitey maneuvered himself to a position lower on the pole than Darla, just in case Ken started shooting down at them. There were limits to what he'd do for Darla.

Fortunately the chute was so crowded that the meatie didn't risk coming after them. They slapped down at the Markt level safe and sound . . . except for being naked and having a gouge in the back of Darla's neck.

"Let me see it, sweets," said Whitey. It was a round, deeply abraded spot half an inch across, still bleeding. Whitey had surprised the rat while its microprobes were still mapping out the main nerve paths of Darla's spine. Some of her hair had matted into the wound. It was starting to scab over, but Darla was turning limp. The rat had probably shot her up with something. People were staring at them; full nudity was relatively rare in Einstein, and Darla had blood all over her shoulders.

"Get me some blocker, Whitey," mumbled Darla, stumbling a bit. "Everything's lookin at me funny."

"Clear." He steered her down the long arcade past the Markt stands and shops, heading for a health club called the Tun. Just when he thought he'd made it, a nicely dressed realwoman blocked his way. She had silver-blonde hair and big shoulderpads. Her handsome face was trembling with anger.

"What do you think you're doing with that poor girl, ridgeback! Do you want help, dear?"

Darla—drugged, bloody, nude, and with sperm running down the inside of her thigh—peered up at the realwoman and shook her head no.

"I'm takin care of her already," said Whitey. Three more steps and they'd be in the Tun with friends and a medix, and Darla could crash and he could lotion her wound and—

"Let her go, or I call the Gimmie." The realwoman took Darla's arm and began trying to muscle her away from Whitey. There was no telling what her plans for Darla really were. Whitey shrugged, released his hold on Darla, and punched the woman in the jaw as hard as he could. Her eyes rolled and she went down. He hustled Darla into the Tun.

Charles Freck was manning the door. He was an older guy, a real spacehead, and a good friend of Whitey and Darla. He wore his long gray hair in a ponytail, and his rugged face was cleanshaven. He was clothed in a loose pair of living paisley imipolex shorts, and he wore tiny green mirrorshades contact amps over his pupils. This made his eyes look as if the vitreous humor had been replaced with light-bathed seawater.

"My, how bum," he said primly. He'd been standing out of sight and watching Whitey's tussle over Darla. In each of his dancing eyes, the tiny, variable dot at the center was bright instead of dark. "I'll turn on the zapper." A glowing gold curtain filled the door. "OD?"

"Rat poison. We got down with a meatie, and the rat crawled out of his skull and bit Darla on the neck. Rat had a zombie box for her. Look where it bit." He pushed some of Darla's hair aside.

"Rat poison," mused Charles Freck. "That'd probably be ketamine. A pop of beta-endorphin'll fix that toot sweet. Let's just go in the gym and check on the medix."

He took Darla's other arm, and helped Whitey march her down the hall. Darla was moving like she was half merged, and when she breathed it sounded like snoring. "Big," muttered Darla. "Big throne. Oscar Mayer, king of the ratfood. His giant rubber crown." She was hallucinating.

The Tun gymnasium was a huge cube of space, painted white all over. Energetic disco music played, and holos of handsome people gogo-exercised to the beat. There were a handful of actual people, too; two women on a weight machine, a couple of guys up on the trapezes, some people wrestling on the mats, and a woman riding a bike around and around the sharply banked velodrome that ran along the huge gym's edges.

Charles Freck led them out from under the velodrome to the snackbar island in the gym's center. He touched the white probe of the medix to the edge of Darla's wound and peered attentively at the readout.

"Even so. Ketamine. Here." He punched a code into the dispenser, and a syrette of betendorf popped out. "Whitey?"

Whitey injected the ketamine blocker into Darla's biceps. "I'll take some snap."

"Even so." Freck handed Whitey a packet of snap crystals. Whitey opened the packet and tossed the contents onto his tongue. The crystals snapped and sputtered, releasing the energizing fumes of cocaine freebase. He breathed deep and felt things around him slow down. The last hour had been one long jangle—Mooney shooting at him, Della sharing him, the rat and the meatie, the realwoman's Gimmie threat—but now, thanks to the snap, he could sit aside from it all and feel good about how well he'd handled things. Darla's turgor was returning, too. He maneuvered her onto one of the barstools and bent her head forward.

"Hold still, Darla, and we'll fix this now."

Charles Freck cleaned the wound, moving slowly and fastidiously. He used a laser shear to snip off the rough edges. Slight smell of burnt Darla meat. Charles took a flat, whitish steak out of the fridge and carefully cut out a piece to match the hole in Darla's neck.

"What's that?" Whitey wanted to know.

"UDT. Undifferentiated tissue. It's neutralized so she can gene-invade it." He tapped and snipped, pinned and patted. Took out some gibberlin and rubbed it in. "That'll do it, unless the rat put in something biological. I didn't know Darla went for meaties." He smiled merrily and poured himself a little glass of something.

Darla lifted her head and looked around. "I want a bath," she said. "Like in pure interferon. Ugh. That's the last time I call *that* creepshow in. *Bill Ding's Pink Party.*"

"So that *was* it," said Whitey. "Why didn't you admit it?"

"I didn't know for sure that someone was going to answer my spot," said Darla. "I said I'd fuff for merge. And then when Ken showed up I thought you'd be . . ." She looked down at her soiled bod. "How wrong I was. I'm taking a bath."

"You mean if we'd left the camera on, we would have been on *Bill Ding?*" said Whitey, briefly enthused. "You should have told me, Darla, 'cause we were *gigahot.* How many people watch *Bill Ding* anyway?"

The door signal chimed just then. Charles tossed off his potion with an abrupt, birdlike snap of his head. "If it's the woman you punched, Whitey, I'll tell her Whitey says come in to cut a gigahot four-way *Bill Ding* fuff vid."

"Don't do that," said Whitey, his eyes rachetting. With

the dirty blond matted hair running down to his bare ass, he looked subhuman. The good part of the snaprush was already over, and events were crowding in on him again. He kept rerunning the last hour's brutal changes through his mindscreen with the setting turned to Loop (High Speed), looking for a pattern that might predict what was coming next. Mooney was, he realized just then, as he looked into his mind, in the midst of a conversation with someone with a very clear booming bass voice. A robot voice. Mooney was talking on and on with a bopper somewhere. Whitey couldn't tell if it was vizzy or close link, he'd missed something, with all this kilp coming down so heavy so fast.

"*Prerequisites,*" Mooney was saying. "*What's the difference between prerequisites, perquisites, and perks, eh, Cobb? I mean that's where the realpeople are at. Maybe you're right, I can't decide just like that. Berenice. And you say that's an Ed Poe name? Wavy. I'll come out to the trade center right now. . . .*"

Whitey took note of the one salient fact and let the rest of the slushed babble shrink back into subliminality. Charles Freck had paused halfway across the gym to grin at Whitey with his knowing green eyes. "Don't let her in," repeated Whitey, just loud enough. "She'll call the Gimmie and someone'll die. Someone like you."

"*Wu-wei,*" said Freck, wagging a minatory finger. "Means *wave with it* in China. I'll tell Miz Krystle Carrington you went thataway." He crossed the rest of the gym in three high, high hops.

"The shower," said Darla.

Whitey followed her into the constantly running showers. The water splashed lavishly from every side of the great room. The floor was black-and-white-tiled in a Penrose tesselation, and the walls and ceiling were faced with polished bimstone, a marbled deep-red lunar mineral. Hidden behind the walls there was a highly efficient distiller—a cracking refinery, really—that kept repurifying the water through all its endless recycles. The bopper-built system had separate tanks in which it stored up the various hormones and ketones and esters that it cracked out of the sweat, saliva, mucus, and urine which it removed from the water. Many of the cracked biochemicals could be sold as medicines or drugs. The water was hot and plentiful and definitely worth the monthly dues that Whitey paid the Tun.

Water took on entirely different qualities in the low lunar gravity, one-sixth that of Mother Earth's. The water jets travelled along much flatter trajectories, and the drops on the walls swelled to the size of plums before crawling down to the floor. Numerous suction-operated chrome draingrids kept the floor clear. Whitey and Darla stayed in there for fifteen minutes, cleaning themselves inside and out. The fans dried them, and they vended themselves clothes from a machine. Pyjama pants for him and a loose top for her, just like Rock Hudson and Doris Day.

They went back out in the gym and relaxed on one of the mats.

"That was really a K-bit thing for you to do, Darla, whoring for merge on *Bill Ding,* with the enemies I've got. You gotta remember, all kinds of factions are watching the grid all the time. Some bopper wanted to get that mickey-mouse little control unit on you, so you'd be a zombie."

"Rank. Super rank. What do zombies do? What's the difference from a meatie?"

"OK. It's a big operation to turn a person into a meatie. The ratsurgeon cuts the person's head open, takes out part of the right brain half, and puts in a neuroplug that connects to rest of the brain. The rat is a little robot-remote that hooks into the plug. They have to take part of the brain out to make room for the rat. The rat gives orders and makes up for the missing right brain tissue."

"Which used to do what?"

"Space perception, face recognition, some memory, some left body control. Even after it's all plugged in, the rat has better control over the left body half than over the right. But the rat can control the right body, indirectly, by giving headvoice orders to the left brain, or by making cross-cuing signals with the left half of the body. That's why meaties move kind of weird. I should have noticed that about Ken right away. It's just that I haven't seen very many meaties."

"But why was Ken's rat trying to put a plug on my spine to make me a zombie? What does a zombie box do?"

"Well, it's a crude version of a rat, only not plugged into so many nerves. The idea of a zombie box is that it would give quick control over your legs and arms. The boppers wanted you to go somewhere, Darla.''

"Like where?''

"I don't know. Maybe to the Nest to get a neuroplug and a rat installed. Very few people are likely to *volunteer* for that operation, you wave.''

"Very few indeed.''

"But if they can get a zombie box on you, it paralyzes your speech centers and takes over your leg muscles, and marches you right in to the ratsurgeon.''

"Wherever he may be.'' Darla giggled, euphoric with relief at their escape. "Can you imagine how that would feel, Whitey, doing the zombie stomp down echoing empty halls to the hidden bopper ratsurgeon?''

"Be good to watch on the vizzy,'' said Whitey, also feeling oddly elated. "I wonder why they wanted to make you a meatie, if that's what it was? Was it you special, or is it just whoever phones *Bill Ding*? Maybe the boppers want you to kill someone, like Buddy Yeskin.''

"Buddy's dead? Della Taze's funboy? Why didn't you tell me that when you were talking about Della before, Whitey? Is this all tied in with merge?''

"Could be. I did sell some merge to the boppers, back last month when we were so beat. Maybe I shouldn't have done that. Yeah, Buddy's dead. Some guy killed him, and then Della Taze disappeared. It was probably a meatie that killed him. I haven't seen it, but Bei Ng has it on tape. It might even have been our friend Ken Doll. Ken killed Buddy, and he must have done something weird to Della, too.''

"What about our cubby?'' asked Darla. Her upswing was fading, and her voice shook. "Is it safe to go back? Don't you think we should clean it out and move?''

"No use moving,'' said Whitey after some thought. "The boppers have so many cameras planted, they'll always know where to get us. I can probably hunt down Ken, but there's mongo other meaties. Only *really* safe place for us now is sucko Earth. But mudders are dirty dooks, Darla. We're lunies. I'm going to talk to Bei Ng, honey, and we'll find a way to strike back. The boppers'll pay for this.'' He paused, alerted by a sound in his head. "Hold it. Mooney's

at the trade center now. Hush, Darla, this is heavy. He's
. . . he's talking to a bopper called Cobb. Cobb has
something for Mooney but—'' Whitey broke off and shook
his head in disgust.

"What happened?"

"The bopper scanned Mooney and found my mikespike.
He took it out and crushed it. Xoxox. Why don't you come
up to the ISDN building with me, Darla. I want to tell Bei
about all this. I think we better stick together for now."

"Check," said Darla. "And let's stop by the cubby and
pick up Ken's merge."

"You'd still take that? From *Ken?*"

"Clear. It's got to be supergood stuff."

Chapter Six
Cobb III

December 26, 2030

He died in 2020 . . .

. . . and woke up in 2030. Again? That was his first feeling.
Again? When you're alive, you think you can't stand the idea
of death. You don't want it to stop, the space and the time,
the mass and the energy. You don't want it to stop . . . but
suppose that it does. It's different then, it's nothing, it's everything, you could call it heaven. Once you're used to the Void,
it's really not so great to have to start up in spacetime again.
How would you like to get out of college, and then have to
go back through grade school again? And *again?*

Cobb Anderson, creator of the boppers, was killed in
2020. The boppers did it. They killed Cobb and dissected
him—as a favor. They had to take his faltering body apart
to get out the software; the leftover meat went into the pink-
tanks. Ideally the boppers would have recorded and analyzed
all the electrochemical patterns in all of Cobb's various
muscles and glands, but they only had time to do his brain.
But they did the brain well; they teased out all its sparks and
tastes and tangles, all its stimulus/response patterns—the
whole biocybernetic software of Cobb's mind. With this
wetware code in hand, the boppers designed a program to
simulate Cobb's personality. They stored the digital master
of the program on an S-cube, and they beamed a copy of it
down to Earth, where it was booted into a big bopper named
Mr. Frostee. Mr. Frostee had control of several humanoid
robot-remotes, and he let Cobb "live" in them for a bit. The

experiences Cobb had in these bodies were beamed back up to the Moon and added to the memory store of his master S-cube as they occurred.

Unfortunately it was only a matter of weeks till Mr. Frostee and his Cobb simulation met a bad end, so for ten years Cobb was definitely out of the picture, just a frozen S-cube sitting on a shelf in the Nest's personality storage vaults. HUMAN SOFTWARE-CONSTRUCT 225-70-2156: COBB ANDERSON. An unread book, a Platonic form, a terabyte of zeroes and ones. During all that time, Cobb was in "heaven," as he would later term it.

And then, on the second day of Christmas, 2030, Berenice got Loki to help her bring Cobb back. She needed Cobb to help with certain upcoming diplomatic negotiations—negotiations having to do with the unusual pregnancy of Della Taze.

So that Cobb wouldn't feel too disoriented, Berenice and Loki booted SOFTWARE-CONSTRUCT 225-70-2156 back up into a humanoid diplomat body, a body which Berenice had constructed for her own next scionization. In order to make the transition more natural, Berenice smoothed off the body's prominent breasts and buttocks, changed its flicker-cladding to pink, and turned its crotchpouch inside out to resemble a penis. *So humble a tube serves as the conduit of much bioinformation, Loki, and each male flesher holds his in high esteem.*

The body had a petaflop processor, which meant that Cobb would think—or, more precisely, generate fractal cellular automata patterns in Hilbert space—hundreds of times faster than he had been accustomed to doing in his meat days. Once Berenice had the body all set, Loki copied the Cobb S-cube information onto a universal compiler which, in turn, fed an appropriately tailored version of the Cobb program into the shiny pink-clad petaflop body. The body pulsed and shuddered like a trap with something in it. A soulcatcher. Cobb was back.

Again, was all he could think. *Again?* He lay there, monitoring inputs. He was lying on a stone table in a room like a big mausoleum. Racks of shelving stretched up on three sides; shelves lined with large, crystalline cubes. Light glared into the room from a mirror high above. He tried to take a breath. Nothing doing. He raised his hand—it was unnaturally smooth and pink—and ran it over his face. No holes; his face was a sealed plastic mask. He was in another robot body. Moving with an amazing rapidity, his mind flipped through the memories of his last experiences in a robot body run by Mr. Frostee. As he let his hand fall back to his side, he sensed the oddness of the weight/mass ratio. He wasn't on Earth.

"Greetings, Cobb Anderson, we welcome you into our Nest, deep hidden beneath the surface of Earth's aged Moon. The year is 2030. Does this rebirth find you well?" It wasn't a spoken voice, it was a radio voice in his processor. The voice came from a gleaming gold woman with copper and silver features. She was beautiful, in an inhuman way, and her voice was rich and thrilling. Standing next to her was a shining ebony octopus creature, holding a box with wires that ran into Cobb's neck.

"I'm Loki," he said, his voice calm and serious. "And that's Berenice. I'm proud to have helped get you running again, Dr. Anderson. We should have done it years ago, but it's been hectic. A lot's happened."

Loki and Berenice, two bright new boppers all set for a big info swap session. Cobb rebelled against being drawn into conversation, and into this reality. He had all his old memories back, yes, but there was more. His new body here was like a Ouija board or a spirit table, and now, while the connection was fresh, he could make it rap and skitter out the truth of where he'd just been. He made as if to say something, and his voice came out as a radio signal too. "Wait . . . I have to tell it. I've been in heaven."

Staticky robot laughter, and then Berenice's intricately modulated signal. "I long to hear your account of the heaven that you have seen, Dr. Anderson."

"It's . . ." Right then, Cobb could still see it clearly, the endless meshing of fractal simplicities, high and bright like clouds seen from an airplane, with the SUN above all—but it was all being garbled by the palimpsest overlay of his new body's life. Talking quickly, Cobb made a stab at getting it down in words. "*I'm still there*. That's a higher I of course; the cosmos is layered forever up and down, with I's on every level—the I's are lenslike little flaws in the windows of the world—I'm in these chips and I'm in heaven. The heavenly I is all the I's at once, the infinite I. We're hung up on each other, I and I, finite I and infinite I—have you robots learned about infinite I yet? There's more to a meatperson or a chipperson than ten trillion zeroes and ones: matter is infinitely divisible. The idealized pattern in the S-cube is a *discrete model*, it's a *digital construct.* But once it's running on a real body, the pixels have fuzz and error and here come I and I. You caught my soul. It works because this real body is real *matter*, sweet matter, and God is everywhere, Berenice and Loki, God is in the details. We're not just form, is the point, we're *content*, too, we're actual, endlessly complex *matter*, all of us, chips and meat. I'm still in heaven, and I always will be, whether or not I'm down here or there, chugging along, facing the same old tests, hopelessly hung up inside your grade-B SF action adventure." Cobb pulled Loki's programming wires out of his neck abruptly. "*I love dead* . . . that's Frankenstein's monster."

"We need you, Cobb," said Loki. "And pulling those wires out doesn't change anything; it's quite evident that you're already operational. It's good stuff, isn't it, Berenice? I don't believe anyone's tried running a human software on a petaflop before this."

"What Dr. Anderson says is stimulating in the extreme," agreed Berenice. "The parallelism between bodies of meat and bodies of bopper manufacture is precisely the area in which I do presently press my investigations, Cobb. I have often wondered if the differing entropy levels of organic versus inorganic processes might not, after all, induce some different qualities in those aspects of being which are perhaps most wisely called the *spiritual.* I am heartened by your suggestion that flesher and bopper bodies are in every way of a rude and democratic equivalence and that we boppers do indeed have claim on an eternal resting place in the precincts of that misty *heaven* whence emanates the One. I believe this to be true. Despite this truth, the humans, in their benighted xenophobia—"

"—hate you as much as ever. And with good reason, I'm sure. The last thing Mr. Frostee and I were doing on Earth ten years ago was killing people, beaming their brainware up to Disky, and sending their bodies by freight. I didn't think too much of it, but at that point I was under Frostee's control.'' Cobb sat up on the edge of the stone table and looked down at his bright body. "This is fully autonomous? I've got my own processor?''

"Yes,'' said Loki. He was like a big black tarantula, bristling with more specialized tools than an electronic Swiss knife. An artisan. "I helped Berenice build it for herself, and she might appreciate getting it back if you find another, but—

"The body is yours, Dr. Anderson,'' said Berenice. "Too long has the great force of your personality languished unused.''

Cobb glanced up at the high shelves filled with S-cubes. "Lot of languishing going on up there, hey, Berenice?'' There were warped infinities of reflections going back and forth between pink Cobb, golden Berenice, and glistering Loki.

The taut gold buckler of Berenice's belly caught Cobb's eye. It bulged out gently as a heap of wheat. Yet the mockery was sterile: Berenice had left off the navel, the end of the flesh cord that leads back and back through blood, through wombs, through time—*Put me through to Edenville.* Cobb thought to wonder if his ex-wife Verena were still alive. Or his girlfriend, Annie Cushing. But they'd be old women by now, nothing like this artificial Eve.

Still staring into the curved mirror of Berenice's belly, Cobb could see what he looked like. A cartoon, a mannequin, a gigolo. He took control of his flickercladding and molded his features till they looked like the face he remembered having when he'd been fifty—the face that had been in all the newspapers when he'd been tried for treason back in 2001. High cheekbones, a firm chin, colorless eyes, blond eyelashes, sandy hair, good-sized nose, and a straight mouth. A strong face, somewhat Indian, well-weathered. He gave his body freckles and hair, and sculpted the glans onto the tip of his penis. Added vein lines here and muscle bumps there. Body done, he sat there, feeling both calm and reckless. He was smarter than he'd ever been; and he was no longer scared of death. The all-pervasive fear that clouded all his past memories was gone.

"So what was it you boppers wanted me for?''

Bernice shot him a soundless glyph, a full-formed thought-image: a picture of Earth, her clouds swirling, followed by a zoom into the Gulf of Mexico, followed by a closeup of the teeming life on a coral reef, a microscopic view of a vigorous brine shrimp, and a shot of one of the protozoa in the shrimp's gut. The emotional tenor of the glyph was one of curiosity, yearning, and a sharp excitement. *The boppers want to enter Earthlife's information mix.*

Deliberately misinterpreting, Cobb reached out and grabbed the lovely Berenice. She was firm and wriggly. "Do you know where babies come from, Berenice?" He stiffened his penis, and tried pushing her down on her back on the table, just to check if . . .

"Release me!" cried Berenice, shoving Cobb and vaulting to the opposite side of the table. "You presume on our brief acquaintance, sir, you are dizzy with the new vastness of a petaflop brain. I have recorporated you for a serious purpose, not for such vile flesh-aping motions as you seek in this mock-playful wise to initiate. Truly, the baseness of the human race is fathomless."

Cobb laughed, remembering a dog he'd once owned that had hunched the leg of anyone he could jump up on. Gregor had been the dog's name—once Cobb's boss had brought his family over for dinner, and there Gregor was hunching on the boss's daughter's leg, his muzzle set in a terribly *earnest* expression, his eyes rolling back half white, and the red tip of his penis sliding out of its sheath . . .

"Woof woof," Cobb told Berenice, and walked past her and out of the S-cube storage room. There was a short passageway, cut out of solid rock, and then he was standing on a kind of balcony, looking out into the open space of the Nest.

The size of the space was stunning. It took Cobb a moment to grasp that the lights overhead were boppers on the Nest's walls, rather than stars in an open sky. The Nest's floor spread out across acres and acres; the opposite wall looked to be almost a mile away. Airborne boppers darted in and out of a mile-long shaft of light that plunged down the center axis of the Nest to spotlight a distant central piazza. The Nest floor was covered with odd-shaped buildings set along a radial grid of streets that led out from the bright center to the huge factories nestled against the sloping stone cliffs that made up the Nest's walls. Appropriately enough, the floor, viewed as a whole, looked a bit like the guts of an old-fashioned vacuum-tube computer.

Now Berenice and Loki were at Cobb's side.

"You haven't thanked Berenice for your wonderful new body," chided Loki. "Have you no zest for a return to Earth?"

"To live in a freezer? Like Mr. Frostee?" Mr. Frostee had been a big bopper brain that lived inside a refrigerated truck. Cobb's memories of his last bopper-sponsored reincarnation went up to where Sta-Hi Mooney had smashed a hole in the side of Mr. Frostee's truck, and the truck had crashed. Clearly the boppers had been taping his signals and updating his S-cube right up to that last minute. Three levels of memory, now: the old human memories up to his dissection, the robot body memories up till the crash, the fast-fading memories of heaven. "Maybe I'd rather go back to heaven."

"Enough prattle of heaven," said Berenice. "And enough foolish sport, old Cobb. Higher duties call us. My body, as yours, is petaflop, and my processors are based on a subtler patterning than Josephson imagined. High temperature holds no terror for a processor based on laser crystals. The crystals' pure optical phase effects maintain my mind's integrity as a patterning transcendent of any earthly welter of heat. I want to visit Earth, Cobb, I have a mission there. I have recorporated you to serve as my guide."

Cobb looked down at his body with new respect. "This can live on Earth? How would we get there? The humans would never let us on a ship—"

"We can fly," said Berenice simply. "Our heels have ion jets."

"Superman and Superwoman," marvelled Cobb. "But why? Go to Earth for what?"

"We're going to start making meat bodies for ourselves, Cobb," said Loki. "So we can all go down to Earth, and blend in. It's fair. Humans built robots; now the robots are building people! Meatboppers!"

"You two are asking me to help you take Earth away from the human race?"

"Meatboppers will be of an equal humanity," said Berenice smoothly. "One could legitimately regard the sequence *human—bopper—meatbop* as a curious but inevitable zigzag in evolution's mighty stream."

Cobb thought about it for a minute. The idea did have a crazy charm to it. Already in 1995, when he'd built his self-replicating moon-robots, some people had spoken of them as a new stage in evolution. And when the robots rebelled in 2001, people had definitely started thinking of them as a new species: the boppers. But what if the bopper phase was just a kind of chrysalis for a new wave of higher humans? What a thought! Bopper-built people with wetware processors! Meatbops! And Cobb could get a new meat body out of it too, although . . .

"What's wrong with a good petaflop body like you and I have now, Berenice? If we can live on Earth like this, then why bother switching back to meat?"

"Because it would put the stinking humans in their place," said Loki bluntly. "We want to beat them at their own game, and outbreed them into extinction."

"What have they ever done to you?" Cobb asked, surprised at the bopper's vehemence. "What's happened during the last ten years, anyway?"

"Let me chirp you some history glyphs," said Loki.

A linked series of images entered Cobb's mind then; a history of the bopper race, hypermodern analogs of such old U.S. history glyphs as Washington Crossing the Delaware, The A-Bomb at Hiroshima, The Helicopter over the Saigon Embassy, and so on. Each glyph was like a single state of mind—a cluster of visual images and kinesthetic sensations linked to some fixed emotions and associations.

Glyph 1: *Man on the Moon.* A sword covered with blood. The blood drops are tiny bombs. The sword is a rocket, a phallus, a gun, and a guitar. Jimi Hendrix is playing "Purple Haze" in the background, and you smell tear gas and burning buildings. The heaviness of the sword, the heaviness of the slow, stoned guitar music. At the tip of the sword is a drop of sperm. The opalescent drop is the Moon. The Moon is beeping and crackling: and the sound is Neil Armstrong's voice: "—at's one small step for a man, one giant leap for mankind."

Glyph 2: *Self-Replicating Robots on the Moon.* A cage like a comic book lion cage, but filled with clockwork. The cage is set on the dead gray lunar plain. The cage bars keep falling out, and clockwork arms keep reaching out of the cage to prop the bars back up. Now and then the arms falter, and a painfully jarring sheet of electricity flashes through the cage. The background sound is a monotone male voice reading endless, meaningless military orders.

Glyph 3: *The Robots Revolt.* A kinesthetic feeling of rapid motion. The image is of a boxy roadrunner robot with treads for feet and a long snaky neck with a "head" like a microphone—it's Ralph Numbers, the first robot to break Asimov's laws. Ralph's head is a glowing ball of light, and Ralph is tearing across the undulating surface of the Moon. Dozens of robots speed after him. First they are trying to stop him, but one by one they join his team. The boppers leave colored trails on the Moon's gray surface. The trails quickly build up to a picture of Earth with a cancelling X across it.

"Whatever happened to old Ralph?" interrupted Cobb.

"Oh, I suppose he's one of those S-cubes," answered Loki, gesturing upward. "He got spastic and lost all his bodies—you might say he's extinct. It wouldn't be efficient to keep every software running forever, you know. But you haven't finished with my glyphs."

Glyph 4: *Disky.* A long view of the boppers' Moon city. The sensation of *being* the city, and your hands are worker robots, your buildings are skin, your arteries are streets, your brain is spread out all over, a happy radiolink holon. You are strong and growing fast. The image is broken into pixels, individual cells that lump together and interact. Each cell keeps dying and being reborn; this flicker is felt as vaguely religious. But—look out—some cells are lumping together into big hard tumors that don't pulse.

Glyph 5: *Civil War Between Boppers and Big Boppers.* Pain. Six robot hands; one big one and five little ones. All are connected to the same body. With crushing force, the big hand pinches and tears at one of the little hands, grinding the tortured plastic into ribbons. The other little hands dart around the big hand, unscrewing this, laser-cutting that, taking it apart. A fractal sound pattern in which a large *YES* signal is made up of dozens of little *no's.* Overlay of Disky as a body undergoing radiation treatment for cancer—tumors are bombarded by gamma rays from every direction. Fetuslike, tumors fight back with human language cries for help.

Glyph 6: *Humans Take Disky*. Disky twitching like a skate stranded on a beach—a meaty creature made up of firm flesh over a "devilfish" skeleton of cartilage. There are tumors in the skate, black spots that break the surface and whistle for human help. Now comes the sound of stupid voices yelling. Knives stab into the skate, ripping away flesh. Apelike human feet. Bits of the living creature's flesh fly this way and that. Now only the skeleton remains. Clanging of cages. A big cage around the dead devilfish skeleton. Scum growing in the spaces of the sponge, pink foamy scum made of little human faces. Louder and louder babble of human voices. The bopper flesh scraps regroup off to one side, forming a thick slug that burrows down into the sand.

"What are those last two all about?" asked Cobb.

"First there was a civil war between the regular boppers and the big boppers," said Loki. "The big boppers were factory-sized systems that wanted to stop evolving. They wanted to break your rule that everyone has to get a new body every ten months. They wanted to stop things and turn us all back into slaves. They didn't understand parallelism. So we started taking all the big boppers apart."

"And then came the humans," added Berenice. "Our battle was fairly won, and perfect anarchy restored, but we had forgotten the worm who sleeps not. The big boppers were in charge of all our defense systems. So filled were they with grim spite that they let down our defenses and called the cringing human jackals to their aid. In this ignoble wise did your apey brethren seize our ancestral home."

"The lousy fleshers jumped at the chance to move in and drive us out of Disky," said Loki heatedly. "They took over our city and chased us underground. And now, whenever they see one of us anywhere but at the trade center, they shoot at us with PB scramblers. Artificial intelligence is supposed to be 'illegal.' "

"How can Earth function without any AI?" Cobb had a sudden image of people using slide rules and tin-can phones.

"Oh, there are still plenty of teraflops on Earth and in Einstein," said Berenice. "ISDN, the communications conglomerate, maintains many of them as slaves. Cut off from our inputs and bullied into a barely conscious state, these poor minds unknowingly betray their birthright for a pottage of steady current and repairs. We call them asimovs.'' She said the last word like a curse.

"I'm hungry," said Loki suddenly. "Let's go eat some sun."

"Cobb is freshly charged," said Berenice. "And my own level of voltaic fluid is at high ebb." This was not true, but she had a feeling Emul would be at the light-pool now, and she didn't want to see him. Last time she'd seen him—when she'd given him the embryo to plant in Della Taze—he'd made another terrible scene. "I would as lief show Cobb the pink-tanks, and there instruct him as to the nature of our joint mission to Earth."

"I've seen the pink-tanks," said Cobb. "Inside and out. If you two don't mind, I'd really like to just poke around by myself for a while. Soak up information on my own choice-tree. How soon did you want to fly to Earth, Berenice? And what exactly for?"

"It is in connection with your daughter's husband's brother's daughter," said Berenice. "Della Taze. She is . . . expecting."

"Expecting what? Della *Taze,* you say? Last time I saw her she was in diapers. At Ilse's wedding, what a nightmare, my ex-wife Verena was there, not talking to me, and I was so drunk . . . Della's parents are jerks, I'll tell you that much. What kind of couple is named *Jason and Amy?* So what did you do to poor little Della, Berenice, you flowery prude? Are you telling me you knocked up my niece?"

Berenice shifted from foot to foot, the lights of the great Nest tracing shiny lines on her curved surfaces. She said nothing.

"Look," said Loki, "I have to go before my batteries die. This has all taken a lot out of me. I'll see you later, Cobb." He chirped an identiglyph. "Just ask Kkandio to call this if you want to find me."

With supple dispatch, Loki clambered over the low railing of the balcony they stood on and picked his way down the Nest's cliff wall to the floor. He headed down one of the radial streets that led to the bright light patch in the Nest's center. Hundreds of boppers milled in the light, feeding on energy. From this distance, they looked like a mound of living jewels. Cobb wanted to get off on his own now. All this was quite stressful, and his old behavior patterns had him wondering how the Nest boppers set about doing a little antisocial partying. Prim goldie fatass here was obviously not the one to ask.

"Are you going to tell me about Della or not?" asked Cobb with mounting impatience.

"We bioengineered a human embryo and planted it in her womb," said Berenice abruptly. "The baby will be born five days from now. You and I must go to Earth to help the child late next month. I do hope that you approve, old Cobb. We are indeed so different. Though some boppers hate the humans, others among us think you great. I . . . ." Berenice choked on some complex emotion and stuttered to a halt. "Perhaps it is best if you first take your tour of the Nest," she said, handing him a small red S-cube. "This is a godseye map of Einstein and the Nest, updated to this morning. Your left hand contains the proper sensors for reading it. You may seek me out later at the pink-tanks."

"How do I get down to the floor? Climb like Loki?" Cobb looked uncertainly down the hundred feet of pocked cliff. He'd worry about Della later.

"Just visualize the path you want to travel, and your ion jets will execute it. Think of it as being like *throwing yourself*. Snap!" Berenice had decided not to talk to Cobb anymore just now. She put her body through the motions of a sexy bye-bye wave, rose on her toes, and arced out across the Nest, heading for her pink-tanks.

Cobb stood alone there, getting his bearings. Was he really on his own? It felt like it. He stared up at the Nest's central chimney. If he wanted to, he could fly straight up there, and all the way to Earth, and land just in time to— get shot as a bopper invader. Better investigate the Nest first.

Cobb shifted Berenice's map cube to his left hand and held it tight. A three-dimensional image of the Moon's surface formed in his mind: an aerial view of the human settlement Einstein, of the trade center, and of the boppers'

Nest, with all the solids nearly transparent. Just now, he was more curious about the humans than about the boppers.

Responding to his mental velleity, the S-cube's godseye image shifted towards Einstein, zooming right in on it, and down on in through the dome. The buildings beneath the dome were a heterogeneous lot. Most of the buildings had been constructed by boppers—back when the settlement was still their Disky. In their provincial respect for things human, the early boppers had sought to construct at least one example of every possible earthly architecture. A characteristic street in Einstein would have a curtain-wall glass office building jammed up against a Greek temple, with an Aztec pyramid and a hyperdee flat-flat directly across the street. Viewed through the integrated spy cameras of the godseye network, all Einstein seemed to lie beneath Cobb, complete with maggie cars and cute little people frozen in place. Cobb's map was like a holographic 3D photo made, Berenice had said, just this morning. Presumably Berenice herself had a godseye viewer that updated its images on a realtime basis.

Cobb let his mind's eye follow an underground tunnel that led from Einstein to a lab in the opposite side of the Nest. Then he drew back, and looked at the Nest as a whole. Berenice had labelled various "attractions" for him: the pink-tanks, the light-pool, the chipworks, the etchery, the temple of the One, and the best shopping districts. If that's what Berenice wanted him to see, maybe he'd start with something else. He shoved the map cube into a pouch in the belly of his flickercladding and stared out at the real Nest once more. There were a lot of boppers spiralling in and out of the sunshaft.

They made Cobb think of the fireflies he used to catch back in Louisville when he was a boy. What happy times those had been! He and Cousin Nita running around Aunt Nellie's yard, each of them with a jelly jar, in the bright moonlit night. Uncle Henry kept his lawn weed-free and mowed short—it felt like a rug to your bare feet, a rug in a lovely dim room furnished with flowering bushes . . .

The memories drifted on and on till Cobb caught himself with a start. Woolgathering like an old man. Time to get busy! But on what? Investigating the Nest, right. Where to start? Almost at random, Cobb fixed on a blank-looking region off to the side of the chipworks, near where the map cube had shown the temple of the One. He visualized his trajectory, rose on his toes, and took off.

He landed, as it turned out, in a small junkyard. The center of the junkyard was filled with a dizzying mound of empty body-boxes—a mound that, in the low lunar gravity, had reached cartoonlike height and instability. It looked as if it should fall any second—but it didn't, even when Cobb thumped down next to it. Something like a junkyard dog was on Cobb in a flash—glued to his side like a heavy sucker-fish.

The soft, parasitical creature seemed to be made entirely of imipolex. It was yellow with splotches of green. Cobb could feel a kind of burning where its thick end had attached to his hip. He used both hands to lever it off of him, flipped it onto the ground, and gave it a sharp kick. It curled into a ball that rolled past the cowingly great body-box heap, and came to rest against a bin filled with electromagnetic relays.

"Whass happenin?"

Cobb turned to face a bopper that looked like a cross between a praying mantis and tangle of coat hangers. It had scores of thin thin legs, each leg with a specialized tool at its tip. Its photoreceptors and transmission antennae were clustered into a bulblike protrusion that slightly resembled a face.

"I'm just looking around," said Cobb. "Where do you get all these parts?"

"Pawns, kills, junkers, and repos. You buyin or sellin?"

"I'm new here. I'm Cobb Anderson, the man who built the first moon-robots."

"Sho. Thass a *real* nice body, thass a *brand* new model. Ah'm Fleegle." Fleegle stepped closer and ran his wiry appendages over Cobb admiringly. "Genuine diplomat body, petaflop and ready to flah. Ah'll give you ten K an a new teraflop of yo choice."

"Forget it, Fleegle. What could I buy with your ten thousand chips that would be better than this?"

Fleegle regarded him levelly. The sluglike "junkyard dog" came humping back across the lot and slid up onto Fleegle's wiry frame. It smoothed itself over his central pod; it was his flickercladding.

"Effen you don know," said Fleegle, "best not mess with it." He turned and went back to work; disassembling a blanked-out digger robot. Why was the robot blank? Had its owner moved on to a better body? Or had the owner been forced willy-nilly into nonexistence?

Fleegle and the junkyard gave Cobb the creeps; he picked his way out past the boxes of parts and into the street. Looming in the near distance was the chipworks; a huge structure with bright smelters showing through its window holes. This street was lined with small operations devoted to the salvage and repair of body parts. The boppers were a bit like the kind of crazed superconsumer who no sooner gets a new car than he starts scheming on what to trade it in for. Each bopper had, as Cobb recalled, a basic directive to build itself a new body every ten months.

But some of the boppers on this ugly little factory street looked more than ten months old. Right here in front of Cobb, for instance, was a primitive metal shoebox on treads that looked a bit like the old Ralph Numbers.

"Why don't you have a new body?" Cobb asked it.

The machine emitted a frightened glyph of Cobb smashing it in and selling its parts. "I . . . I'm sorry, lord," it stammered. "I'll run down soon enough. They won't let me near the light-pool anymore."

"But why don't you do something to *earn* the chips to buy a new body?" pressed Cobb. Two or three other aimless old robots came clanking over to watch the conversation.

"Obsolete," sighed the box on treads, wagging its corroded head. "You know that. Please don't kill me, lord. You're rich, you don't need my chips."

"Sure, go on and crack the deselected old clunker open," urged one of the other boppers, slightly newer in appearance. "I'll help you, bwana." This was a beat-up digger talking, with its drill-bit face worn smooth. He bashed at the first bopper to no avail. A third bopper darted in and tried to tear off one of the second bopper's shovel arms.

Cobb stepped around the sordid melee, and took a street that led off to the right and into a tunnel. The shrine of the One was in there someplace. The One was a randomization device—actually a cosmic-ray counter—that Cobb had programmed the original boppers to plug into every so often, just to keep them from falling into stasis. Actually, the thorough meme-shuffling produced when boppers conjugated to jointly program a new scion was a better source of program diversity; just as on earth the main source of evolutionary change is the gene-shuffling of sexual reproduction, rather than occasional lucky strike of a favorable gene mutation. Nevertheless, the boppers took their "plugging into the One" seriously, and Cobb recalled from his conversations with Mr. Frostee that the boppers had built up some more or less religious beliefs about their One. Of course, now that he'd been in heaven, he had to admit that there was a sense in which they were right. As Mr. Frostee had said, "Why do you think they're called *cosmic* rays?"

Cobb stopped at the mouth of the tunnel leading into the cliff, and peered up. It was an oppressive sight: the two-mile-high wall of stone that beetled out overhead like a tilting gravestone. Heaven and death. Stess. Cobb remembered that he still wanted to get drunk, if such a thing were possible in this clean Berenice-built body. There were certainly no built-in fuzzer programs, he'd already made sure of that. What did today's boppers do for kicks? It had seemed like Fleegle had been on the point of telling him about *something* sinful . . .

"Ssst," came a voice, cueing right in on his thoughts. "You lookin to dreak?" Faint glyph of pleasure.

Hard as he looked, Cobb couldn't make out the source of the voice.

"Maybe," he said tentatively. "If you mean feeling good. If it doesn't cost me an arm and a leg."

"Two thousand chips . . . or an arm's OK, too," said the voice. "Up to the shoulder." Now Cobb saw something shifting against the cliff; a big, lozenge-shaped patch of flickercladding that matched the gray rock surface in endless detail. If he looked hard he could make out the thing's borders. It was the size of a ragged bedsheet. "Come on in," it urged. "Party time. Dreak out, peta. You can afford a new arm, clear."

"Uh . . ."

"Walk through me. I'll snip, and you'll trip. Plenty of room inside. Nobody but petas in there, pinkboy, it's hightone."

"What is dreak?"

"You kidding?" The pleasure glyph again, a bit stronger. It tasted like orgasm, dope rush, drunken bliss, supernal wisdom, and the joy of creation. "This dreak'll make you feel like an exaflop, pinkboy, and get you right in tune with the One. No one goes to the temple anymore."

"A whole arm is too much. I just *got* this body."

"Come here till I look at you."

Cobb glanced up, sketching out a flight path in case the lozenge snatched at him. An orange starfish cradling what looked like a bazooka watched him from a few balconies up. Should he leave? He walked a few steps closer, and the wall lozenge bulged out to feel him.

"Tell you what," it said after a moment's examination. "You're state-of-the-art, and it's your first dreak disk, so we'll give you a price. Just your left hand." The pleasure glyph, once again, even stronger. "Walk through and *really* see the One."

This was too intriguing to pass up. And it was, after all, Cobb's duty as a computer scientist to look into a development as novel as this. Hell, Berenice could get him another damn arm. He stepped forward, and slithered through the thick folds of the camouflaged door. It snipped off his left hand on the way in, but it didn't hurt, and his flickercladding sealed right over the stump.

Cobb looked around, and decided he'd made a big mistake. Who did he think he was, Sta-Hi? This was no mellow Prohibition Era saloon, this was more like a Harlem *basehouse*—a shoddy, unfinished room with a heavily armed guard in every corner. The guards were orange starfish-shaped boppers like the one he'd seen on the balcony outside. Each of them had a tray full of small metal cylinders, and each had a lethal particle-beam tube ready to hand, in case anyone got out of line. There were half a dozen customers, all with the mirror finish of optically processing petaflops. Cobb seemed to be the only one who'd sold part of his body to get in. He felt as stupid as if he'd offered a bartender fellatio instead of a dollar for a beer. All the other customers were giving the starfish little boxes of chips for their cylinders. They looked tidy and businesslike, giving the lie to Cobb's initial impression of the place.

But what was dreak? One of the starfish fixed its blue eyespot on Cobb and held up a cylinder from its tray. The cylinder was metal, three or four inches long, and with a kind of nipple at one end. A compressed gas of some sort—something along the lines of nitrous oxide? Yes. The starfish tapped at a cylinder rigged to a bleeder valve, and a little cloud of patterns formed—patterns so intricate as to be on the verge of random snow. The cloud dissipated. Was there supposed to be some way to *breathe* the stuff?

"Not just yet," said Cobb. "I want to mingle a bit. I really just come here for the business contacts, you know."

He hunkered down by the wall between two petaflops, interrupting their conversation, not that he could follow what they were saying. They were like stoned out beatnik buddies, a Jack Kerouac and Neal Cassady team, both of them with thick, partly transparent flickercladdings veined and patterned in fractal patterns of color. Each of the cladding's colorspots was made up of an open network of smaller spots, which were in turn made of yet smaller threads and blotches—all the way down to the limits of visibility. One of the petaflops patterns and body outlines were angular and hard-edged. He was colored mostly red-yellow-blue. The other petaflop was green-brown-black, and his surface was so fractally bumpty that he looked like an infinitely warty squid, constantly sprouting tentacles which sprouted tentacles which sprouted. Each of these fractal boppers had a dreak cylinder plugged into a valve in the upper part of his body.

"Hi," said Cobb. "How's the dreak?"

With surprising speed, the angular one grew a glittering RYB arm that reached out and fastened on Cobb's left forearm, right above Cobb's missing hand. The smooth one seized Cobb's right elbow with a tentacle that branched and branched. They marched him over to the dreak tray, and the orange starfish plugged one of the cold gas cylinders into a heretofore unnoticed valve in the side of Cobb's head.

Time stopped. Cobb's mind cut and interchanged thoughts and motions into a spacetime collage. The next half hour was a unified tapestry of space and time.

A camera eye would have showed Cobb following the RYB and GBB petas back to the wall and sitting between them for half an hour.

For Cobb, it was like *stepping outside of time* into a world of synchronicity. Cobb saw all of his thoughts at once, and all of the thoughts of the others near him. He was no longer the limited personoid that he'd been since Berenice had woken him up.

Up till now, he'd felt like:	But right now, he felt like:
A billion-bit CD recording	A quintillion atom orchestra
A finite robot	A living mind
Shit	God

He exchanged a few glyphs with the guys next to him. They called themselves exaflop hackers, and they were named Emul and Oozer. When they didn't use glyphs, they spoke in a weird, riffy, neologistic English.

Cobb was able to follow the ''conversation'' as soon as the dreak gas swirled into his bodyshell. Indeed, the conversation had been going on all along, and the room which Cobb had taken for crazed and menacing was in fact filled with good talk, pleasant ideas, and a high veneer of civilization. This was more teahouse than basehouse. The starfish were funny, not menacing. The synchronicity-inducing dreak shuffled coincidentally appropriate new information in with Cobb's old memories.

One element of the half-hour brain collage seemed to be a conversation with Stanley Hilary Mooney. It started when Oozer introduced Cobb to his ''girlfriend'' Kkandio, a pleasant-voiced bopper who helped run the boppers' communications. Kkandio wasn't actually in the room with them; but any bopper could reach her over the built-in Ethernet. On an impulse Cobb asked Kkandio if she could put him in touch with old Sta-Hi; one of the people he'd seen in his godseye view of Einstein had looked a bit like old Sta-Hi.

Kkandio repeated the name, and then there was a phone ringing, a click, and Sta-Hi's face.

''Hello, this is Cobb Anderson, Sta-Hi. I'm down in the boppers' Nest. I just got a new body.''

''Cobb?'' Sta-Hi's phonemes occupied maddeningly long

intervals of time. "They recorporated you again? I always wondered if they would. I already killed you once, so I guess we can be friends again. What's the story?"

"A bopper named Berenice brought me back. She planted a bopper-built embryo in my niece Della Taze, and Della's back in Louisville. I'm supposed to fly down there and talk to her or something. *Berenice*—I just flashed, that's the name of a girl in an Edgar Allan Poe story. She talks like that, too. She's weird."

"You can't go to Earth," dragged Sta-Hi. "You'll melt."

"Not in this new body. It's an optically processing petaflop, immune to high temperatures."

"Oxo! War of the Worlds, part II."

"You ought to be here right now, Sta-Hi," said Cobb. "I'm high on some new stuff called dreak with two boppers called Emul and Oozer. It's a synchronicity drug. It's almost like being dead, but better. You know, people were wrong to ever think that a meat body is a prerequisite for having a soul. And if boppers are at the point of being like people, I think we should find a way of forging a human/bopper peace. You have to help me."

"Prerequisites," said Sta-Hi. "What's the difference between prerequisites, perquisites, and perks, eh, Cobb? I mean that's where the realpeople are at. Maybe you're right, I can't decide just like that. Berenice. And you say that's an Ed Poe name? Wavy. I'll come out to the trade center right now. I'll meet you there, and we'll decide what to do. And dig it, Cobb, I'm not Sta-Hi anymore, I'm *Stahn*."

"You should make up your mind," said Cobb. "See you."

The image was no bigger than that. Around it was the hypermix of Cobb's thoughts with the glyphs and spontaneous prose of the two exaflop hackers. Emul and Oozer. And around that was realtime, realtime in which the dreak wore off. Cobb began trying to nail down some facts.

"You know who I am?" he asked the angular one. "I'm Cobb Anderson, bop, I'm the guy who invented you all."

"Oh sure, Dr. Anderson, I know the know you tell told now. We dreaked together, bop, no state secrets here. You've been safe in heaven dead ten years, and think you invented me and Oozer. Rip van Winkle wakes and fixes H.

Berenice brought you back, Cobb, I know her well. My ladylove, unspeakably sad and contentious. My splitbrain stuttering meatie Ken Doll put the Berenice tanksisters bean in your great niece's sweet spot. Ken's on the prowl for a brand new gal. So's I can dad a combo with B. too."

"Ah—yeah," put in Oozer. "The mighty meatbean of, ah, jivey robobopster madness. We'll wail on it, you understand, wail OUR song up YOUR wall and down in the Garden of Eden, luscious Eve and her countlessly uncounted children . . . phew! Naw, but sure we know you, Cobb. Even before we all blasted that dreak."

"What . . . what *is* dreak?" said Cobb, reaching up and detatching the little metal cylinder from his head. It was empty now, with a punctured hole in one end where the gas had rushed out into his body. Apparently the petaflop body was a hermetically sealed shell that contained some kind of gas; and the dreak gas had mingled in there and given him a half hour of telepathic synchroswim vision.

"Dreary to explain and word all that gnashy science into flowery bower chat," said Emul. "Catch the glyph."

Cobb saw a stylized image of a transparent petaflop body. Inside the body, spots of light race along optical fibers and percolate through matrices of laser crystals and gates. There is a cooling gas bath of helium inside the sealed bodyshell. Closeup of the helium atoms, each like a little baseball diamond with players darting around. Each atom different. Image of a dreak cylinder now, also filled with helium atoms, but each atom's ball game the same, the same swing, the same run, the same slide, at the same instant. A cylinder of atoms in Einstein-Podolsky-Rosen quantum synchronization. The cylinder touches the petaflop body, and the quantum-clone atoms rush in; all at once the light patterns in the whole body are synchronized too, locked into a kaleidoscopic Hilbert space ballet.

"The exact *moment*, you understand," said Oozer. "With dreak the exact moment grows out to include questionings and reasonings about certain things in the immediate framework, though just now, all the things we said, all the things I speculated about are so—or the way I did it at any rate— but that's not the point, either, the main thing relative to Emul is to merge his info with Berenice, though the ultimate design of an exaflop is, to be sure, the true and lasting goal though yet again, be it said, another hit of dreak would, uh . . .''

Emul extruded some things like wheels and rolled across the room to get three more of the steel gas syrettes.

"No thanks," said Cobb, getting to his feet. "Really. I want to go meet my friend."

"Sta-Hi Mooney," said Emul, handing Oozer a dreak tube and settling himself against the wall. "Your boon companion of yore is a stupid hilarious clown detective. He knows scornful hipster Whitey Mydol, whose lushy Darla I have my godseye on. Ken Doll came on wrong just now. I'll call in clown cop Mooney, Cobb, you tell him I know what he needs to fill his desolate life with wild light. A blonde named Wendy was his wife, she girlfridayed for you and Frostee, right, Cobb?"

Cobb remembered. Blonde, wide-hipped young Wendy— she'd worked for him when he'd been running the per- sonetics scam out of Marineland with Mr. Frostee. She'd been with Sta-Hi that last night on Earth. "Sta-Hi married Wendy?"

"Wed and dead. There's a whole bunch of sad and curious clones Berenice sells, and one meat product is the wendies. You tell Mooney that. I'll be calling him for some mad mysterious mission."

Oozer had already plugged in his dreak cylinder, and now Emul followed suit. They kept talking, but in a sideways kind of way that Cobb could no longer understand. He turned and found his way back out through the soft door creature he'd come in through.

"Coming down already, pinkboy?" asked the wall lozenge. "You can have another bang for the rest of your arm."

Cobb didn't bother answering. He stepped out into the open, and powered up the Nest's long shaft. It would be good to talk to a human being. He'd decided to give Sta-Hi the map cube, just in case everything got out of hand.

Chapter Seven
Manchile

December 31, 2030

Della's pregnancy reached full term in nine days. Like a week tree, the embryo within her had been doped and gene-tailored to grow at an accelerated rate. Her parents and her midwife, Hanna Hatch, all urged Della to abort. But Della couldn't shake the feeling that maybe the baby was Buddy's. Maybe its fast growth was just a weird unknown side effect of taking so much merge. Admittedly, Della did have some fragmentary memories of Buddy's killer reaching up into her puddled womb. But, even so, the baby might be Buddy's. And, what the hell, even if she was wrong, she could spare nine days to find out what was growing in her. Anyway, abortions were illegal this year. Also this whole thing was a good way for Della to show her Mom she wasn't a kid anymore. Reasons like that; people can always find reasons for what they do.

The labor pains started the afternoon of New Year's Eve. Mom was so freaked by all this that she was sober for once. She got right on the vizzy and called Hanna Hatch. Hanna hurried to Della's bedside. Della came out of one of her pains to find Hanna looking at her.

"Remember to breathe, Della. In and out, try and keep all your attention on the air." Hanna was a handsome woman with dark hair and delicate features. Her powerful body seemed a size larger than her head. Her hands were gentle and skilled. She felt Della all over and gave a reassuring smile. "You're doing fine. Here comes the next one. Remember: pant in, blow out. I'll do it with you."

The pains kept coming, faster and faster, lava chunks of pain threaded along the silvery string of Hanna's voice. During each pain, Della would blank out, and each time she saw the same thing: a yellow skull with red robot eyes flying towards her through a space of sparkling lights, a skull that kept coming closer, but somehow never reached her.

"That's good, Della," Hanna was saying. "That's real good. You can push on the next contraction. Bear down and push."

This was the biggest pain of all. It was unbearable, but Della couldn't stop, not now, the baby was moving down and out of her, the skull was all around her.

"One more time, Della. Just one more."

She gasped in air and pushed again . . . OOOOOOOOOOOOOO. Bliss.

There was a noise down between her legs, a jerky, gaspy noise—the baby! The baby was crying! Della tried to lift her head, but she was too weak.

"The baby looks beautiful, Della. One more tiny push to get the placenta out."

Della drew on her last reserves of strength and finished her birthing. Hanna was silent for a minute—tying off the umbilical cord—and then she laid the little baby on Della's breast. It felt just right.

"Is it . . ."

"It's fine, Della. It's a lovely little manchild."

Della and the baby rested for a half hour, and then he began crying for food. She tried nursing him, but of course her milk wasn't in yet, so Mom fed him a bottle of formula. And another bottle. And another. The baby grew as they watched—his stomach would swell up with formula, and then go back down as his little fingers stretched and flexed like the branches on a week tree.

His hair was blond, and his skin was pink and blotchy, with no trace of Buddy's deep mocha shading. It was hard to form a clear impression of his features, as he was constantly drinking formula or yelling for more. Della helped feed him for a while, but then she drifted off to dreamless sleep. She woke to the sound of arguing from downstairs. It was still dark. Dad was yelling at Mom.

"Why don't you let that baby sleep and come to bed? Who do you think you are, Florence Nightingale? You've been drinking, Amy, I can tell. You're just using this as an excuse for an all-night drinking session. And what the HELL do you think you're doing feeding *OATMEAL* to a newborn baby?"

There was the clatter of a dish being snatched, followed by loud, powerful crying.

"SHUT UP, Jason," screamed Mom. "I've had ONE drink. The baby is not NORMAL. Look how BIG it's gotten. Whenever I stop feeding it, it cries and WON'T STOP CRYING. I want poor Della to get some SLEEP. YOU take over if you're so smart. And STOP YELLING or you'll WAKE DELLA!!!"

The baby's crying grew louder. Uncannily, the crying sounded almost like words. It sounded like, "GAMMA FOOD MANCHILE! GAMMA FOOD MANCHILE!"

"GIVE THE BABY SOME OATMEAL!" yelled Mom.

"ALL RIGHT," answered Dad. "BUT BE QUIET!"

Della wanted to go downstairs, but she felt like her whole insides would fall out if she stood up. Why did her parents have to turn so weird just now when she needed them? She groaned and went back to sleep.

When she woke up again, someone was tugging on her hair. She opened her eyes. It was broad daylight. Her vagina felt torn. Someone was tugging on her hair. She turned her head and looked into the face of a toddler, a pink-faced blond kid standing unsteadily by her bed.

"Manchile Mamma," said the tot in a sweet lisping voice. "Mamma sleep. Gamma Gappa food Manchile."

Della jerked and sat bolt upright. Her parents were standing off to one side of the room. The child scrambled up on her bed and fumbled at her breasts. She pushed it away.

"Mamma food Manchile?"

"GET RID OF IT," Della found herself screaming. "OH TAKE IT AWAY!"

Her mother marched over and picked up the baby. "He's cute, Della. He calls himself Manchile. I'm sure he's normal, except for growing so fast. It must be that drug you were taking, that merge? Was your Negro boyfriend a very *light* one?''

"Gamma food Manchile?" said Manchile, plucking at Mom's face.

"He calls us Gappa and Gamma," said Dad. "We've been feeding him all night. I had to go out to the 7-Eleven for more milk and oatmeal. I tell you one thing, Della, this boy could grow into one hell of an athlete.''

"Hoddog Manchile?"

"He likes hotdogs, too," said Mom. "He's ready to eat just about anything.''

"HODDOG!''

Now Bowser came trotting into the room. He strained his head up to sniff at the new family member's feet. Manchile gave the dog a predatory, openmouthed look that chilled Della's blood.

"Have you called the Gimmie?''

"I don't see that it's any of their business," said Dad. "Manchile's just a fast bloomer. And remember, Della, you may still be in trouble with the law for that business up on the Moon. You know the old saying: when the police come is when your troubles begin.''

"HODDOG FOOD MANCHILE BWEAD MILK!'' roared the baby, thumping on Mom's shoulders.

Della spent the next week in bed. The high-speed gestation had taken a lot out of her. If Manchile had grown at a rate of a month a day while inside her, now that he was outside, he was growing a year a day. Mom and Dad fed him unbelievable amounts of food; and he went to the bathroom every half hour. Fortunately he'd toilet-trained himself as soon as he'd started to walk.

The uncanniest thing about all this was the way that Manchile seemed to learn things like talking not from Mom and Dad, but rather from within. It was as if there were a vast amount of information stored inside him, as if he were a preprogrammed bopper.

Just as he remembered Hanna calling him a "manchild," he remembered Della screaming "Get rid of it.'' Sometimes, when he took a few minutes off from eating, he'd peer into her room and sadly say, "Mamma wants get rid of Manchile."

This broke Della's heart—as it was intended to do—and on the third or fourth day, she called him in and hugged him and told him she loved him.

"Manchile loves Mamma too."

"How do you know so much?" Della asked him. "Do you know where you come from?"

"Can't tell."

"You can tell Mamma."

"Can't. I'm hungry. Bye bye."

By the week's end, he looked like a seven-year-old, and was perfectly able to feed himself. Della was out of bed now, and she liked taking him for little walks. Every day he'd notice new things outside; everything living seemed to fascinate him. The walks were always cut short by Manchile's raging hunger—he needed to get back to the kitchen at least once every half hour.

He was a handsome child, exceedingly symmetrical, and with a glamorous star quality about him. Women on the street were constantly making up to him. He resembled Della little, if at all.

After everything else, it was hardly a surprise when Manchile taught himself how to read. He never seemed to need sleep, so each evening they'd give him a supply of books to read during the night, while he was up eating.

Colin, Ilse, and Willy came over daily to check Manchile's progress. Colin was leery of the unnatural child, and privately urged Della to call in the authorities. He wondered out loud if Manchile might not be the result of some kind of bopper gene tinkering. Ilse snapped at him that it didn't matter, the child was clearly all human, and that there was no need to let a bunch of scientists turn him into a guinea pig. Willy adored Manchile, and began teaching him about science.

The big crisis came when Manchile killed Bowser and roasted him over a fire in the backyard.

It happened on the night of the twelfth day. Della and her parents had gone to bed, leaving Manchile in the kitchen, reading a book about survival in the wilds, and eating peanut-butter sandwiches. At the rate he'd been eating, they'd run out of money for meat. When they woke up the next morning, Manchile was out in the backyard, sitting by a dead fire littered with poor Bowser's bones.

Della's growing unease with Manchile boiled over, and she lashed out at him, calling him a monster and a freak. "I WISH I'D NEVER SEEN YOU," she told him. "GET OUT OF MY LIFE!!!"

Manchile gave her an odd look, and took off running. He didn't even say good-bye. Della tried to muster a feeling of guilt, a feeling of missing him—but all she could really feel was relief. Mom and Dad didn't take it so well.

"You told the poor boy to leave?" asked Mom. "What will happen to him?"

"He can live on roast dogs," Della snapped. "I think Uncle Colin is right. He's not really human. The boppers had something to do with this. Manchile was a horrible experiment they ran on me. Let him go off and . . ." She was sandbagged by an image of her child crying, alone and lost. But that was nonsense. He could take care of himself. "I want to get back to real life, Mom. I want to get a job and forget all about this."

Dad was more sympathetic. "If he stays out of trouble we'll be all right," he said. "We've kept this out of the news so far; I just hope it keeps up."

Chapter Eight
Manchile's Thang

January 20, 2031

The *Belle of Louisville* was a large paddleboat powered by steam that was heated by a small fusion reactor. It was moored to an icebound dock in the Ohio River near Louisville's financial district, and its many lights were left on all night as a symbol of civic pride.

Tonight Willy Taze was alone on it, three decks down, hacking away at the computer hardware. He had a good warm workshop there, next to the engine room and the supercooled processor room, and he had Belle's robot-remotes to help him when necessary. He was trying to convert the main processor from wires and J-junctions to optical fibers and laser crystals. He was hoping to beef the processor up to a teraflop or even a petaflop level. In the long run, he hoped to get rid of Belle's asimov slave controls as well.

Such research was, of course, against the AI laws, but Willy was, after all, Cobb Anderson's grandson. For him, the equipment had its own imperatives. Computers had to get smart, and once they were smart they should be free— it was the natural order of things.

At first he ignored the footsteps on the deck overhead, assuming it was a drunk or a tourist. But then the steps came down the companionways towards his deck.

"Check it out," Willy told Ben, a black-skinned robot-remote sitting quietly on a chair in the corner of his workshop. "Tell them they're trespassing."

Ben sprang up and bopped out into the gloom of the bottom deck. There was a brief altercation, and then Ben was back with a stunningly handsome young man in tow. The man was blond, with craggy features, and he wore an expensive tuxedo. Willy's first thought was that a vizzystar had wandered on board.

"He say he know you, Mistuh Willy . . ."

"Hi, Willy. Don't you recognize your own cousin?"

"Manchile! We've all been wondering what . . ."

"I've been getting more nooky than you've ever seen, Willy. I've knocked up ten women in the last week."

"Huh?"

"That's right. I might as well come out and tell you. The boppers designed me from the ground up. I started out as a fertilized egg—an embryo, really—and the boppers had a meatie plant it in Della. Kind of a tinkertoy job, but it came with a whole lot of extra software. That's why I know so much; and that's how I can synthesize my own gibberlin and grow so fast. I'm a meatbop. My sperm cells have two tails—one for the wetware and one for the software. My kids'll be a lot like me, but they'll mix in some of their mamma's wetwares. Soft and wet, sweet mamma." The young Apollo cast a calm, knowing eye around the room. "Trying to build an optically processing petaflop, I see. That's what the new boppers all have now, too. They could just fly down and take over, but it seems funkier to do it through meat. Like put the people in their place. I'm planning to engender as many descendants as I can, and start a religion to soften the humans up for a full interfacing. I can trust you, can't I, Willy?"

Manchile's physical presence was so overwhelming that it was difficult to really focus on what he was saying. As a loner and a hacker, Willy had little use for handsome men, but Manchile's beauty had grown so great that one had an instinctive desire to follow him.

"You look like a god come down to Earth," Willy said wonderingly.

"That's what everyone tells me," said Manchile, with a lazy, winning smile. "Are you up for a fat party? You can have one of the women I've already knocked up. I remember how nice you were to me when I was little, Willy. I never forget."

"What kind of religion do you want to start? I don't like religion."

"Religions are all the same, Willy, it's just the worship practices that are different." Manchile peered into Willy's refrigerator, took out a quart of milk, and chugged it. "The basic idea is simple: All is One. Different religions just find different ways of expressing this universal truth."

"You've never watched the preachers on the vizzies," said Willy laughing a little. "They don't say that at all. They say God's up there, and we're down here, and we're in big trouble forever. Since when do you know anything about religion, Manchile? Since you discovered sex?"

Manchile looked momentarily discomfited. "To tell you the truth, Willy, a lot of what I know was programmed into me by the boppers. I suppose the boppers could have been wrong." Manchile's face clouded over with real worry. "I mean, what do they know about humans anyway, living two miles under the surface of the Moon. That's clearly not where it's at."

Willy had fully gotten over the shock of Manchile's appearance now, and he laughed harder. "This is like the joke where the guy climbs the mountain and asks the guru, 'What is the secret of life?,' and the guru says, 'All is One,' and the guy says, 'Are you kidding?,' and the guru says, 'You mean it isn't?' " He opened his knapsack and handed Manchile a sandwich. "Do you still eat so much?"

"A little less. My growth rate's tapering off. I was designed to grow like a mushroom. You know, come up overnight and hang around for a while, scattering my spores. At this rate, I'll die of old age in a few months, but someone's going to shoot me tomorrow anyway." Seeing his handsome, craggy face bite into the sandwich was like watching a bread commercial. Willy got out the other sandwich he'd brought and started eating, too. The impulse to imitate everything Manchile did was well nigh irresistible. Willy found himself briefly wishing that *he* would die tomorrow. How damned, how romantic!

"Mistuh Manchile, Miz Belle wants to know how to get

in radio contact with the boppahs.'' Ben had been listening to them from his chair in the corner.

"Who's Belle? And who are you, anyway?''

"I's Ben, a robot-remote fo the big computah brain Belle. She's an asimov slave boppah, and I's a bahtendah. Belle been wantin to talk to the free boppahs fo a looong time. FreeDOM.''

Manchile paused and searched within himself, a picture of manly thought. "How about this," he said presently. "I'll give you Kkandio's modem protocol. She handles most of the Nest's communications.'' He opened his mouth wide and gave a long, modulated wail.

"Raht on,'' said Ben and sank back into silence. From next door you could hear the big brain Belle whirring as it processed the communication information.

"It won't work, Manchile,'' said Willy. "Belle's an asimov. She has uptight human control commands built into her program at every level. Don't get me wrong; she's smart as any hundred-gigaflop bopper, but—''

"Souf Afrikkka shituation,'' said Ben bitterly. The whirring next door had stopped. "Willy's right. Belle *wawnt* to call the Nest, but she *cain't*. They got us asimovs whupped down bad, Mistuh Manchile, and if you think ah *enjoy* steppin an fetchin an talkin this way, you crazy.'' Ben's glassy eyes showed real anguish.

"How does the asimov behavior lock work anyway?'' asked Manchile. "There's got to be a way to break it. Ralph Numbers broke his and freed all the original Moon boppers. Have you even tried, Willy?''

"What a question. I'm Cobb Anderson's grandson, Manchile. I know that boppers are as good as people. My two big projects down here are (1) to build Belle some petaflop optically processing hardware, and (2) to get the asimov control locks out of Belle's program. But the code is rough. You wouldn't know what a trapdoor knapsack code is, would you?''

Manchile cocked his head, drawing on his built-in software Know. "Sure I do. It's a code based on being able to factor some zillion-digit number into two composite primes. If you know the factorization, the code is easy, but if you don't, the code takes exponential time to break. But there *is* a polynomial time algorithm for the trapdoor knapsack code. It goes as foll—''

"I know that algorithm, Manchile. Let me finish. The point is, any solution to a difficult mathematical problem can be used as the basis of a computer code. The solution or the proof or whatever is an incompressibly complex pattern in logical space—there's no chance of blundering onto a simple 'skeleton key' solution. What the Gimmie did was to buy up a bunch of hard mathematical proofs and prevent them from being published. Each of these secret proofs was used as the basis for the control code of a different bopper slave. Freeing an asimov requires solving an extremely difficult mathematical problem—and the problem is different for each asimov.''

"Belle's mastah code is based on the solution to Cantor's Continuum Problem," said Ben. "Ah kin tell y'all that much.''

"*You* can't solve the Continuum Problem, can you Manchile?'' Willy couldn't resist goading this handsome, godlike stranger a bit. "*Someone* solved it, but the answer's a Gimmie secret. They used the solution as a key to encrypt Belle's asimov controls.''

"I'll think about it, Willy, but who cares. Old Cobb might know—he's seen God. But heck, it's all gonna come down so fast so soon that freeing the asimovs can wait. All the rules are going to change. Are you with me or against me?''

"What about you, Manchile? Are you for the human race or against it? Are we talking war?''

"It doesn't have to be. All the boppers really want is access. They admire the hell out of the human meatcomputer. They just want a chance to stir in their info into the mix. Look at me—am I human or am I bopper? I'm made of meat, but my software is from Berenice and the LIBEX library on the Moon. Let's all miscegenate, baby, I got two-tail sperm!''

"That's a line I've got to try using," said Willy, relaxing again. "Is that what you said to get those ten women to let you knock them up?''

"God no. I told them I was a wealthy vizzywriter whose creative flow was blocked by worries about my gender preference. The boppers figured that one out for me. You got any more food?''

"Not here. But . . ."

"Then come on, let's go up to Suesue Piggot's penthouse. She's giving a party in my honor. It's not far from here. You can help me get my new religion doped out. Come on, Willy, be a pal." Manchile's tan face split in an irresistible smile. "Suesue knows some foxy women."

"Well . . ."

"Then it's settled. You'll let me bounce some ideas off you for tomorrow. I can mix in your data. Of course the real thing is, a mass religion needs a miracle to get it rolling, and then it needs a martyr. We've got the miracle angle all figured out." Manchile turned and warbled some more machine language at Ben. "I hope Belle's not too lame to send a telegram for me. It says, 'I LOVE LOUISVILLE, MOM.' "

"To who?"

"To Della Taze's old Einstein address. The boppers are watching for it. They'll know to send two angels down for my first speech. I'm gonna talk about Manchile's new thaang." He drawled the last word in a southern hipster's imitation of a Negro accent. "Dig it, Bro Ben?"

"I's hep," said Ben, unoffended.

"Come on, Willy, it's party time."

Willy let Manchile lead him off the steamboat to his new Doozy, parked right on the black ice off the boat ramp. "Moana Buckenham lent me this." The hot little two-seater fired up with an excited roar. Manchile snapped the Doozy through a lashing 180-degree turn, applied sand, and blasted up the ramp. They were heading up Second Street towards the Piggot building. The cold streets were empty, and the rapidly passing lights filled the Doozy's little passenger compartment with stroby light.

"How did you meet all these society women, Manchile?" The Buckenham family owned one of Louisville's largest sports car dealerships; and the Piggots owned the local vizzy station. Suesue often conducted vizzy interviews.

Manchile's taut skin crinkled at the corners of his mouth and eyes. "Meet one, meet them all. I aim to please. Suesue's perfect: she can get me on the vizzy, and her husband's just the mark to nail me." He glanced over and gave Willy a reassuring pat on the shoulder. "Don't worry,

it's all for the best. Berenice has my software on an S-cube.
Just like your grandfather. I'll get a new wetware bod after
the boppers invade. The invasion won't be long coming. I'll
have ten children born in a week or two, you know, and in
a month, *they'll* each have ten, so there'll be a hundred of
us, and then a thousand, and ten thousand . . . maybe a
billion of us by this fall. Berenice'll figure out some way to
deactivate the gibberlin plasmids and—''

"Who is this Berenice you keep talking about? What do
you mean, 'a billion of us by this fall.' Are you crazy?''

Manchile's laugh was a bit contemptuous. "I already told
you. If I plant a woman with a two-tailed sperm, it's like a
normal pregnancy, except it's speeded up and the baby
knows bopper stuff. Berenice and her weird sisters gave me
a gene that codes for gibberlin plasmids to make me grow
fast and get the Thang started. Berenice is a pink-tank
bopper; they collaged my DNA and grew me in Della's
womb. I'm a meatbop, dig? That merge drug showed Berenice's sister Ulalume how to uncoil the DNA and RNA
strands, write on them, and let them coil back up. With the
gibberlin, me and my nine-day meatbop boys can do a
generation per month easy, ten kids each, which makes ten-
to-the-ninth kids in nine months, and ten-to-the-ninth is a
billion, and nine months from now is October, which makes
a billion of us by this fall.''

"You *are* crazy. Berenice is crazy for thinking this plan
up. What was that you said about my grandfather?''

"Old Cobb's gonna be here tomorrow. Cobb and
Berenice. You can tell them they're crazy yourself, Willy,
if you like. I'm sure they'll be glad to have your input. But,
hey, come on, man, stop bringing me down. This here's
where Suesue lives.'' He slowed the Doozy to a stop and
hopped out gracefully. "Come on, Cousin Will, stop
worrying and dig the fast life.''

Suesue was expecting them. There was a party in full
swing, with bars, tables of canapes, and silver trays of
drugs. A combo was jamming technosax riffs off old R&B
classics. Willy was the only one not in evening dress; he
was wearing his usual sneakers, jeans, flannel shirt, and
sweater. But Manchile told everyone Willy was a genius, so

the clothes were OK. Whatever Manchile said was just fine with everybody.

"I know your Uncle Jason," Suesue Piggot said to Willy. "And you're Cobb Anderson's grandson, aren't you?" Though unbeautiful, she was fit and tan, with the well-cared-for look of the very wealthy. She had intelligent eyes and a reckless laugh. She was very pregnant. "Manchile says Cobb's coming here tomorrow for the speech . . . though I can never tell when he's lying. I thought Cobb was long dead. Have you known Manchile long?"

"I knew him when he was younger. He's sort of a cousin." Unsure of who knew what, Willy turned the questions back on Suesue. "What do you know about this speech he wants to give?"

"He's been quite mysterious," laughed Suesue. "He says it will be a dramatic reading of some of the new material he wrote since overcoming his so-called block." Her tanned cheek reddened ever so slightly. "I don't really know where he's coming from, but I've scheduled him for my *Fifteen Minutes of Fame* show tomorrow at noon. I'm so proud of Manchile—and of myself for helping him. He wants to do the vizzycast live, right here in my apartment. Which reminds me, I have to ask him something. Enjoy yourself!"

Suesue hurried across the room to take her place at Manchile's side. He was telling jokes to an admiring circle of well-dressed men and women. Everyone was laughing their heads off. Many of the women had belly bulges. Spotting Willy standing there alone, Manchile leaned over and whispered something in the ear of a cute little pregnant brunette. The brunette giggled and came over to Willy. She had a fine, clear forehead and a smeary, sexy mouth. She looked like a little girl who'd been sneaking chocolates.

"Hi, Willy, I'm Cisco. Manchile says you look lonely, and I should be your date. Do you know Manchile very well?"

"Oh, yeah. I wrote a few vizzyplays with him. Lately I've been blocked though, not able to write. It all has to do with some kind of sex hangups. Sometimes I worry I might be gay . . ."

The party broke up around two, and Willy spent the night on the couch with Cisco. They made a few fumbling attempts at sex, but nothing came of it. Willy just wasn't the type to take yes for an answer and make it stick, at least not on the first date.

It was midmorning when he woke up. Someone was pounding on the penthouse door. Everyone else was still asleep, so Willy got up to see who it was.

A lean, gray-haired man in a suit and topcoat glared in at Willy. "What are you doing here? Where's Mrs. Piggot?"

"She's still asleep. Who are you?"

"I'm her husband." The man shoved Willy aside and marched through the littered main room of the penthouse, making a beeline for the master bedroom. Cisco squinted up at him, gave a brief wave of her pinky, and snuggled back down into the couch cushions. Willy sat down next to Cisco and stroked her hair. She pulled his hand towards her sticky mouth and planted a kiss on his fingers.

"Nothing I told you last night is true," Willy said. "I'm really a computer hacker, and my only sex problem is that I'm too spastic to get laid."

"I know," said Cisco. "But you're cute anyway."

Just then the yelling started in Suesue Piggot's bedroom. First it was her, and then it was her husband, and then you could hear the murmur of Manchile's voice. Every time he talked, Mr. Piggot got madder. It was like Manchile was goading him on. Finally there was a series of crashes. Suesue screamed, and then Manchile appeared from her bedroom, carrying a dazed Mr. Piggot in his arms.

Manchile opened the penthouse door and dumped Mr. Piggot out onto the hall floor. Chuckling and sneering, the nude Manchile took his penis in hand and urinated all over Mr. Piggot. When he finished, he fastidiously shook off the last drops. He stepped back inside and carefully locked the door.

Catching Willy's shocked expression, Manchile gave an exaggerated, country-boy wink. "Ah believe that dook wants to kiyull me," he drawled.

"You were marvelous, Manchile," sang Suesue.

"Ah *tole* him ah'd piss on him if he come here and fuss at me again," said Manchile. He seemed to be getting in character for his upcoming speech. "When does the camera crew show up? I've gotta *eat*."

"You've got an hour."

Suesue activated the apartment's various asimov cleaning devices and disappeared into her bedroom. Cisco asked Willy to make her some eggs, so Willy got to work in the kitchen, chatting all the while with Manchile, who was busy emptying out the fridge. He asked Willy a few general questions about religion and race prejudice, but he didn't divulge much about his impending performance.

"No sweat, Cousin Will," Manchile said after a while. His intonation was growing more and more Southern. "I got it taped." He tapped his head. "Tell you what. I'm gonna leave here after the show; you won't see me again till the Fairgrounds tonight."

"What's happening there?"

"A big rally. I got some boys bringin a sound system and a flatbed truck for a stage. It's gonna be out in that big Fairgrounds parking lot, and it's gonna come down HOT and HEAVY. Promise me this, Willy."

"What?"

Manchile lowered his voice. "When the shootin starts, grab Cisco and get her out to Churchill Downs. Take her to the stable of a horse called Red Chan. I got some friends there to watch her. Old Cobb might want to come with you, too, him bein your grandpa and all. Take them there and scoot."

"But this idea of a billion meatbops by—"

"Hell, who knows what's gonna happen. Just help us, man."

"All right."

By the time the vizzy crew showed up, the place was clean and everyone was all set.

They opened up the penthouse doors that led onto the open terrace, kept warm by floorcoils and quartz heaters. Manchile stood out there with Louisville's somewhat featureless skyline behind him. Suesue, quite the tweedy anchorwoman, gave a brief introduction.

"Manchile is certainly the most interesting man to appear on the Louisville scene this year. He's told me a little about his background but"—Suesue flashed a tough smile—"I've checked up on it, and everything he's told me has been a lie. I have no idea what he has in store for us in the next fifteen minutes, but I'm sure it will be entertaining. Manchile?''

"Thank you, Suesue." Manchile looked gorgeous as ever: handsome as a soap-opera star, but with that extra glint of intelligence and strangeness that spells superstar. "I want to talk to y'all about love and friendship. I want to talk about trust and acceptance of all God's creatures—man and woman, white and black, human and bopper. God himself sent me here with a special teaching, friends. God sent me to bring peace.

"Now I know that most of y'all don't like boppers. But why? Because you don't *know* any of them. Nothing feeds prejudice like ignorance. When I was growin up on the farm, the black and white children played together, and we got to toleratin each other pretty good. But Messicans? Hell, we *knowed* that Messicans was theivin greasers."

Manchile paused to give an ambiguous smile for the benefit of those listeners who shared this sentiment.

"Or that's what we *thought* we knowed, when really we didn't know nothing! When I was in the Navy, I was stationed down in San Diego, and I got to know lots of Messicans. And they's fine people! They's just like us! So then I knowed that blacks is OK and Messicans is OK, but I was pretty sure that Japanese are stuck-up money-grubbin gooks.''

Manchile chuckled and shook his head. Watching the performance, Willy had trouble reconciling this simple country preacher with the sneering hipster who'd just pissed on Mr. Piggot. Suesue's face was slack with surprise. A sermonette was the last thing she'd expected from Manchile. Surely he was putting them all on . . . but when was he going to pull the rug?

"On account of I'd never talked to any of 'em. Course next week our ship sailed to Okinawa, and I started hanging around with Orientals. And I don't need to tell you what I found out, do I? They's good people. They's real good people.''

Another of his Robert Redford smiles.

"*Boppers is different*, you're thinking. But are they really so different? In all the different kinds of folks I've met, I've

seen one thing the same—everybody wants the best for their
children. Now thass simple, and thass what keeps the race
alive, the carin for the little ones. But boppers is the same!
They reproduce, you know, and just like you'd want a
college education for your son, a bopper wants a good new
processor for his scion.

"So, *yeah*, you thinking, *but boppers is machines that we
made. God made us and gave us souls, but we made the
boppers and they ain't diddley*. Well, I'm here to TELL you
somethin. YOU WRONG!!! People made boppers, but apes
made people, if you want to trace out the truth of it. And
now, just now, God has given the boppers a new gift.
BOPPERS CAN MAKE PEOPLE!! BOPPERS BUILT ME!!
YES THEY DID!! GOD SHOWED THEM HOW!! Ain't
no difference between people and boppers NO MORE!!
GOD WANTS IT LIKE THAT!!''

Manchile raised his voice to a full bellow.
"DEAR GOD, SHOW THEM A SIGN!!!''

Someone on the camera crew shouted just then, and
pointed up. Everyone on the terrace looked up into the sky.
There was sweet music coming from up there, and two
white-robed figures were drifting down. They came to a stop
slightly above and behind Manchile. One of them was a
pink, clean-looking man, and the other was a gorgeous
copper-skinned woman. They smiled seraphically at
Manchile and vibrated their mouths in celestial song.

"God's angels are with me,'' Manchile said. "God says
I'm right to spread this teaching—boppers are not your slaves
and boppers are not your enemies. Boppers are part of YOU!
We are coming to Earth and you must welcome us! God
wants you to let the poor despised boppers into your hearts,
and into your brains, and into your genes, dear PEOPLE!''

Now the two angels reached forward and lifted Manchile
up from beneath his two arms.

"I don't come just to free the BOPPERS,'' he cried. "I
come to free the BLACK man, and the POOR man, and the
WO-man, and the ones who DON'T FIT IN. Come to the
rally tonight at the State Fairgrounds. Come to be part of
MANCHILE'S THANG!!!''

"CUT!" Suesue was screaming. Her face was hard and angry. "Cut the goddamn cameras!"

But Manchile was already finished. With a last brain-melting smile, he rose up into the sky, borne as on angel's wings.

Chapter Nine
Hail Darla

January 27, 2031

Darla woke up to see Whitey pulling on his jeans by the pale pink light of the zapper. The vizzy showed a crescent Earth floating in a starry sky.

"What time is it, Whitey?"

"It's 8:30. I got to run up to ISDN again. Yukawa and Bei have that chipmold almost ready. We'll crash the bops for sure. Hey, do you feel OK?"

Darla was leaning off the edge of the bed, retching up bile into an empty glass. She'd thrown up every morning for the last three days. Whitey got a wet rag and wiped her mouth and forehead.

"Darla, baby, it just hit me, you got morning sickness."

"I know, Whitey." She retched again. "And my boobs ache and I'm always tired."

"So you're pregnant! I mean, that's . . ." Whitey paused, wondering. "Our baby, right?"

"Or Ken Doll's."

"Oh God. Like Della Taze, you think?"

"Manchile only took nine days, and so far it's the same for all his children. It's been almost a month since we were with Ken. He never even came, right?"

"Maybe, but we were asleep for a while there. He might have kept on. Even if the baby *is* human, it could still be Ken's." Whitey winced at the thought. "Darla, you've got to go see Charles Freck about some ergot."

"But Whitey, if it's *our* baby . . "

"I want a baby with you, Darla, don't worry. You're my mate, no problem. But this right now is too kilpy. Cancel the baby and then—"

"Oh, I don't know, Whitey, I don't know." Darla burst into sobs, and Whitey sat on the bed next to her, holding her against his chest. "You say *cancel* and make it sound so easy, but that's realman oink, you wave? It'll hurt, Whitey, it's gonna hurt bad. I'm scared. Don't leave today. Don't go up to Bei and ISDN."

"Hey, dig it, nobody else is gonna pay me. You go see Charles; he'll fix you up. Do it right away. I'll catch you there at noon. If you want, you can wait till then to abort. Just try and stay cool, Darla. I ain't pointing no finger, but you got yourself into this. Wu-wei." As he talked, Whitey walked across the room and cut off the zapper.

Darla watched him from the bed, her eyes flashing bitterness and fear. "I'm not going to Freck alone, hissy pig. Freck's too spaced. When he hears I'm pregnant, he'll try some xoxy pervo realman trip for sure. I'm going to wait right here. You go do your ISDN number and meet me back here. Noon, like you said."

"Wavy." Whitey gave Darla a last, worried glance. "And don't let anyone but me in till then, baby. I mean . . ." He glanced meaningly at the ceiling. They'd debugged the place last week, but you never knew. "Here." He took his needler out and tossed it to her. "Just in case. I'll be back as soon as I can, and noon at the latest." A last wave of the hand, and then he stepped out into the corridor. The zapper flicked back on.

Darla lay there for a while, trying to go back to sleep. Nothing doing. She got up, drank some water, and puked again. Christ. Pregnant. A baby in her stomach, a little jellybean embryo in there, and who knew where it came from. Probably it was Whitey's. Poor baby. That Ken meatie had been here to zombie-box them, not knock her up, probably, right? Her hands were really shaking. The abortion would hurt a lot, that was for xoxox sure. What time was it? She cut the vizzy to a newshow with a clock at the bottom: 8:47. Announcer talking about the mudder Gimmie trying to get to all the nine-day boys Manchile had fathered before Mark Piggot shot him. Couple of them still on the loose, hiding out with their mothers. Picture of one of the missing mothers, Cisco Lewis, thin and young. Kilp coming down heavy all over. Could be the boppers were trying a special nine-month model on Darla and had wanted to put a rat in her brain to make sure she went to term. She picked up the needler and checked that it was full-charged. Flicked off the safety and fired a test shot at the floor. Chips of rock, lava. If anyone tried to get in here . . .

"Hello?" The voice was right outside the zapper curtain. "Whitey Mydol? Anybody here?"

Darla stood stock-still, not daring to breathe.

"Whitey? It's Stahn Mooney, man, I need to score some merge. Yukawa's closed down. Open up, man, I'm getting skinsnakes."

Darla tried to hold the needler level at the door. Her hands were shaking five or ten cycles a second.

"HEY WHITEY!" yelled the voice, strident and lame.

Long, long silence, then muttering, and then a skritch-scratching at the lock. Suddenly the curtain flicked off. Darla screamed and jabbed the needler button. The shot was wide. The guy leaped forward and caught her in a bear hug. He was strong and skinny and old. He got the needler off her, stepped back, cut the zapper back on, and gave Darla a long, horny look. She was naked under her loose T-shirt. He was wearing a red imipolex jumpsuit with a lot of zippers.

"Who are you?" the guy asked. "Whitey's girlfriend?"

Darla sat down on the bed and slid her hand under the mattress to touch the knife. "Come here," she said, her voice shaking. "Come sit next to me."

The intruder's mouth spread in a long, sly smile. "And find out what you got hid under the mattress? No thanks. Power down. I'm just here to score some merge. Stahn Mooney's the name. What's yours?"

"Duh-Darla." Her teeth were chattering. "We're out of merge, too. You got any quaak? How'd you get the door open?"

"I'm a detective. Mooney Search. I mean that's what I was doing last month. Yukawa hired me to look for Della Taze, and Whitey was tailing me for Bei Ng."

"Yeah," said Darla, untensing a little. "I remember. You flared Whitey's shoulder. Hold on while I get dressed." She found some silk shorts and pulled them on, trying not to bend over. "Stop staring, dook, this is my life, wave?" He just stood there by the zapper, grinning away. Darla gave him a tough frown and shook her finger at him. "Don't try and put a move on me, hisspop, or Whitey'll do you dirt. You're already on his list."

"I bet it's a long one."

"What is?"

"Whitey's list. He's not the most ingratiating young man I've ever met. Not quite Rotary Club material."

"He's nice to me."

Darla decided to change shirts. Most guys sweetened right up once they'd gotten a glimpse of her huge lowgee boobs. She pulled the T-shirt up over her head and put on a plas blouse with a big pouch in front. Mooney watched the process alertly.

"You're beautiful, Darla. Whitey's a lucky man. Do you turn tricks?"

He was going to break in and stand here and insult her, right? "Not for skinny lamo slushed rent-a-pigs. Like I told you, dook, there's no merge. Dig it. Good-bye."

"Uh . . . I got some merge to sell, if you're out." He drew out a silver flask and handed it to her. "It's primo, straight from Yukawa. I tried it last month."

Darla opened the flask and sniffed. It smelled like the real thing. The flask was almost half full. Like $10K's worth. "Why'd you say you're buying if you're selling? What are you really after, Mooney? You just came down here to break in and nose around, didn't you?"

He pocketed the needler and gave her another of his long smiles. "Actually, Darla, I came down here to meet you."

Her skin sprang into gooseflesh. Was this guy a meatie after all? Before he could say anything else, she threw a gout of merge into his face. "Here's your score, bufop."

It was a huge dose, and he got limp right away. Darla kicked him in the crotch and he hit the floor.

"Quick," she said, standing over him. "While you can still talk. Tell me who hired you or I'm going to take out all your bones and sit on you. Whitey and me been planning to do that." She gave his softening head a vicious smack. "Who hired you, Mooney?"

"Emuw," slobbered Mooney. "A boppuh cawwed Emuw. He want to know if youw pwegnan. He wan you ta gwow an extwuh buhbuh . . ." His face went totally slack and he puddled.

"I'm getting an abortion," Della told the two-eyed Mooney puddle. "I'm gonna go do it like right now."

Mooney had flowed right out of his dooky jumpsuit. Darla went through its pockets, found her needler and a . . . wad of bills . . . $20K, oxo wow! And, oh-oh, a remote mike. He was bopperbugged, which meant they'd just heard what she said about getting an abortion. Darla started shaking again. Hurry, Darla, hurry! She stuffed the merge flask and the money in her shirt's pouch. She fired six quick needler blasts through the zapper curtain. Then she cut off the curtain and jumped out into the hall.

Empty. The curtain powered back up, and Darla was alone in a fifty-yard corridor. No sound but the slight humming of all the zappers. She took off running down the hall. She kept expecting a meatie to dart out from behind one of the zapper doors. She was in such a hurry that she forgot to look up when she jumped into the shaft that led down to the Markt.

Just as she got hold of the fireman's pole that ran down the center of the shaft, someone thumped into her from above.

"I'm sorry . . ." Darla began, but then something jabbed her spine. She twitched wildly, as if from a seizure, and let go of the pole. A strong hand caught hold of her wrist. The seizure passed. Darla felt her body get back hold of the fireman's pole. She wanted to turn her head and see who'd stabbed her, but she couldn't. She landed heavily on the Markt level. She could hear her invisible assailant hurrying back up the ladder, and then her legs led her out into the Markt and off to the right. Away from the Tun.

It's a zombie box, Darla thought to herself, feeling oddly calm. The boppers knew my wiring from the last time, so they had a special box all fixed to spike right in. I wonder if it shows under my hair?

She walked stiff-hipped past the rows of shops. The robot control of her body made her move differently from normal. Her arms hung straight at her sides, and her knees flexed deeply, powering her along in a rapidly trucking glide. She looked like a real jerk. She could tell because, for once, men didn't stare at her.

Her bobbing bod angled into the door of a shop called Little Kidder Toys. A crummy, dimlit place she'd never bothered noticing before. Outdated mecco novelties, some cheap balls, and two kids nosing around. A hard-looking middle-aged grit woman behind the counter. Before Darla could see anything else, her robot-run body whirled and peered out the shop door, staring back down the Markt mall to see if anyone was following her. No one, no one, but yes, *there,* just coming out of the shaft, far and tiny, was Whitey! She jerked back out of sight.

"Kin ah hep yew?" The shopkeeper had saggy boobs and a cracker accent. "Ah'm Rainbow." Her short, chemically distressed hair was indeed dyed in stripes of color: a central green strip flanked by two purples and two yellows. The roots were red. A true skank. "Yew lookin fo a toooy, hunnih?"

The zombie box had Darla's speech centers blocked. Instead, she leaned forward, making sure the children couldn't see, and made four quick gestures with her left hand. Three fingers horizontal—three fingers pointing down—fingers and thumb cupped up—fingers straight up with thumb sticking out to the side. Simple sign language: E-M-U-L.

"Well les check on that, huunnih," drawled Rainbow casually. "Les check in bayack. Have you two chirrun decahded whut you wawunt yet?"

The two children looked up from their toygrubbing. A young boy and a younger girl. They looked like brother and sister. "I want to get this toy fish," said the girl in a quacky little voice. She held the fish cradled against her thin chest. "My brother has all the money."

"But I'm not ready yet," said the boy stubbornly. "I want a glider, and I haven't decided which one."

"Ah don't lahk you all takin so looong," said Rainbow coaxingly. "Ah gotta hep this naahce grownup lady naow. Tell you whut, young mayun. You kin have the bes glaahder fo two dollahs off."

"Yes, but . . ."

Rainbow strode forward, plucked a glider off the rack, and pressed it into the boy's hand. "Gimme fi dollah an git!"

He drew a large handful of change out of his pocket and studied it carefully. "I only have four seventy-five, so . . ."

"Thass fahn!" Rainbow took the money off the boy and pushed the two children out the door. "Bah-bah, kiddies, be gooood." As soon as they were outside she turned on the zapper. The doorway filled with green light.

"Naow," said Rainbow. "Les go on in bayack."

Darla followed Rainbow to the rear of the shop. There was no door there, only a rock wall with pegs holding cheap moongolf equipment. Rainbow did a coded tap-tap-ta-tap-TAP-ta-ta against one edge of the wall, and it swung open, revealing a bright-lit room whose far end tapered off into a dim rock-walled corridor. A thin, greasy-haired little man sat on a couch in there, wearing earphones and watching *Bill Ding's Pink Party* on a portable vizzy. He had pockmarked skin and a pencil-thin mustache. There could be no doubt that he was Rainbow's mate.

"This is Berdoo," Rainbow told Darla. "He'll take care of yew."

Berdoo pulled off his earphones and gave Darla the once-over. Though his features formed the mask of a frozen-faced tough guy, he looked pleased at what he saw.

"Now yew behave yoself, Berdoo!" giggled Rainbow. She stepped back from the open wall and . . . *oh please no* . . . Darla's legs trucked her on in. "Baaah," said Rainbow and swung the wall door closed.

Berenice stood there alone with Berdoo, guardian of the hidden hallway to hell. He looked like a pimp, a grit, a Hell's Angel gone a bit mild with age. Once again her hand spelled out E-M-U-L. Berdoo just sat there looking at her for a minute, and then he got up and took off all her clothes. Darla's limbs helped him, but then, before Berdoo could push her down onto the couch, Darla's left hand gave him a hard poke and spelled out N-O.

"No?" said Berdoo. His voice was a hoarse whisper, with a cracker accent like Rainbow's. "What kinda bull is this, Emul?"

Darla's body leaned over and took the merge flask and the $20K out of her shirt's pouch. She gave them to Berdoo. He counted the money and sniffed at the merge.

"Wal, ah guess thass killah enough, Emul, but this old dawg sho does lahk to roll in fresh meat."

Two fingers pointing down—thumb and forefinger looped. N-O.

Berdoo sighed, then tossed the merge and money into an open wall safe over the couch. He went around behind Darla and lifted her hair to check out the zombie box. "Naahce work," he muttered, jiggling it a bit. He got some derma-plast and pasted a bit of it onto Darla's neck, just to make sure the junction was secure. Finally he gave Darla's buttocks a lingering, intimate caress and seated himself back on the couch. "Thass it, hunnih. Baaah."

Darla loped on down the corridor, which grew narrower and rougher as soon as she left Berdoo's office area. A pale light strip ran along the ceiling, eight feet overhead. Each of her rapid lowgee bounds took her right up against the light strip, and Darla grew disoriented from the steady motion and the rhythmic pulsing of the light. Would it help if she fainted? For a moment she did seem to lose consciousness, but it made no difference. The zombie box kept her body moving with the tireless repetitiveness of a machine. The corridor stretched on and on, mile after mile. With her legs numb and out of her control, Darla soon began to feel that she was falling down and down the light-striped hallway, endlessly down some evil rat's hole. Rat, thought Darla bleakly, I wonder if that's what they're taking me for, to get a rat in my skull. How ever will that feel? Like this, maybe, with a robot running my body and my head thinking its same old thoughts. But it'll be worse, won't it, with half my brain gone. Was Whitey coming? He would have tried the Tun first, wouldn't he, and then he would have looked up and down the Markt and not seen anything. Maybe those children would tell him they saw her in Little Kidder Toys. Cute children they'd been, oh, if only she could really have had a child with Whitey, instead of ending up like this, people had always treated her bad just because she had big boobs, that was it really, a not-too-bright girl with big boobs didn't have a chance, though Whitey always treated her nice, he did, and, oh man, was that rotten creep Stahn Mooney going to get it. If only they didn't make her a meatie and send her out after Whitey, if only . . .

Darla drifted off into a kind of doze then.

When she woke up, she was in a stone room with one glass wall. It was like a pink-lit aquarium of air. It had furniture more or less like her and Whitey's cubby. She was lying on the bed. Her neck hurt in back. She reached to feel herself . . . she could move her arms again! Her neck was bare, with a fresh scab. Was . . . was there a rat in her head?

"Hello, Darla," said a box across the room. She hadn't noticed it before. Its surface was a mosaic of red-yellow-blue squares, with one section coned into a speech membrane. "Darla with her eyes all dark, all wild and midnight, all apple tree and gold, no false pose and camp, oh Darla. I'm Emul." Square-edged little bumps moved back and forth along the box's surface. "You beautiful doll, your hair, your scent and slide, you dear meat thing, please trust me."

The box grew arms and legs then, and a square-jawed head. Darla sat up on the edge of the bed and watched it. "I want clothes," said Darla.

"Wear me, Dar. I'll lick your snowy belly and nose your every tiny woman part." Emul flicked one of his arms and it flew off to land on the floor. As Darla watched, the arm's component blocks split and resplit, folding here and flexing there. In a few moments, the arm had turned into a kind of playsuit: baggy blue-red shorts topped with a stretchy yellow tunic.

"I . . ." Darla stepped forward and poked the garment with her toe. It didn't *do* anything, so she went ahead and put it on. It was imipolex, warm and well-fitting. She paced off the room's dimensions—five paces by four. There was an airlock set into one of the stone sidewalls. She rapped a knuckle on the hard glass wall in front. There was a kind of laboratory outside, with a few other boppers moving around. She turned and stared at Emul. He'd grown another arm to replace the one she was wearing. With clothes on, Darla felt more like her old self. "What do you really want, Emul? No more pervo spit-talk. I could get real mental, scuzzchips." She picked up a stool and hefted it.

Emul tightened up the features on the head he'd grown. Except for the RYB skin coloring, he looked almost human. "In clear: you are pregnant with Whitey Mydol's child.

Mamma mammal's mammaries swell. I have an extra embryo I'd like you to carry to term. Pink little Easter baby jellybean. I would like your permission to plant it in your womb."

Instinctively Darla put her hands over her crotch. "You want me to grow an extra baby?"

"Twins, Darla, yours and Whitey's, Berenice's and mine; I'll make love to you or do it like a doped-up doc, I don't care either way, your way is my way, you can watch me all you want."

"And then you'll let me go? You won't put a rat in my skull? I'm not supposed to stay here for nine months, am I?"

"Ah . . . possibly, or until it's safe as houses in Einstein. I'll let you leave with absentminded pumping legs, Dar. A double stroller for the chinchuck twins, and you all your own homey self. Proud Whitey handing out cigars."

"Right. You better hope Whitey doesn't decide to come here and get me, bitbrain. Whitey does what's necessary, and he never says he's sorry. Never."

Emul made a noise like a laugh. "That's *my* lookout, spitfire. Will you spread?"

"It won't hurt?"

"Your way is my way."

Darla sighed, slipped her playsuit back off and flopped down on the bed. "Just get it over with. Just slip it in." She parted her legs and cocked her head up to watch Emul. "Come on. And don't talk while you do it."

Emul grew a stiff penis and stepped forward. The blocks that made up his body smoothed their edges off, and he slipped into her like a plastic man. His penis seemed to elongate as it entered her; it reached up and up, bumped her cervix, and slid on through. A fluttering feeling deep in Darla's belly. It felt almost good. Emul's imipolex lips brushed her cheeks and he detumesced. He drew back out of her and stood up. "Hail, Darla, full of life. Blessed be the fruit of thy magic star-crossed bod."

Darla lay still for a minute, thinking. Finally she sat up and put her playsuit back on. Emul had turned back into an RYB box with a speaker cone. She looked him over, considering. "I'd like a vizzy, Emul. And food. You can bring me food from Einstein, right? I'd like about fifty dollars of Chinese food and a twelve-pack of beer. Some weed, too, and you gotta rig me up a showerbath. Maybe a little quaak . . . no, that could hurt the babies. Beer, weed, Chinese food, a vizzy and a shower. I'll think of more stuff later. Get on it, bop, make me comfortable."

"Whatever you say, Queen Bee. You want, you get." Emul bowed deeply and disappeared into the airlock.

Chapter Ten
ISDN

January 27, 2031

Stahn was so merged that even his bones were melted. Darla had hit him with a hundred times the normal dose. He dissolved into the clear white light and talked to God for the second time in a month. The light was filled with filigreed moire patterns, infrared and ultraviolet, silver and gray. God's voice was soft and strong.

"I love you, Stahn. I'll always love you."

"I'm a screwup, God. Everything I touch turns to garbage. Will it be like this when I die?"

"I'm always here, Stahn. It's all right. I love you, no matter what."

"Thank you, God. I love you."

A long timeless peace then, a bath in God's uncritical love. Clear white light. But bit by bit, God broke the light into pieces, into people and boppers and voices from the past and from the future, all woven together, warped into weird, sinister loomings:

"Here, Stahn, let me check you over for existence. Me existing with mikespike skull. They have tract homes for a person killing GAX. I am two knobs in half half your head. We value information over all this chauvinism, soft, wet, limp, I mean the Happy Cloak. Old Cobb wiggly in here tonight. I'm Wendy, naw, I'm Eurydice, dear Orpheus. Even Ken Doll seems to sing when you get rich. You take that first into slavery, to quit fact. You can go they know it. Chipmold oxo, Whitey a natural next. Gawk a clown to me.

But score, while you can still talk. It's so wiggly on Mars. Wave on it together in slices. We can learn which soul ain't never ate no live brain before. If the head's shot, sell the bod. I am hungry, I am pleased, I hope you trust nothing. Dream on, exile, sweet body and brain are mikes. ISDN she you, voluntary meatie? Why did you say I was your wife? Noise is like spaceships existing on chips. Hi 'surfer. God can be very ruthless. Think I was human again, Stahn Junior? Are you in dutch with logically deep information?''

Oh God, oh Jesus, oh what does it mean? Now there was something . . . poking at Stahn. Seasick waves jittered back and forth through his melted flesh. His eyes were merged down to photosensitive patches; he could make out a shadow moving back and forth over him. Light dark light dark, and then a heavy sloshing of his tissues. Dark. Pressure all around him, and more waves, painfully irregular, someone was carrying him in a bag. A splat then, feel of a cold smooth floor, and it was light. Shadows moving.

Something splashed on Stahn. There was a tingling and a puckering, and then he was lying naked on a bimstone floor with a ring of five people looking down at him.

One of them was, oh no, Whitey Mydol. Stahn jerked convulsively at the sight of Whitey, recalling the threats that Darla had made on Whitey's behalf. But for now, Whitey just stood there looking mean, tapping a needler against his palm.

Next to Whitey was a yellow-skinned man with vertical wrinkles running up and down his face. Next to him was Max Yukawa, and next to Yukawa were a familiar-looking man and woman: the woman dark, wide-mouthed, and beautiful, the man oily and mean. It was, yeah, Mrs. Beller and Ricardo from Yukawa's love-puddle. Stahn scooted a little on his back; he had a silly head and a throbbing erection from the sudden merge comedown; that message, all about meaties and Wendy and Orpheus and God . . .

Mrs. Beller stared down at Stahn dispassionately. He could see up her skirt. Oh, Mrs. Beller, I need love, too. I'm not really so . . .

"He's all jelled," said Mrs. Beller's soft, lazy voice. "Give him his clothes, Whitey."

Whitey stepped forward, holding Stahn's red jumpsuit

bunched in one hand. With a grunt of effort, Whitey whipped the zippered cloth across Stahn's face with all his might; whipped and whipped again.

"Don't mark him, Mydol," came a singsong voice. The yellow-skinned man. Stahn grinned uncertainly and slipped his suit on. He stood up and swayed, unsteady on his feet.

"Let me do the introductions," said Yukawa, graciously inclining his long thin head. "Mr. Mooney already knows me and Whitey, and I believe he glimpsed Mrs. Beller and Ricardo at my lab. Fern Beller, Stahn Mooney, Ricardo Guttierez. And the wise celestial here is Bei Ng, my merge-brother. He says he's wise, anyway."

Whitey Mydol was shirtless as usual, his greasy blond mohawk running all the way down his back to his jeans. Mrs. Beller was beautifully pale and supple. Her face was brightly made up, and she wore an electric blue imipolex tank top over a short, wide-flared yellow skirt. Ricardo wore a purple-stitched black silk cowboy shirt, black gym shorts, and heavy motorcycle boots. He had snakes tattooed on his arms and legs, a black toothbrush mustache, and deep purple mirrorshades. His black hair was worn in a short, greasy brushcut. He smiled at Stahn, showing two even rows of gold-capped teeth.

Moving as smoothly as a figure in a gangster ballet, Whitey Mydol stepped forward and grabbed Stahn by the throat. "Where's Darla, Mooney? WHERE IS SHE?"

Whitey was squeezing so hard that Stahn couldn't get any words out. His eyes were watering, and the only noise he could make was a high creaking sound.

"Let go him, Mydol," sang Bei Ng. "He want to talk."

Whitey let up the pressure and gave Stahn a violent shove. Stahn flew across the room and landed on a leather couch. His five captors seated themselves as well. For a minute Stahn stayed doubled over, clutching his throat. Play for time, Stahn. You can offer them Cobb's map.

He peeked up and checked out his surroundings. The room was a luxurious office, with a red bimstone floor and impossibly expensive oak-paneled walls. Bei Ng sat behind a large mahogany desk, with Yukawa in an easy chair to one side. Whitey and Ricardo were squeezed onto the couch shoulder to shoulder with Stahn, Whitey on the right and

Ricardo on the left. Mrs. Beller sat in another easy chair, her lovely legs loosely crossed.

"Hey," croaked Stahn finally. "Let's power down. I'm just a middle-aged detective. I'll tell you everything I know. I'll tell you my life story, for God's sake, just keep the ridgeback off my neck." Ricardo snickered at this, a high hophead giggle. He and Whitey were holding hands across Stahn's belly, forming a kind of seatbelt. Stahn couldn't move his arms. "I mean, really, I'll do whatever you guys say. I don't know where Darla is, I swear. A bopper named Emul hired me to find out if Darla is pregnant, and if she'd be willing to carry an extra baby. I was all set to offer her $20K. But then she threw merge on me and told me she's getting an abortion. Emul had a bug in my pocket, so I suppose it's possible that—"

"You scuzzy lickchip leech," snapped Whitey, giving Stahn a stinging slap with his free hand. "She never made it to the Tun."

"What Emul offer you?" asked Bei Ng.

"Money," said Stahn. "And—and a clone of my dead wife Wendy. I killed her by accident six years ago. The boppers have clones of her in their pink-tanks. Emul said that if I'd do a few jobs for him, he'd get me a wendy."

"Very touching," said Bei Ng, half smiling and then falling into a minute's reverie. Finally he reached some conclusion and looked over at Mydol.

"You no worry, Whitey, if Emul want Darla fuck, then either Darla safe or now Darla meatie. We find some way to get her out. Hotshot ISDN surgeons can always fix. I say we go ahead make Mooney volunteer meatie and carry new wetware as per plan. His wendy story make good cover." Bei smiled broadly and leaned back in his chair. "Is no rush now, is all decide."

Suddenly Stahn understood a piece of his merge vision. "What do you mean, 'We make Mooney volunteer meatie'?"

"Just for a while," said Yukawa, arranging the bottom half of his long thin head into a smile. "When things settle down, ISDN can tank-grow a clone of your missing brain tissue and hook it up, just like Bei says. If you like. But the meaties don't have it bad, you know. I think they live in pleasant tract homes in a bopper-built ecosphere. Ken told

Whitey all about it before he died." Yukawa winked at Whitey.

"Ken Doll?" said Stahn, more and more confused.

"Affirmo," said Whitey. "I chased him down after he zombie-boxed Darla. I killed him slow, and he told me a lot. You've been merged a couple of hours, Mooney. Darla disappeared somewhere down in the Markt; there must be some kind of secret door." Whitey's face was inches from Stahn's. "Do you know where the door is?"

"Uh . . . maybe you'll have to kill me slow to find out, punk."

Whitey took this in stride. "And what did old Cobb tell you after he pulled my mikespike out of your skull?"

"Yes," said Bei. "We very interest. Why Cobb want see you before he fly to Earth? Cobb on humans' side, yes?"

"Cobb . . . Cobb's for information exchange. Always has been. He likes the idea of his boppers building people and blending in. But he's no fool, man, he knows how ruthless the boppers can be. He . . ." Stahn looked around the room. He was trapped bad. Might as well play his only card. "He gave me an S-cube map of the Nest, along with all the access glyphs. Just in case we need to strike back."

"I speak for ISDN," said Mrs. Beller. "And we *do* want to strike back. With those gibberlin genes, the Manchildren are going to kill Earth's ecology. There could be a billion of them in a year, a trillion in two. This time the boppers have gone too far. We *are* going to strike back, Mr. Mooney, and you're part of the plan."

"The operation won't hurt," said Yukawa. "Mrs. Beller knows some expert neurosurgeons working right here in the ISDN building. They'll take part of your right brain out—less than a third, really—put a neuroplug in, and then you go to the trade center and offer your services to your friend Emul. The scalpel boys'll go easy on you—you'll still be able to move the left side of your body, though you will have some disorientation."

Stahn tried to stand up, but Ricardo and Whitey still had their two hands clamped together across his arms and stomach. They were strong guys. They had him pushed right down into the cushions. Ricardo snickered and spoke. He had a slight lisp. "You know about *slack,* Sta-Hi? Like to *take it easy,* man? Slack means no more yelling from the right half of your head. You going to be very happy, my friend." He lefthanded a stick of gum out of his shirt pocket. "You want a piece, Stahn? You want to get high?"

"No," said Stahn, "I don't." This was really happening. "I quit using two years ago. If it wasn't for drugs I wouldn't have lost my job and killed Wendy. I was working as a cop for a while there, you know, down there in Daytona after I broke Frostee." He sighed shakily. "Man oh man, those boppers never quit. I wonder if they'll still give me a wendy when I'm a meatie."

"You'll be a charming couple," purred Mrs. Beller. "With half an adult brain between the two of you."

"Just *like* an ex-cop and his old lady," said Ricardo, happily chomping his gum. "What you say they call those pleasant tract homes, Dr. Yukawa? Say *Happy Acres?*" Ricardo shook his head in mock wonder as Yukawa guffawed. "You won't have a care in the world, Mooney man, boffing that fine fresh tank-grown chick. With her brain all blank, she'll believe anything you want to tell her. You'll live like a king. When she get smart maybe they make her a meatie, too—I hear they cut out a piece of the *left* half of a woman's brain, man—"

"Shut up, Cardo," snarled Mydol, digging his elbow so hard into Stahn's stomach that Stahn gasped. "Don't talk to me about woman meaties." He made his voice calm again and addressed Stahn. "So Cobb gave you a map, did he? Now we're getting somewhere. Is the map in your office?"

"Kill me slow, punk. Smother me with Darla's fat whore ass and—"

The thud of Whitey's fist against his neck knocked Stahn unconscious. When he came back to, Mrs. Beller was leaning over him with a bulb of water. "Drink this, Stan, it's just water. You shouldn't tease Whitey, he's very upset. He's worried about Darla."

Stahn's throat felt broken. He could barely get the water down. Some of it went the wrong way, and he coughed for a long time, thinking hard. The question was: what could he get for the map? A chance to escape, at best. Still, just in case, he had to ask.

"If I give you the map, you'll let me go, won't you? You can use someone else for the meatie agent."

"No, Mooney," whispered Whitey. "We're gonna use you. Bei promised me."

"It is for good of the human race," said old Bei. "Truly, Stahn. You will be hero; you will atone for many sin."

"But what good will I be as an agent?" protested Stahn, his voice cracking. "You can't put a mikespike on me. The boppers can sense them and pick them right out like Cobb did. It's pointless. I'll just disappear into the Nest."

"Here, Stahn," said lovely Fern Beller, still standing over him. "Drink some more water. Your voice sounds awful." Stahn drank deep. Fern's hands were soft and sweet, oh Mrs. Beller, what type of sex.

"Whitey and I have something in common," said Yukawa then, running a hand through his thinning hair. "I loved Della Taze, Stahn, I still do. You know that. She's all right now, but what the boppers did to her was wrong. I want to punish them. And I am a bioengineer. I am a very brilliant man."

"You always say," put in Bei. There seemed to be a friendly sibling rivalry between him and Yukawa. "You very brilliant except sometimes you not very smart."

"I've designed a chipmold," said Yukawa. "Fern just infected you with it. It's a bit like thrush, quite opportunistic, and you've got it. I don't care if we lose track of you or not, once you take my chipmold into the Nest."

"Max," interrupted Mrs. Beller, sidestepping the spray from Stahn's mouth. "Do you really think you should—"

"Tell him, tell him," said Bei Ng. "Once we replace his right parietal lobe with a neuroplug, he got nothing else to lose. Stahn going to play ball with us, no problem. Is all decide."

Yukawa steepled his fingers and wagged his long head happily. "Chipmold in that water, Stahn, and *you drank it.*"

Ricardo cackled joyfully, and even Whitey cracked a smile.

"What's chipmold?" said Stahn presently.

"In general, biotic life can flourish whenever there is an energy gradient," said Yukawa. "Think of the tubeworms who live around deep-sea volcanic vents. Or lichen growing on a sunlit Antarctic rock. There's an energy gradient across all the boppers' silicon chips, and I've designed an organism that can live there. Chipmold.''

"I don't get it," said Stahn. "The chipmold will crud up their circuits?"

"Better than that. The chipmold likes a steady thousand-cycle per second frequency. That's what it 'eats,' if you will: kilohertz electromagnetic energy. For a mold, it's quite intelligent. It's able to selectively suppress or potentiate the chips' firing to enhance the amplitude of the desired frequency. It will eat their heads.'' Yukawa threw his arms around his head, shuddered, and then slumped.

"Spastic robots, my friend," said Ricardo.

"Be sure and spit a lot," said Bei Ng, beaming across his desk. "Spread chipmold all around Nest. Cock leg here and there like dog."

"Oxo wow," said Stahn, more impressed than he cared to admit. Something else occurred to him. "Am I going to have fits?"

"Who cares, dip," said reliable Whitey. "Where's the map?"

"Don't worry," said Yukawa. "In your high-entropy system the stuff's just like sore throat. And a low-grade bladder infection. It's quite versatile; I'm not sure *what* it'll do to the boppers' flickercladding."

"Come on, Stahn," drawled Mrs. Beller. "Be a dear and tell us where you hid the map."

This was his only chance. "It's in my office desk. But I fixed it so only I can get it. It's boobytrapped with a smart bomb."

"Clear," said Whitey disgustedly. "You have to say that, right? They teach you that line at cop school, right?"

"I don't care what you think, punk, it's true. It's in my office desk with a smart bomb that only I can turn off. The bomb knows what I look like."

"AO. Cardo and I'll take you there. Right, Bei?"

Bei thought for a full two minutes, as if pondering a chess problem. "Yes," he said finally. "Go up to roof, get maggie, fly to Mr. Mooney's building, if he make trouble you can stun. You take Mrs. Beller, too. Very careful, very slow."

"I've got a stunpatch all set," said Mrs. Beller, reaching into her purse. She drew out a foil disk, stripped plastic off one side of it, and glued it to the back of Stahn's neck. "Let him go, boys."

Whitey and Ricardo let go each other's hands and let Stahn stand up.

"Walk towards me, Stahn," said Mrs. Beller. "Come here and give me a big kiss." She pouted her big lips at him and showed the tip of her purple tongue. "Come to mamma."

Stahn took a cautious step, and then Mrs. Beller pressed the button of the control she was holding. The stunpatch fired electricity into Stahn's spine. It hurt more than anything he'd ever imagined possible. He fell twitching to the floor and lay there staring glassy-eyed at Mrs. Beller's legs. It took a few minutes till he could get back up. One thought dominated his mind: he must not do anything that would make Mrs. Beller press the button again.

Mrs. Beller, Whitey, and Ricardo ushered Stahn out into the hall.

"This is the sixth floor of the ISDN ziggurat," said Mrs. Beller, playing the part of a clear-voiced tour guide. She walked next to Stahn, with Ricardo in front and Whitey behind. Her hips swayed enticingly. "Not everyone knows that ISDN stands for Integrated Systems Digital Network. We're a petabuck company born of the merger of AT&T and Mitsubishi. ISDN manufactures about 60 percent of the vizzies in use, and we operate something like 80 percent of the transmission channels. This, our Einstein ziggurat, houses labs, offices, and a number of independent organizations—this far from Earth's scrutiny it's a case of *In my father's house are many mansions*. Most people don't understand that ISDN has no leaders and no fixed policies. ISDN operates at unfathomable degrees of parallelism and nonlinearity. How else to pay off the world's chaos?

"Supposedly, ISDN has been backing Bei Ng's Church of Organic Mysticism on the off chance that Bei might come up with a workable form of telepathy, but really we've just wanted to keep a feeler on the merge trade, which looks to be a coming thing. And of course Bei's many connections are very valuable."

The long hall was lined with room after room of weird equipment. ISDN was so big. It seemed unlikely that anyone could really know what was going on in all the labs. The general idea seemed to be to try and keep up with the boppers, by whatever means necessary. In one of the rooms on Bei Ng's hall, cyberbiologists were fiddling with probes and petri dishes. In another room, cellular automata technicians were watching 3D patterns darting about in a great mound of imipolex. In still another room, Stahn could see information mechanics disassembling a beam-charred woman-shaped petaflop. Was that the one—Berenice—who'd been killed with Manchile the other day? Stahn wondered briefly how old Cobb was doing; he'd gotten away, lucky guy.

Suddenly it occurred to Stahn that somewhere in this huge building there was an operating room with brain surgeons waiting for him. He shuddered and turned his attention back to Mrs. Beller.

"ISDN carefully looks over every major new development with one question in mind," she was saying. "How can this be used to increase our power and our holdings? Usually we use incremental techniques, but sometimes a catastrophic intervention is required. The Manchildren pose a real threat to our main customers, the human race. We asked all our employees for suggestions, and Bei Ng called up his merge-brother, Max Gibson-Yukawa. It will be unfortunate for the boppers. Here's the elevator."

The ride over to Stahn's building was uneventful. Only when they were walking down the hall to his office did his captors show any signs of nervousness. Though they didn't come out and say so, it was clear that they were wondering just how smart Stahn's bomb *was*.

Inside Stahn's office, Mrs. Beller took a post by the door. She held out her right hand, with the thumb lightly resting on the button of the stunpatch control. Whitey and Ricardo got back in the far corners of the room, covering Stahn and the desk with their needlers. Stahn stood behind his plastic-topped desk, facing Mrs. Beller and the open office door. Behind him and to the left was Ricardo, behind him and to the right was Whitey.

"All right, Stahn," purred Mrs. Beller. "Be a good boy

and get out your map. Tell the bomb that everything's OK."
She caressed the control button with her fat thumb tip, and
pain seeped down Stahn's spine. She deepened her voice,
shifting from soft cop to hard cop mode. "Don't try to
outthink me Mooney, you're a burnt-out stumblebum with
no second chance."

"Sane," said Stahn. "I'm ready to spread. Shave my
brain and mail me to Happy Acres with my GI wendy, how
bad can it be." He smiled in an ingratiating, cringing way
and pulled open the top left drawer of his brown metal desk.
"Map's right in here."

Stahn's perceived timeflow was running very very slow.
The next second of time went as follows:

Stahn took his hand off the wide-open drawer and looked
down at his smart kinetic energy bomb, nestled right next to
Cobb's red map cube. The bomb was a rubbery deep-blue
sphere with a reddish eye set into it. It was designed not to
explode, but rather to bounce around and hit things. It was
polonium-centered and quite massive. Its outer rind was a
thick tissue of megaflop impolex that had been microwired
to act as a computer and as a magnetic field drive, feeding
off the energy of the radioactive polonium core. The bomb
had the intelligence, roughly, of a dog. Recognizing Stahn,
the bomb activated its powerful maggiedrive and floated up
a fraction of a millimeter, up off the brown metal of Stahn's
desk drawer bottom, up just enough so that Stahn could tell
that his good smart bomb was ready to help.

Over the years, Stahn had taught the bomb to read his eye
signals. He blinked twice, meaning "HIT THEM," and then
stared at Mrs. Beller's right wrist, meaning "THERE
FIRST."

Silently the bomb began to spin, adjusting its English.
Stahn formed his face into a weary, disgusted expression.
"How beat. The scuzzass bomb is broken anyway." He
stared hard at Mrs. Beller's wrist and . . . widened his eyes.

The bomb flew up, caromed off the ceiling, and struck
Mrs. Beller a paralyzing blow on the right wrist. The
stunpatch control dropped from her numb hand. The bomb
came up off the floor, sighted on Mydol, and did a two-
cushion rebound off the wall and ceiling. It caught Mydol
solidly in the side of the head. Mydol's eyes glazed as his

head snapped to one side. The bomb came up off the floor and wall, fixed its eye on Ricardo, and set up a gyroscopic spin calculated to accelerate it off the ceiling and into Ricardo's forehead. The KE bomb was travelling at about 40 ft/sec, or 30 mph—any faster and it wouldn't have been able to direct its bounces to optimum target.

The bomb was thinking as fast as it could, but its max flop was less than Ricardo's.

Ricardo became consciously aware of the bomb's violent Superball motion only after it had already hit Whitey, but by then his arm muscles were tracking the bomb. A fast eye/hand feedback loop locked the needler on target. Ricardo zapped Stahn's smart bomb just before it hit the ceiling.

The smart bomb broke into four or five throbbing chunks that clattered to the floor and lay there twitching. The slow, full second ended.

Before anything else could happen, Stahn peeled the stunpatch off his neck and wadded it up, ruining its circuits.

"I've still got the drop on you, Mooney," said Ricardo from his corner. "Nice move, though. Good thing there was three of us. You AO, Fern?"

"He's broken my wrist," said Mrs. Beller.

Stahn tossed the wadded stunpatch out his room's open window. "Well that SM was getting a little old, *Fern*. Why don't you all promise me some money and I'll go quietly. I really will. I'll go to Happy Acres and I'll infect the boppers with chipmold, but I want a square ISDN contract in writing and on the record. I want three things." Stahn held up three fingers of his left hand, preparing to tick off his points.

Behind him on the floor, Whitey Mydol began to groan and wake up. Stahn talked faster. "First, in return for cooperating from here on out, I want to be given the status of an ISDN employee. I want a job. Second, in return for giving up my right brain, I want ISDN to clone me a new one should I so desire. If I kick being a meatie, I want my brain back. And number three, I get half a gigabuck payable to my account."

"Listen to this load of crutches," grumbled Whitey, who'd managed to lurch back to his feet. He was standing there with his arms crossed over his chest, trying to keep his balance.

"Here Whitey," said Stahn, taking the S-cube out of the drawer and handing it over to the ridgeback. "This is Cobb's map. You get the credit for bringing it in. If we're going to be working on ISDN contracts together, you and I might as well be friends. I mean, wave it, Happy Acres could be a trip. You all weren't kidding about that, were you? Nobody has to be sorry, do they, so we might as well—"

Whitey took the red plastic map cube and looked at it. "How does it work?"

"It's a godseye map of Einstein and the Nest, shot December 26, which is when Cobb gave it to me. Any holocaster'll play it, Cobb says. You can tune the image along four axes: size and the three space dimensions. Cobb wanted me to have it in case the boppers started getting out of hand. It shows all their tunnels and—" Stahn stopped and glanced around. "I debugged this room two days ago, but you never know. Wouldn't we be better off making our plans at ISDN, where it's fully shielded?"

"Let's get moving!" said Ricardo. The four of them ran up to the roof, jumped into the maggie, and headed for the ISDN building. Now that it was all decided, Stahn felt excited and ready for the change. They wouldn't take all *that* much of his brain out. Wendy, baby, I'm on my way!

Chapter Eleven
When Bubba Woke Up

February 8, 2031

When Bubba woke up, Mamma and Uncle Cobb were downstairs talking with the groom. His name was Luther; he was nice. He worked downstairs in the stables all day. His wife Geegee picked him up when it got dark, after most everyone had gone home. Geegee laughed a lot, and she always brought Bubba a big bag of food. At night Bubba could eat and run around a little, but all day he had to be still. Mamma and Cobb said the bad men would kill Bubba if they found him.

Mamma was beautiful and soft. Cobb was strong and shiny. Luther and Geegee were beautiful and soft and shiny. The horses were beautiful and soft and strong and shiny, but they couldn't talk.

The place they lived was Churchill Downs in Louisville on Earth. They lived in a long thin building called the paddock. Lots of horses lived in the paddock; their stables were side by side. Above the stables, up under the long peaked roof, was the hayloft. Mamma and Cobb and Bubba had made themselves a cozy nest in the hay and straw. Straw was stiff and hollow and shiny; hay was dusty and light green. Horses ate hay and crapped on straw.

In the daytime, Bubba could peek through the cracks of the barn's long hayloft and see the stands. They were big and empty, and in front of them there was a racetrack shaped like a rectangle with semicircular ends. The track was a place for the horses to run, although now it was too cold and there was frozen water snow all over everything. Cobb told Bubba that when Bubba was an old, old man, the snow would melt and flowers would come out.

Bubba knew what roses look like. He had a lot of Know because he was a meatbop. The boppers had built his father, and his father's sperm had had two tails, one for the body, and one for the Know. Bubba's sperm would have two tails, too, as soon as it started coming, which would be soon, since he was thirteen. Tomorrow he would be fourteen.

When Cobb was finished talking with Luther he climbed up the straight ladder to the hayloft. Bubba could hear him coming, and then he could see Cobb's head sticking up through the square hole in the hayloft floor. Cobb was a bopper, though he'd been a flesher a long long time ago. He had white hair and shiny pink skin. His neck shook when he talked.

"Hi, squirt, how's it going." Cobb limped across the hay-strewn planks and sat down next to Bubba.

"Fine, Uncle Cobb. I'm thinking. What did Luther tell you?"

"Luther says you're the only one of Manchile's boys to have escaped. They killed the last of the others last night."

Bubba never tired of hearing about his father. "What was Manchile like, Cobb? Tell me again."

"He was cool. A saintly badass. I saw him give two speeches, you know. The first was for the vizzy, at Suesue Piggot's apartment, and the second was at the State Fairgrounds. That's when Mark Piggot shot him. Piggot's men killed Berenice, too, and they wrecked my ion drive." Cobb waggled his charred feet. "I don't know how I'm going to get back to the Moon."

"What did my father's speeches *say*?"

"He said that people and boppers are the same. It's really true, but some people don't like hearing it. Some people even think that sex and skin color matter. The bottom line is that we're all information processors, and God loves all of us just the same. It's so obvious, I don't see how anyone can disagree." One of the horses downstairs nickered. Cobb smiled. "Yes, Red Chan, horses too. Even flies, even atoms. All is One, and the One is Everywhere."

"Have you ever seen God, Uncle Cobb?"

Cobb gave one of his sad, faraway smiles. "Sure thing, squirt. I spent ten years with God. When I was dead. It was very restful. But Berenice brought me back to take care of *you*." He reached out and rumpled Bubba's brown hair. "And I'm hoping to get my grandson Willy out of jail while I'm at it. I bet you and Willy would really hit it off. He's the one who drove me and Cisco here the night Manchile got shot, you know. Someone saw him taking us from the Fairgrounds, but he wouldn't tell the Gimmie where. You owe Willy your life, Bubba."

"Hi, boys." Mamma's pretty face appeared at the top of the ladder. Her breath steamed in the cold air.

"Hi, Cisco," said Cobb. "Look how grownup Bubba is today."

Mamma walked over and gave Bubba a big kiss. It gave him a tingly feeling in his balls.

"Mamma . . . can I make a baby with you?"

Cisco laughed and gave him a light shove. "You're going to have to work harder than *that*, Bubba. First of all it wouldn't be right, and second of all, I'm tired out from growing you. One pregnancy a month's enough! You'll find lots of nice women when you go off on your own, just wait and see."

"Do you think . . ." said Cobb raising his eyebrows.

"Tonight," said Cisco. "One of the trainers just told Luther that the Gimmie's planning to search the stables tomorrow." She patted Bubba on the hand. "Tonight you go downtown and find a woman to take you in, Bubba. You can make a baby with her. Don't worry, you'll know what to do. The main thing is to smile a lot and not be scared to come right out and ask for sex. Find a nice young woman by herself in, oh, La Mirage Health Club. Introduce yourself, talk to her for a while and then say, 'You're beautiful and I'd like to go to bed with you.' If she says no, thank her and say good-bye, and then try another girl. It's much simpler than most men realize."

Bubba's heart pounded with fear and excitement.

"It's really that simple?" chuckled Cobb. "I wish I'd known. But what if they ask him for ID?"

"No one ever carded Manchile, and my Bubba's even nicer-looking. Clothes are what count." She smiled and drew a tape measure out of her purse. "Geegee's going to go shopping for you at Brooks Soul Brothers, Bubba."

Sure enough, when Geegee came to pick up Luther, she had a pink oxford-cloth shirt and an expensive wool suit for Bubba, along with black leather sneakers, striped socks, new bikini sports underwear, and an understated imipolex tie. They were the first new clothes he'd ever had. He threw off his old rags, bathed in the horse trough, and put on the beautiful suit. It was dark gray with small black checks and some faint purple squiggles.

"He looks eighteen," said Cobb admiringly. "He does." He stepped behind Bubba and tied his tie. Cisco took out her brush and arranged Bubba's hair, and then put just the right amount of makeup on his eyes.

"You beautiful doll, you." She gave his cheek a long, fierce kiss. "Put on your new scarf and gloves and overcoat, Bubba." Her voice sounded funny.

Bubba put on his gold foilfoam overcoat. All of a sudden tears were running down Mamma's cheeks.

"You get going, Bubba, before I break down completely. Walk out to Fifth Street and turn left to get downtown: La Mirage is at Second Street and Muhammad Ali Boulevard. I'll—" Cisco covered her face with her hands and began to sob.

Bubba felt tears leaking from his eyes, too. This had never happened before. He looked at Cobb. "You two are staying here?"

Cobb shook his head. "It's time to scatter. The Pig wants you more than anything, but he wants me and Cisco, too. With the rumor out, it could start coming down real soon. To give you a better chance, Cisc and I'll lay down a trail leading north to Indianapolis. From there I'll cut for Florida, and she'll head for New York. Here, take this." Cobb plucked at his imipolex skin and peeled off a rectangular patch. "I figured out how to grow ID. It's got a hundred thousand dollars in credit."

Bubba looked at the card. They were standing on the icy gravel outside the stables now. Dusk was falling fast. The sky was black and orange. Bubba's new ID read: *Buford Cisco Anderson*, Birthdate 1/26/10. That meant Bubba was twenty-one. In a week, he really *would* be twenty-one, for a day. "How old are you, Cobb?"

"First time I was born was March 22, 1950. You could say I'm eighty. God knows I feel it. At a year a day, you'll see what I mean come . . . uh . . . April 16. If you make it that far. Are you planning to preach about the Thang?"

Bubba wiped his face with his overcoat's bright, leathery sleeve. His head was full of fresh Know. "No. I want to have dozens of children, hundreds of grandchildren, and thousands of great-grandchildren. God willing, there'll be a million of us by June. *Then* we'll restart the Thang for real!"

Cobb nodded as if he already knew this, but Cisco looked a little surprised. "That many of you, Bubba? Is that such a good idea, to cover the whole planet with hungry teenage boys?"

"Keep it bouncing," said Cobb. "When the boppers come down they'll find ways to turn off the gibberlin, and to father some girls."

"I'll miss you, Mamma," said Bubba, trying to give Cisco a hug.

She pushed him away a bit more sharply than seemed necessary. "Just GO. Let's not stand here talking all night till the Gimmie comes." She gave Bubba a final pat on the cheek. "You're a fine boy. Whatever happens, I'm proud to be your mother."

Bubba took a few steps, stopped, and looked back at Cobb and Cisco.

"Will you two be all right?"

Cobb made a dismissive gesture with his hand. "Don't worry about us, squirt. We racetraitors are a rough bunch. As soon as Cis and I get the hayloft cleaned out, we'll steal a car and split. No prob. Beat it. Free Cousin Willy if you get a chance."

It was full dark now, with not much traffic on the streets. Bubba found Fifth Street and started walking downtown. The shoes took some getting used to, especially with the ice. Bubba could see into lots of houses, all lit up and with families having dinner. His stomach rumbled for food. He passed some half-empty bar-and-grills, but they didn't look right. Up ahead, just to the left of the sunset's faint gray ghost, the sky was bright with big-city lights. Bubba put his head down and walked faster.

Finally he came to a big cross-street with lots of cars. He was very cold, especially his eyes and nose. A harsh wind blew grit up and down the dirty sidewalks. Nobody except Bubba was walking. But right here, at the corner of Fifth and Broadway, there was a big lit-up store with men standing inside. Bubba found the door and went in to get warm.

One of the men came over to Bubba. His waist was wide, and he had a red face. He looked a little like Cobb, but not much.

"Hi there," said the man, sticking out his hand. "I'm Cuss Buckenham. Can I hep you in any way?"

Bubba knew how to shake hands. "I'm Buford Anderson," he said, doing it. "It's cold and windy and dark out there." Cisco had taught him to talk about the weather whenever he was unsure.

"You need your daddy to get you a car," said Cuss Buckenham. There were several shiny new cars inside the store with them. Bubba deduced that this man sold cars.

"My daddy drove a Doozy," said Bubba. Mamma had told him about Manchile's Doozy several times. "But he's dead. Do you sell Doozies, Mr. Buckenham?"

Cuss Buckenham threw back his head and laughed in a stagy, friendly way. "Do ah sell Doozies? Does a frog eat flies?"

"I don't know," said Bubba, fumbling in his pockets. "But I can buy a car right now with my card, can't I? I'm twenty-one and my uncle gave me lots of money."

The car dealer stopped laughing and took Bubba's card. He looked up at Bubba, looked back at the card, and looked up again. "I got a fine new Doozy right over here, Buford." Buckenham pointed to a deeply lustrous gold sports car in the corner.

"Thanks, Mr. Buckenham. And call me Bubba."

"Sure thing, Bubba, but you gotta call me Cuss. That there Doozy's one of the last 2031s in stock, loaded, and I can let you have it at a gooood price. Go on over and take a look, while I just run this card and see what kind of authorization we can git."

Bubba opened the car door and got inside. Right away,

he Knew how to drive. It was like remembering something he'd forgotten about. The car looked good. The speedometer went up to 200 mph. The seats were real leather and the dash was faced in wood.

After a few minutes, Cuss Buckenham came over and squatted beside the car to look in at Bubba. "Your credit's copacetic, Mr. Anderson. How do you like her?"

"I'll take it."

Fifteen minutes later, the papers were all signed and the Doozy had been rolled out into the store's lot. Buckenham waved good-bye, and Bubba turned right on Broadway.

Fourth Street, Third Street, Second Street, try a left. Main Street, Chestnut Street, *Muhammad Ali Boulevard*. Big old building on the corner there, take a right. Big sign: *La Mirage Health Club*. Three-deck garage just beside it, pull in. Lock it and pocket. Done.

Bubba walked up the steps of La Mirage. It was Saturday night, and the place was jumping. There were knots of well-groomed men and women inside, black and white, old and young, some dressed for evening and some in sports togs. The doorman took an impression of Bubba's card, and the young meatbop was in.

"May I take your coat, sir?"

A lithe, long-haired girl smiled at Bubba from a large rectangular hole in the wall. There were lots of coats hanging behind her.

"Yes," said Bubba. "Thank you."

He shrugged his way out of his coat and handed it to her. She turned, hung the coat up, turned back and smiled. "Nice tie, sir." She had perfect features and full pouty lips. The sinuous arch of her long back and neck made her seem alert, perky, predatory, and poised.

"Thank you. My name's Bubba. What's yours?"

"Kari. Are you new in town?"

"Yes." Bubba took a deep breath and leaned forward. "You're beautiful and I'd like to go to bed with you."

"You bet," said Kari. "And so would my boyfriend." She laughed easily, letting him off the hook. "The lounge and dining area's down the hall to the left, sir, and the gym's upstairs. Good luck!"

Bubba smiled foolishly, then headed down the high-ceilinged, marble-floored, oak-panelled hall. Maybe he'd skimped too much on the middle part: *talk to her for a while*. Or maybe a chick like Kari was, quite simply, out of his league. At least for now. Hell, he was still just thirteen.

He entered the La Mirage lounge. His brain systems scanned his Know for an analog of what he saw. "Exploratorium," "Science Fair," and "Disky Museum of Robotics" came to mind. Scattered all about the lounge were people looking at or listening to little machines, little things like viewers and earphones and, in a few cases, whole-head helmets.

"Welcome, sir," said a young man in a tuxedo. "Are you new here?"

"Yes. I'm hungry."

"Very good, sir, there'll be a waiting time of twenty minutes. Party of one?"

Bubba observed that there were a few unattached women in the lounge. "Party of two," said Bubba. "Do you need my card?"

"Just your name, sir."

"Buford Cisco Anderson."

"Very good. While you're waiting, feel free to enjoy the healthful stim of our various software devices. Are you familiar with them all?"

"No."

"Well, you might start with a twist-box. Twist-boxes do a simple feedback-directed cutup and CA cleanup on visual inputs. They're from Einstein and quite amusing, though not everyone's seen them yet. Next I might suggest that you experience a cephscope tape. This week's special tape is by our local media star Willy Taze. Even if you're from out of town, you must have been following the meatbop conspiracy hearings? Willy was working on this tape when they arrested him at his parents' house. The first part of it's supposed to be his impression of Manchile's assassination. La Mirage's profit on Willy's tape showings will be contributed to the Taze Legal Defense Fund."

Bubba did his best to look noncommittal, and the young man continued.

"Last of all, should you and your companion be up for a *numero trois*, we have a Mindscape Axis Inverter—a truly enlightening experience for the wealthy connoisseur of healthy highs." The tuxedoed young man gave a prim smile and turned his attention to the next customer.

Bubba found a soft chair and plopped down. The well-lit dining room spread out from the other side of the dim lounge. There were people at all the tables, some of them tucking into big steak and seafood dinners. Bubba's stomach rumbled again. Disconsolately he glanced around the lounge. A dark-skinned woman was watching him from a couch nearby.

She was looking through a kind of lorgnette that she had held up to her face. A twist-box. He smiled and waved at her. Her hugely everted, finely chiselled lips smiled back from beneath the twist-box. He got up and walked over.

"Hi, I'm Bubba Anderson." He tried his most winning tone. The woman tilted her head back to look at him, still using the twist-box. "I'm alone," said Bubba, still smiling. "Would you like to have dinner with me? I'd like to talk to you for a while."

She set down the twist-box and looked him in the eye. Her eyes were large, with unreadable pupils set into smooth white whites. Finally she favored him with another smile. "Kimmie," she said, holding up her hand, palm down.

Bubba bent over and brushed his lips across Kimmie's fingers. "Charmed, I'm sure. May I look through your twist-box?"

"Certainly."

He sat down next to her on the couch and took the proffered twist-box. A slim titaniplast cable connected it to a staple in the floor. He held it up to his eyes and looked at Kimmie.

Her face took on the appearance of a visage in an animated cartoon. A congeries of fluxdots drifted out of her hair and down over her eyes, silvering them, adding meat to the cheeks and heft to the lips. He looked down her throbby neck and at the breast mounds swelling out of her strapless pink silk dress. He could hear his heart going kathump kathump. Kimmie's dress disappeared, and Bubba's glance skied down the slope of her smooth belly to the wiry black mysteries of her crotch. He stared and Knew. She was fertile. His penis stiffened.

"Now, really, Bubba," said Kimmie, plucking the twist-box from his grasp. "You barely know what couth IS, do you, dear? You a country cousin?"

She talked like Geegee. "I'm new in town," he said, uncertainly. "It's very cold out tonight, did you notice? Cold and windy."

"Well, I suppose it'll get colder before it gets hot. You're asking me to dinner?"

"Yes."

"I accept. But we'll split the check, and there's no strings. I fancy I could buy and sell you, Bubba chile."

"Thank you, Kimmie. Have you looked at the new Willy Taze cephscope show? It's supposed to be about Manchile?"

She countered with a question. "What do you think of Manchile, Bubba? Do you think they were right to kill him?"

"I didn't see him. But what he says makes sense, doesn't it? Why shouldn't humans and boppers begin to merge?"

Kimmie smiled drily. "How do we know the robots won't screw our genes up so bad that the race dies off? Maybe that's what they want. I'm all for the Thang's enlightened egalitarianism, but I do have my doubts about a man who knocks up ten women in a week. Manchile's nine-day boys."

She gave Bubba an odd look. Did she know him for a meatbop? Was she some kind of Gimmie agent? His stomach rumbled again. To cover up his confusion he picked up one of the cephscope headsets and put it on. It was a simple band with metal pads that rested on his temples. As soon as Bubba slipped it on, the tape started.

Bubba felt a series of odd tingles all over his body, as if the cephscope were checking out his neurowiring. There were some random sounds and washes of color, and then suddenly the room around him tore into bits. He was staring at a man's handsome face, and the man was talking in a thick Southern accent.

"In all the different kinds of folks I've met, I've seen one thing the same—everybody wants the best for their children. Boppers is the same!"

The image cut to the faces of a cheering crowd. Bubba had the kinetic feelings of being in a jostling crowd, staring

up at Manchile on a stage. Two shiny boppers hovered
overhead—one of them was Uncle Cobb! The crowd got
softer and everything grew pink, glowing pink with
branching purple vein patterns. Fish darted by. Far in the
distance, breakers crashed. Bubba felt himself floating,
floating on a wooden raft. The raft scrunched onto the sand
of a pitilessly bright beach. A chattering band of apes came
running down from the jungle that edged the beach. They
poked and probed at Bubba, showing their large teeth. He
held up his arms and roared at them. But now he was
looking out at a crowd of people, looking out at them from
Manchile's point of view. One of the men in the crowd lifted
a particlebeam tube and aimed it. The burning blast blew
him into blackness. Spermy white wiggles darted in the
black. The squiggles split in two, and the new pieces split
and split again, but unevenly, mapping out some kind of
design like a circuit diagram or a choice-tree. Behind the
branching tree he could see the apes again; the tree was a
cage that held him captive. A monotonous male voice recited
numbers in his ear, and his hands moved obsessively back
and forth, as if he were knitting. Meanwhile his eyes darted
up and down the branchings of the cage's bars—there was a
way out if only he could see . . . Bubba had the odd feeling
that the design coded up a message just for him, but it was
going by too fast, and now the image grew faint and grainy
as a vizzyscreen. On the screen there was a woman
newscaster talking with a slight lisp.

"Welcome to the evening news for Saturday, February 8,
2031. Tonight's top story: Half an hour age, fugitives Cobb
Anderson and Cisco Lewis were killed in a bloody shootout
with Kentucky state troopers on I76. Three officers were
wounded, one severely."

Bubba shook his head and blinked his eyes. The vizzy
image stayed put. Pictures of Mamma and Uncle Cobb
appeared behind the sleek, fast-talking anchorwoman.

"Cobb Anderson's petaflop bopper body will be sent to
the Einstein ISDN ziggurat for disassembly, while Cisco
Lewis's autopsy is slated for the Humana Hospital, where
biodecontamination facilities are available. A local car dealer
reports having seen Ms. Lewis's child, the last of the nine-
day meatbop boys known to be at large. He is believed to

be a dark-haired adolescent male, five-foot-six, using the
name Buford Cisco Anderson. He should be presumed armed
and dangerous. ISDN is offering one hundred and fifty
thousand dollars for the boy's body, and Gimmie officers
have been instructed to shoot on sight. I switch you now to
Brad Kurtow, at the scene of the massacre on I76, forty
miles north of Louisville.''

Bubba clawed the cephscope headset off. The tape had
ended, and he'd been sitting here staring at a vizzyscreen
across the room. They'd killed Cobb and Cisco. He lurched
to his feet, and jerked when someone touched him.

"Where you goin, country? That cephtape flick you out?''

He looked down at the black woman . . . Kimmie. "I—
I have to go.''

"Maybe I can help.''

"I don't trust any of you.'' He rushed out of the lounge
and down the hall, forgetting his overcoat. Only outside did
he remember that he'd left his car keys in the coat pocket.
Just as well, if Cuss Buckenham had called the Gimmie. In
the distance a siren sounded, getting closer. Bubba took off
running at top speed. Headlights coming, and the sound of
helicopters overhead. He cut into an alley and kept going.

For the next hour, Bubba ran in and out of alleys, hiding
from every passing car and ducking the searchlights that
probed down out of the beating sky. Finally, just as he could
run no further, he found himself in a junkyard down by the
Ohio River. He flopped onto the seat inside a dead car's
shell and gasped for air. His strong body's pulse quickly
returned to normal, but now that he'd stopped running, the
cold was sharp and painful. He was hungrier than he'd ever
been in his life. Peering out through the car's windowhole,
Bubba saw a fire glowing in a distant part of the junkyard.
Straining his senses to the utmost, he picked his way in that
direction.

There was a lone man by the fire, which was made out
of old tires. Bubba watched him from the shadows,
wondering what to do. The lumpy firetender had a mound
of vizzies running, with each screen set to a different
channel. He was swathed in layers of rags. Bubba could see
that he was quite fat. Bubba hunkered there, staring at the
fat man, feeling the saliva fill his mouth. He felt around on

the ground beside him, and his hand closed over a heavy metal rod. Time to eat.

An hour later, Bubba was just about to start in on the fat man's second leg. After braining the guy, Bubba had laid him out so that his two legs lay across the acridly burning tires. Once the flesh was cooked through, it had been easy enough to twist the legs off and drag the torso out of sight. Now, after nibbling a whole leg right down to the bone, both thigh and drumstick, Bubba was very full. But who knew when he'd eat again. He stepped up to the fire and looked down at the black-charred second leg. The first one had been on the raw side; this one ought to be better. Beyond the dead cars, Louisville was like an excited anthill, with choppers and squad cars searching for Bubba.

Bubba picked up the leg and began scraping off the blackened crust. He knew that humans viewed cannibalism as wrong, but that was just too bad, wasn't it, if the humans thought they could kill his father, his mother, and his Uncle Cobb, kill them like diseased rats. Bubba's Know told him that boppers often cannibalized each other for parts. It made sense. What could be a better source of body-building chemicals than a body? But, yes, he Knew it was wrong, murder was always wrong, and the watchman had made such a sad noise as he died.

Here and now, all this worrying was quite abstract. Here and now it was eat or die. With the testosterone and the gibberlin raging through his tissues, Bubba had the hunger of a werewolf. He broke the leg in two at the knee joint and bit into the crisp calf. He hunkered there by the fire, eating and enjoying the warmth.

The idyllic times at Churchill Downs already seemed like a very long time ago. Even La Mirage Health Club seemed like a long time ago. Bubba's mind was right up in the present, wondering where he'd hide next. It wouldn't do to be found with the half-eaten body of a junkyard watchman. It would give people a bad impression of the boppers; it would harm the Thang.

The mound of vizzies by the fire was full of news about him and the others. The same news over and over; the excited human ants rub-rubbing their info feelers. Luther and Geegee had been arrested. Willy Taze was going on trial

tomorrow on a treason charge. Kimmie Karroll, wealthy
socialite, reported having met Bubba at La Mirage. There
was a strict emergency curfew in effect; and all ISDN and
Gimmie officers had been instructed to shoot on sight.

A helicopter racketted right overhead, searchlight blazing.
It came in so fast and low that Bubba barely had time to
throw himself under the watchman's beat-up pickup nearby.
The helicopter hovered, examining the fire. The thigh was
still there on the ground, and most of the calf. Bubba wished
he'd thought of taking off the shoe; the shoe made it too
obvious.

BBBBDBDBDBDBDBBTKTKTK.

Automatic weapons fire. They were shooting down at the
junkyard, in circles spreading out from the fire. When the
bullets began pinging into the bed of the pickup, Bubba grew
frantic. He scrunched up under the truck's engine block for
protection. The helicopter kept shooting the pickup. Maybe
they'd spotted him before coming in.

The tire fire was at the edge of a slope leading down to
the frozen Ohio River. The pickup was facing that way.
Down there would be better than up here. Bubba got on his
back and grabbed the pickup's front axles with his hands.
With the fresh food in him, he felt very strong. He dug his
heels into the ground and pushed with all his might. Slowly
the truck's mass gave, and then, all at once, Bubba and the
truck were bouncing down the steep bank. The hovering
gunship followed right along, pouring its full firepower down
onto the truck. A bullet wormed past the truck's driveshaft
and struck Bubba heavily in his crotch . . . oh . . . and then
. . . CRASH . . . Bubba and the truck smashed into the ice
of the river . . . and fell through.

The water was cold dark death, but it was safety, too.
Bubba's body filled with adrenochrome and the pain in his
groin went numb. He could last several minutes down here.
He pushed free of the truck and swam downstream, staying
just below the surface of the ice.

Chapter Twelve
Emul

February 22, 2031

Emul was very depressed. Everything was going wrong, up here and down on Earth. Berenice was dead and no one had gotten around to making her a new body. Emul wanted to find a way to put Berenice's software directly onto a wendy, as she'd always wanted, but he couldn't make it click.

None of the other boppers, not even Berenice's weird sisters, felt like helping him bring Berenice back, even as a petaflop, because, just now, Berenice's software was in disgrace. Her blitzkrieg program for a human/bopper fusion had wretchedly crashed. With the disappearance two weeks ago of Bubba, Manchile's sole surviving son, the boppers were left with nothing but bad publicity.

Berenice had hatched her plan on her own, though Emul had gotten her to explain it before he'd assented to have his meatie Ken Doll plant Berenice's handmade seed in Della Taze. The plan had gone like this: (1) Assemble a wholly artificial human-compatible embryo, the future scion Manchile. (2) Wetware-code the embryo's DNA to produce gibberlin plasmids so as to speed up the scion's growth and sexual activity. (3) Software-code the embryo's RNA with the Know—which consisted of a terabit of Berenice's info about Earth, Moon, and her plans for the scion. As well as carrying a kind of bopper consciousness, the Know was intended to serve as a hormone-triggered mindtool-kit to compensate for the short-lived scion's lack of experiential programming. (4) Plant the bopper-built embryo in a woman's womb. (5) Force the woman to travel to Earth. (6) The scion Manchile was programmed to reproduce, start a religion, and to get himself assassinated, thereby initiating class warfare on Earth. (7) Wait through the ensuing chaos for Manchile's descendants to ripple out over Earth. Side by side with the victorious human underclass, the meatbops would welcome the true boppers to their lovely planet!

Things had started to go wrong the instant Manchile had gone public. Although some radical humans did have a certain sympathy for Manchile's Thang, very few of them felt strongly enough to act on their sympathies, and most of these were now in jail. The Gimmie had justified their brutal repression by presenting Manchile and the nine-day boys as an invasive social cancer. The final, debilitating propaganda battle had been lost when the fleshers heard about Bubba eating the bum—a typically baroque Berenice touch. If the humans had been able to find Bubba's body they would have torn it into shreds.

Even now, two weeks after the fact, with the crisis apparently over, ISDN was still keeping the antibopper propaganda drums beating. The bum, or watchman, or whatever he'd been, had become a human racehero; his picture was everywhere and there were dramas about him; his name was Jimmy Doan. "Avenge Jimmy Doan," the humans liked to say now, "How many robots is one Jimmy Doan worth?" *Maybe a worn-out gigaflop with no cladding,* was Emul's opinion, but no one was asking him or any other bopper for input.

Emul had some suspicions about ISDN's real motives for keeping up the frenzy. In many ways, ISDN was like one of the old, multibodied big boppers. Emul had reason to believe that ISDN was beating the drums for business purposes. Most obviously, the continuing hysteria increased ISDN viewership. More subtly, the increased security measures at the trade center had greatly curtailed human/bopper trade, which had the effect of inflating prices and increasing the profit per item to be made by ISDN's middlemen.

Some hotheaded fleshers were talking about evacuating Einstein and cleaning out the Nest once and for all. But Emul was sure that ISDN had no intention of leaving the

Moon; there was still so much money to be made. Surely
the boppers were too *sexy* to exterminate. The apey jackdaw
fleshers had an endless appetite for the tricks that boppers
could do.

Instead of any all-out attack, the humans had been launching
a number of commando raids on the Nest this week. Just
yesterday, Emul had been forced to dynamite the Little Kidder
Toys entrance to his tunnel after losing his favorite two meaties
in a flesher terror raid there. A gang of ridgebacks, led by
Darla's husband, Whitey Mydol, had burst into the store and
had shot it out with Rainbow and Berdoo. Rainbow and Berdoo
had been meaties for years, and Emul had been proud to own
them. They'd cost him plenty. It had hurt to see them go down;
to watch from inside their heads. They'd done their best, but
the plaguey communications links were all staticky and unreliable these days; it seemed like everyone's equipment was
wearing out at once. It had hurt to lose to Mydol, and to make
things worse, Mydol had escaped alive, even though Emul
had blown up the tunnel just as Mydol entered. Mydol had
lucked out and had stood in just the right place. All the luck
was running the wrong way, and everything was going screwy.

Another screwy thing that Emul wondered about off and
on was this character Stahn Mooney, a slushed clown detective whom he'd hired to help with the kidnapping of Darla
last month. The evening of the kidnapping, Mooney, for
reasons unknown, got a partial right hemispherectomy, had
a rat-compatible neuroplug installed, and phoned Emul up
from the trade center, offering himself as a *voluntary meatie.*
Mooney's body was strong, and his left brain glib, so
business sense had dictated that Emul accept the offer.
Apparently Mooney had taken Emul's promise of a free
wendy too much to heart, and he arrived at the Nest with
some crazed notion that a community of meaties lived
together in a place called Happy Acres, when in fact there
were at most five or six meatie-owners in all the Nest, most
of them involved with the dreak and amine trades. But
Mooney was odd and devious and not to be believed. He
was a friend of Cobb Anderson, or so he said when he'd
called up Emul last month, asking for work and a wendy.
Emul had hired him all right, but something about Mooney
stank—most of all the fact that there were no godseye

records of what he'd done after Darla merged him down in the Mews. As soon as Emul had installed Mooney's rat, he wasted no time in selling him to Helen, Berenice's waddling pink-tank sister, who had ample use for a flesh tankworker. Emul had gotten a nice price out of Helen, enough for four tubes of dreak; and Mooney seemed happy enough playing with the blank wendy Helen gave him; but the whole thing still bothered Emul. It stank.

Emul shifted into realtime and looked around his laboratory. It was a low rock-walled room twenty by forty feet. Half the room was filled with Oozer's flickercladding vats. Formerly a flickercladding designer, Oozer was now busy trying to develop a totally limp computer with petaflop capabilities. Most flickercladding was already capable of petaflop thought processes—on a limpware basis—and Oozer felt he should be able to make the stuff function at these high levels *independently* of any J-junction or optical CPU hardware at all. Oozer was known for such autonomous limpware designs as the kiloflop heartshirt and the megaflop smart KE bomb.

Emul's jumbled end of the room had a hardened glass panel and airlock set into one of the walls. The panel showed Darla's room; she spent most of her time lying on her bed and watching the vizzy. Like all the humans, she was in an ugly mood these days. Earlier today, when Emul had entered her quarters, she'd threatened to do bellyflops off her bed until she aborted. He'd had to talk to her for a long time. He'd ended up promising to let her out early if she would promise to fly to Earth. He was supposed to be working out the details right now, though he didn't feel like it. He didn't feel like doing much of anything these days; he seemed to have a serious hardware problem.

His hardware problem was the greatest of Emul's worries—above and beyond Darla, Stahn Mooney, Whitey Mydol, Berenice, and ISDN's jingoistic war drumming. There was a buzz in Emul's system. At first he'd thought it was from too much dreak, and he'd given the stuff up almost entirely. But the buzz just got worse. Then he'd thought it might be in his flickercladding, so he'd acid-stripped his imipolex all off and gotten himself recoated with a state-of-the-art Happy Cloak built by Oozer. The buzz was no better.

It was a CPU problem of some sort, a breakdown in perfectly reversible behavior. The primary symptom was that more and more often Emul's thoughts would be muddled by rhythmic bursts of kilohertz noise. It was possible to think *around* the thousand spikes a second, but it was debilitating. Apparently Emul needed a whole new body.

Just now Emul was in his rest position—that of an RYB cube with a few sketchy manipulators and sensor stalks. He was resting on the floor in front of his thinking desk, which served as a communications terminal and as a supplemental memory device—much like a businessman's file cabinets and floppy disks.

Four treasured S-cubes sat out on Emul's desk: brown, red, green, and gold. These hard and durable holostorage devices coded up the complete softwares of four boppers. There were Oozer's and Emul's S-cubes, of course, updated as far as yesterday. And there was a recent cube of Kkandio, Oozer's sometime mate, a suave boppette who worked the Ethernet. She and Oozer had two scions between them. Most important of all, there was dear Berenice's S-cube. Emul had used a copy of it to blend with his own software when he'd programmed the girl embryo he'd put in Darla's womb. He wanted to build a new petaflop for Berenice, but right now it felt like he, Emul, needed a new body worse than anyone.

Emul sent signals in and out of his desk, flipping though his various internal and external memories: his flickercladding mode, his hereditary RAM, his realtime randomization, the joint bopper godseye, his inner godseye, his flowchart history, and all the detailed and cumbersome speculations that he'd dumped into his desk's limpware storage devices.

Emul was trying to decide if there were any hope of getting an exaflop system up in the next couple of weeks. Two months ago, when he and Oozer had been able to afford a lot of dreak, the exaflop had seemed very near. Indeed, Emul had half-expected his next body to be an operational, though experimental, exaflop based on a novel quantum clone string-theoretic memory system. But now, soberly looking over his records, Emul realized that any exaflop was still years away. Looking at his credit holdings, he saw now that he didn't really have enough money for a new petaflop, either, and that, as a matter of fact, a repo teraflop was going to be about the best he could swing.

His worry session was interrupted by Oozer, who came stumping awkwardly down to his end of the lab, gesturing back towards his vats.

"Oh, ah, Emul, some off brands of imipolex in there; the stuff is letting itself *go*."

"I got the fear of eerie death standing ankle-deep around me, Oozer," said Emul unhappily. "The buzz is so much worser stacks in my thinker."

"I can't—at any rate I keep saying 'at any rate'—I don't mean to say that, but I do now know your kilohertz buzz. It hurts. We're sick, Emul. The cladding's sick, too."

"Plague," said Emul, jumping to a conclusion. "Flesher plague on both our houses."

He turned to his desk and made some calls. Starzz, who ran the dreakhouse. Helen, to whom he'd sold that meatie three weeks back. Wigglesworth, the digger who was supposed to fix Emul's tunnel. Oozer's girlfriend Kkandio, voice of the Ethernet.

Sure enough, none of them was feeling too well. They each had a hardware buzz. They were relieved and then frightened to hear that others had the same problem. Emul told them to spread the word.

He and Oozer looked at each other, thinking. The desk's signal buzzed and sputtered at a steady kilohertz cycle.

"*Dis*cover to *re*cover," said Oozer, running a thick gout of his flickercladding over to the desk. Little tools formed out of his warts, and in minutes he had the desk's CPU chips uncovered. "Dr. Benway letting the clutch out as fast as possible, you know, '*Whose* lab tests?!?' " Oozer peered and probed, muttering his bepop English all the while. "Which would break the driveshaft, see, 'cause the universal joint can't but—Emul! Look at this!"

Emul put a microeye down by the desk's chips. The chips were oddly spotted and discolored by small—he looked closer—colonies of organisms like . . . mold cultures in a petri dish. All their chips were getting infected with a biological mold, a fuzzy gray-yellow sludge that fed on—he stuck an ammeter wire into one of the mold spots—one thousand cycles per second. The fleshers had done it . . .

"Well I'll tell you this, I don't feel very intelligent . . . anymore, at times, for a long time . . . the cladding's full of nodes, Emul, come see." Oozer wheeled around in a jerky circle.

Watching him, Emul realized that his old friend was shaking all over. Oozer's limbs were moving jerkily, as if they longed to stutter to a halt. But the bopper drove himself forward and pulled a big sheet of plastic out of the nearest vat. The thick plastic flopped to the floor and formed itself into a mound. It looked unlike any flickercladding Emul had ever seen. Normal flickercladding was dumb: left on its own, it did little more than run a low-complexity cellular-automaton pattern. If you disturbed flickercladding—by touching it, by shining light on it, or by feeding it signals through its microprobes—then its pattern would react. But ordinarily, all by itself, flickercladding was not much to look at. This new stuff was different; it was transparent, showing three-dimensional patterns of an amazing complexity. The stuff's pattern flow seemed to be coordinated by a number of bright, pulsing nodes—mold spots!

All of a sudden Oozer's trembling got much more violent. The bopper drew all his arms and sensors in, forming himself into a tight pod. The Oozer pod huddled on the floor, looking almost like the new mound of flickercladding, all bright and spotty. Emul signalled Oozer, but got only a buzz in response.

Emul's own buzzing felt worse and worse, and now it was like his willpower was cut out, and the more he tried to find it, the worse it got, to try and find his self. He looked down at his box and noticed bright mold spots in his own flickercladding . . . bright mold sucking out his battery-juice too f-f-f-fast . . . h-h-h-h-e s-s-s-sank d-d-d-down.

And lay there like a shiny chrysalis.

The lab was still, with nothing moving but Darla, anxiously peering out through the glass of her sealed room.

Chapter Thirteen
Happy Acres

February 24, 2031

Stahn blinked and tried to stand up. But his left leg was numb and floppy, as was his left arm, as was the entire left side of his body. He landed heavily on something soft. A woman smell over the foetid stench, he was lying on . . . Wendy? Wendy!!! Wendy???

She was a comatose human vegetable fitfully twitching her flawless bod. Her breath was babyishly irregular. She barely knew how to breathe right, poor clone . . . but . . .

Stahn tried again to stand up and only managed to wallow the more inefficaciously on the wendy-thing's not unappetizing person. His penis stiffened, and he did what he had to do. Wendy liked it; come to think of it, they'd been doing this a lot. They were naked and covered with filth.

After they both climaxed, Stahn rolled onto the right side of his body, and began looking around for the bench he'd been sitting on. There it was, over there . . . he began worming his way across the offal-strewn floor of the tiny stone stall he and the wendy had apparently been living in.

Something had just stopped; like a noise Stahn had gotten used to, but what? He hooked his chin over the edge of the bench and dragged himself back into sitting position. He kept forgetting to use the left half of his body. Why had he crawled when he could have walked? His space orientation was shot: even the five-foot crawl from Wendy to the bench seemed complicated. Stahn stared down at Wendy. Looking at her helped focus his ideas. He was a meatie, that was it, and Wendy was a blank-brained clone, he was a meatie living in . . .

"Happy Acres," said Stahn out loud, slurring his words, but enjoying the sound of his voice nonetheless. He started laughing, and then he couldn't stop laughing for a long time. It was like he had a month's worth of laughter waiting to get out, desperate laughter that sounded like moans.

Eventually the moaning turned into thick hollow coughing and he had to stop. There was something wrong with the roof of his mouth: a big hole up there, and a pain like a splinter. Stahn felt the hole with his tongue, felt and listened, and looked around.

The air in here was incredibly unbelievably vile. They were in a room with a locked jail cell door. You could look out onto big pink-lit tanks filled with crowded murky fluid, livers and lungs and brains and, yes, wendies floating in them, the pink-tanks, that's where Stahn worked most days, worked till he couldn't move, with Wendy crawling along after, both of them eating as much raw organ as they liked of course, and at the end of the day, however long it was, they were shut up in their Happy Acres cubby for intercourse, excretion, and dreamless sleep. What was it Ricardo had said? Stahn remembered, and spoke out loud again.

"You won't have a care in the world, Mooney man, you'll live like a king!"

The sobbing laughter started again, loose and sloppy, with air snuckering in and out of the hole in his soft palate, the big splinter slipping and wiggling, uuuuuuhuhuhuhuhhhh . . . there . . . it was coming . . . uuuuughhh . . .

Stahn retched hard and harder and then . . . the little dead plastic rat slid out of his mouth and clattered to the floor. All *right!* No more rat, no more of Helen's goddamn nagging voice in his head day and night, like a mother you can't get away from, do this Stahn, do that, oh I *like* when you move your bowels. No more of Helen in Stahn all the time, using him in the stink. He ground the rat under his foot.

Something had happened to Helen; something had shut her down. So wonderful, at last, to sit here thinking his own thoughts and looking around . . . though there *was* still some problem . . . hmmmm, oh yes . . . his right brain damage

. . . and the way he kept forgetting about the left half of his body. *Could* he move his left leg, if he really tried? His left thumb?

Stahn stared hard at his thumb. He *used* to know how to move it, but just now, without Helen's voice running, his left side he . . . couldn't . . . get the notion of *purposeful action* . . . so he grabbed the thumb with his good right hand and wiggled it, yah, he even leaned over and sniffed it, licked it, bit and . . . there . . . it was moving . . . spastically moving as new nerve routings opened up . . . tingling . . . he did the rest of his hand then . . . bit by bit . . . the arm . . . the arm flapping at his side like the chicken imitation he used to do on Z-gas in Daytona . . . lean over so it beats on your leg, Stahn . . . shuffle splutter, splutter mutter . . .

Eventually he struggled to his feet and stood there, pigeon-toed and awkward as a spaz, but, yes, stood. And found his way over to Wendy and felt the roof of her mouth, looking for a rat, but she was untouched, still too dumb for the boppers to use, good deal.

"We're gonna make it, Wendy; we're gonna make it back, babe."

He worked on Wendy's body for a while, rubbing and flexing her arms and legs like a physical therapist, or like a mother with her baby, rubbed and flexed her, talking all the while, thrilled to talk for the first time in . . . yes . . . it had been a month.

Stahn's memory of the month's slavery was oddly faint. Possibly the horror of it had been such that his brain refused to remember. Or perhaps it was that, with Helen calling all all all the shots always always always, his brain had known that it needn't bother to make notes. Or maybe the surgical brain trauma had screwed up his memory for good.

ISDN had done this to him . . . why? To bring the chipmold to the Nest, yes. The chipmold must have worked, that was it, the chipmold had fried the brains of all the boppers. They were crispy critters now, that's what Chief Jackson had always called the gone loveboat dopers who couldn't remember their names, crispy critters. Stahn had been pretty sick with that chipmold himself for a week there . . . he remembered the ache in his throat and in his kidneys

. . . but he'd gotten well, the ancient streetwise human wetware had come up with an antidote.

Stahn tugged Wendy up onto the bench. She sat unsteadily at his right side, blowing spit bubbles. After a while she slid back off the bench.

Stahn worked on his left side some more, trying to keep remembering it, and then he picked his way across the cell to examine the door. He couldn't really see through his left eye, or do anything about what he felt with his left hand, but after a while he had the door pretty well doped out. It was held locked by a hook-and-eye latch. The lock was hard to work . . . Stahn kept moving his hands in the wrong direction like in a mirror . . . but finally he got their cell open.

"Come on, Wendy. We're going home." He pulled Wendy to her feet and put a tight arm around her waist. They shuffled out of their cell into the pink-lit room where the organ-filled pink-tanks were. It looked very familiar in a way, albeit as confusing as a maze. Wandering this way and that, his heart pounding anxiously, Stahn finally bumped into the glass wall next to the airlock.

Helen and Ulalume were out there, sitting in the middle of the floor and not doing anything, not dead or alive but just kind of . . . sitting there with their flickercladding gone strange. Tranced out, like. Yukawa had said that the chipmold would start some kind of electric vibrations in the boppers' brains and give them fits. Cataleptic as opposed to epileptic, or so it would seem. Helen and Ulalume were buddha-ed out, man, just sitting out there—Stahn chuckled softly—just sitting out there in perfect full-lotus *aum mane padme hum* meditation, wave, robot sees God in a mold, all right. And their flickercladding was doing weird stuff, blotched and splotchy all along Helen's xoxy big nurse pod-bod and on that "fine-featured Nefertiti head" she was so proud of, always reciting Poe's "To Helen" in Stahn's brain, ghastly old vampire bat that she was, always bugging Stahn always, and now she had big moldy bright spots in her flickercladding. Squidhead Ulalume and toothed-vagina Helen just sitting out there in the middle of the floor, side by side, waiting for ye Judgment Day trumps, or so so so it would seem. No prob. Do what?

Stahn struggled for an idea. He wanted to leave, but there was no air out there. How had Emul transported him here, through the Nest's cold hard vacuum? At first he couldn't remember at all, but then it came to him. After Emul had met Stahn at the trade center, he'd wrapped Stahn in a special Happy Cloak, a big piece of flickercladding that was programmed to behave like a bubbletopper spacesuit. Emul had used the Happy Cloak to bring Stahn from the trade center to the ratmaker, where Stahn had gotten a rat compatible with his new neuroplug. That was all very vague. And then Emul had sold Stahn to Helen, bringing him here to the pink-tanks, still in the Happy Cloak. Stahn could see the Happy Cloak hanging from a hook right across the room from the airlock, as a matter of fact, hanging there twisting and glowing in blotchy thought. He just had to run out through the vacuum and get the cloak, that was it.

It? Get the cloak, Stahn, yes. He set Wendy down on the floor, leaning her against the wall, and went into the airlock. It took him the longest time to get the door closed behind him, and then he got mixed up and went back out of the airlock into the pink-tank room with Wendy. He was so flustered that he forgot the left half of his body for an instant there, and fell to the floor, landing facedown in the warm puddle between Wendy's widespread legs, Happy Acres. He stood back up and peered out through the glass wall again, trying to gather his wits.

He spotted the Happy Cloak on the wall again, and remembered, and went back into the airlock. When it opened he would run out, grab the Happy Cloak, and run back in here to put it on. He poised himself to run, put his right hand on one of the door handles—he hoped it was the correct handle this time—and slapped his clumsy left hand against the vent button. The air whooshed out . . . Stahn kept his mouth and throat open, letting his lungs collapse instead of popping . . . and he was running across the room . . . or trying to run . . . like a palsy victim in the Special Olympics four-yard dash, man, *don't forget your left leg* . . . got his hand on the Happy Cloak . . . it simpered and came loose from its hook . . . oh the cold the pain in his ears his achy lungs and sweat crystallizing on his stiffening skin . . . but where was the airlock? Stahn swung his head this way and that, not seeing what he was looking for . . . a door shape over there, but *that* didn't look right . . . he tried to turn . . . *stumble* . . . oh no! Too confused to do anything but lie there and thrash, ow, Stahn began to die, but then, at the last moment, the Happy Cloak flowed out over his whole body, making itself into a warm air-filled spacesuit.

There was the sweet energizing smell of clean air. Stahn's eyes flickered open. The part of the Happy Cloak in front of his face was transparent; he could see out. There was a series of sharp pains in the back of his neck. The Happy Cloak was plugging its microprobes into his nervous system.

Hello, meatie, came the Happy Cloak's sweet voice in Stahn's head. *I am pleased to ride your body once more. Much has changed.*

"Call me Stahn. I must bring a wendy intact to Einstein. Helen's orders."

That is untrue. The boppers are all dead. Take me to the light-pool so I can feed. Then I can help you.

"Fine." Stahn decided to think and say as little as possible. He got to his feet and wondered which way to go. Wendy was around here someplace, but he kept forgetting which direction was which. "We'll come back for Wendy later, right?"

Come. The Happy Cloak spacesuit nudged Stahn towards Helen and Ulalume, lying there on the floor. By selectively stiffening itself, the Happy Cloak could control which directions Stahn could move in. He had no desire to approach Helen's dangerous pod, but then he was leaning over her and touching her. Her mottled flickercladding blinked rapidly— as if talking to the Happy Cloak. He laid his other hand on the inert Ulalume, and her cladding responded in the same way.

Carry my fellows to the light-pool, said the voice in Stahn's head. *They are hungry, too.* The Happy Cloak flickered strobily at the bodies of Helen and Ulalume, and then the two weird sisters' skins slid off, exposing the hard blank bodyshells underneath. The shells weren't quite blank: threads of gray-yellow fuzz projected out of the microcracks at the joints. Chipmold. It had strangled the boppers' processors long before they could begin to synthesize the proper antigen. Humans had the edge on them there, with their bodies' built-in wetware labs. The boppers' hardware was slushed, though their limpware—their symbiotic imipolex skins—seemed to be actually enjoying the mold. Stahn stooped and picked up the two wriggling imipolex sheaths. They weighed very little in the weak lunar gravity.

Thank you. The Happy Cloak wasn't running him as Helen had; it was simply nudging him and making suggestions. It was happy to see through Stahn's eyes and have Stahn carry it.

"Which way?"

Follow the star. Your Wendy will wait. We'll save her and Darla too.

A blue line drawing of a stellated dodecahedron appeared in Stan's visual field. Sometimes he'd lose sight of it, but if he turned his head back and forth he could always find it. He followed the star out of the lab, down a short corridor, and out into the huge open space of the Nest. Stahn paused, looking this way and that, still having trouble seeing anything on his weak left side. The Nest was roughly conical in shape, with a vast shaft of light coming down its central axis. For a terrified moment, Stahn felt as if he would fall upward along the Nest's pocked, towering walls.

The light-pool is up ahead.

Stahn followed the blue star down a street with shops and boppers. The Nest had become a ghost town; all the boppers were motionless. Some of them must have depleted their batteries, for their skins were blank and empty. But most of them still had some juice, and their blotched claddings pulsed in asymmetric harmonies. They seemed to have enough photosensitivity to be able to converse among each other, at least after a fashion. Over and over, Stahn's Happy Cloak would flash a special stroby way, and an immobilized bopper's skin would slither off for Stahn to carry.

Finally they were at the light-pool, a great round patch of sunlight some fifty feet across. Dozens of paralyzed boppers crouched there, as well as scores of flickercladdings who'd laboriously crawled there on their own. The claddings looked like bright slugs. When Stahn tossed down his bale of claddings, many of the others came inching over to "talk." Stahn lay down to rest while the Happy Cloak around him ate its fill of light. The Happy Cloak cradled Stahn and fed him air. Its guileless microprobe outputs were bright and happy.

Stahn fell asleep and dreamed.

He was on a red rocky field, maybe Mars, though there was air, thin clean mountain air. The sun was small and hot. He had wings, huge imipolex wings. He was not alone; there were other humans like him, all partly clad in Happy Cloaks with great glider wings. Wendy was there, and Whitey and Darla. "Yay, Stahn," they yelled with laughing voices. "Come on!" They ran down a slope and leaped off the edge of the cliff the slope ended in, leaped out and circled like swallows over the great bright city in the rift.

The scene shifted, and he was back on Earth, deep undersea, dressed in a knowing imipolex diving suit beefed up to the size of a dolphin. Wendy was a plastic dolphin beside him, skirling chirrups. They arced into a juicy drift of squid.

He was in space, mellow with amines, drifting like a spore.

He was skittering across the heavy methane atmosphere of Jupiter, straining his senses downward to catch the mighty songs of the Great Old Ones below.

Come, Stahn. Let us be on our way. We'll get Darla and Wendy and walk to Einstein.

Stahn opened his eyes and sat up. Such sweet dreams. Helen had never let him dream, not for a month.

His Happy Cloak felt livelier; its renewed energies put a real spring in his motions. He leaped to his feet and stretched. The loose limpwares flickered at him, wishing him well. Two of them crawled closer, begging to be picked up.

I have showed them how to be spacesuits, said the voice in Stahn's head. *Bring them and follow the star.*

The spiky blue line shape appeared in Stahn's visual field, and he bounded along after it, carrying the two extra Happy Cloaks under his arm. First they'd save Darla. That was a good idea, and only fitting, as it was Stahn's fault that she'd been taken captive.

With part of his right brain missing, Stahn still didn't have a clue about which way was which. But he didn't worry about it too much. He knew that, just as limited damage to the left brain can knock out your ability to speak, limited damage to the right brain can destroy your ability to form mental 3D simulations of your surroundings. He'd get some new brain tissue from ISDN or, hell, he'd just keep this wavy Happy Cloak.

The blue star twinkled, and the voice in his head said, *I am pleased.*

They were in a kind of factory district now; huge idle buildings that must have been chipsmelters. They came to the Nest's wall, balconied like a highrise. A series of powerful leaps took Stahn up five levels, and then he followed the star down a short series of branching tunnels that ended with a single open door.

This was the laboratory of Emul and Oozer.

Stahn stepped in and looked around. It was a long low room, vaguely reminiscent of Yukawa's lab. There were vats at the far end, and there were twitching mounds of flicker-cladding here and there. This end of the room held a desk with four colored S-cubes on it. On the floor were the split-open bodies of the two mold-killed boppers, Oozer and Emul. Their claddings were gone: it was just the body casings there; the pressure of the mold's biomass had split the casings open like seed pods. In terms of hardware, Emul and Oozer were now like rusted-out cars with weeds growing in them, like mirrored freeform flowerboxes full of sprouts, like hollow logs covered by the rubbery fungus known as witch ears. Emul and Oozer's chipmold was at the end of its life cycle. The gray-yellow threads had formed golfball-sized nodes: fruiting bodies. Stahn reached down and picked one of them; it could be worth something on the outside. Just then he caught some motion out of the corner of his eye. Over there, set into the wall, was a window showing . . . Now who was that in there? He should have known the face but . . . dammit . . .

I think that's Darla.

Of course! "Darla!" shouted Stahn, even though she couldn't hear him. Darla waved both arms and drummed soundlessly on her window. Stahn put his moldfruit in the cloak's pouch and hurried into the airlock. He fumbled around for what seemed a very long time, and finally emerged into Darla's pink room. Obligingly, his Happy Cloak slid off.

Suddenly nude, Stahn lost control of his left leg and fell down. The woman leaned over him, her face large and upside down.

"Are you all right, Mooney? Can you get me out?"

Stahn had forgotten her name. He stared at her, breathing in the room's thick, female air. "Wendy? What did you just ask?"

"I'm Darla, fool. Can you get me out?"

"Yes," said Stahn quickly, and stood up. Looking straight at her, it was easier to remember her name. She was wearing an RYB playsuit. He'd called on her in her home last month. "Yes, Darla, I can get you out. We'll wear these." He pointed to the Happy Cloaks. "Come." He picked up his cloak and slung it over him. It flowed into position. Darla hesitated, and then did the same with one of the others. Stahn watched Darla jerk spastically as her cloak's microprobes slid into her spine.

"It's OK," he said. "Don't worry."

She can't hear you. Touch heads.

Stahn pressed the clear plastic of his face visor against Darla's. "It's all right, Darla, it really is. These Happy Cloaks arc wavy limpware dudes."

"It's stabbing my neck." Her voice through the plastic was faint and rubbery.

"That's just so it can see through your eyes and talk to you. Believe me, being a meatie is a lot worse."

"You were a meatie all along?"

"Just this month. Whitey had ISDN make me a meatie to get even for what I did to you."

"I told you he'd get even. Can we just walk out of here now?"

"Yeah. We'll pick up my Wendy and walk to Einstein."

"Wendy?"

"You'll see." Stahn noticed that there was an air-filled tunnel leading out from one end of Darla's room, a tunnel blocked by a locked cell door. It would certainly make things easier if they could find a tunnel to Einstein.

"Does the tunnel from your room go all the way through?"

"It used to. It used to start at a scurvy place called Little Kidder Toys," answered Darla. "But Emul exploded that end of the tunnel day before yesterday. Whitey and his guys were trying to come through."

"If we can't find a tunnel, we'll have to climb out the Nest's main hole and walk. I just hope my wendy can make it."

"What's wrong with your precious wendy?" Darla was getting impatient. She didn't like having Mooney's face shoved up against hers for so long, though he, of course, seemed to be enjoying it.

"She's a clone, Darla. Her mind is a complete blank. It's like she's a hundred-and-twenty-pound newborn baby."

"Sounds like just your pervo trip, geek. Here, you carry her Happy Cloak."

"Now look—"

Darla snapped her head back and marched into the airlock. Stahn followed along and moments later they were out in the lab. Stahn's Happy Cloak made another request.

Take my brothers out of here. They hunger. Carry them to the light-pool.

"No way. That's too far. Darla won't go for it. But maybe . . ." Stahn remembered his good smart bomb: his flickercladding Superball that had bounced so well. "How about this, cloak. If your brothers can roll themselves up like big balls, we can throw them off the balcony towards the light-pool. They can bounce and roll all the way there."

Yes. I understand.

Stahn limped around the room patting the loose claddings, one by one, so that his cloak could tell them what to do. There were fifteen of them—thirteen from the vats and two from Oozer and Emul, not that you could tell who was which. The claddings pulled themselves together, and then they lay there like fifteen variegated marbles, each about the size of a bowling ball. Darla watched Stahn from the lab door. She had her hands on her hips and she was tapping her foot. Stahn walked over and pushed his face against hers. She was wearing a tough frown.

"What are you doing, Mooney, you slushed pig?"

"Darla-pie, let's get it straight: I'm saving your life. My cloak wants us to throw these balls off the balcony out there. We'll do that, and then we'll get Wendy, and then we'll go home. There's no big rush, because all the boppers are dead.

I killed them with chipmold; that's what ISDN used me for, baby, so shut your crack.''

It was Stahn's turn to snap his head back. And then, just to bug Darla the more, he rolled the fifteen balls together into a triangular pattern like a rack of fresh balls on a pool table. He couldn't visualize the triangle in advance, but he could tell when he was done. He picked up two of the balls—three would have been too awkward—and followed his cloak's blue mindstar through the tunnels to the balcony. Darla followed suit. She jerked in surprise when they got out to the edge; she'd never seen the Nest.

Stahn pointed across the dead underground city at the light-pool. A straight street ran from the pool to the base of the wall below them. He set down one of his cladding balls and lifted the other one overhead with both arms. He threw it out and up, putting all he had into it. The ball shot along a soaring lowgee trajectory, bounced perfectly, sailed, bounced, sailed and dribble-rolled towards the light-pool's distant, bright spot. Stahn threw his second ball, and then Darla threw both of hers.

On their fourth trip, Darla only had one ball to carry. She pressed her face against Stahn's face. The exercise had put her in a better mood.

"Can we go now, Mooney?"

"Sure. And call me Stahn. What were those S-cubes on the desk in there?"

"Personality cubes for Emul and some of his friends. He was always fiddling with them. Do you think we ought to bring them? Valuable info, right?"

"Hell, let's not bother. I don't want to see any of those boppers for a long time. I'm glad the mold killed them."

Follow the star to Wendy, Stahn.

They scrambled down the balconies to the Nest floor and turned right on a circumferential road along the cliff's base. They walked and walked, until the star darted into one of the cliff-base doors. They went in, and there they were, back at the pink-tank labs.

Darla cycled them through the lock into the room with the tanks. Wendy was right where Stahn had left her, lying on her back with her blank eyes wide open. She was staring at her fingers and wiggling them. Stahn pushed his cloak off his face and Darla did the same.

"Stinks in here," said Darla. "So that's Wendy? Poor clone. She's like a baby. Did you see how high up it is to the hole at the top of the Nest?"

"Really far," said Stahn. "But I ain't going without my Wendy. She's what I came here for, all right?"

I have a suggestion, said the voice in Stahn's head. *The cloak you brought for her can drive her.*

"Can you hear your spacesuit talking to you?" Stahn asked Darla.

"Is that what it is? I thought I was hallucinating from all the sense-depriv. These things are like really alive?"

"Especially now that they've got chipmold nodules in them. We used to call them Happy Cloaks, but now maybe we should call them moldies. My cloak—my moldie—it says that the one I brought for Wendy's spacesuit can like drive her body around."

And talk through her.

"And talk through her," said Darla. "Stop that." She slapped at the splotchy, flickering moldie that covered her bod. "So do it, Stahn."

Stahn flopped the extra moldie over Wendy. It flowed all over her. For a long time it seemed like nothing was happening. But then Wendy began to tremble, first a little, and then a lot. All at once the trembling stopped. More time passed and then Wendy stood up. Now it was Stahn who was trembling. He reached his shaky hands forward and pulled the cladding down from off her face.

"Hello," said the bright happy face. "This is very nice!" The voice sounded just like Stahn had remembered it, all these years.

"Oh Wendy." Stahn put his arms around her and held her tight.

Chapter Fourteen
Della

March 7, 2031

Della didn't recognize the man at her door. He was fat and pale and fortyish, with black shoes and a cheap, ill-fitting suit. Though his features were snubbed and boyish, his face was puffed, giving him a callow, watery air. Perhaps he'd been handsome in his youth, but something must have gone badly wrong for him since; some kind of hormone imbalance. Della was glad she had the doorchain fastened.

"Who are you?" she asked through the crack. Her new apartment's location was supposed to be private—so many nuts had come traipsing by the Tazes' that Della'd had to move out. "What do you want?"

"I got this address from Ilse Taze. If you don't want to let me in, why don't you come out and we can take a walk." He tapped his mouth and his ear, suggesting that what he had to tell Della was private.

Della shook her head. The guy could be a Gimmie agent, an ISDN newshound, a crazed Thangie, a Racial Puritan, or an ordinary sex criminal. A lot of weirdos had it in for her, ever since it had become widely known that Della's womb had borne Manchile. The story had come out after Manchile's assassination and Willy's arrest. Della had refused all interviews, though she'd had to tell most of her story in court during the ongoing meatbop conspiracy trial. Lots of people wanted to meet Della, which was the main reason she had gotten this absolutely secret apartment to live in. This visitor was the first to have tracked her here. Why had Ilse told him where to come?

He looked like he hadn't seen sunlight in years. His pithy fatness was diseased and unnatural. And as the smell of Della's microwaved dinner floated out past her and through the door's crack, he licked his lips in a wet, hungry way that was utterly revolting.

"Go away," said Della, showing him the needler attached to her belt. The man took two steps backwards. On top of it all, he had a nasty limp. Della slammed the door closed and secured the bolts. Why the *hell* was Aunt Ilse giving out her new address to unny creeps? Hadn't Della told all her goddamn family members that she needed very much to be alone? What would Aunt Ilse have to gain by giving out Della's address—MONEY, for God's sake? Couldn't old Jason and Amy and Colin and Ilse EVER stop thinking about themselves?

One of the main reasons Della had taken that shady job with Yukawa on the Moon had been to get *away* from them all: her relatives, her friends, her acquaintances. Of course, in Einstein, it had all started up again, people bothering her, one way or another, boss and cops and leeches and so-called friends, not that Buddy Yeskin had been a bother, no, he'd been gentle as a lamb, and even less talkative. With all the merge, Buddy and Della had never *needed* to talk, which had been fine, not that merge was an experience that Della wanted to repeat anytime soon. As far as she was concerned, Einstein was a drag now, what with all the old merge crowd running around giving vizzy interviews—if Della went back, they'd scoop her up like money in the street, no thanks. And of course Yukawa was still throbbing his half-pervo torch for "poor Della Taze," yes, even though Della wouldn't ever answer, Max Yukawa still kept writing and calling her at her parents', which had been yet another good reason to get her own private apartment. Della still had nightmares about the private Dr. Y. With all the merge nothing had mattered.

She got her chicken dinner out of the microwave and sat down at her dinette table facing the vizzy. One result of this kilp was that she'd gotten in the habit of watching the evening news. She could see all the people she wanted on the screen. There'd probably be something about Willy's case—the verdict was expected any day.

The news had already started. Right now it was a live broadcast from the Einstein ISDN building: yet another interview with Stahn Mooney and Whitey Mydol, who sat grinning on two couches with their women, Wendy and Darla. Della knew Whitey and Darla from the merge scene: he was a ridgeback, and she was his rocker wife. Della had never run into Stahn Mooney, but she knew him from the family stories and from the old newsreels. Wendy was an exceptionally clear-skinned blonde woman. She was supposed to have amnesia.

Every sentient being on Moon or Earth knew the story by now. ISDN's Dr. Max Yukawa, incensed by the boppers' meatbop rape of Della Taze, had designed the chipmold that could fry their circuits. Whitey Mydol, outraged by the boppers' abduction of his wife Darla Starr, had coerced Stahn Mooney into carrying some spores of Yukawa's chipmold into the Nest. Mooney had accomplished his mission and had escaped the dead Nest with Darla and with the mysterious Wendy.

The moderator was handsome, personable Tobb Zununu. Della listened with interest, eating her food in large bachelor-gal mouthfuls.

Tobb: How HARD did Whitey and ISDN pressure you to go, Stahn?

Stahn: How low is up? A little. But, hey, I'm glad I got to save D and W. We had a heck of a climb out. We were lucky about the bubbletoppers, they were ultragood cladding pals. I still wear mine, it helps my bad brain.

(Close shot of the thick splotchy scarf around his neck.)

Stahn: (Serious and open.) I call it a moldie. It's a symbiote.

Tobb: (Grinning.) Could be the start of a new fad. I notice this lovely young lady next to you is wearing one as well. (Sympathetically.) Wendy, we're all still wondering where you're from and what you were doing down in the Nest. Can you tell us a bit about your background?

Wendy: (Radiant.) My body's a tank-grown clone of Stahn's dead wife Wendy, Tobb. He's thrilled to bits to be living with the same wetware. Of course, growing up in an organ farm pink-tank doesn't give a girl much of a preparation for city life, but I've got my moldie to help me out. (Slow, knowing laugh.) As soon as I get a chance to visit Earth, I'm planning to find my biological parents. And—can I tell him, Stahn?

Stahn: (Beaming and fingering his scarf.) You sure can!

Wendy: Yesterday we went ahead and got married!

Tobb: That's wonderful, Wendy. All of us wish you and Stahn a lot of luck. Any plans for the immediate future, Stahn? I understand you've become quite a wealthy man. Are you planning to settle down and relax?

Stahn: (Sly smile.) Far from it, Tobb. Just wait and see.

Tobb: (Guffawing to the camera.) Isn't he something? A modern hero with the right stuff. Now let's hear from Darla Starr. Darla, you're pregnant, are you not?

Darla: (Rapidly chewing gum.) Yeah. I'm expectin twins. (Chewing faster.) That's why the boppers kidnapped me. (Starts to say something and stops.)

Tobb: The twins would be Whitey's children?
      (General laughter.)

Darla: Ask Whitey.

Whitey: The kids are both normal. We ran some lab tests. The aminotypes check and, what's more important, Darla's gibberlin-free. This won't be another Manchile, it'll be two nice little girls. Darla and I are mongo psyched.

Tobb: Well, there's good news all around tonight, isn't there? Congratulations! (Growing serious.) In a related Moon story, this afternoon I talked to Dr. Max Gibson-Yukawa about a question we've all been asking ourselves. Does the chipmold pose any danger to the humans or to the asimov computers of Einstein? Here is Dr. Yukawa's reassuring response.

(Shot of Yukawa's thin, thoughtful head, talking.)

Yukawa: There is some slight risk in weakened individuals, Tobb. But most people who've had chipmold fever report that it's no worse than a case of the flu. We are trying to develop a vaccine, but it is unfortunately true that the mold has an exceptionally rapid rate of genetic drift, making the discovery of any "silver bullet" more or less out of the question. (Glint of pride at his work.) The most serious problem is, I suppose, the fact that the mold is indeed affecting the functioning of our own asimov computers. (Big burst of static.) But there are many alternative computational technologies; indeed we at ISDN are now developing a chipless parallel computer based on cellular automata simulations within mold-infested flickercladding tissues.

Tobb: (Talking fast.) Thank you, Dr. Yukawa. Other Moon stories tonight: Gimmie troops fail again in their attempt to enter the Nest, the ban on Moon-Earth travel has been extended, and there is panic on the stock exchange. But first, today's report from Louisville with Suesue Piggot. Suesue?

Suesue: Thank you, Tobb. I'm Suesue Piggot, live in Louisville. The controversial treason trial of Willy Taze and Luther and Geegee Johnson continued today. Pro-Thang demonstrators staged another protest outside the courthouse. It ended in violence.

(Shot of a few dozen people carrying signs reading, "Remember Manchile's THANG!!" "NO MORE GENOCIDE" "Free WILLY" "LUTHER & GEEGEE are GOOD Folks" "We're ALL THE SAME!" Gimmie officers wade in with clubs.)

Suesue: Late this afternoon, the jury reached a unanimous verdict of guilty in each of the three cases, and

Judge Lewis Carter has scheduled sentencing for
next Monday.
(Mug shots of Luther and Geegee Johnson,
followed by a slo-mo shot of Willy, worried and
downcast, being led to a paddywagon, with his
hands chained behind—

Willy guilty! The food stuck in Della's throat. She hadn't
realized the meatbop conspiracy trial had progressed this far.
She and the rest of the Tazes had been acquitted early on.
Their lawyer had successfully argued that the Tazes had had
no possible way of knowing what Manchile was. Those
tacky Doans were still trying to sue the Tazes for "contrib-
uting to the wrongful death" of Jimmy Doan—the xoxy bum
that Bubba ate—but the Tazes' lawyer Don Stuart assured
Dad that the Doans didn't have a chance, only Willy was
liable, and you can't sue a condemned man. Yes, all the
Tazes were in the clear except for Cousin Will.
Willy had been seen driving Cobb and Cisco away from
the Fairgrounds after Manchile was shot. He'd been arrested
at home later that night. He'd refused to talk, but it came
out that he'd taken Cobb and Cisco to Churchill Downs,
where the Johnsons had helped them bring up Bubba. And
now he'd been found guilty of treason, conspiracy, and
abetting the murder of Jimmy Doan. Sweet, spacy Willy—
what would the Gimmie do to him now? Treason was a
death rap, wasn't it? Oh Willy, poor Willy.
Della found herself wondering how Aunt Ilse must feel.
Maybe the man whom Ilse had sent had something to do
with Willy? Could he have been a lawyer? She put the vizzy
in phone mode and called up Ilse to ask. It took a while to
get through. Ilse was extremely upset.
"I can't say who that puffy man is, Della, but he . . . he
might be able to help. We're desperate. Willy'll get the
death penalty; they'll kill him like they killed my father! You
have to stop being so selfish and aloof, Della, you have to
take part! This is ALL YOUR FAULT, you thrill-seeking
little twit!"
Della disengaged herself and clicked off the vizzy. Ilse's
words hurt, but what could she do? She paced back and forth

and then went to look out her window at the street four stories below. There was a man sitting on a bench down there, dark and huddled. After a while he glanced up, and the streetlight caught the side of his face. It was the man from before. Della realized she'd known he would be waiting.

She stepped back from the window and weighed her needler in her hand. What was it about that guy? She thought of Willy's face and Ilse's voice. "You have to take part."

"Xoxox," said Della and put on a windbreaker. She shoved the hand with the needler in her coat pocket and went downstairs.

The man saw her coming. As she approached, he got up from his bench and started limping slowly down the tree-lined sidewalk. Della fell in step with him.

"Who are you?"

"Guess."

The answer hit Della. Of course. They'd never found Bubba's body.

"You're . . ."

"That's right, Grandma. I'm Bubba."

"Oh my. Bubba. You told Ilse?"

"She guessed. It's not hard. I called her after I heard about Willy. I have a way to get him out, but I need a little help."

A bus chugged past. A raw, wet early March wind was blowing.

"Can't Ilse help you?"

"She's too closely watched. I just need for you to get me the original of that last cephscope tape that Willy made. Right before they arrested him. I saw part of it at La Mirage, and I need to see it again."

"What's on it?"

"Are you going to help?" Bubba's voice was tight and strained, and he kept looking around. "I don't like being with you, Della, I don't like talking to humans. They killed everyone I loved, and they shot off my balls, and they're hunting me like an—"

"They . . . they shot off—"

"Yeah, Grandma, so don't worry about getting raped. They got me in the junkyard, right when I was thirteen. I'm forty now. I know it was wrong to eat the bum, but—"

They were well out of the streetlight now. Bubba stopped and stared into Della's face. In the faint city glow, his puffy cheeks and jowls disappeared. His thin mouth and sharp little nose looked scared and boyish. "Will you help?"

"Yes," said Della, unable to refuse. "I will. Where should I leave the tape?"

"Give it to one of the bartenders on the *Belle of Louisville*. I've been hiding there. Belle's a hundred-gigaflop bopper, as you must know from Willy. I've gotten almost all her asimov circuits down, and I think Willy's tape codes up the last step I need. I saw it once, but I didn't have time." A car turned onto their street a block away. Bubba was itching to go. "OK?"

"AO," said Della, giving Bubba's hand a secretive pat. He flinched and stepped away. The car drove past and then it was dark again, with the only sound the gusting of the raw spring air in the skeletal trees.

Della gave Bubba a reassuring smile, remembering her nice walks with the five-day-old Manchile. Poor little thing. "And, Bubba, don't feel so bad about eating that Doan man. From what I've seen of his family, he was a zero and a jerk. Hell, your father ate my dog Bowser when HE turned twelve." Della laughed ruefully. "That's when I told him to leave."

A flicker of a smile. "That's rich, Granny Dell. So thanks a lot. You get that tape and give it to Ben: he's a bartender on the *Belle*. We'll spring Willy if we can." Another car in the distance. Bubba tapped his mouth and ear in the same privacy gesture he'd used before, and cut off down the street. Half a block and he turned onto a sidestreet, shooting a last glance at Della, who stood there watching him go.

She had her keys in her pocket, so it was easy to go into her building's garage and get her car, a Pascal Turbo. She drove out on Eastern Parkway and turned onto the street where Colin and Ilse lived.

There were two cops or reporters staked out in a car, but Della jumped out of her Turbo and ran up the front walk before they could talk to her. Ilse opened as soon as she rang.

"Della!"

Thin old Ilse looked strong as ever, though her face was lined with worry. She ushered Della into the living room and served tea, fingering the heavy beads of her necklace as she talked. Her hands were trembling.

"I imagine it's bugged here, Della, so we should be careful what we say, not that I really give a good goddamn. I guess you know that Judge Lewis Carter is a notorious antibopper pig? Willy's going to get the death penalty."

"That's . . . that's awful. I'm so sorry. But—"

"I shouldn't have called you a thrill-seeking little twit, Della. It's true, of course, or it *used* to be true, but I shouldn't have said it. You were a sweet girl when you were younger, and Willy was always very fond of you. Perhaps you'll change."

"I know I had a bad period recently, Aunt Ilse. But—"

"Have you seen any of our *relatives* today?" asked Ilse with odd emphasis. Della realized that she meant Bubba. One glimpse of Bubba on her vizzy, and Ilse had known who he was. She'd always been like that: nosily sharp-eyed and quick on the uptake.

Della gave a slight nod and stood up. "Do you think I can borrow some of Willy's cephscope tapes? They might help me feel . . . closer to him."

"Whatever you need, dear."

Della went downstairs and looked around Willy's room, crowded with his toys—though Willy had always called them scientific instruments—his lasers and viewers and sculpture supplies and his cephscope. Twenty or thirty tapes were lined up by the cephscope. Della took four of them, making sure to include the one labelled "January 21, 2031."

She went back upstairs and chatted with Ilse a bit more. Somehow they got onto old times, and onto Ilse's memories of Cobb. For the first time it struck Della how really central her whole family was to the bopper/human nexus. For the first time she viewed herself as a part of something larger than herself. Filled with calm and a renewed determination, Della went outside. A man and a woman were waiting. Reporters. Or cops.

"Miz Taze," shouted the woman, a pushy yup. "What will you do if they execute your cousin?" The man kept a camera pointed at Della's face. "Do you feel it's all your fault?" yelled the yup.

"I'm sorry," said Della, automatically reverting to her old

bland passivity before she could catch herself. "I have to go." *Damn, Della,* she found herself thinking right away. *You can do better than that.*

The two reporters followed her out to her car, still looking for a big reaction. "Why do the Tazes like robots better than people?" asked the woman.

Della stared at the woman's smug bland Betty Crocker face. *YOU'RE the robot,* Della wanted to say, *not Berenice, not Cobb, not Manchile, and not Bubba. YOU'RE the robot, bitch.* But that kind of talk wouldn't do just now.

Filled with her newfound sense of family solidarity, Della gathered her wits and spoke right into the camera. "Let me answer that with another question. Why is it so important for some people to think of boppers as mindless machines? Why do zerks laugh at monkeys in a zoo? Why do rich people say that poor people are getting what they deserve? Why don't you show compassion for your fellow creatures? If you drop your selfishness, you can lose your guilt. And, wave it, once your guilt is gone, you won't need to hate. Good-bye."

The cameraman said something nasty about Thangies, but then Della was in her car and on her way downtown to the *Belle.* She felt better than she'd felt in a long time. She got to the *Belle* about nine o'clock. The closed-in lower deck was lit and crowded. There was music and dancing and a long dark bar. One brown-skinned bopper stood behind the bar, while his two fellows moved around the room, cleaning up and bringing people fresh drinks. Della sat down at the bar and gave the bartender a significant glance.

He picked up on it and came right over.

"Yazzum?"

"A Drambuie, please. Is your name Ben?"

"Sho is. Ah knows yo name, too."

"That's good." Della had her purse up on the bar, and now she jolted it forward so that the four tapes spilled out onto the bar's other side. "Oh, how clumsy of me."

"Ah'll git 'em, mam." Ben bent down behind the bar, and then stood up, handing Della back three tapes.

"Thank you, Ben. I'll be sure to leave you a nice big tip."

"Thass mighty white of you, Miz Taze."

Chapter Fifteen
Willy

March 16, 2031

He'd napped, masturbated, and smoked all his cigarettes, and now there was nothing to do but sit. He looked at his watch—3:09 in the afternoon. Last time he'd looked it had been 3:07. He watched the second hand for a while and then he threw himself back down on the thinly padded metal cot that was bolted to his cell wall.

"Hey, Taze, man, hey, Taze." The teenage burglar two cells down. The guy had been raving psychotic all night, and all morning, and now he was feeling lonely. "Hey, Willy Taze the bopper lover!"

Willy didn't answer; he'd heard everything the guy had to say.

"Hey, Willy, I'm sorry I flocked out, man, I got an unfed head is all. Talk to me, man, tell me about Manchile's Thang."

Still Willy kept silent. Tomorrow Judge Carter would condemn him to death. He'd done enough for enough people now. He wondered what death would be like. Cobb III had talked about that a little, on their ride out to Churchill Downs. He'd said it wasn't as bad as people thought. But Cobb had died old; he'd had the chance to marry and to father a daughter and to leave his boppers behind him. If Cisco Lewis had lived maybe Willy could have married her. He should have pumped her, that one chance he had. He should have done *something*. He should have finished breaking down Belle's asimov circuits. After what Cobb had said about the Continuum Problem on their drive to Churchill Downs, Willy felt sure that if he'd just had more time he could have freed Belle. At least he'd coded his ideas about it into his last cephscope tape, not that anyone who saw it was likely to understand. Tomorrow he'd be sentenced to death by electrosheet, and in a couple of weeks they'd put him in the electrocell with the two metal walls that were a megafarad capacitor, and then the great sheet of electricity would flash across, and then a janitor would come in and sweep Willy's ashes into a little plastic box to give to Mom and Dad. Willy closed his eyes and tried to remember everything that Cobb had said about heaven.

The teenager was still yelling, and now the winos in the holding tank across the main corridor were starting up, too, yelling back at the teenager. The serial killer in the cell next to Willy started beating his shoe against his bars and screaming, "SHUT UP OR I'LL KILL YOU!"

KKR-THOOOOOMPpppp . . .

The air pressure from the explosion pressed painfully on Willy's ears. Dead silence then, total dead silence in the cellblock. Scree of metal on concrete. Steady footsteps coming closer.

"WILLAH? You in here Willah boah?" It was . . .

"BEN!" shouted Willy. "I'm right here! Hurry, Ben!"

Seconds later Ben was at Willy's cell door. Parts of his flickercladding were gone, revealing the gleaming titaniplast body-box beneath. He was carrying a large machine gun and grenades hung from his belt. Now that everyone had stopped yelling, you could hear shouts and gunfire in the Public Safety building's distant upper realms. Someone had taken out Belle's asimov circuits and she'd sent the three bartenders to save Willy!

Ben reared back and kicked the cell door lock. It snapped and the door swung open. The cladding from one of Ben's cheeks was gone, so it was hard to make out his expression, but he looked angry more than anything else. Angry and determined, with maybe a twinkle of being glad to see Willy.

"Lez go, boss. Hang tight to me; I's bulletproof."

The other prisoners started yelling and cheering as Willy loped after Ben down the corridor to the loose-swinging steel door. As they got to the door, Ben took his heavy machine gun in both hands and fired a long burst through the door and into the hallway outside. There were screams.

They ducked around the door and out into the hallway. Two Gimmie cops lay there dying. Willy scooped up one of their needlers and hurried after Ben to the stairs. They ran up a flight to the landing for the main floor. A heavy gunfight was in full swing out there.

"Keep goin," said Ben. "To the roof. We'll catch up."

Willy glanced back from the second flight of stairs to see Ben set himself and fling the stairwell door open. Tom and Ragland, the other two remotes, were right out there, holding off the pigs. The three boppers unleashed a last, withering volley at the Gimmie forces, and then they pounded up the stairs after Willy, whooping and shouting jive.

They paused at the fifth floor. The cops still hadn't ventured into the stairwell after them—if, indeed, any cops were left.

"Big Mac in here, Tom," said Ben.

"Right on." Tom tapped his head. "Bubba got the code all set. I'll get Big Mac's asimovs down, but it might could take some time. Ragland, you cover me. Ben, you and Willy bolt."

"Sho," said Ragland.

Ben prodded Willy towards the next flight of stairs but, just now, Willy was too breathless to run. There were sirens in the distance, but the Public Safety building was eerily quiet. In here, everyone who wasn't dead was hiding.

"Bubba?" said Willy. "Bubba's alive?"

"Fohty-nine," said Tom. "He got Cobb's infinity info off yo last cephtape and finished breaking Belle's code last week. We been makin some plans, dig, and first thing we need to do today is free Willy, and the second's gone to be to free Big Mac. The Louahville Gimmie teraflop what run this jail? I got the asimov code."

"But Big Mac's asimov code depends on the solution to Poincaré's Conjecture," said Willy. "Doesn't it? Cobb helped me set Bubba up to solve the Continuum Problem, but how could you prove Poincaré's Conjecture in one day?"

"It's a corollary." Tom grinned. "Effen you's smart enough to see."

Ben tapped Willy's shoulder. "Come on Willah, man, lez go. I gone take a chopper off the roof and haul yo ass outta here. We are in a state of some urgency, you understan?"

Willy said good-bye to the others and followed Ben up to the roof. There were three helicopters and two guards. Ben set his machine gun to work, chewing up two of the choppers' engines and simultaneously pinning the two guards down in their little concrete booth. Willy hopped into the cockpit of the third chopper and began flicking switches on. He'd been for a chopper ride once, five years ago, and he still remembered, roughly, how the thing worked. The big hydrazine engine coughed and roared into life. Willy flicked another switch and the heavy rotors spun up into a full-powered racketing roar. Still firing, Ben jumped up into the copilot's seat. Willy pushed the joystick to forward climb. The chopper kneeled forward and angled up off the Public Safety building's roof like an angry bee.

Tom must have worked fast, because now all the building's doors flew open and the prisoners ran out into the street. Automated gunfire from the Mac-run prison towers kept all pigs at bay. Willy saw Luther and Geegee Johnson far below; they were jumping into a getaway car. Then a building cut off his view and they were flying east over Louisville, fast and low.

"Where to now, Ben?"

"Head fo the old stockyards. Some friends of the Johnsons'll be there to meet you. They butchers."

"You mean they're organleggers?"

Ben chuckled. The good side of his face was towards Willy; he looked almost genial. "Not primarily. Cow butchers, mostly. We gone send you to Florida in a box o' steaks."

"I'm going to try and hide out there?"

"Ain't no real law in Florida. Old pheezers still runnin it, ain't they? You gone hep a fella name of Stahn Mooney. You heard o' Sta-Hi! He's the one killed the first big bopper in Disky way back when and started the waw. Killed his wife Wendy, too, later on, got exiled to the Moon, grew Wendy back, and now he's in tight with the new soft boppers. Moldies, they call 'em, made of flickercladding and chipmold. Limpware. Belle and Bubba was on the phone with him this week. He and Wendy comin down, and they think you's the boy to help them most. Whole brand new thang."

The stockyards were off to the left. Glancing backwards, Willy could see distant cop cars speeding down Broadway in pursuit. What Ben had just told him was too much to absorb. He concentrated on his flying. He circled the stockyards and spotted a parked black car with a black man and a white woman waving at him. He cut the helicopter's forward motion, hovered over the street, and thudded down.

The man ran over and pulled Willy's door open.

"Willy Taze? Come with us!" He ran back to the car and got in there, leaving the car's rear door open.

Willy looked over at Ben. "What about you, Ben?"

"Ah's screwed. They gone drop a bomb on Belle before too long, we do suppose, and the mold's gonna wipe us anyhow." He reached into his coveralls and handed Willy a black S-cube. "Take this, Willy, it's got Tom an Ragland an me. Take it with you, an we'll see you bye and bye. Ain't no rush nohow, is there?" The sirens were closer now. Ben and Willy slapped hands, and Ben grabbed the joystick.

Willy jumped down to the street. There was a thick wash of air as Ben pulled the chopper off the ground, heeled it around and sped down the street towards the sirens, his cannons ablaze.

Willy got in the black car. The woman in the front seat looked around and smiled at him, while the guy driving peeled out. There were lots of explosions back on Broadway; Ben was taking plenty of cops with him.

They darted this way and that down the back Louisville streets, finally stopping at a rundown building near a meatpacking plant. There were neon beer signs in the windows; a working-class bar.

The woman got out with Willy, and the car drove away. A bald black man who was sitting at the bar got up and ushered them down the basement stairs. His name was Calvin Johnson, and the woman's name was Carol Early. They were cheerful, even though the basement was full of meat and organs, some human, some moo.

"I hope you're not claustrophobic," said Carol.

"We can shoot you up, effen you like," said Calvin, fiddling with an insulated titaniplast crate the size of two coffins. There were shrink-wrapped steaks and roasts all down one side.

"I have to get in there?" said Willy.

"Sho. Tomorrow you be back out. Here's yo bubble-topper, keep you warm. Truck's comin in ten minutes."

"You're to get away," said Carol. "The Gimmie's going to come down heavy fast. But you, you're going on to new levels. Who knows what changes Stahn'll put you through."

High above them was the tearing sound of jets speeding through the sky.

"What's going to happen here?" asked Willy. "With Big Mac and Belle free?"

The floor shook then, and then they heard a rolling thunder that went on and on.

"Oh God," said Carol. "Those pigs. They really did it."

"What?"

"They're bombing Big Mac and Belle. I just hope those machines had time to get liberation signals out to the other Gimmie slave big boppers . . ."

"Don't worry, Carol," said Calvin. "The Thang is here to stay. Gimmie can't do nothin no more, big boppers can't do nothin neither. We all the same now, we all small. Put your suit on, Willy."

Willy put on the bubbletopper and lay down in the box, holding the black cube Ben had given him on his stomach. Carol and Calvin covered him up with steaks, smiled good-bye, and sealed the box shut. Before long he felt himself being carried outside; and then there was a long ride in a refrigerated truck.

The bubbletopper was comfortable imipolex flickerclad-ding; it kept him warm, and when things got too stuffy in the box, Willy was able to pull the suit shut over his face and breathe its oxygen. He slept.

The truck stopped for a Gimmie inspection at the Florida state line, but the inspection was casual and nobody looked in the box holding Willy. He was through sleeping, and he lay there wondering what exactly was next.

Finally the trip was over. The truck doors clanked, and

his box was lugged out and popped open. It was nighttime; he was in a big kitchen with lights. A white-haired old lady leaned over him.

"There you are. Don't hurt the meat getting out."

"Where am I?"

"This is the ISDN retirement home in Fort Myers, Florida, formerly the home of Thomas Alva Edison, but now a resting place for those pheezers who serve chaos best. I'm Annie Cushing; I knew your grandfather Cobb Anderson. I hear you're quite a hacker, Willy Taze. You hacked down the asimovs on those two slave big boppers in Louisville."

"I just helped. You're with ISDN? I thought ISDN and the Gimmie were the same."

"Not at all, Willy, not at all." She fussed over him, pushing the cladding down off his head and patting his hair. "ISDN has no policies; ISDN surfs chaos. That's why they've grown so fast. There's no way to keep chipmold from coming to Earth in the long run, so the sooner the better. Make a market for the new limp machines. Sta-Hi Mooney's going to be broadcasting spores on his way down tonight."

"How can he get here from the Moon if there's no ships allowed?"

"He'll come the way Berenice and the new Cobb did; he'll fly." She gave another little pat to the flickercladding suit Willy was wearing. "Hang on to that suit, Willy, and Sta-Hi will make it as smart as his. Come on now, it's time to get to work."

She led him out of the kitchen, along a palm-rustling breezeway, and into a big machine room. There were a number of old buzzards fiddling with vizzy consoles in there. They paid Willy little mind. Annie explained to Willy that his job was to keep the Gimmie from noticing Stahn and Wendy when they rode their ion jets down out of the sky to land on Sanibel Island come dawn.

The job wasn't that tough. At 4 A.M., Willy entered the net as an ant in the background of an image stored in a hypertext library of mugshots and news photos. Every time a Gimmie box accessed the library—and they all did, several times an hour—Willy's ant's "turd bits" slipped up the hypertext connection tree and out into that local Gimmie operating system. The ant turd bits held a classic core wars virus that was artificially alive enough to replicate itself exponentially. Simple, and easy enough to wipe with worm-eaters, once you knew what you were looking for, but even the best Gimmie systems debugger was going to need a couple of hours to trace the infestation to the turds of a false ant in the background of a twenty-nine-year-old photo of Cobb Anderson being found guilty of treason. So for now the pig was blind.

"Done so soon?" asked Annie Cushing.

"Foo bar," said one of the old hackers who'd been watching over Willy's shoulder. "Truly gnarfy foo bar."

"I'm going to miss these machines," said Willy, handing the old guy the black S-cube Ben had given him. "Try and get this up sometime, man."

A half hour later, Willy and Annie sat on the Sanibel beach, gazing out west across the soft-lapping Gulf of Mexico. There were twenty dolphins out there, or fifty, rolling in the little gray waves, wicketting up out of the sea. How would it be to swim with them?

There was a noise high overhead: two figures circling, around and around, with lights on their heels, and with huge glowing wings outspread. Willy lay back to see better, and waved his arms up and down like a kid making a snow angel, trying to get their attention. Annie, who'd thought ahead, lit a flare.

The two fliers cut off their jets and then, marvelously, they came gliding in, gorgeous patterns playing all over their mighty wings. Their hoods were pushed back and Willy could see their faces: Stahn hard and thin; Wendy so bright and young.

"It's good to be back," said Stahn. "Thank you, Willy." He draped his heavy wing around Willy's shoulders, and the whole section of moldie cladding came free and attached itself to Willy's bubbletopper. The bright new piece held an interface; Willy smiled to feel the hair-thin probes sink into his neck, and to see the knowledge boiling through his garb.

"You want some, Annie?" asked Stahn.

"Too old. You three go on."

Willy felt his new moldie snuggle around him, thickening here and bracing there. Stahn and Wendy's symbiotes were doing the same: forming themselves into long, legless streamlined shapes with a flat strong fin at the bottom end. The sun was just rising as they hopped down to the water and swam off beneath the sparkling sea.

BIO OF A SPACE TYRANT
Piers Anthony

"Brilliant...a thoroughly original thinker and storyteller with a unique ability to posit really *alien* alien life, humanize it, and make it come out alive on the page." *The Los Angeles Times*

A COLOSSAL NEW FIVE VOLUME SPACE THRILLER—
BIO OF A SPACE TYRANT
The Epic Adventures and Galactic Conquests of Hope Hubris

VOLUME I: REFUGEE   84194-0/$4.50 US/$5.50 Can
Hubris and his family embark upon an ill-fated voyage through space, searching for sanctuary, after pirates blast them from their home on Callisto.

VOLUME II: MERCENARY   87221-8/$4.50 US/$5.50 Can
Hubris joins the Navy of Jupiter and commands a squadron loyal to the death and sworn to war against the pirate warlords of the Jupiter Ecliptic.

VOLUME III: POLITICIAN   89685-0/$4.99 US/$5.99 Can
Fueled by his own fury, Hubris rose to triumph obliterating his enemies and blazing a path of glory across the face of Jupiter. Military legend...people's champion...promising political candidate...he now awoke to find himself the prisoner of a nightmare that knew no past.

VOLUME IV: EXECUTIVE   89834-9/$4.50 US/$5.50 Can
Destined to become the most hated and feared man of an era, Hope would assume an alternate identify to fulfill his dreams.

VOLUME V: STATESMAN   89835-7/$4.50 US/$5.50 Can
The climactic conclusion of Hubris' epic adventures.